PICTURE PERFECT WEDDING

LYNNETTE AUSTIN

sourcebooks
casablanca

Published by Sourcebooks Casablanca, an imprint of Sourcebooks, Inc.
P.O. Box 4410, Naperville, Illinois 60567-4410
(630) 961-3900
Fax: (630) 961-2168
www.sourcebooks.com

Printed and bound in Canada.
MBP 10 9 8 7 6 5 4 3 2 1

Chapter 1

IN A PERFECT WORLD OR, HECK, EVEN IN A MOVIE, music would play softly in the background. The SUV's windows would be down, her auburn hair blowing softly in the breeze. Her hero would wait at the road's end, arms open and welcoming.

They'd kiss…

Tansy Calhoun Forbes's cell rang, and, startled, she glanced in the rearview mirror. Gracie, her four-year-old daughter, slept soundly, a welcome respite from today's endless are-we-there-yets.

"Hello?" she practically whispered.

"You unpacked yet?" Jenni Beth Beaumont, her best friend forever, sounded stressed.

"Still a few miles from town, but almost there."

"Good. Great. Listen, I know this has been a stressful day, heck, a stressful year, and you're tired…"

Tansy smiled. She could practically see her friend squirming. "What do you need, Jenni Beth?"

"Oh, Tanz, I have two weddings and a sixteenth birthday party coming up this week. Magnolia Brides is booked solid for the next nine months—my dream come true—but I'm dying here! I need cakes. Phenomenal cakes. Your cakes!"

"I don't have—"

"Kitty said you can use the bakery's kitchen."

Tansy sighed and ran her fingers through already-mussed hair.

"I know, I know." Jenni Beth's tension vibrated over the airwaves. "I'm putting you on the spot. Big-time. I'm a horrible person. An even worse friend."

"No, you're not." Determined, Tansy sat up a little straighter. "This is exactly what I've insisted I want. Part of the reason I'm on my way home. Color me stupid, but I'm in."

Her friend let out a quiet squeal. "Kitty has all the details—colors, design ideas, size—but if you have any questions—"

Tansy laughed. "I'll call."

As the city-limits sign loomed, she hung up and removed her dark glasses. Misty Bottoms, Georgia. The Low Country. Even slowing to a crawl didn't stop the inevitable.

Home, sweet home.

Right back at the starting gate.

Waiting for her? No music, no hero, and no kiss.

And no one but herself to blame.

Tansy pushed her sunglasses back in place and glared at the brilliant sunshine that bathed the beyond-gorgeous autumn day. The humidity had dropped, and a few white clouds drifted high in the bluebird sky. *Shouldn't it be raining, the sky dark with ominous thunderheads?*

Divorced for fifty-three days, five hours, and—she checked the dashboard clock—six minutes, and here she was, hell-bent on creating the cake for a bride's special day.

She'd had her own shot at the dream and lost—because the wrong groom stood beside her at the altar.

A self-absorbed, compulsive gambler, her ex had lost their house along with all their savings and investments.

She'd supported Emerson through multiple rounds of rehab because he was her daughter's father, but when two goons showed up at the front door demanding her jewelry for money owed, her first call had been to the police, the second to her attorney. At that moment, Emerson Forbes became nothing more than a footnote in her life.

In the blink of an eye, she'd gone from a forty-five-hundred-square-foot home to her SUV and the contents of a few suitcases and boxes. All without a single regret because, from her perspective, she'd drawn the Golden Ticket. She'd left the marriage with Gracie Bella, her daughter.

The wedding and engagement rings, the for-show-only anniversary necklace and earrings she'd refused to hand over to the goons? After her first-ever trip to a pawnshop, the jewelry had financed her and Gracie's move and given her some essential seed money.

For the next little bit, she and Gracie would stay with her mom. Since Tansy's dad's death almost five years ago, her mother'd been lonely. She'd provide a haven for Tansy and her daughter, and they'd fill a void for her. A temporary one. Tansy intended to start searching for a place of her own right away. Until she found something and the movers delivered the few things she'd stored, she and Gracie would live out of their suitcases.

Walking out of her supersized house that morning had been confusing. She'd expected a huge weight to lift, and it had. Still, that was the house she'd brought Gracie home to after she'd been born. Where her first four birthdays had been celebrated. Christmases and Thanksgivings.

And so much unhappiness and deceit.

Tansy massaged her temples where a screaming headache had taken up residence. How long since she'd had a decent night's sleep or a good meal? Driving one-handed, she rooted around on the passenger seat with the other till she found the bag of almonds. Maybe some protein would give her a boost.

A building off to her right caught her attention and caused a hitch in her heart. Elliot Construction and Lumberyard. She tossed the almonds aside untouched, any semblance of appetite deserting her.

Beck Elliot, the groom behind door number one, the door she hadn't chosen.

Oh boy. She rested a hand on her stomach. Was she making another mistake? Should she have started over somewhere else?

Ding, ding, ding. The low-fuel indicator chimed, and the little red light blinked on. Shoot! She'd meant to get fuel a while ago, but Gracie had been sleeping so soundly, she'd hesitated to take a chance on waking her. Gracie was the sweetest, most easygoing child on earth, but one more question, no matter how innocent, might be enough to send Tansy over the edge. She felt totally wrung out—from the move, the emotions and uncertainty of the past months.

"Months?" she whispered. "Oh, Tansy Calhoun Forbes, you are still lyin'. Nothing's been right for years. At least be honest with yourself!"

Tommy's Texaco loomed.

Relieved, she flipped on her turn signal, veered into the lot, and pulled up to the gas pump.

And there it sat.

A big red truck with Elliot Construction on the side.

The door to the gas station opened, and Beck Elliot, looking hotter than any man had a right to in dusty jeans, a faded T-shirt, and old work boots, stepped outside.

He tore the wrapper off a candy bar and took a bite.

Then his intense, midnight-blue eyes met hers. The chill had her rubbing her arms even though the temperature read seventy-five in the shade.

As she got out, her gaze collided with Beck's again.

His eyes radiated resentment and betrayed hopes.

Hers? She figured they held remorse, hurt, and impossible-to-deny desire.

—⁄⁄⁄—

Beck nearly choked on the bite of chocolate. What the hell?

He tossed the bar into the trash barrel outside the door.

Months ago, he'd heard rumblings that Tansy'd enrolled her daughter in the local preschool, but since no one had said anything else about it, he'd figured she'd changed her mind. That fancy SUV of hers was loaded to the roof, though, way more than she'd need for a quick visit.

His chest constricted, and he swore under his breath. Why would she return to Misty Bottoms? She looked like one of those emaciated French models in the magazines his mom read. A good strong wind off the coast would blow her from here to Atlanta.

The strong, carefree Tansy he'd known had disappeared. She'd become... He didn't know. Ethereal came to mind.

Not his business—and she'd be the first to tell him that.

"Hey, Beck," Tommy said. "Got your truck filled for ya."

"Thanks. I left the money on the counter. Later, pal."

Without another word, without another glance toward the woman he'd once expected to marry, Beck hopped in his truck, turned the key, and pulled out of the gas station, reminding himself that Tansy Calhoun—no, make that Tansy Forbes—was history. Ancient history.

―〰―

Tommy watched as first Beck, then Tansy headed down the road. He dug out his phone and hit speed dial. "She's here."

Chapter 2

TOO RESTLESS TO HEAD BACK TO WORK, BECK TURNED off the main drag and drove along one of the smaller ones that led toward the river. Spotting the sign for Whiskey Road, he made a quick right. If his pal Cole was home, he'd probably have the inside scoop since Tansy and his fiancée had been best friends from kindergarten on. If Tansy was, indeed, moving home, Jenni Beth would know.

He'd have thought somebody would have given him a heads-up.

Beck pulled into the drive behind Jenni Beth's '65 Vette and studied the renovated barn his friend called home. Since Cole owned a huge architectural salvaging company in Savannah, he'd filled the house with some really unique pieces, like the granite-covered trough in the master bath.

Right now, though, Beck didn't care about that trough. He had an inexplicable—and unwelcome—pain in his chest. Climbing out, he slammed the truck's door.

Cole rounded the corner. "Hey, Beck, figured you'd be at work." His eyes narrowed. "What's wrong? Your family okay?"

"Yeah, everyone's fine."

Jenni Beth stepped out of the house, a glass of iced tea in one hand, a ring of fabric swatches in the other. "Hey, Beck, maybe you can help. I'm tryin' to decide on table covering colors for my New Year's Eve bride.

She can't make up her mind between blue and purple."
She held up the ring. "What do you think?"

He shrugged. "No clue."

"Want some tea?"

"Yeah. No. I don't know." He jammed his hands in
his pockets.

Her face clouded with concern.

Kicking his front tire, he said, "Tansy's in town."

His friends shared a look, and it wasn't one of surprise.

"How long have you known she's movin' back, Cole?"

"Jenni Beth told me last night."

"And you didn't call?"

"At midnight?"

"How 'bout you, Jenni Beth?"

"She told me a couple weeks ago she was comin'
today."

"Son of a—"

Not in the least intimidated by his scowl, she walked
to him and threaded her arm through one of his. He
didn't move a muscle, hands still tucked in his pockets.

"Sam said you were with him when Lucinda spilled
the beans about preschool."

"Yeah, I was." He scuffed his booted foot over the
pebbles. "But, hell, when nothin' happened, I assumed
she'd come to her senses." He raised his head and met
her gaze. "Why would she move back here?"

"Because she *did* finally come to her senses. Now
that she's divorced the loser, she wants to start over."

"Why here?"

Jenni Beth shrugged. "Same reason I came back.
Misty Bottoms is home. Did you run into her, Beck?"

A muscle worked in his jaw. "Yep. Stopped at

Tommy's for some gas and she pulled in with Gracie and a jam-packed SUV."

Cole dropped onto a wooden chair and nodded for Beck to sit. "Thought you'd moved past all this, bud."

"I have. It's just—I don't know. Damn, she looked beat—and would hate that I noticed."

Jenni Beth sighed. "And I've added to her load."

"What?" Beck looked confused.

"She hadn't even hit the town limits when I begged her to tackle three cakes. This week."

Cole took her hand, ran his thumb over the back of it. "Probably best she stays busy, sugar." Turning to Beck, he changed the subject. "You still gonna be able to help me on that new Savannah project this week?"

"You bet." He checked his watch and gave Jenni Beth a quick hug. "Gotta run. Take care of Tansy. And don't you dare tell her I said that."

"Okay." She hugged him back. "I know this is hard for you."

"I'll be fine."

"You seemed pretty fine last week when that hot brunette you've been seeing down in Savannah showed up on the job site." Cole shot a look toward Jenni Beth. "Not that I noticed her."

Jenni Beth just shook her head.

"I like Rachel," Beck said.

"But?"

"I'm not sure it's gonna work. I told her it might be time for us to start seein' other people."

Cole tipped his head. "Kind of like Roxy?"

"Yeah."

"And Cindy?"

Beck rolled his eyes skyward. "You sayin' there's a pattern here?"

"Nope." Cole smiled. "You did."

"Point taken."

"You don't still love her?"

"Who?"

Cole snorted. "Who?"

"No." Beck shook his head. "That's long ago over and done with. But I *was* in love with her. She left, I mourned, and we both moved on."

"Glad to hear it."

Something in Cole's tone warned Beck his pal didn't believe him. "It's true."

Jenni Beth chimed in. "Thou doth protest—"

"Too much," Beck finished. "Yeah, yeah. I took Mrs. Fitzgibbon's English lit class, too." He tapped Jenni Beth on the top of her head. "Don't you have something to cook or clean?"

She narrowed her eyes. "Once."

"What?"

"You get a pass on a comment like that once."

He laughed. "So noted."

"Seriously, Beck—"

"I'm good. I've got this covered. Thanks for listening." He slapped his thighs. "I've got to go. It's a workday. Jobs to do, people to see."

With a single wave, Beck hopped in his truck and headed toward the Savannah River. Forcing himself to drive sanely, he acknowledged the fact that specters of days past rode with him. How many times had he and Tansy stolen off to the riverbank to snag a few kisses? Hot kisses. Kisses that ripped him up inside.

Now? Hadn't his life just turned on its ear! Tansy. So slick and polished, except for that unruly, tousled head of auburn curls. He'd teased her no end that her hair gave her away, hinted at what lay beneath her cool exterior and exposed the wild child locked away.

And that wild side had driven him nuts. Even now, memories of the two of them steaming up the windows in the old truck he drove in high school spiked his blood pressure.

Then Tansy'd given that wild side away. To Emerson Forbes.

He pulled onto the verge, under the shade of a weeping willow. Time he let go of the anger. She'd moved on and so had he.

Still, pinching the bridge of his nose, he tussled with the reality of a newly divorced Tansy who'd returned to Misty Bottoms. And with her? Gracie, Emerson's daughter.

Every time he saw that beautiful little girl with either Tansy or her grandma, it tore him up. She should have been his, should be little Gracie Elliot, not Gracie Forbes. But she wasn't, and that was that.

He and Tansy? Past tense. Still, he'd just as soon not run into her when he turned a corner in the grocery store or walked into Dee-Ann's Diner.

Shit!

———

Whew! Tansy's knees went wobbly when Beck stepped out of Tommy's. Even after everything that had happened, her fingers itched to run through all that curly blond hair. But his eyes had changed. They used to be full of love—for her. One look and she felt cherished. Not anymore.

"Mama? I'm thirsty." Gracie, wide awake now and blissfully unaware of her mother's turmoil, caught Tansy's eye in the rearview mirror.

They'd already pulled out of the Texaco station, and the drinks in their tiny cooler had gone warm after Gracie'd played around in it and left the top off.

"We'll stop at Kitty's, honey. You can get a drink there."

Since she had three cakes to create this week, she'd take a few minutes to talk to Kitty about them. She'd work up some designs after Gracie fell asleep tonight.

She also needed to pull herself together a bit before she hit her mom's. Even though she'd run into Beck occasionally when she'd visited, it felt different this time. It *was* different. She was now a single mother with no home and no job.

Jeez.

"Are we almost there, Mama? I'm hungry, too."

"Another couple minutes. Pinkie promise."

Gracie grinned. "'Kay."

Driving along Main Street, Tansy noticed a change, an air of hope. Yes, the brick sidewalks still buckled in places, but no empty storefronts stared back at her. People she'd never seen before wandered along the street, shopping bags in hand. A new gourmet wine and cheese shop had opened in the old five-and-dime building. The drugstore had a fresh coat of paint.

The town looked good. Vibrant. Darlene, the owner of Quilty Pleasures, walked her pair of Cairn Terriers, dressed today in jaunty green-and-blue-plaid sweaters that matched hers.

Tansy slowed and lowered her driver's side window. "Hey, Darlene."

"Hey, yourself, Tansy. Welcome home!" She scooped up first Mint Julep and then Moonshine, waving their paws. Her voice raised three octaves as she slid into baby talk. "Tell Gracie we're glad to see her. Yes, we are." She kissed each of the dogs' noses.

In the backseat, Gracie Bella giggled and waved. "Can I have a doggie, Mama?"

"Maybe someday." A red Volkswagen beetle came up behind her, so with a promise to stop by Darlene's shop, she continued down the street, a smile tugging at her lips. Jenni Beth Beaumont, with her dreams and hard work, had put Misty Bottoms back on the map. Magnolia House, her renovated antebellum home, had become *the spot* for destination weddings, engagement parties, proms, reunions, birthday parties, you name it.

Tansy's heart fluttered. With this week's cakes, she'd be part of that.

Live oaks, heavy with Spanish moss, shaded the sidewalks and added an air of gentility to the street. A hint of fall in the air, the little park that separated the two sides of Main Street burst with the golds and russets of autumn flowers. The Ladies' Garden Club had clustered chrysanthemums, zinnias, and pansies around an old wooden wheelbarrow. Scattered pumpkins added a festive flair.

Autumn. Her favorite season.

As she drove slowly past Dee-Ann's Diner, the old building all but smiled at her in its red-and-white finery. Geraniums bloomed in planters out front, and Lem Gilmore sat at a table by the window. No doubt he was mooching something off Dee-Ann even though he had nearly as much money as Croesus.

Misty Bottoms. So different from the glitzy shops and malls she'd grown used to. The town felt comfortable, like slipping into a pair of favorite slippers.

The big question? Could she fit into life here again, or had she been gone too long?

Only time would tell if those slippers welcomed her or pinched her feet.

She turned onto Old Church Street, past the pretty little periwinkle railroad car that boasted a florist and gardening center, and slid to the curb in front of Kitty's Kakes and Bakery with its funky, pink-and-green awning. The shop's huge front window proudly displayed today's temptations and looked exactly as it had when she and Beck had stopped in for a treat before Saturday's football game a lifetime ago.

The bell above Kitty's door jingled welcomingly when Tansy pushed it open.

Gracie squeezed around her to run inside. "Ms. Kitty, we're here!" Her soft child's voice was high-pitched with excitement.

Kitty peeked around the kitchen doorway, her full face breaking into a sunny smile. "Well, you certainly are, Gracie Bella."

Wiping her hands on the batter-smeared apron that covered her girth, she stepped around the corner of the display case, arms wide to catch the grinning child. "Welcome home."

Tansy watched as Kitty kissed her child and fussed over her.

"Don't you look a picture?"

Gracie's brows drew together, and the older woman laughed.

"You're as pretty as any picture I've ever seen," she amended.

"Mama bought me a new dress for today." Twirling, she showed off the pastel-flowered smock. "I gots ribbons to match." She reached up to her long, dark hair and fingered the silky ties in her ponytail.

"You sure do." Kitty turned her gaze to Tansy. "You doin' okay?"

She nodded.

"Been to your mom's yet?"

"No." She pointed to the packed vehicle. "That's our next stop. Gracie and I decided a drink and a snack were in order first."

"Then you've come to the right place." Kitty studied Tansy. "I know this has been hard for you, sweetie, but it sure is good to have you home."

Tansy gave her a wobbly smile. "It's good to be home."

"One of these days, you'll be able to say that and mean it," Kitty said.

Tansy nodded sadly.

"It'll be okay." She patted Tansy's shoulder, then turned to her daughter. "Why don't you come over here and show me what you want, sweetheart?" Kitty took Gracie by the hand and led her to the rows of baked goodies.

"I think, as much as I'd like one of your maple-iced doughnuts, we should both stick with bagels," Tansy said. "Neither of us has had much today." She glanced at her daughter. "A sugar high's probably not a great idea, so we'll save the doughnuts for another time."

"Smart." Her gaze ran over Tansy. "You're way too thin, though, honey. I think a few calories might be exactly what the doctor ordered."

When she opened her mouth to protest, Kitty shook her head.

"But not today. Understood." Her tongs reached inside the case for a bagel. "Toasted?"

"Yes, please."

"I have some maple-flavored cream cheese." She eyed Tansy.

Laughing, Tansy said, "Why not?"

"To drink?"

"A glass of milk and a cup of coffee. Black."

"Can I have a soda, Mama?"

Tansy shook her head, and the little girl's lip stuck out in the beginning of a pout.

"Kitty has the best milk in the county," Tansy said.

"You got that right. Maybe in all the South."

"You do?" Gracie pressed her face against the display case.

"Yes, ma'am." As Kitty prepared their order, she spoke over her shoulder. "You still want to do this?"

Nerves sizzled. "Yes, I do, but the location's crucial."

"Not much to choose from. The town's booming!"

"Jenni Beth's dream has been good for Misty Bottoms, hasn't it?"

"A blessing. And Cricket? Hard worker, that girl. I liked her right off. Our new deputy's warmed up to her, too."

"So I hear." Tansy pulled a couple napkins from the holder. "I'll call Quinlyn Deveroux tomorrow. See if she has anything that might fit my needs. I'm really hoping to find something with living quarters above. My budget would be a whole lot happier paying one mortgage."

"Thought you were livin' with your mama." Kitty placed their drinks in front of them and went back for the bagels.

"Only till I find something." Tansy unwrapped Gracie's straw. "I need to be on my own."

"Understood." Returning with their food, Kitty dropped into a chair beside her, buttered the bagel for Gracie, and cut it into quarters.

"Jenni Beth says you're swamped."

"I am. Honey, to be honest, the only reason I'm still open is because I don't want to let her down. She needs somebody to bake her cakes and such, but I'm too old and too tired."

"You're not old!"

"I am. I checked my mirror this mornin'. Above my head, the name *Methuselah* flashed on and off." She opened and closed her hand in a flashing gesture.

Tansy laughed. "Quit."

"That's exactly what I want to do." Kitty sipped the coffee she'd poured for herself. "This is a young person's job. Besides, Harvey's finished his treatments. He beat the Big C. Got a clean bill of health on his last visit."

Tansy squeezed her hand. "Mom told me, and I can't tell you how happy I was to hear that."

"You and me both. It's time I retire. Time somebody else takes care of this town's sweet tooth and caffeine addiction. Harv and I don't plan to leave Misty Bottoms right away, but eventually we'd like to sell that big old house we're in and downsize. We're thinkin' to move to Charleston to be close to our daughter. She and Joe have two little ones now." Kitty pulled a phone from her pocket and brought up the latest pictures of her grandchildren.

Tansy looked at them while she picked at her bagel. Gracie demolished hers, and Tansy felt a prick of guilt. She should have realized sooner how hungry Gracie was. But then, she'd been asleep, right?

Ah, the perils of parenthood. Tansy did guilt extremely well.

Beck, stepping out of the gas station, that heated moment when their eyes met, popped into her head. Regret, stepsister to guilt, washed over her. Yep, she was an expert at guilt and all its relatives.

She yanked herself back to Kitty's conversation.

"If I owned this place, honey, I'd let you have it for a song. But, stupid me, I've leased it all these years. Made a small fortune for Howard Greene. Like I said, though, the equipment's all mine, and you're welcome to whatever you can use. You can have it dirt cheap."

"I appreciate that." Tansy stacked their plates, then stood and carried their trash to the wastebasket. "So we have three cakes to make, huh?"

"*You* have three cakes," Kitty said. "Let me get the order forms, and we can go over them. And you." She pointed at Gracie. "I've got a *Frozen* coloring book and some crayons."

Gracie clapped her hands. "Is Olaf in it?"

"Yes, he is." She carried the book and crayons to Gracie, then held up a finger to Tansy. "I have one quick call I need to make."

"Fine. I'll get another coffee if you don't mind?"

"Help yourself. Pour me a refill, too, would you?" Kitty pulled her cell from an apron pocket and punched in a number. She moved behind her bakery case. "Hey, you out and about?" She listened a minute, then said, "I've got some of my date-filled cookies here—your mom's favorite. If you could stop by in the next little bit, I'll send them home with you." She nodded. "Wonderful."

Moving to a filing cabinet, she pulled out three folders. "There you go." She set them on the table beside Tansy. "I've got a hunch you can put some magic in these."

Tansy flipped open the first. "Betsy and Clem. They want a Vegas-themed wedding?"

"Roulette table and all. Beck managed to find everything Jenni Beth is gonna need to turn the barn into a Vegas gambling hall for the day—minus the actual betting, of course. That would be against the law."

"I didn't realize she was using the old barn."

"You know Cole and old buildings. Nothin' he likes more than to get his hands on one. He and Beck have worked miracles with Jenni Beth's. It's like a blank canvas. She can turn it into anything she—or her brides—want."

"Hmmm." She flipped open a second file. "A vintage-style wedding?" She rubbed her hands together. "I know exactly what I want to do with this one."

Before she could take a peek at the notes for Tanya and Ray Miller's daughter's sweet-sixteen party, the door opened.

"Do you know what Coralee's...up to?" Beck stopped, one foot in, one foot out of the bakery shop as he caught sight of Tansy. He swore all the oxygen in the place had been sucked out.

"Beck." The page Tansy held fluttered, and she laid it on the table.

"Hey, Gracie, how are you?"

"Hi, Beck. I'm coloring."

"I see that."

Tansy studied her daughter. "Gracie, how do you know Beck?"

"He goes to see Grandma."

Tansy met Beck's midnight-blue eyes. "Seriously?"

He shrugged. "I like your mom. The problem was between you and me, Tanz. Never with me and your mom or dad."

Beck glanced toward a very innocent-looking Kitty.

Beaming, she hustled behind the counter, then handed him a coffee. "Here you go. On the house. Look who just got into town. Why don't you two catch up while I box those cookies?"

"Your timing's off, Kitty."

The older woman plumped her gray hair. "I don't think so, honey. Have a seat. This won't take but a minute."

He'd rather stand. Hell, he'd rather eat Dee-Ann's liver and onions or walk barefoot through a fire ant hill. But since neither was an option, he walked stiffly to where Tansy sat, staring with those damn big, blue-green eyes of hers.

Taking a deep breath, coffee in hand, he headed into enemy territory. Nodding at the empty chair beside Gracie, he asked, "You mind?"

"Not at all." Tansy set down her cup.

He nearly spewed the sip he'd just taken. If her voice

had been any chillier, that snowman Gracie was coloring would turn to a chunk of ice.

Tapping the picture, he asked, "Whatcha doin' there, Gracie?"

"I'm drawin' a necklace for Olaf, Beck."

Raising a brow and ignoring the question in Tansy's incredible Caribbean-blue eyes, he returned his gaze to Gracie. "You do know Olaf's a guy, right?"

"Yeah, but he wants one."

"Okay." He drew out the word, then lifted his gaze to meet her mama's.

"What were you saying about Coralee?"

"Your crazy aunt's up to somethin', Tanz, and knowin' her?" He shook his head. "Could be anything."

"Well, you know what they say. Here in the South, we don't bother to hide crazy. We plop it right down in a rocker on the front porch with a big old glass of sweet tea."

"If Coralee would stay on the front porch, I'd be good with that," Beck answered. "Problem is she carries that crazy all over town."

"Don't I know it." Tansy sipped her coffee. "Remember the time she marched down to the old swimming hole where the Sunday school class was splashing around, stripped down to her skivvies, and insisted Pastor Jeremiah baptize her? I about died of embarrassment."

He laughed. "And if memory serves, you hid behind me so she couldn't see you. But she waded right over to you and pulled you along beside her, insisting you be witness."

"I swore I'd disown her."

"But you didn't."

"No. Deep down, she's a wonderful woman."

Gracie tugged at Beck's sleeve. "She bought me a BB gun."

His mouth dropped open. "For a four-year-old?"

"Mama put it away. She said I had to be older to shoot it." She turned that beautiful smile on him. "I think I should have it now. Don't you?"

Despite himself, he grinned. "Oh no, you don't." He tapped the end of her nose. "I'm not gettin' into this. What your mama says goes."

The child's smile turned to a pout.

"And will the real Gracie Bella please stand up?" Tansy sighed.

"Why do you want me to stand up, Mama?"

Tansy looked toward the ceiling and shook her head. "It's just a saying."

"'Kay." She bent her head to her coloring, tongue slipping out between her lips as she concentrated.

He nodded toward the papers Tansy had spread over the table. "What have you got there?"

"Cake orders. Jenni Beth called on my way into town. It seems our unflappable Ms. B. is quite flapped."

Beck threw her a lopsided grin. "Yeah, it's that old 'be careful what you wish for.' She said she'd thrown herself on your mercy."

Kitty swiped at some powdered sugar on the counter. "Afraid that's my fault. I can't keep up with both the bakery and all the fancies for Magnolia House's events."

"Nonsense. You can still run circles around all of us," Tansy said.

"Harv's cancer took a lot out of me."

"But he's good now," Beck said.

"He is. And looking forward to my retirement. Says

he intends to chase me around the bed mornin', noon, and night." She blushed like a schoolgirl.

"You play tag?" Gracie asked.

Everybody chuckled.

"Somethin' like that," Beck answered. To Kitty, he said, "Enviable goals, you ask me." His gaze settled on Tansy. "Chasin' is fun." He arched a brow. "Catchin' is even more fun."

She choked on her coffee. "Beck, you can't say things like that."

"Sure I can. I just did."

He looked up to see Kitty holding a white baker's box, a twinkle in her eyes. An uneasy thought slithered through his mind. Had she called him when she did fig-uring Tansy would be gone by the time he got here, or was the old gal up to something?

Nah. Everybody knew he and Tansy were past tense.

The bell over the door tinkled as Beck left.

Tansy watched him walk to his truck, admired his fine butt in those worn-nearly-white jeans. The man had a sexy stride. Confident. Easy.

Kitty cleared her throat. "My guess is you two are worn out. Go. Get that child settled. Your mother's probably pacing the floor. I know for a fact she can't wait to get her hands on her granddaughter again."

Tansy laughed. "I wouldn't argue that." She held up the files. "Where do you want me to put these?"

"Take them with you. They're yours now. Magnolia House cakes are in your capable hands as of today, and I, for one, can't wait to see what you'll do with them."

The idea of starting her own business sent a mixture of ecstasy and full-blown panic through Tansy. But she was good, very good, with pastries and cakes. Left alone, day after day, in that cold mausoleum of a house Emerson's folks had purchased for them as their wedding gift, the one he'd lost in a high-stakes poker game, she'd worked hard on her baking skills. She'd honed them with some daytime classes she'd sneaked in.

This venture was her dream. It would be her salvation and allow her to support her daughter.

Waving good-bye to Kitty, her daughter's hand in hers, Tansy walked to the loaded-down SUV.

Once she had Gracie buckled in her seat, Tansy decided to drive down Main. She'd take the roundabout way to her childhood home. Somewhere, there had to be an available building.

Nothing caught her eye.

At the end of Main, she spotted the Elliot homestead and fought the wave of nostalgia that swept over her. She'd dreamed of one day living in the two-story home with its cupola and wraparound porch—with Beck.

And that would never happen.

Still, the house called to her. She slowed, then gasped out loud.

"What's wrong, Mama?"

"Nothin', sugar. I'm just lookin' at the pretty house."

"Are we gonna live in it?" Gracie struggled against her restraining harness to get a better peek.

"No."

"Why not?"

She gave the parent's age-old fallback answer. "Because."

Still, she pulled up in front of the house, beneath the shade of the big live oak that fairly dripped with Spanish moss. A for-sale sign had been planted in the front yard right beside a monstrous azalea bush. In the spring, it would fill the yard with the most incredible shade of pink. Now, as they headed into fall, zinnias and chrysanthemums bloomed, their deeper colors heralding the changing of the season.

Memories assaulted her. How many times had she come here for dinner or to deliver one of her mom's pies to Pops and NeeNee, Beck's grandparents? She smiled remembering the time she and Beck had sneaked out the back door after dinner, away from his parents and grandparents, and out of sight of the house. God, Beck could kiss. One touch from those lips and she was a goner.

Beck. Her smile wavered.

Jenni Beth insisted he looked more like Dierks Bentley than Dierks did. Maybe she was right. To Tansy, though, Beck was Beck with his curly, blond hair and eyes the color of a starry night sky.

Motor still running, a window down to let in the somewhat cooler breeze, she concentrated on the present. Struggling to set emotion aside, she studied the house with a more critical eye.

Pops had lived there alone the last few years. After NeeNee died, he must have been lonely. A few months ago, he'd moved in with Beck's parents, where he'd have life around him again.

Her own mother, living alone now, was suffering the same loneliness. Hopefully, it would be better with her and Gracie back in town.

Idling at the curb, Tansy struggled for details, tried to

bring the floor plan into clear focus. If she remembered right, the entire house had hardwood floors. The windows in the back? Perfection. Upstairs, it seemed to her the ceiling slanted a bit and peaked in the center. But she might be wrong. She'd only been on the second story a time or two. No dummies, the adults had kept the two of them away from the bedrooms.

Her heartbeat accelerated. She and Gracie could live upstairs, and she'd turn the bottom floor into her business.

The more she thought about it, the more excited she got. It could work. She knew it could. Amazed that someone hadn't snatched the place up immediately, she wanted to hop out of the SUV, tear down the for-sale sign, and stow it in the back of her vehicle so no one else would be tempted.

She'd paint it even though either Beck or his dad had given it a fresh coat recently. While the white on white looked good, the place was a grand old lady and needed a style that better suited a Victorian. She'd look so much snazzier with something more colorful, something just this side of garish.

Beck would hate that. Truth? Even though he'd been civil at Kitty's, he'd no doubt hate anything she did, must hate that she'd come home to Misty Bottoms. Maybe. And maybe he didn't give a flying fig what she did.

Somehow that would be worse.

Thumbing open the bottle in her center console, she popped a cherry-flavored Tums.

Chapter 3

BECK SWORE A DRUMMER HAD TAKEN UP PERMANENT residence in his head, and his chest hurt. Jeez, he felt like he'd been run over—by a beautiful witch driving an SUV. Make that a beautiful, unsettling witch. Shouldn't the calendar have had a warning note on today's date? Beware the ides of September.

Why had she really come back?

He shook his head and smiled ruefully. Stupid, stupid question. She'd divorced a multimillionaire. Guess she could do whatever she damn well pleased, wherever she pleased. And didn't that just suck dust?

Why now? He'd been honest with Cole. He *was* over her and had been for a long time. Still, it didn't sit well to have her moving home.

He hit his Bluetooth button when his cell rang and barked, "What?"

"Something crawl up your butt this morning?" his cousin's fiancé asked.

"Yeah, as a matter of fact, something did, Sam. Rather, someone." He rubbed a hand over his forehead. *Shake it off*, he told himself. "How's my favorite cousin?"

"Cricket's wonderful as always. Those rose-colored glasses she has permanently affixed to her face guarantee it."

Despite himself, Beck laughed. "Yeah, you got that right."

Cricket had moved back to Misty Bottoms and opened a flower-and-garden center, then fell in love with Sam DeLuca, a New York City detective who'd come to town for some R & R. Now he was a small-town deputy—and loving it.

"What can I do for you, Sam? This an official or unofficial call?"

"Official. Seems a couple kids got to tossing a football around and put the pigskin through old Mrs. Macy's window."

"Oh boy. I had her for eighth-grade math. Those kids picked the wrong person to mess with. She's got a tongue sharp as those Ginsu knives they sell on TV at Christmas and a temper to match."

Sam chuckled. "It took me all of three seconds to figure that out. Anyway, I managed to talk her out of pressing charges, but only if I can get a new window installed before nightfall. You up to playing hero? Saving a couple kids from the slammer?"

Beck glanced into the rearview mirror and looked into his own eyes. A little sweaty labor and a go-round with Mrs. Macy might be exactly what he needed. The job would let him work off some steam. "I'll head over now and measure her window, then pick up what I need at the store. We should have the right size in stock. If not, I'll rush order it and nail some plywood in place till it comes in."

Actually, he had a well-hidden soft spot for his former teacher. He'd left his backpack in her classroom one afternoon. When he'd returned for it, she was still there, with Wilson Potts. Poor as dirt, Wilson's beat-up shoes stayed together with only a wish and a prayer.

While Beck peeked through the door's window, Mrs. Macy handed Wilson a brand-spankin'-new pair along with new jeans and a T-shirt.

Beck had slipped back down the hall with no one the wiser.

And the next day, when the homework he'd left in that backpack wasn't finished, he took the tongue-lashing she laid on him without a single complaint.

He'd let the kids or their folks pay for the window and materials, but he'd eat the labor himself. A little paying it forward.

———

More excited than she'd been in a long time, ideas bouncing around in her head, Tansy drove on automatic pilot the rest of the way to her mom's. When the tidy, ranch-style house came into view, though, her mind jerked back to the present. The future would save for later.

"Grandma's!"

"Yes, honey, we're here. Finally."

As she turned into the drive, the front door opened and her mother stepped out. Tansy smiled. Her mother, dark-blond hair cut stylishly short, looked chic in a sleeveless dress, the elongated top black, the skirt wide black-and-white bands. Low-heeled black pumps completed her outfit.

Tansy, in her dark-green silk top and fitted slacks to match, felt road weary and rumpled.

Having just turned fifty-two, Rexanna Calhoun was still young and attractive. For the first time, Tansy wondered if her mom might be dating, if she'd consider marriage again. The idea rattled her. She wanted her mother happy, she really did. But Daddy…

The thought evaporated when her mother opened the SUV's back door to hug her granddaughter. Through the happy confusion of unbuckling Gracie, she asked, "How was the trip?"

"Great. Uneventful."

"Wonderful. I prayed you'd have no rain and no problems."

"Your prayers were answered, Mom." *Unless you included me not running into Beck Elliot*, Tansy mentally added as she slid from the front seat.

Inside her childhood home, Puddles, her mother's gray tabby, greeted them, winding in and out of their legs and purring wildly. Gracie dropped on her belly right in the center of the hallway to give the cat a kiss and a hug. Tansy and her mom skirted the little girl and carried in the first of the bags.

Surrounded by familiar furniture and doodads, Tansy relaxed for the first time in way too long. Gracie, cooped up for hours in the car, hit the backyard like a whirling dervish.

Once she was out of earshot, Tansy said, "I've been thinking a lot lately." She reached for her mother's hand. "I'm sorry."

"Sorry? For what?"

"For making such a mess of everything. I let you and Daddy down."

"Never." Rexanna's voice, usually so quiet and soft with that heavy Southern drawl, turned hard and determined. "I don't ever want to hear you say that again. Since the day we found out I was carrying you, Daddy and I loved you with all our hearts. Nothing you've done, nothing you ever could do, would change that."

"But—"

"But nothin'. You are our pride and joy, Tansy. Forever. And not just because I birthed you, but because you've earned it."

"I got pregnant before I walked down the aisle."

"Yes, and because of that, you blessed me with the most precious grandbaby on the face of this earth."

"I'm divorced, Mom." Her voice grew small. "There's never been a divorce in our family. Until now. Until me."

"You are divorced, and the only thing I have to say about that is thank God!" Rexanna dropped her voice. "That nincompoop might be the father of that darlin' little girl out there," she said, tipping her head toward the backyard, "but as far as I'm concerned, Emerson Forbes doesn't deserve to see either you or her ever again. The man's a toad—a toad you left a prince for, I feel obliged to add."

A surprised laugh erupted from Tansy. "He's not a toad. Unfortunately, on the outside anyway, he's attractive…and knows it. As to being a nincompoop? At the very least. And Beck? A prince? Seriously?" Tansy set her purse beside her overnighter. "Mom, does Beck visit you?"

Her mother looked sheepish. "Yes, he does."

"Mom." She drew out the word.

"Beck did nothing wrong, honey."

"You're right." She threw up her hands. "It was me. All my fault."

"I didn't say that."

"You didn't have to."

"Emerson took advantage of you at a very vulnerable time."

"There were two of us involved, Mom. Whatever the circumstances, I participated."

Her mother blushed. "TMI, sweetie. Still…after your daddy died, Beck came around from time to time to see if I needed anything, and sometimes I did—the bathroom door started to stick, the back porch roof sprung a leak, that kind of thing."

"You told me everything was fine."

"And it was, but occasionally I owed that to Beck. He refused to charge me anything more than a batch of his favorite oatmeal raisin cookies."

"I could have paid someone to do the work, Mom."

"Why should you do that? Beck's a good man, and he's extremely handy when it comes to home repairs. It's how he earns his living. He's also the son of one of my best friends. Here in Misty Bottoms, that's how it's done." She tipped her head. "Have you forgotten your roots so quickly?"

Tansy said nothing. Without a voice raised, she'd been well and thoroughly chastised. Her mother was right. Misty Bottoms, small town that it was, took care of its own.

"Now, want a cup of coffee?" Mom hopped to her feet, changing the subject. "I just brewed a fresh pot."

"I'd love that." Tears misted her vision. "I love you."

"And I love you right back!"

After a heartfelt hug, her mother busied herself at the counter.

Watching her, Tansy made a decision. "I'm going to do something else that's crazy, Mom."

"Is it something you want to do?"

"Yes."

"Good. About time you did what you want."

"Well, this is a doozy." She paused for a heartbeat, let out her breath in a huff. "I want to buy Lamont Elliot's house."

Coffee sloshed over the edge of the cup Rexanna had just filled. "Tansy—"

"Gracie and I can live upstairs, and the downstairs is absolutely perfect for my new business."

"Beck will have a fit."

"Yes, he probably will."

"And you're okay with that?"

Tansy shook her head. "No, I'm not. I've already hurt him enough. But I have to live my own life. Do what's best for Gracie and me." She straightened her shoulders. "I forgot that for far too long. I lived my life around Emerson's needs. No more, Mom. I'm taking back my own life."

"Oh, honey." Coffee forgotten, Rexanna pulled her daughter into another tight embrace. "I'll be forever sorry I didn't stop you from marrying that odious man. I should have brought you home with me."

"I wouldn't have come."

"I know."

"But I learned a valuable lesson." She peeked into the backyard at the little girl on the swing. "And I have Gracie." She turned back to her. "I'm home now. Home to stay."

"You say that, but already you're making plans to move out."

"To start my own home right here in Misty Bottoms. We'll go to Gracie's school plays together and sit in the

stands to watch the soccer games she'll be the MVP of.
It'll be great!"

Her mother laughed and, for that brief space of time,
life was nothing but good.

Slowly, Tansy sank onto the edge of her bed. The cover
was new, but the walls were still the pale lavender she'd
fallen in love with standing in the paint aisle at Elliot's
Lumberyard. That had been her junior year of high
school. Beck preferred forest green, but she'd held out
for lavender. A sad smile lifted the corners of her mouth
as she glanced at the deep-green lampshade, the green
in the drapes she'd begged her mother to buy. A little
bit of Beck.

She'd loved him so much. Just the thought of him
had been enough to set her heart pounding. How many
nights had she lain in this very bed and dreamed of the
day she'd share her nights with Beck?

When she'd left for college and he'd stayed home to
help with the family business, she'd been devastated.
Pops had just lost his NeeNee, and Beck had an obliga-
tion and responsibility to the family. But it had broken
her heart to drive away alone when they'd planned to
go together.

He'd promised to wait; she'd promised to return.

She'd broken that promise. After her father's funeral,
she'd met Emerson, and everything had changed.

Water under the bridge.

Dragging her suitcase to the closet, she hung up the
few things she'd brought with her.

While Gracie, Puddles, and her mother played in the

backyard, Tansy gave her friend Quinlyn a quick call. A Realtor now, her name had been on the for-sale sign at the Elliot home. After Tansy explained her plans, they agreed to meet the next day. There were no available properties on Main Street, but they'd take a peek at a building several blocks off it and at another on Old Church Street. They'd also look at the Elliot homestead.

She knew where her heart lay, but she owed it to herself to make sure it was the right choice. A lot rode on this. She had to use her head, not only her heart and emotions. Because of that, she'd also consider Kitty's present location. She didn't want to rent, but Howard wasn't a spring chicken anymore, and maybe he'd consider selling the place to her.

If she did that, though, she and Gracie would still have to find a place to live. As much as she loved her mother, as much as she'd missed her, Tansy couldn't see herself living under the same roof permanently. She and Gracie needed their own home. If they couldn't live above the business, that meant two mortgages and two properties to maintain. The mere idea of that made her headache return.

The topper, though, was that if she set up shop in Kitty's place, it would always be just that. Kitty's Kakes and Bakery. It wouldn't matter if she ran the store for the next fifty years. Misty Bottomers would continue to think of it as Kitty's. She wanted it to be hers. Tansy's Sweet Dreams.

So rather than waste Quinlyn's time, she'd cross Kitty's off the list. It wasn't what she wanted. And by darn, her mom was right. It was past time she started standing up for herself again. Time she had a little of what *she* wanted. Time to stop bowing to the pressure of what she felt others thought she should do.

Folding the last of her lingerie, she placed it in the dresser drawer.

Right now? She'd join the others in the backyard for a game of hide-and-seek. Fitting since she'd been hiding too long. It was about time she was found.

Chapter 4

EVERY SINGLE BUILDING INVITED TANSY TO STEP INTO the past. Exploring the empty stores turned into a walk down memory lane. As she and Quinlyn checked off the pros and cons of each, Tansy realized it was wasted time.

She already knew what she wanted.

Pops Elliot's house.

Sherman's March to the Sea couldn't have stirred up more dust than her decision would.

Could she do this to Beck?

Yes, their *thing* had happened long enough ago to be the past. She winced. Her sense of justice wouldn't allow her to trivialize what they'd had by calling it a *thing*. They'd been in love. Deeply.

One look at him in that second before he shuttered his eyes and blocked her out was all it took to realize he still harbored feelings for her. Not love anymore. No. She'd killed that, and she'd be forever sorry. He'd behaved well in front of Kitty and Gracie, but he didn't fool her. It was anger she read in his eyes now, anger and hurt.

Yet Pops's house had a for-sale sign in the front yard, and she was in the market for a house. Her money was every bit as good as anyone else's. Wouldn't it be better if she bought it, because no other buyer could possibly love the house as much as she did? Nobody would take better care of it.

Quinlyn, who'd been in the same class as her and

Jenni Beth, locked the door on the once-affluent men's clothing store. She bounced the keys in her hand and looked cool as a cucumber, her hair pulled up in a loose twist, her makeup expertly applied. Jewel-toned rings winked on every perfectly manicured finger.

Beside her, Tansy felt frazzled and disheveled.

"This building didn't do it either, did it?"

"No, it didn't. Sorry." She started to dig in her bag for a Tums.

"Don't be sorry. This is what I do. Real estate is a big investment, and it's important to get it right." Quinlyn tapped a suicidally high-heeled shoe on the uneven brick sidewalk. "So, what next? You want to take a peek at the Elliot place?" She fished another set of keys from the pocket of her crisp cotton dress and dangled them in front of Tansy. "I've got the keys right here."

Tansy tried to hide the shiver of delight mixed with apprehension that ran through her. Quinlyn was more than aware of the stumbling block, though, of Tansy's history with Beck.

Clasping her hands beneath her chin, Tansy said, "You know I do. Everything else aside, the house is a perfect fit for Gracie and me. That yard is simply crying out for a young child to play in it. We can live upstairs, and I can work down. One mortgage. Although…" She hesitated. "I'm almost afraid to ask the price."

Quinlyn threw out a figure.

Tansy nodded thoughtfully. "More than I'd hoped, but not as much as I'd feared. I think I can swing that." She laughed. "Thankfully, Gracie likes mac and cheese. We might be eatin' a whole lot of it while I get the business off the ground."

"I thought your husband—"

"Ex-husband," Tansy inserted. "And, no, he's not helpin'. I'm doin' this on my own, and you don't need to spread that around." She knew only too well how tongues wagged in a small town, and as she spoke and her stress grew, so did her drawl.

Her friend made a zipping gesture across her blush-pink lips. "I won't tell a soul."

Tansy knew better than to believe that; sooner or later it would come out anyway. But she wanted that house. She'd go through the motions of looking it over and having a building inspector check it out, but as far as she was concerned, the place was hers.

She'd already talked over the phone to the new manager of Coastal Plains Savings and Trust about a loan, but she would need to stop in today.

On the ride to the Elliot house in Quinlyn's pink MINI Cooper convertible, Tansy tried really, really hard to squelch the quick spurt of envy at her friend's carefree life. She loved her daughter, but the responsibility of being a mom never went away. Now that she was a *single* mom, the load felt far heavier.

Quinlyn's younger sister lived with her, though. So maybe her friend's life wasn't quite as carefree as it seemed.

When they pulled up in front of the house, the two sat in almost reverent silence.

Finally, Quinlyn cleared her throat. "This house means a lot to you, doesn't it?"

Tansy nodded. "I spent a lot of time here with Beck and his family."

"Have you seen Beck?"

"He was at Tommy's when I stopped for gas. Then he showed up while Gracie and I were at the bakery."

"You talked?"

"A little. Mostly, he talked to Kitty and Gracie." She turned to look at Quin. "Is he happy?"

"He seems okay, keeps busy. He's dated quite a bit, but if anything starts to look long-term, it ends. His choice, not the women's."

"I'm sorry about that." Even as she spoke the words, Tansy wondered at the truth in them. She wanted Beck happy. She really did. But it would kill her to see him with someone else, and wasn't that hypocritical?

"You want to go in?"

"Absolutely." She opened her car door and slipped out.

As the front door swung open, Tansy stepped across the threshold and smiled. Exactly as she remembered, minus the furniture. The big front room with its massive fireplace and white, carved mantel took up the front of the house. She wandered into the dining room with its ornate crystal chandelier. Beck's grandma had told her it was original to the house, which had transitioned from gas lighting to electricity somewhere in the early 1900s. Reaching up, she ran a fingertip along a sparkling crystal.

The living room and dining room could be used to seat customers. And the library? She wandered into it, her grin growing. This would be where she could let her love of all things girly run free. While she'd work hard to keep the other areas gender neutral, she'd set this room aside for the ladies. For their showers, luncheons, and get-away times.

The kitchen? She studied it with a critical eye. She'd

need to take down one wall and open it for counter and display cases. If she could find them, she'd replace the appliances with retro fixtures, preferably colored ones. Maybe red. Or pink. Cole might be able to help her with that.

She'd like to redo the bathroom, too. Take it back a few decades. She understood why Pops and NeeNee had updated everything, but for what she wanted, older was better.

The room behind the kitchen would make a phenomenal office and keep everything work related on this floor. None of it would have to travel to their living quarters.

This was a huge step. Once she decided on this, there'd be no turning back. It would take money for the remodeling, for the furnishings and supplies to start her fledgling business. It would also take a lot of hard work. She was up for that. In fact, she couldn't wait to roll up her sleeves and jump in.

With her mother's help, Gracie Bella would be fine, too. The two of them had discussed this during long, late-night phone chats. The money would be her biggest problem.

And then there was Beck. If she bought this house, he'd no doubt see it as another betrayal. Could she live with that?

Did she have a choice?

Both her heartburn and her headache returned.

She climbed the curved staircase, her hand trailing along the smooth, worn banister. This she'd leave just as it was, nicks and all. That assurance the house had been well lived in added a special touch to the ambience.

Five rooms and two baths made up the second floor. She'd turn one into an eat-in family kitchen and the largest into their living area. The others she'd use for bedrooms.

At the bottom of the second narrow flight of stairs, she pulled a string to light a bare bulb and gripped the simple railing. When she reached the top, she stared at the empty third-floor attic, dusty and long unused. Maybe she'd finish it off as a playroom for Gracie. It would make a fun place for her and her friends to watch TV or talk and eat pizza. This home was perfect in every way—except, of course, for the matter of Beck.

"Can I bring Kitty over after she closes today?"

"Absolutely."

"I'd like her take on the business aspect of it. But I want it, Quin. I really want this house."

"It's been on the market for a month now, and no one's made an offer. It's a bit more than most Misty Bottomers want to spend, so I don't see anyone coming along and nudging you out."

"You sure?" Tansy chewed her bottom lip. "Maybe I should put in an offer right now. Sign a paper. Give you some earnest money."

Quinlyn laughed. "I've got the listing for it, Tanz. If anyone makes an offer, I'll let you know. My goal is to sell the house, but this is a huge decision. I'd feel a whole lot better if you talked to Kitty first. Maybe bring your mom to see it. Sleep on it."

"Okay." Tansy nodded hesitantly. "If you're positive."

"I am."

Tansy called Kitty, feeling like a kid on Christmas

Eve. Waiting for Kitty to close for the day proved excruciating. Tansy went to the post office to check on her change of address, then to the bank to open a new account. The clock dragged, and she swore time had ground to a halt.

She checked her watch. One o'clock. A quick call ensured everything was well with her mom and Gracie. Her stomach grumbled. A trip to the Dairy Queen would fix that, and she'd still have time for a consult with Jenni Beth at Magnolia House.

An hour later, ensconced in Jenni Beth's wonderful carriage house office, Tansy slipped her sketchbook from her bag and flipped it open to the first of her drawings, the sweet-sixteen cake.

A squeal erupted as Jenni Beth pulled it toward her. "Olivia will love this!"

"She wanted something fun, and I think this should do it."

"Oh yeah."

"Since it's coed, I didn't figure girlie pink or frilly froufrou would work, so I went with neon—pink, green, and yellow. I thought I'd cover the bottom layer in white, then stripe it in the other colors. The middle layer? Neon green with a deeper green fondant bow. The top layer will be white with fondant polka dots in the pink, green, and yellow."

"Outstanding. And I love the little guitars and musical notes. She loves that guitar of hers—and she's got an outstanding voice." Jenni Beth leaned toward Tansy and hugged her. "This is good. So, so good! I can't wait till she sees it."

"So it's a go? I can move ahead on this one?"

"Absolutely. The layers are a little tipsy looking. On purpose?"

Tansy nodded. "I thought I'd cut them at angles to give them kind of an edgy look, then bead the colors around where the layers meet."

"What else do you have?" Eyes shining, Jenni Beth slid her chair closer.

Tansy flipped to another drawing, grinning when her friend clapped. "The vintage cake. Soft green for the bottom layer and soft lavender for the top. The middle layer I'll leave in ivory. I'll have fondant lace spilling over the sides of the first layer, then add sugar-paste violets to the middle. The top layer I'll cover in lace fondant. Since they're not using a topper, I'll do more sugar-paste violets and some old-fashioned roses there. A few strands of fondant pearls draped here and there, and it should be good to go."

"You can do this?"

"I can."

"Oh, Tansy, have I told you how happy I am you're here? For this, yes, but I've missed you so much."

Tansy blinked hard and fast to hold the tears at bay. "Don't make me cry, Jenni Beth. I'm not sure I'll ever stop if I give in to it."

"Okay." Jenni Beth breathed deeply. "Back to business. A groom's cake?"

"They don't want one, but I thought I'd make some cute little cupcakes incorporating the same colors. I'll put flowers on some, bows on others, pearls, whatever. I'll do them all a little differently. It should look good."

"It will look spectacular." Jenni Beth leaned back in her chair. "And the last? Betsy wanted Vegas but pretty. I'm thinkin' if you can pull that off, you're Wonder Woman."

Tansy laughed. "I'll show you what I have in mind. Then you can let me know whether or not I've earned my indestructible bracelets."

"The bride and groom both love Elvis, too."

"I saw that on the notes Kitty passed to me—with glee, I might add. I was concerned about stepping on her toes. Not the case. She's more than ready to pass the baton." She made to turn the page, then stopped. "Close your eyes."

Jenni Beth did.

"Remember, they want a groom's cake. So…" She laid two drawings on the table. "What do you think?"

The sides of the round groom's cake were decorated to look like piano keys. The top was a replica of Elvis's "Love Me Tender" vinyl, RCA Victor logo and all.

"This wasn't a Sun Records song?" Jenni Beth asked.

"Nope. RCA bought Elvis's contract from Sun for $35,000. Can you imagine? I'm kind of glad. It'll be fun doing the Nipper and gramophone logo."

"Nipper?"

"The dog on the logo. He liked to bite the back of visitors' legs. My grandma had a dog just like that called Baby."

"How do you know this stuff?"

Tansy simply smiled and tapped the side of her head. "Mind like a steel trap."

"Right."

They both laughed, knowing her words for the fish story they were.

"And this." Jenni Beth rested a finger on the

three-layer, square wedding cake done in red, white, and black. "Very Las Vegas. Very pretty. You did it."

"On paper, anyway. Now I've got to translate all this into cake." She poured more iced tea for herself, then held the pitcher up toward Jenni Beth who shook her head. "Let me tell you what else I've decided today."

Beck turned into Magnolia House's oak-lined drive. Damn, this place was fantastic. It never got old. His eyes drifted down the lane, and he hit his brakes. What the hell?

Tansy's SUV sat parked crookedly in front of Jenni Beth's office. With his thumb and forefinger, he rubbed his eyes beneath his dark glasses. The temptation to back out of the drive and come back later prodded him to put his truck in reverse.

No, that would be stupid. Charlotte, the Beaumonts' housekeeper, had called him about repairing the back door screen. Zeke, their old yellow Lab, had run through it. His eyesight was going, and he hadn't realized it was shut.

After all Ms. Charlotte had done for him over the years, he owed it to her to take care of it quickly. The temperature had mellowed some, but the kitchen would still heat up with the oven on.

He pulled up to the big house, hopped out of his truck, and grabbed the roll of screen and the tools he'd need. Even though he and Cole and Wes, Jenni Beth's brother who'd been killed in the war, had run wild here when they'd been kids, he knocked on the front screen door.

"Ms. Charlotte? It's Beck."

"Come on in." She stuck her head around the kitchen door, gesturing to him. "I'm puttin' the finishing touches on a big bowl of potato salad. I'll dish up some for you to take home."

Practically salivating at the idea of it, he grinned. "I'd appreciate that." Striding toward the door, he said, "Let's take a look at the screen." Kneeling, he studied the damage. "This is a straight-line cut. What was Zeke doin'? Carrying his Boy Scout knife?"

"Stranger things have happened." With that, she went back to her salad.

What kind of an answer was that? He studied the tear a little closer. Damned if it didn't look like a cut. Whatever. If she intended to pay him with potato salad for tonight's dinner, he didn't care how it got there. Besides, he needed to finish this and disappear before Jenni Beth and Tansy took it in their heads to come inside the main house.

The less he saw of Tansy Forbes, the better.

In no time, he had a new screen installed. "There you go. Good as new."

"Thank you. You're a good boy, and you can tell your mama I said so."

"You can be sure I will. Let me take this stuff out to the truck, then I'll come back for that potato salad."

Whistling Tim McGraw's "Real Good Man," he laid the rest of the roll of screen in the bed of his truck and set his tools in beside it. Despite himself, he glanced toward the carriage house. Tansy was still there. Didn't matter. It had nothing to do with him.

He did want that potato salad, though, so he headed back inside.

Charlotte stood at the counter, the plastic container in hand. "The girls are out at the office workin' hard, and my guess is they could use a snack about now. You won't mind runnin' it out to them, will you?"

"Ah, Ms. Charlotte..." He rubbed the back of his neck. "I've got a couple more stops to make."

"This won't take but a minute."

Before he could blink, he held his potato salad in one hand and a tray of cheese and crackers in the other. Seriously? She wanted him to play waiter to Tansy?

Charlotte limped across the kitchen for napkins. Had she been limping before? Huffing out a huge breath, he met her halfway, took the napkins, and headed for the door.

"Thank you, honey. Like I said before, you're a good boy."

"Right. Have a nice day, Ms. Charlotte. Tell Mr. and Mrs. Beaumont hello for me."

"I surely will."

"You might want to get off that leg for a bit."

"I'm gonna take a few minutes right now."

The front screen door slammed shut behind him as he crossed the porch. He hustled down the stairs and across the lawn. He'd dump these damn things inside and leave. Nothing said he had to talk to Tansy. He'd played nice at Kitty's. That was enough.

He gave a quick knock at the door, opened it, and peeked in. "Everybody decent?"

Jenni Beth laughed. "We're dressed. Decent? Probably."

"Charlotte sent me with fuel for you. She said you were workin' hard." He pointedly ignored Tansy. He was still PO'ed that she'd come back. He'd been doing just fine; he didn't need or want her here.

Not that he still had a thing for her.

Tansy, however, wasn't having it. She jumped up. "Are you following me?"

"Am I—hell, no, I'm not followin' you. Why would I want to do that?"

Hand on her hip, Tansy said, "You tell me."

"I don't have a reason because I'm not followin' you. I came to fix the back screen door for Charlotte. Zeke ran through it."

Jenni Beth's forehead creased. "When?"

"A little bit ago. Charlotte said the kitchen gets hot and asked if I could fix it before dinner."

"But Zeke's been gone all day. My dad took him to the groomer."

Beck threw his hands in the air. "I don't know. I don't care. She asked me to fix it, and I fixed it. End of story. I'm leavin'."

Jenni Beth held the tray out to him. "Have a few."

"No thanks." Without another word, he left.

The whole damn town was going crazy.

———

Tansy pulled up in front of the bakery. A quick check of her watch showed she was only ten minutes early. Not too bad, considering she'd wanted to come an hour ago.

She'd nearly died when Beck had walked in on her and Jenni Beth. Her guilt-ometer had spiked into the red zone. She'd been certain he'd found out about Quinlyn showing her the house and had come to tell her he'd yanked it off the market.

So she'd gone on the defense. Still, it was darned strange how he kept showing up. Well, she'd worry about that later. Right now, she had a date with Kitty to walk through the Elliot house again. She'd wondered if some of her initial excitement might wane, but it hadn't. If anything, she was more certain than ever she'd found her new home.

Hers and Gracie Bella's.

The bell tinkled overhead as she pushed open the door. "It's me," she said.

"I'm almost done here, sweetie," Kitty called from the back room. "Want coffee or iced tea?"

"Nope. I don't want anything to slow us down."

Kitty chuckled. "Understood."

A few pans banged, a drawer opened and closed, then Kitty stepped out from the back room, untying her apron. Tossing it in the laundry basket, she ran both hands through her short hair. "I look okay?"

"Yes, you do."

"Then we're out of here."

Tansy practically danced to the door. Kitty flipped the sign to read "Sorry, we're closed" and locked the door behind her. They'd both drive, so Kitty could leave for home from there.

Quinlyn waved from the steps of the Elliot house when they pulled up.

Kitty, hands behind her back, walked slowly through the first floor. Waiting for her verdict, Tansy could barely breathe. Like a puppy, she followed the older woman into the kitchen and outlined her idea for removing the wall.

"So you'd do all your bakin' right here in front of

folks? Sell directly from here?" She stood in the middle of the kitchen, arms outstretched.

"That's what I thought, yes."

"Ask me, that's not a good idea. I mean, where you gonna wash your dishes and pans? You don't want to be doin' that in front of customers while they're enjoying their baked goods."

"*Hmmm*. Good point." She turned to the older woman. "What would you do?"

"I'd use the kitchen for exactly that. This is where I'd do my work. That beautiful dining room with the huge window lookin' out onto the backyard and the gardens? Half of it would make a perfect salesroom. That's where the display cases and racks should go. Set it up to look like a kitchen if you want, but do the real work right here. Use the rest of the space for tables."

Eyes narrowed, Tansy imagined that plan and had to admit it worked. It worked very well, in fact. "You're right."

"Of course I am." Kitty grinned. "Been doin' this a couple years now. It's always best, honey, to separate the spaces. Nobody wants to see the actual work that goes into the treats they're eatin'. Takes away all the magic."

They walked through the rest of the space and then wandered upstairs. "I know this doesn't have anything to do with the business, but I'd appreciate any advice you can give me. I really need this to work."

"You young girls are puttin' us all to shame." Kitty rested her hands on her hips. "Quinlyn here builds her own real estate business. Jenni Beth rips into Magnolia House and practically rebuilds it, then turns it into one of the most beautiful wedding destinations imaginable. Then Cricket shows up and completely transforms the flower business in town." She turned to Tansy. "And now you've come home to start your own bakery and tea shop. I'm proud of you girls. Misty Bottoms is back on the map, thanks to y'all."

Tansy wrapped an arm around Kitty's waist. "I'm kind of riding on the others' coattails…and yours."

"Nonsense."

Quinlyn nodded. "This is big, Tansy, and a whole lot riskier than what I did."

Tansy popped an antacid.

Kitty looked out at the street and noticed the day had grown long. "I've got to be goin', girls. Time to fix dinner for Harvey and me, then put these old feet up for a bit. That alarm goes off awful early." She eyed Tansy. "You ready for that? In order for the bread to rise, you have to, too. Early."

"I've always been an early riser."

They stepped onto the front porch just as Tansy's mom pulled up out front with Gracie.

Tansy ran down the front porch steps to meet them.

Rexanna and Kitty spoke for a few minutes, then Kitty left.

Tansy's mom stood in the front yard studying the house while Gracie hopscotched up and down the walk.

"I've got to say this feels rather strange, honey," Rexanna said. "Your dad and Beck's were friends from first grade on. Judy and I were friends, too. So I've been in this house too many times to count. Still, looking at it as an investment and a business rather than as a friend's home puts everything in a new light, doesn't it?"

Tansy nodded.

"You have your heart set on this, don't you?"

She nodded again.

"You have a lot of memories here, too. You and Beck."

"Yes."

"Why don't Gracie and I go out back while you two take a tour and talk about this?" Quinlyn suggested. "I've got my sister's soccer ball in the trunk of the car along with a pair of old sneakers. We can kick it around."

"Can we, Mama?"

"Of course! Thank you, Quin. I appreciate it."

Her friend smiled. "Always easier to concentrate without—" She tipped her head toward the child.

"Yes, it is."

"You said Gracie would be a soccer star. Guess it's started, huh?" Her mother watched Quinlyn walk away, the little girl's hand in hers.

Rexanna and Tansy stepped inside and closed the door behind them. Their footsteps echoed in the big, empty space.

"What do you think, Mom?"

Her mom moved to the center of the living room, turned a slow three-sixty, and breathed deeply. "I think this place is amazing. Always have." Her eyes sparkled when she faced Tansy. "Walk through it with me." She took her daughter's hand as Quin had taken her granddaughter's.

"Let me tell you what I'm thinkin' about doing here. Kitty gave me some great ideas."

They spent the better part of an hour exploring and inspecting, stopping to study a room, discussing how it might be used and changes that needed to be made.

Tansy dropped onto the top step of the second-floor landing. "I love it, Mom."

Her mother sat beside her, looping an arm around her daughter's waist, and drew her close. "So why are you hesitatin'?"

She leaned into her mom's warmth and dropped her head to her shoulder. "A couple reasons, really."

"Let me guess. Would the first be Beck?"

Wordlessly, she nodded.

"Honey, what happened between the two of you is an old story. Beck wants you to be happy."

"I wonder."

"Tansy Elizabeth!" Rexanna swiveled to look her daughter in the eye. "Beck's too good a man to hold a grudge."

Tansy turned slightly, rested her back against the railing. "Not where I'm concerned. The truth? I deserve it, Mom. He loved me, and I cut him to the core. You know what they say about that line between love and hate. It's a very fine one. I shoved him—hard—and pushed him to the other side."

When her mom opened her mouth to speak, Tansy shook her head.

"No. Don't say anything. Beck *is* a good man, but not around me, and I can't blame him one bit. At best, he's coolly indifferent."

"Coolly indifferent?" Her mother studied her for a moment, tapping a finger on her chin. "Okay, let's table that for now. What else is keeping you from making an offer tonight? You said you had a couple reasons."

Uneasy, Tansy ran the toe of her shoe along the grain in the oak stair tread.

"Honey, what else?"

Running her fingers through her already-tousled hair, she sighed. "Money."

"Ahhh."

"Yes, ahhh. Everybody in town thinks I'm practically swimmin' in it."

"But we know better."

She nodded.

"I still say you need to take that jackass to court." Rexanna's face flushed. "I know he has no money now, but in time, he will. And he has a trust fund. How you allowed him to talk his way out of payin' any alimony or child support is beyond me."

"I wanted out, Mom."

"Understood, but practicalities still need to be considered. The law would have been behind you."

"And the divorce would have dragged out for months, years even." Her voice dropped to a whisper. "I couldn't have stood that."

Her mom patted her knee. "You always were headstrong. Another reason your marriage to Emerson never made sense to me."

An unexpected tear plopped onto Tansy's pant leg. "I can't explain it." She sniffed. "I don't understand it, either. I loved Beck and wanted more than anything to marry him. Then Daddy died and… I don't know. Timing, I guess. Emerson showed up, and before I could surface for a deep breath, I was pregnant." She swiped at her eyes.

"And it's in the past." Her mom squeezed her tightly. "Here we sit." She waved her other arm, indicating the house. "In your future."

"Maybe."

"Nonsense. Will this house work for you?"

"Yes."

"Then go tell Quinlyn you want it."

"But—"

"No buts." Putting both hands on her daughter's shoulders, she turned her. "Look at me, baby. The day you were born—" Her voice caught, and she drew in a deep breath, let it out. "Oh, I do miss your daddy, sugar."

"I know, Mom. So do I." Tears burned Tansy's eyes, and she blinked them away. "I wish he were here with us right now."

"Me too. He always wanted what was best for his little girl. From the day you were born, he doted on you." Her lips trembled. "So this house is a gift from him."

"What?" Tansy's brows drew together.

Rexanna cleared her throat and took her daughter's hand. "The day you were born, your daddy went down to see old Mr. Carson. Remember him?"

"I do. Gosh, I haven't thought about him in years."

"Yes, well, he passed on quite some time ago. Anyway, Mr. Carson ran a small investment firm. Financial advising, that sort of thing." She flicked a hand in the air. "Daddy, God bless him, invested some money with Mr. Carson that very first day you drew breath. Over the years, your father's picks did well, and he found he enjoyed playin' the market." She wet her lips and gripped Tansy's hand a little tighter. "He asked me to wait till the time was right to tell you all this. I think that time has come."

"What are you sayin', Mom?"

"I'm sayin' you have the money to pay cash for this house if it's what you want, darlin' girl."

Ignoring Tansy's silence and, Tansy was sure, her slack-jawed expression, her mom continued. "Of course, you'll need to borrow some money for the remodeling, the equipment you need and such, but I think you can manage that, don't you?"

Still, she could find no words.

Her mother snapped her fingers in front of Tansy's face, and she flinched.

"Mom, I can't take that money. You need it."

She shook her head adamantly. "It's not my money. It's yours and always has been. I've just been sittin' on it, waitin' for you to leave Mr. High-and-Mighty. I didn't want him to have a nickel of it to throw away on the horses or whatever."

The look on Tansy's face stopped her.

"Sorry, but I'm not goin' to pretend to ever have liked that man. And me? I don't need the money, Tanz. Your dad was a little bit of a wizard when it came to the stock market. He left me with everything I'll ever need—except him."

"Oh, Mom."

They sat at the top of the stairs and watched the sun settle low in the sky outside.

Finally her mother said, "You think it's time we save Quin? My guess is that Gracie has her worn to the bone by now."

"Yeah." She knuckled away a stray tear. "I don't know what to say."

"Thanks will do."

"Then, thanks, Mom." Lower lip quivering, she raised her eyes heavenward. "And Daddy, thank you, too." Walking down the steps, she said, "Even with the changed circumstances, I think I'll take Quin's advice and sleep on it. And tomorrow? I'll give Beck another reason to hate me."

Chapter 5

UP WITH THE DAWN, TANSY SCRIBBLED A NOTE FOR her mother and headed to Kitty's.

Time to watch a master at work. Kitty had no doubt been at the bakery a good hour already, but she wanted to see firsthand what went on behind the scenes, and hopefully, it would take her mind off the call she'd make the minute Quin's office opened.

An hour later, a borrowed apron tied around her waist, Tansy flipped the door sign to "Open" and took her place behind the counter.

"You're sure you trust me to do this?"

Kitty raised a brow. "Honey, if you can't run a counter and cash register, you need to reconsider plunking down good money on that house 'cause this is the easy part. The fun part."

She was right. As friends and neighbors came through the door, Tansy caught up on their lives and families, their views on politics and world events, on the happenings in town.

"Kitty, do you have any more glazed doughnuts?" she called over her shoulder.

"Sure do. I'll be right out with a tray."

The door opened again, and Tansy's heart dropped to her toes. Beck.

He stopped, hand on the knob.

Gathering her courage, she smiled. "Good morning, Beck. You can come in. I promise not to bite."

He said nothing.

"Grab your coffee and doughnuts and get over here, Beck," Sam called. "I need to pick your brain about siding for the house. Cricket and I are at odds."

"You're gonna pit me against my own blood?" Beck replied.

"Heck, yeah."

"I don't know." Beck glanced at Tansy. "Loyalty's awful important to me."

Tansy, heart sinking, met his gaze. "And it should be," she said quietly. "Sometimes the people who hurt most are the very ones who break our trust—and who regret the mistake they've made."

His eyes narrowed, then he seemed to shake himself. "I'll have a coffee and two raspberry-filled doughnuts."

"Beck—"

"Not now." He tossed some money on the counter. "Not a good time for this talk, Tanz."

"But I—"

He scooped up the doughnuts, grabbed his coffee, and walked over to Sam's table.

"A little hard on her, weren't you?" Sam said.

Tansy didn't want to hear Beck's answer, so she stepped into the back for that tray of glazed doughnuts.

———

At his office, the doughnuts sat in Beck's stomach like two lumps of concrete. Sam was right. He had been hard on Tansy. But looking at her, talking to her—it was almost more than he could bear. She'd been his world, and he'd have done anything for her.

Did she really regret what she'd done? Did she hurt, too, because of it?

Argh, he was a mess! She did that to him. Scrambled his brain.

Since she'd been gone, he'd dated. Lots. Heck, that first year, he'd gone through women like a junkie went through crack. Then he'd got his feet under him and slowed down, but it was never quite right. He'd never found what he'd had with Tansy, someone who completed him, and he'd decided he probably never would.

Yet he'd walked into the bakery this morning and *wham*! It'd hit him right between the eyes. He finally felt it again—for Tansy.

But now that he understood, he'd get over it, wouldn't he? He had to because she sure had.

The day could only get better, right?

His office door stood open, and he glanced up to see his dad making his way down the paint aisle.

"Hey, Dad, you're up early. Mom got you paintin' another room? The kitchen again?"

"Nope, and thank Jesus for small favors on that one." His father, at fifty-five, was the picture of health—blond, tanned, and trim. He'd started taking more and more time off as Beck grew into the job. He still came in three days a week, but he wasn't scheduled today.

Beck grinned. "Glad to hear it. Thought I'd have to avoid the house for a while."

"Don't want you doin' that. In fact, why don't you stop by after work? I'm grillin' a couple racks of ribs tonight, and your mom's makin' some of her baked beans. Her sweet potato casserole, too."

"Say no more. About six?"

"That'll work."

He eyed his dad. "Anything else?"

Stanton shook his head. "Nope. See you later." With a wave, he headed back outside.

Beck stood in his office doorway and watched him go, a little voice nagging at him the whole time. Something was up. He suspected more than an invite to dinner was on the table. If he wasn't mistaken, his folks had something up their sleeves and whatever that something was, they'd share it with him tonight over one of his favorite dinners. Oh, yeah. That made him more than a tad nervous.

Another trip? If so, good for them. But he didn't think so. His dad would have told him if that were the case. No, this was more than the two of them flying off to the Caribbean.

Was his mom or dad sick? Pops?

Anxiety gnawed at him and promised a long day.

The phone rang. "Elliot's Lumberyard and Construction." He listened, then asked a couple questions.

When he hung up, he shook his head. It seemed the workday would start with a plumbing project at Lucinda Worthington's preschool. A couple of the boys had decided to try out their own plumbing skills and had somehow managed to unscrew the plastic pipes under the little boys' room vanity.

Then, just for giggles, they'd turned on the spigot. By the time they'd exited the bathroom for morning milk and cookies, using the dismantled pieces of pipe for horns, water was already streaming into the hallway.

Beck had to laugh. While the landlord wouldn't be amused, he had to give the boys credit for a job well done. Damn! He might have to hire those tykes in a few years!

"Jeeters!"

"Yeah, Boss?" Jeeters stuck his head inside the office.

"We've got an emergency job over at the preschool." He explained the situation. "Gather up the supplies and stow them in the truck. I'll take Darrell along."

"Got it."

"They've shut off the water, so I'll take a minute and finish this order. Have everything ready to go in five."

Jeeters nodded and closed the door behind him.

A few minutes later, Beck shut down the computer. No doubt Lucinda was well on her way to a nervous breakdown by now. He stuck his head out the door. "Jeeters, is the truck loaded?"

"Yep, and Darrell's waitin' for you."

"Good enough."

When they arrived, even though he'd promised himself he wouldn't, he looked for Gracie. She was nowhere in sight. Guess that made sense. Tansy probably figured she needed a couple days at home before sending her into another new environment.

Whatever else he thought about Tansy, he had no doubt she was a great mother.

What in the hell had she been doing at the bakery this morning? Working for Kitty? She couldn't need the money.

Unconsciously, he rubbed at a spot over his heart, then set thoughts of her aside and grabbed a length of PVC.

—*∿*—

Beck hadn't been wrong about it being a long day but not because he'd worried over what his parents intended to spring on him. Instead, he and his crew had put out one fire after another. First the preschool fiasco, then a very rattled Mrs. Stuckey called and asked for a ladder. She'd climbed out the bedroom window to clean some gutters and, somehow, the window had closed behind her. She hadn't been able to open it and found herself stuck on her roof.

Fortunately, she'd had her cell in her pocket. Her son had run into some legal trouble a few months back and, even though things had been ironed out, she hadn't wanted to call Sheriff Jimmy Don. Since Beck sold ladders, she'd called him.

He'd taken one over himself to save her any more embarrassment and suggested next time she let her son, Jeremy, do the gutter cleaning. She agreed, then promised Beck a fresh blackberry pie later in the week, a more-than-fair trade.

Potato salad yesterday for a repaired screen and blackberry pie today for helping a damsel in distress. Sounded like something out of *The Andy Griffith Show*. Whatever. Misty Bottoms was, despite the changes happening, still a small town. His small town. And he loved it.

He hadn't been back to the store ten minutes when his delivery truck pulled in from Atlanta. Unfortunately, not everything they needed for a job the next day had been on it. Three phone calls later, he was assured the materials would be there before closing.

Now, though? Time to head to his mom and dad's for a home-cooked meal.

It was the question of what they intended to serve up with it that bothered him.

Well, just like the missing supplies, they'd work it out.

As he cranked up the air in his truck, he decided he'd better run home, shower, shave, and change into some clean clothes before he showed up at Judy Elliot's table.

———

Beck had to hand it to his folks. They were good. Academy Award–winning good. They'd finished dinner and were working on wiping out a pan of his mom's brownies drenched in vanilla bean ice cream and not a word about upcoming events. Still, he'd bet his new Dodge truck there was a hidden agenda behind this dinner.

"Have they announced the Oscar nominees yet?" he asked.

Frowning, his dad swiped the last of the ice cream from his bowl. "Don't think that happens till mid-January, Son. Why? You see a good movie?"

"Nope, haven't had time." He looked from his dad to his mom. Pops wasn't home. He'd gone somewhere with Lem. "Thought I might see your names on the list."

"What do you mean?" His mom looked toward her husband, the tiniest hint of apprehension in her eyes.

Beck pointed his spoon at her. "You two are up to somethin'. I know it as sure as I'm sittin' here. What's goin' on?"

"We've had an offer on Pops's house."

He took the blow, telling himself that was a good

thing. Yeah, it would hurt to see someone else in the house he'd practically grown up in, but he'd known this was coming.

"Okay." He dragged out the word. "A good offer?"

"Full price."

"But?" His stomach wrapped itself in knots. Something was wrong here.

His mother stacked their bowls and carried them to the sink.

"Dad?"

His mother came back to the table and laid a hand on her son's. "You know we love you more than anything in this world."

"I do."

"Your grandfather does, too."

He tilted his head. "Now you're scarin' me."

His mother went pale, and his dad's face flushed.

"We can't keep the house."

"Understood."

"We offered it to you," his dad said.

"You did, but I have a house, and I don't need another."

"Right." His dad took another sip of coffee. "There isn't much of a market in Misty Bottoms for a house that big."

"Again, understood. Is the buyer somebody from out of town?"

"In a sense. It's somebody who's moving back."

The tumblers clicked into place. "Tansy."

"Honey, I know this must seem like a betrayal to you, but Tansy's had a hard time of it, too. She needs to come home."

"To Pops's house?"

"Apparently she wants to start a business on the first floor and live upstairs."

"This is okay with you two?" He looked from his mom to his dad.

"To be really honest, I wish it were different, that someone else had made an offer," his dad said.

"They will," Beck insisted. "Give it time."

"I know this is hard, Son. Tansy broke your heart, and don't think for a second I've forgotten. But that sweet little girl needs a home," his mother said.

"Tansy is far from sweet. I—"

"I'm talkin' about Gracie Bella."

That shut him up for about three seconds.

"That sweet little girl's daddy can afford to build her a new house."

"He won't lift a finger or a cent to help them, and you know it."

Surprise jolted through him. He *didn't* know that. He'd assumed Tansy had taken the jerk for everything she could get. That she'd left with a pile of cold, hard cash. Of course, his mother could have things all wrong. It wouldn't be the first time.

His father studied him over his coffee cup.

"What?"

"Thought you were over her."

"I am."

"Uh-huh."

"I have to be honest here. I'm angry. Very angry," he said slowly, emphasizing each word. "Her coming back has stirred up things I thought I'd buried. You're gonna have to give me some time—and some space." A muscle ticked in his jaw.

"Beck—"

He pushed back his chair and stood. "Dinner was great. Thanks." Woodenly, he bent down and kissed his mom's cheek. "I need to head home. If I don't get some laundry done, I'm gonna have to go to work buck naked."

"Drop it off here in the morning, honey."

He shook his head. "I can handle it. I'm a big boy."

———

Beck hopped into his pickup and turned the key, then sat a minute, rubbing his eyes. His grandfather's house? He and Tansy had planned to move into that house together, had talked about raising their kids there. Instead? If the sale went through, she'd be moving in with her kid.

He'd asked around this afternoon, and rumor had it she was taking over for Kitty, that she planned to open a bakery in Misty Bottoms. That surprised him. For the life of him, he couldn't figure why she'd work. Maybe his mom had been right.

No. No way had she left that gold mine without a few hefty nuggets of her own.

It didn't matter. What she did or didn't do wasn't his concern. But why'd she have to pick Pops's house to do it in?

Had his grandfather signed off on it? Didn't blood count for anything anymore? It would probably be best if he stayed away from his family for a few days. The last thing he wanted was to argue with them. If he was lucky, Tansy would change her mind and it would all be a moot point.

Having her in Misty Bottoms would take some getting used to, but he didn't know if he'd ever get used to having her in his grandfather's house. The sign for

Duffy's Pub came into view, and he whipped into the parking lot. Stuffing his keys in his jeans pocket, he headed in. He'd have one beer, then go home. It had been a long day and another was coming tomorrow.

He took a small table in the corner, away from everybody else.

"Hey, Beck, how you doin' tonight?" Binnie, the pub's waitress, came up behind him. "You want a menu?"

"Nope. Already ate at my folks' place. I'd like a beer. Whatever you have on tap."

She frowned. "Everything okay?"

"Just dandy."

"Why don't I believe that?"

He sighed and planted his fingertips at his temples. "Binnie, I don't mean to be rude, but what I really need is a beer and a little thinkin' time."

"Fine." Nose in the air, she crossed the room and placed his order.

Behind the bar, Duffy drew his drink and carried it across to Beck himself. "There you go. Won't solve your problem, though, whatever it might be."

"That's not a very good sales pitch."

"You're a friend first, a customer second."

Beck swore. "You make it damn hard to nurse a mad, Duffy. So tell me this. What's your take on loyalty?"

"It's invaluable—regardless of the situation."

"There you go." Beck lifted his glass in a salute. "I agree."

———

Beck sat alone, nursing both the drink and his hurt.

Tansy Calhoun Forbes, of the red hair and Caribbean-blue eyes, of the brilliant mind and nimble tongue. He'd thought he was going to die the day he found out she was pregnant and marrying another man. He kept thinking she'd call and tell him she'd changed her mind, that she was coming home to him.

She hadn't.

At some point, he'd pronounced himself cured. Oh, sure, she'd waltz back into town for a quick visit, and one look—one single Tansy sighting—was all it took to put him in a nasty mood. But he'd always known it was temporary. That by the next day she'd be gone again, back to her husband. It didn't look like that was going to happen anymore.

Not if she truly had come back to Misty Bottoms to stay.

Not if she intended to buy Pops's house.

The door opened and Sam stepped inside to dark lighting, loud music, and the chatter of diners. Not in uniform, he wore a pair of worn denims and a Maroon Five T-shirt.

Their eyes met and held.

In quick strides, Sam crossed the pub and slid onto a chair across from him. "What's going on, bud?" He raised his voice over the din. "How about a couple coffees here, Duffy? Black."

"I don't want or need coffee, Sam. This is my first and only beer of the night, so I'm good, Deputy. Believe me when I tell you I've earned this one."

"Make that one coffee, Duffy. And a burger, medium well. With fries."

"Gotcha." Duffy came over with the coffee. "Burger'll be about five minutes."

After he left, Beck asked, "Did my parents call you?"

"Your parents?"

"Yeah."

"No." Sam shook his head slowly. "Cricket's at Jenni Beth's. They're talking weddings. One's coming up soon. I'm hungry, figured I'd grab a burger."

Neither man spoke again for a few minutes. Beck felt a grim sense of satisfaction when Sam winced at his first taste of the brew Duffy passed off as coffee. Another Misty Bottoms ritual, he guessed. Anybody who'd been in town long enough knew not to order the stuff in here.

The song on the jukebox ended and another started.

Finally, Sam asked, "You're not yourself tonight. What's up?"

"No deep, dark secret. Tansy's back in town."

"I heard that."

"She left. She was supposed to stay gone."

"Don't you think you're being a little unreasonable?"

"So?"

A bark of laughter erupted from Sam.

Beck shrugged and grabbed a handful of peanuts from the bowl he'd snagged from the bar. "Okay, before you ask, here's the *Reader's Digest* version. Tansy and I dated all through high school. I asked her to marry me, and she said yes. I saved up months for the ring I gave her. Our folks insisted we wait to get married till after we'd graduated from college."

Sam grunted, mostly, Beck supposed, to let him know he was listening. Or maybe it was a technique they taught in detective school. *Don't interrupt. Keep the suspect talking.*

Whatever.

"I loved her, Sam. I've never loved anyone like that. I waited to start college till she graduated from high school so we could go together. Then my grandmother passed away, and Pops got sick. Dad needed help, so I thought, what the heck. I didn't need a degree to run the family business. I already knew it inside and out. We agreed she should go, though. The day she left for college, it damn near broke my heart."

He grew quiet.

"But Tansy didn't come back," Sam said into the void.

"Nope. She met the very wealthy Emerson Forbes, and before you could say 'spit,' she was pregnant and they had themselves a wedding. Guess I didn't rank high enough on the financial or societal ladders to make the cut."

"People change, Beck."

"You on her side?"

"No. She did you wrong. I've only ever met her a couple times, but she doesn't seem like a snob to me. Oh, she dresses well and is kind of formal, but I don't see her choosing money over love."

"Just goes to show what you know, Mr. Big-City Detective, 'cause she did exactly that."

Beck hadn't wanted company, but Sam was easy to be with. His cousin had chosen well.

Or *did* you choose your mate? Maybe it was some predestined thing. Nah. It just felt that way right now because he was in a funk.

One of these days, he might find the right woman. It wasn't Rachel in Savannah, though. Or Cindy or Roxy or Lucinda.

"Time to go." Sam pushed his plate aside. "You good to drive?"

"Like I said, one beer, Deputy." He lifted his right hand. "I swear. And I've been nursin' it for the better part of an hour now, so I'm good to go. That's not somethin' I mess with. One drink's my limit if I'm getting behind the wheel."

He and Sam threaded their way through the tables, speaking to several acquaintances as they passed.

Halfway across the parking lot, Beck jerked to a stop. "You still drivin' that rust bucket you bought from Lem Gilmore?"

"Yep."

"Cricket deserves better than that."

"Strangely enough, your cousin likes it."

"She probably does. Tansy wouldn't." His chin jutted high, mimicking her nose in the air. Then he patted the truck's ready-to-drop-off bumper. "Too much the lady for a ride like this."

Sam scratched his head. "You know, Beck, if the lady's not interested…"

"I know. Get over her. I honestly thought I was. Now, here she is again. And my world?" He made the sound of a huge explosion and mushroomed his hands to show it expanding.

Beck watched as Sam started the old truck and headed home. To Cricket. The woman he loved.

Him? He'd go home to an empty house. And the knowledge the woman he loved—the woman he *used* to love—would soon be calling the Elliot house her own.

He'd definitely had better days.

Halfway home, he spotted a vehicle pulled over to the shoulder, the hood up. His headlights swept over it and the person standing beside it.

Tansy.

Was the woman everywhere?

He couldn't drive by and pretend he hadn't seen her. He'd stop for any woman stranded on a dark stretch of road. His tires crunched as he pulled up in front of her and rolled down his window. Immediately he saw the panic flare in her eyes.

"It's me, Tansy. Beck."

Instead of welcoming him, she groaned in frustration. "God, I'm so sorry. I'm a real pain in your backside, aren't I?"

"I won't argue that."

"My car just quit. I was driving along, and all of a sudden, the check engine light came on. The car bucked, then nothing. Look, you don't have to stay. Apparently, I left my cell at Mom's, though, so if you'd call a wrecker for—"

"Stop." He held up a hand. "Let me take a quick look. It might be an easy fix. You do have gas, don't you?"

Exasperated, she sighed. "Yes, I have gas. I filled up at Tommy's."

"Before or after you put in a bid on Pops's house?"

A full minute of uneasy silence followed.

"Beck—"

"Forget I asked that. For now." He ducked beneath the hood, shining his flashlight over the engine area. "I don't see anything, Tansy. It's late. I'm tired, I'm more than a little pissed, and I want my bed. Despite the fact that you're the reason I've got a good mad goin', I absolutely refuse to leave you here alone on the side of the road in the dark. Get what you need from your car, then hop in. I'll drive you home. We can call a wrecker to come pick up your car."

"You don't need to—"

"Tansy, don't argue. Just get your stuff and hop in."

When she got in, he turned up the radio to avert any attempt at conversation. Still, she tried.

"About your grandfather's house—"

"My parents told me tonight. I don't want to discuss it." He shot her a sideways glance. "Why'd you come back?"

"This is home."

"It hasn't been for years."

"You're wrong. It's always been home. It just hasn't been where I've been living."

"Semantics."

"No. Heart."

He snorted. "You still have one of those?"

"Yes, I do." She paused. "Beck, a stranger won't ever love Pops's house like I do. I have so many memories there. Not nearly as many as you, but they're all good ones. They're all ones I cherish. I want Gracie to make memories there, too."

"I wanted *our* kids to make memories there. Or have you forgotten that?"

"No," she whispered. "I haven't forgotten anything."

The scent of her wafted to him and filled the truck cab.

The night wrapped itself around them, and Beck had

an incredible feeling of déjà vu. Fate had one hell of a warped sense of humor.

He hit the in-dash phone button and asked to be connected to Elmer's Wrecking. When a very sleepy Elmer answered, Beck filled him in on the location of Tansy's SUV and asked him to pick it up. Elmer promised he'd take care of it right away and deliver it to D&J's. By the time everything was ironed out, they'd reached Tansy's mother's with no blood drawn. He reached across her and opened her door.

"I'd see you in, but your mother might have a shotgun."

"Very funny, Beck. My mother actually called you a prince the other day."

"Oh yeah?"

"Don't let it go to your head."

"I'm sure you corrected her."

"I tried, but she wouldn't listen. Sometimes there's simply no accounting for taste."

"Ha-ha."

One hand on the door, Tansy turned to him. "My mom told me you've helped her out with things around the house." She chewed at her bottom lip. "Thank you for that."

"It was my pleasure, believe me."

"All the same, I appreciate it."

He studied her in the cab's overhead light. "You know, most sons-in-law would realize a widow might need some help now and again, and maybe spend one or two of his valuable weekends here doing a few things for her. But then, Emerson wasn't most sons-in-law, was he?"

Heat crept up her cheeks. "No. He wasn't." She ducked her head, letting soft curls fall over her eyes.

"Again, I thank you. From the bottom of my heart. I don't expect you to believe that, but—"

"Tanz, I'm sorry." He threw his head back against the seat and closed his eyes. Then he rolled his head sideways, drew in a big breath and let it out slowly. "I'm bein' an ass again, aren't I? Might be a terminal condition. What do you think?"

She simply shook her head.

"Not sure what that means." He studied her, that mass of auburn curls, those eyes a man could drown in, and that inviting mouth. If he let her, she'd break his heart all over again. "Maybe you can cure me," he whispered. "You might be just what the doctor ordered. Kiss me, sugar."

"Beck, I can't. I'm the one who's been the ass."

"One little kiss. Right here. Come on. Lay one on me." He leaned toward her and tapped his cheek.

On a sigh, she touched his cheek with those soft, full lips. He angled his head, ever so slightly, so that lips touched lips. One hand moved to the back of her head, cupped it, and drew her closer. The other hand started at her waist and slid south. He groaned.

Tansy pulled away and slipped out of the truck. "Good night, Beck. You saved my bacon tonight. I'm not sure what I'd have done if you hadn't come along." Her voice shook as she added, "Maybe Mom was right, and you actually are a prince."

"Don't get your hopes up, Tansy. You'll be disappointed."

"Disappointment and I are on a first-name basis, Beck. Sleep well. Thanks again."

He sat in the dark and waited till she disappeared

inside. The porch light blinked to let him know all was
well, and he felt something inside him break free. She'd
always done that when he'd dropped her off after a date,
even if he'd walked her to the door and kissed her sense-
less before sending her inside.

As he pulled away, her scent lingered, feminine and
mysterious. Foreign yet familiar. He seriously doubted
he'd sleep tonight.

Chapter 6

BECK DECIDED TO STOP BY HIS PARENTS' ON THE WAY to work. He didn't feel good about the way he'd left things with them last night.

One step inside the kitchen door, his dad looked up from the paper. "You look like heck, Son."

"I didn't get home till late, then I didn't sleep well."

"We laid a lot on you last night."

"Yeah, you did."

"Sit down and let me fix you some eggs." His mother hurried to the fridge.

"You don't need to do that."

"Yes, I do. I never sent you to school without breakfast, and I'm certainly not sending you off to do a day's work without food. Now sit." His mother pointed her spatula, and he sat.

"Where is Pops, by the way?"

"He and Earle Whittaker left on a fishing trip."

"Earle? I thought he was with Lem."

"Nope."

"You let those two go alone? Earle's nuttier than a fruitcake."

"They went out to the old fishing cabin. How much trouble can they get into?"

Beck studied him. "I'm assuming that's a rhetorical question."

"You'd be right. Besides, your grandfather makes his own decisions, Son."

"Speakin' of decisions. You said Pops knows about Tansy putting an offer on his house?"

"Yes, he does. I called him, and we discussed it. He likes Tansy."

"He always did."

Not wanting to fight with his folks, he bit back the rest of his words. Instead, he told them about finding Tansy stranded on the side of the road last night. "I'll call D&J's today. See what they found."

"Thank you, honey, for helping her," his mom said. "I'm sure that wasn't easy for you."

"None of this is easy for me—not that it seems to matter to anybody."

"Son—"

"Let's give it some time, Dad. See what happens."

After he ate, he kissed his mom on the cheek, waved to his dad, and left for work. Outside the lumberyard, dark glasses in place, he rested his hands, fingers laced, on top of his head. He had to get it together. Because right now? Tansy Forbes, without lifting so much as her little finger, was leading him around by the nose.

He scrubbed a hand down his face. He was mad at the world right now about the situation and determined to put an end to it.

Only one way to make that happen.

He put his truck in gear and left the lot.

It was time he had a come-to-Jesus meeting with

Tansy. She'd stirred up all this mess, and damned if he was going to lug around some supersized ball of angst without at least having his say. Logistics became the problem, though. He couldn't drive up to her mother's house and knock at the door. Nope, this wasn't the kind of conversation you had in front of someone's mother or someone's little girl, and they'd both be at the house.

This talk called for privacy.

But how to arrange that was beyond him. The more he thought about it, the more it burned him. Tansy had already stolen his dreams for the future. He didn't want her changing Pops's house and stealing his childhood memories, too. He'd had plenty of time to mull it over while he wasn't sleeping last night.

Over and over, he'd rehearsed what he'd say, imagined how she'd respond. And always, always, always in these scenarios, she told him she was sorry, that it had always been him she loved, and if her buying his grandfather's house would cause further pain, she'd take back her offer.

Yeah, in his mind that's how it worked. In reality? She'd already made her case last night with that whole nobody-will-love-the-house-as-much-as-me thing. Today, she'd probably tell him to go to hell. Well, he had news for her. He'd already been there—and she'd been the driver of that bus.

With her coming back to town? He was perilously close to those raging flames again. It wouldn't take much...

He turned onto Main and about swallowed his tongue.

What did you know? Maybe lady luck had hitchhiked a ride with him this morning after all.

Tansy Forbes closed the realty office's door behind her and started down the walk.

He swerved into an empty parking space and leaned across the seat to throw open the passenger door. "Hop in, Red. We need to talk."

She looked at him warily.

"Well, this looks familiar," a voice said behind her. "The two of you. Just like old times."

Tansy turned quickly. "Good morning, Walter."

She took in his bent posture, the gnarled hand resting on his uniform's belt. How long had he guarded the customers and staff at Coastal Plains Savings?

"Ms. Gloria said you'd been into the bank yesterday to open an account. Welcome home. I'm glad you're back."

Throwing a glance over her shoulder at Beck, she muttered, "That would make one." Despite last night's kiss, she couldn't fool herself. Beck would be much happier if she were gone.

"Pardon?" Old Walter cupped a hand behind his ear. "Hearin' ain't as good as it used to be. You'll bake one? One what?"

"No." She shook her head. "I said—"

"She'd *take* one," Beck put in. "I asked if I could give her a ride, and she said, sure, she'd take one."

Tansy scowled at him, and he threw her that bad-boy grin that melted the soles of her shoes. Then she reminded herself he was simply putting on a show for Walter.

The grin would disappear the minute the bank guard did.

"Well, you two kids have fun." Walter threw them a wink and headed on down the street.

"Hop in, Tansy. Don't make a scene."

"Me?" Openmouthed, she pointed a finger at her chest.

"Come on, get in."

"Why do I feel like I'm stepping into a pit of quick-sand?" The second she took hold of the door handle, she smelled his heat, his masculinity. With his eyes hidden behind dark glasses, a dark-blond curl falling over his forehead, the man practically stopped her heart.

She'd known last night this confrontation was bound to happen, that Beck wasn't going to simply roll over. Still, she wasn't ready. Taking a deep breath, she ran a damp palm along the leg of her rust-colored linen slacks, then set about chewing off the remnants of her lipstick.

The big truck idled smoothly, mirroring its owner's power.

"I—" She wet her lips. "I understand how upset you are. But what happened between us... Beck, I have a business to start, a home to set up for Gracie. Your grandfather's house is perfect for both."

"It is perfect, but it's not for you. Not anymore." He whipped off his dark glasses, and his eyes met hers. "It was perfect for neckin' under that big, old oak tree, away from pryin' eyes. It was perfect for family Thanksgivings and Christmases. Like I said last night, I always figured you and I would be a family, Tanz, that we'd raise our kids there—make a lifetime of memories in that house."

Despite herself, tears threatened, and she blinked hard to hold them back. "That's not fair," she whispered.

"Fair? You want to talk to me about fair? You sure that's a discussion you want to be havin'?"

She turned to open the door, but his hand shot out and caught her arm.

"Rent Kitty's place. It would be a lot easier for everybody."

"Kitty's shop isn't what I want." Her back stiffened, and she met and held his angry eyes. "I want your grandfather's house."

He shook his head. "I don't get it."

"What?"

"I'd think our Podunk town would be too small, too tame, too hick for you."

Hurt coursed through her. This wasn't the Beck she'd known, but then she wasn't the woman he'd proposed to, either. They'd both changed. A lot.

"Then maybe you never knew me at all, Beck. I love Misty Bottoms. I always have."

"Okay, so answer me one question."

"If I can."

"Since you're so dead-set on comin' home, why work?" His forehead creased in question. "Why not stay home with that beautiful little girl of yours? Your ex is a multimillionaire. That not enough for you?"

Shame filled her. Emerson's family was wealthy—stinking, filthy rich. But Emerson? He'd lost every cent he'd had. Lost everything he and Tansy had. What he hadn't left on the craps and roulette tables, they'd spent on his two stints in rehab. He'd lost his job, the house, their savings. His parents refused to help them and blamed her for his problems. Everything had mushroomed; he had no longer made any attempt to hide what he was doing or shield her or Gracie from the rough group he'd fallen into.

With her out of the picture, she hoped his mom and dad would step in and take care of their son. She couldn't. Not anymore. Nor could she chance a custody battle. Unable to afford the kind of lawyer she'd need in order to fight the Forbes family and loath to wait another day to escape, she'd left without one red cent. She would not, though, explain any of that to Beck or the rest of the town. Still, rumors and half-truths were bound to fly, and she couldn't blame any of them for that.

Bottom line, though, she had to work to earn a living for her and her daughter. And to do that, she needed Mr. Elliot's house.

When she said nothing, he growled. "That's what I thought. By the way, I called the mechanic about your car."

"You did?"

"Yeah. Your gas cap was off and you had water in your tank. He'll have it taken care of by late this afternoon."

"Thanks. I'll have Mom take me over to pick it up tomorrow morning."

"You said you filled up at Tommy's?"

"Yes."

"I'll have him stick his tanks today and check for water. So far, nobody else seems to have had any problems."

"What's that mean?"

"I'm not sure."

"Thanks."

"You can thank me by rescinding your offer on Pops's place."

"I can't do that." Without another word, she opened her door and got out.

As he disappeared down the street, she wrapped her arms around her waist. Inside, another small part of her heart broke off. She'd hurt him, had hurt them both.

For nothing. Absolutely nothing.

Her life with Emerson had been hell, but nobody would believe that. They'd see the house she'd lived in, the clothes she wore, and think she had it all. But when those things came without love, they didn't add up to all. They added up to zero.

As she shut the door, she heard a siren and saw Sam in his police car, lights flashing. A strange sight for Misty Bottoms. She prayed no one had had an accident.

Beck slid over to let Sam pass. He refused to check his rearview mirror. He would not feel bad about Tansy standing alone on the sidewalk.

He'd settled nothing. Tansy's soft, slightly floral fragrance surrounded him. Swearing, he rolled down his windows to let in fresh air, to carry away the scent of her.

After all this time, after everything that had happened, the woman still got to him. That, in and of itself, was enough to drive him insane. Why couldn't he let it go? Let *her* go? She'd belonged to another man, had taken his name, and borne his child.

His cell rang, and he checked the display. Jeeters.

Halfway through the call, he pulled a U-turn and headed toward Ms. Hattie's. The rest of the mess that was his life right now would have to wait.

Chapter 7

NERVES PRACTICALLY ATE A HOLE IN TANSY'S stomach. Today marked the beginning of her career as a professional baker. A professional event cake designer and creator.

Unless she failed.

She wouldn't. She couldn't. Failure wasn't an option.

Her mom and Gracie Bella had a full day scheduled. It would be good for both of them.

Before she headed to Kitty's, though, she'd stop to visit her aunt. The whole town seemed certain Coralee was up to something. No surprise there. Coralee was always up to something, wasn't she?

Feeling both sadness and comfort, Tansy slid behind the wheel of her dad's Thunderbird. His cherished 2002 T-bird had been one of the first to roll off the newly restarted production lines. Her mother couldn't bring herself to get rid of it, and this morning, with her vehicle in the shop, Tansy was glad.

She ran in to Tommy's Texaco and picked up two coffees to go.

Turning onto her aunt's street, she slowed and took a minute to simply enjoy the whimsical house. On the very outskirts of town, it sat on a little over an acre of land. Tansy seriously doubted there was a single Misty Bottomer who hadn't driven by more than a time or two to simply see what Coralee was doing.

Fairy gardens bloomed in little clusters throughout the yard, looking as if they'd sprouted up magically. A yellow-brick path wound its way to the front porch. Her aunt was an artist and worked with every possible medium. Statues and colorful, wacky yard art popped up throughout the gardens, alongside fountains and bird feeders. A giant peacock her aunt had created from metal and glass shone in the morning sun, its colors vibrant. Bronze frogs and copper wind art added to the whimsy. As a child, she'd spent hours in that yard. As an adult, she marveled at it.

The house itself was an eclectic mixture of old and new. Stucco siding had been painted in random stripes of blue, green, and yellow. A rooster weathervane perched on the cedar-shingled roof's peak.

She pulled into the drive and parked beside Coralee's rusty, old Jeep.

But when she knocked at the door, she got no answer. Tansy decided her aunt must be out for a walk, so she sat on the front porch stairs to wait, the coffee cooling on the step beside her.

Not five minutes later, she spotted Coralee as she turned the corner onto the street. Her hair redder and wilder than Tansy's own, she wore a purple-and-yellow-polka-dotted *I Love Lucy* dress with black tights and purple-sequined cowboy boots. Beside her, prancing along like a queen, was her Siamese. For the life of her, Tansy had never figured out how Coralee had trained that cat to take walks with her. But hers was not to question why. Coralee and Tempus took a walk every single day.

Tansy could almost feel sorry for the cat. What a

name! *Tempus Fugit*. Time flies. But her aunt was a huge fan of clocks and had literally dozens strewn throughout her house—on the walls, on end tables and dressers. If there was an empty space, Coralee found a clock to fill it.

"Tansy, honey! Have you been here long?"

"Not more than a few minutes." She ran to meet her aunt, hugging her tightly. She smelled like lavender and violets—always had.

"I heard you've come home to stay." Coralee took Tansy's hand in hers as they walked along the bricks.

"I have."

"Your mother is over the moon."

"I should have come sooner."

"You won't get an argument from me on that."

Along with everything else, her aunt was nothing if not outspoken. Tansy smiled and handed her one of the coffees, the one laden with sugar.

Coralee took a drink and grinned. "Thank you, baby. It's perfect." At the door, she hesitated, searching through her pockets. "Uh-oh. I forgot my key again."

"Are your windows locked?" Tansy eyed the one on the porch. "I could crawl through one."

"No need, sweetheart. I'll give Beck a call." She pulled a red-rhinestone-covered phone from her pocket.

"Why would you do that?"

"Because he has a spare key."

"For your house?"

"Sure. I gave it to him for times just like this."

"Can't you hide one somewhere? That would be easier."

"Oh, I have. Several of them, but I've used them all. They're inside the house, too."

"Coralee, Beck's busy."

"He's never too busy for me, sweetie." Her aunt patted Tansy's cheek, then hit one of her speed dial numbers.

Tansy's forehead wrinkled. A headache brewed behind her eyes. Why was it that everywhere she went, people were calling Beck, asking him to stop by? The poor man must be run ragged taking care of the entire Misty Bottoms population.

Despite everything, she found herself more and more impressed with the man he'd become. As a teen, he'd been dependable, but there'd also been a reckless, wild side that, she had to admit, she'd enjoyed. Now? It seemed everyone in town looked to him as the go-to guy. Have a problem? Call Beck Elliot.

After their chat earlier, she wasn't looking forward to seeing him again so soon. Seemed she wouldn't be able to avoid it unless she turned tail and ran before he got there. That idea—as appealing as it was—would hurt her pride. So she stood her ground.

"Come have a seat on the porch, Tansy. It's a hell of a lot more comfortable than those wooden steps. My backside doesn't have as much padding as it used to."

They sat side by side, enjoying the warm breeze, the coffee, and each other. They talked about everything and nothing. For all her eccentricities, Tansy wouldn't have traded her aunt for anyone else's. She loved Coralee, quirks and all.

Tansy heard Beck's truck before she saw it.

Coralee set down her coffee. "Ah, the boy's here."

"He's a man, Coralee. He stopped being a boy a long time ago."

"I'm sure you'd know better than most."

Heat rushed over Tansy's neck and face.

Beck got out of his truck, his brows arching when he saw her. "And we meet again."

"You know what they say about bad pennies."

He simply grunted.

"I told Coralee not to bother you."

"That's okay. I was just comin' back into town. Still haven't made it into the lumberyard. Ms. Hattie had a squirrel in her attic, so I've been crawling around in insulation. I need to stop by my place for a quick shower and a change of clothes."

It was on the tip of her tongue to offer her help with that shower. Fortunately, she came to her senses and offered a bland, "And instead of doing that, here you are."

"Yep, here I am. With the two prettiest redheads in Misty Bottoms—and the most annoying ones." He walked up one step as she descended one and their bodies brushed.

Tansy doubted grabbing an electric plug with wet fingers would have given her a bigger jolt. Wowser! A quick glance at Beck told her he'd felt it, too. He looked like someone in shock.

But he pulled himself together quickly. Withdrawing a key ring from his pocket, he dangled it in front of her. "I've taken to carrying your aunt's door key and Jeep key in my truck. Saves running back to the lumberyard to pick this up every time she calls."

"I told her I'd climb in through one of the windows."

One side of his lip turned up and his eyes went dark. "That I'd like to see."

"I—"

His phone rang, and he lifted one finger. "Hold that

thought." Into the phone, he said, "Yeah?" His smile faded. "I'll be right there."

Hanging up, he said, "I've gotta run. Here." He tossed the keys to Tansy. "I'll get those from you later. Do not let Coralee keep them. I don't want to have to change all the locks again."

Without another word, he was in his truck and backing down the drive.

"Wonder what on earth was that important. I'd hoped he could stay a bit." Coralee stared at the disappearing truck, jiggling something in her pocket.

Tansy's brows drew together. "What do you have in there?"

"I don't know." Coralee withdrew her hand. "Well, would you look at that. I had my key the whole time."

Ten minutes later, Beck wheeled to a stop in front of Jenni Beth's carriage house. Sam, in full cop mode, stepped out to meet him.

"I appreciate you calling me, Sam."

He followed the deputy inside and found Jenni Beth perched on the edge of the comfy upholstered chair. She looked tense enough to snap in half. "You okay?"

"I'm fine."

Beck looked toward Sam for verification and got a slight nod.

"I've checked both the French doors and the windows for any sign of a break-in, but I don't see anything," Sam said.

"That's probably because, like Cricket, she never locks up."

"Touché," Jenni Beth said. "We weren't gone long."

"Charlotte with you?"

"Yes." Her old Lab roused himself enough to crawl halfway into her lap as she rubbed his head. "Zeke here was asleep in his favorite chair on the back porch. He doesn't hear well anymore, so even if somebody had pulled into the drive, I doubt he'd have so much as barked at them."

"Anything missin'?" Beck asked.

"Not that I can tell."

"You're sure somebody was in here?"

"You sound like Sam."

"Sorry."

"I'm not sorry," Sam said. "I'm doing my job."

"A couple files were on my desk. I didn't leave them there."

"Okay," Beck said.

"But…" She hesitated.

"What?"

She frowned. "The copier was warm."

"What?"

"I know. That sounds stupid. Maybe it's from the sun hitting it."

"But you don't believe that."

She shook her head. "No. And the room smelled different."

Sam's chin came up. "You didn't tell me that."

"Sorry. I didn't think of it till just now."

"What did it smell like?"

"I don't know. I can't pinpoint it, but I will."

"I thought you could beef up her security," Sam said. "That's why I called. Of course, nothing you do will help if she doesn't use it." He gave her the stink eye.

"I will. I promise. My files have a lot of information in them, and I can't take a chance on somebody getting their hands on them."

"But you did," Beck said, "when you didn't lock up."

"Jeez, you're not being very nice."

"Sorry." He threw up his hands. "I'm itchy and that makes me short-tempered."

"You contagious?" Sam took a step backward.

"Hell no. I'm covered in insulation from Ms. Hattie's attic."

"Another squirrel?"

"Yep. I'm goin' out there tomorrow with some plywood and caulking to make sure that whole thing is sealed up tight. After that, I'll swing by here and install some motion sensors. Maybe a camera, too."

"And you were on your way for a shower when we bothered you," Jenni Beth said.

"Actually, I was at Coralee's. She locked herself out again. And before you ask, yes, Tansy was there."

"Which totally explains your mood," she said.

"What mood? I'm fine. Thanks for takin' care of Jenni Beth, Sam." With a wave, he hopped in his truck and headed for his place. A shower was exactly what he needed—to wash away both the scratchy insulation and the even more annoying touch of one redheaded pain in the butt.

Had someone really been poking around in Jenni Beth's office? A lot of new people in Misty Bottoms lately, and almost every single one knew about her and Magnolia House. After all, that was the draw, the reason they were coming.

The thought unsettled him.

Driving down Main Street, Tansy decided to pick up sandwiches from the diner for her and Kitty's lunch. Today would be a long day.

She'd emailed the Millers last night, attaching her colored sketches for their daughter's sweet-sixteen cake. Before she started on it, she wanted to verify that both the design and the colors would work. They'd called almost immediately, and she'd heard Olivia in the background, trying to talk her mom into letting her skip school so she could watch Tansy bring the design to life.

Tansy gave the kid kudos for her efforts, but Olivia wouldn't be showing up at the bakery today.

When she pulled into a parking space across from the diner, she spotted Moose Jansen. The former high school football star and old friend grinned at her, and she scrambled out of her car.

"Heard you were back, Tansy. You gonna be takin' over for Kitty?"

"In a sense. You still working at Mr. Harvey's appliance store?"

"Yes, ma'am. Pays the bills. Denise and I just closed on a house with a nice big yard for our boys to play in." He laid a hand on the roof of her dad's T-bird. "It's right down the road from your aunt's."

Tansy held her breath, waiting for the other shoe to drop. It always did when Coralee was involved.

Moose lowered his voice to a loud whisper. "Somethin' goin' on at her house, Tansy."

"I stopped in to see her this morning. Everything seemed to be okay."

"She's acting kind of strange."

"Moose, Aunt Coralee's middle name is strange."

He laughed, the decibel close to that of a sonic boom. "Guess you'd be right about that." After a glance at his watch, he said, "Break's over. Better get back to the store before the boss sends a search team for me. Good to have you back."

"Thanks, Moose. Tell Denise hi for me."

"Will do."

She watched him lumber on down the street; then she scooted into Dee-Ann's.

Luanna handed her a plastic-covered menu when she eased onto a counter stool.

"I like your hair," Tansy said. "That shade of blue is perfect with your eyes."

"Thanks. I got tired of the maroon streaks and decided to try somethin' different."

Dee-Ann swung through the kitchen door. "Order's up, Luanna."

With a thumbs-up, Luanna headed for it.

"What are you gonna have today, Tansy?" Dee-Ann asked.

"Two BLTs with avocado. Make one no L."

"You're still eating BTs?"

"Some things never change."

Dee-Ann's gaze lingered on hers. "Truer words were never spoken."

Tansy frowned. "Why do I get the feeling we're not talking about lettuce or the lack of it?"

"Maybe because we're not."

"Dee-Ann—"

"Tansy—"

They both laughed, and Dee-Ann, with a shake of her head, asked, "Who's the second for? Your mom?"

"No, I thought I'd take one to Kitty. Save her from that cottage cheese she eats for lunch day after day after day." Tansy let out a long breath. "I'm starting my first Magnolia House cake today. A sweet sixteen for Olivia Miller's birthday. Kitty's offered to let me use her kitchen."

"Got your aunt's artistic bent, didn't you?"

"Maybe so. Time will tell, I guess."

"I'd intended to call Kitty this afternoon. Will you ask her if she could make me up a batch of her snickerdoodles? I've never had much luck with them. I swear she must sprinkle a little magic in along with her cinnamon."

"I'll ask her."

"Hey, Dee-Ann, how about you top me off before you head to the kitchen?" From his seat by the window where he could keep an eye on everything inside and outside the diner, Lem held up his coffee cup.

"You know, I should be chargin' you by the pot or, at the very least, for seat rental. Why don't you go bother Lyda Mae for a while?"

"Said she's busy and needs to concentrate. She kicked me out."

"No surprise there." Dee-Ann picked up the coffee-pot and headed to Lem's booth. "Hey, Lem?"

"Yeah?"

"I'm busy and need to concentrate, so why don't—"

He laughed, a gravelly sound. "Won't work. You're a business. You can't lock me out. It's against the law."

"You gonna call the sheriff?"

"Jimmy Don? Nope. His deputy, my pal Sam."

Dee-Ann rolled her eyes, splashed fresh coffee into his cup, and left to put in Tansy's order.

"You sure you know what you're gettin' into, Tansy?" Lem asked. "You heard about the bride who showed up last month two days before the wedding and announced she'd changed her mind about her colors? Jenni Beth scrambled to come up with tablecloths and napkins and what-have-yous to make her happy. Cricket? That little girl had a ton of flowers she couldn't use…and needed ones she didn't have."

"No, I didn't." She imagined the hours that would have gone into a cake—that no one would want. Cricket and Jenni Beth must have been spitting nails—and putting on good faces the whole time.

Dee-Ann stuck her head out of the kitchen. "What are you doin', old man? Tryin' to scare our Tansy away? Stop tellin' tales."

"Ain't tales if they're true."

"Ain't necessary to share everything you know, either."

"All right, all right," Lem placated.

Tansy listened to the exchange and smiled. Coming home had been the right decision. If only she and Beck could reach some kind of an understanding.

Damn! What a day. Beck drove around the block a second time, eyes peeled for an empty parking space. Not too long ago, he'd have been hard-pressed to find more than a couple cars on Main. Now, the place was crawling with them—and people. People who actually spent money in Misty Bottoms' businesses.

Spying a car backing out, he put on his turn signal and waited—impatiently—for the spot. Once parked, he grabbed his tools from the truck bed and headed for Darlene's Quilty Pleasures. Seemed everybody in town was having some kind of trouble today.

Jenni Beth's niggled at his mind, though, and wouldn't shake loose. Then, there was the water in Tansy's tank. Tommy'd checked his at the station and found nothing. It didn't make sense.

He nodded at a couple locals, then followed behind them, an ear on their conversation.

"Did you hear Helen got a hundred-dollar tip last weekend at Frenchie's Beauty Parlor?"

"What'd she have to do for that?"

"One of those out-of-town brides pitched a real hissy fit after Helen colored her hair. Said it wasn't right and made her do it again. After she cooled off, Bridezilla felt bad enough about her poor behavior that she coughed up an extra hundred dollars."

"Humph! I'd hope so. Helen does good work."

"Yes, she does." Effie, the town librarian, fluffed her own curls.

"Did you hear…"

Beck was almost sorry he couldn't listen to the rest of it, but Darlene needed him more than he needed another dose of gossip. The always-impeccable woman looked frazzled. She had a mop and bucket in her back hallway and more than a few strands had escaped her French twist.

Darlene and her dogs were decked out in neon green today. She wore a neon-green sheath, Moonshine wore a vest in the same color, and Mint Julep sported a green knit sweater. Guess that was one of the perks of owning a shop that sold yarn and fabric; every time Ms. Darlene bought a new outfit, she whipped up matching ones for her Cairn Terriers.

"No customers?"

"Not right now, no. It's been a busy morning and then the toilet overflowed—I'm sorry. I'm upset."

"And you have every right to be. Tell you what. Why don't you fix yourself a nice cup of herbal tea? Sit down for a couple minutes and take some deep breaths. Moonshine, Mint Julep, and I will take care of this mess."

"I can't do that."

"Sure you can. Won't take more than a couple minutes to unplug the commode. Since my mama taught me how to run a mop quite a few years ago, I'm pretty good at it. Go on now, and let us do our thing."

"You're sure?"

"Absolutely."

She went to the back room to put on the teakettle, and Beck got out his plunger and snake and went to work. He smiled when he heard her walk past, then soft music wafted through the store.

Peeking around the corner, he saw she'd not only sat down but had pulled up a footstool and taken off her shoes. *Way to go, Darlene*.

Within twenty minutes, the plumbing in Quilty Pleasures was fixed and he'd mopped up the last of the flood. His tool belt slung over his shoulder, plunger and snake in hand, he stepped out front.

"Okay, Darlene, you're good to go. Keep that bathroom door closed, so those dogs don't clog up the toilet with any more of their toys."

"I'll do that. Thanks, Beck."

"You're more than welcome." He chuckled. "Nice outfits today."

"We like them, don't we?" She reached out her hand and both dogs scurried toward her, nails clicking on the wooden floor.

Beck's phone rang. "Better take this. Could be another damsel in distress for me to rescue." He winked at Darlene.

She blushed. "Go on. Get out of here, you rascal."

He stepped out of the yarn shop and closed the door behind him. "Hey, Kitty. How's my favorite girl?"

Listening as he slid into his pickup, he checked the dashboard clock. What were a few more minutes? "Be right there."

Five minutes later, he rolled up in front of Kitty's Kakes and Bakery. When he recognized Mr. Calhoun's T-bird, he groaned. Tansy had been driving it this morning.

Pig feathers!

He headed in. "Hey, Kitty. Darlene had a plumbing problem today, too. A pair of terriers were the culprits there. It's your sink?"

"Yep. The one in the kitchen's drippin'."

"Let's take a look."

He smelled her even before he saw her, that unique all-woman smell that was Tansy's alone. Her hips swayed in time to the Thomas Rhett song on the radio, and she sang along as she created magic with those delicate hands.

The cake in front of her was fun, covered in bright colors, with stripes and polka dots and a fancy fondant *16* perched on top. She'd corralled that wild mass of hair somehow into a stubby little tail. Tendrils escaped and curled at the nape of her neck.

A rolling pin in one hand, she wore a frilly little apron. She looked intense. Hot and sexy.

"'Now, baby, don't you look at me that way'," she sang, fussing with the green fondant ribbon.

The air in the room changed, and she knew. Beck had walked in. Her head jerked up.

"What are you doin' here?"

"Kitty called me."

He crowded her, gave her no space. Instead of moving past, he stopped. His body touched hers, warmed her. Made her think all sorts of forbidden thoughts. A memory of them dancing in the dark out by the old Frog Pond rushed through her. Beck had turned on his truck radio and left the window down. He'd held her in his arms, and they'd swayed to the music beneath the light of a big, fat moon.

And there'd been roses. Wild roses. Their scent had added to the night's magic.

Then they'd gone skinny-dipping.

"Tansy!"

"Huh? What?"

"Where'd you go?" Beck asked.

She swallowed. Oh, if he only knew. "I was, um, deciding what to do next with this cake."

"You seemed a million miles away."

Nope, she thought. *Just a few years away*.

Standing behind her, he peeked over her shoulder. "Looks damned good to me."

His warm breath tickled her bare neck. Instant lust ripped through her, and she almost moaned. Instead, she placed both hands flat on the counter and forced herself to breathe. *In, out, in, out*.

"You smell good. Like sugar and spice and every-thing nice."

She laughed. "Good line."

"I thought so."

Hot. The man was so damned hot. His body radiated heat.

"I'll just slide past you here so I can check out that dripping faucet."

"Dripping faucet?" She glanced toward the sink. Sure enough, water plopped in a slow, steady tune. "I didn't notice that earlier."

He set his hands at her waist and squeezed past. One crank on the handle, and the dripping stopped. Hands tucked in the pockets of his well-worn jeans, he turned to Kitty. "You didn't turn it the whole way off."

Kitty slapped herself upside the head. "Dumb as a dodo."

Tansy's gaze shifted from Kitty to him. *Crafty as a fox is more like it*, she thought.

"Let me get you a couple doughnuts, Beck." Kitty hustled into the storefront. "Cup of coffee?"

"Beck, I had no idea she'd called you."

"I know." Without another word, he followed Kitty out.

She stared after him a moment, then immersed her-self back in her work.

An eternity later, she was riding a high. Olivia's sweet-sixteen cake was finished. She'd deliver it to Magnolia House tomorrow for the party. Although not decorated, the cakes for the upcoming weddings were both baked and in the freezer. It had been a good day.

And she'd be part of people's memories.

She'd help make their special days special. Under her breath, she said, "I feel like a superhero! I did it!"

The high didn't last long, though. Halfway home, the hours on her feet took their toll and she longed for a hot bath and bed. Exhausted, she turned onto her mother's street and hit the brakes.

A familiar red truck sat in her mother's drive.

Her stomach pitched. *Not now*. She'd already dealt with him not once, but twice today. And danged if she hadn't forgotten her Wonder Woman bracelets at Kitty's. She had no defense against Beck right now.

Please, God, she prayed, *don't let my mom have invited him to dinner out of some twisted hope the past would magically dissolve and everything would be as it was*. So not going to happen. She and Beck had both moved on.

Okay, so she'd taken a step, heck, a bazillion steps backward since hitting the city limits, but she'd get it together.

Hands on the T-bird's steering wheel, the heat from this afternoon returned as she thought of Beck. The man was…was…such a man! Why hadn't he married? She felt guilt over that and, if she was totally honest, relief. And that was downright mean-hearted.

He deserved happiness. A wife and children.

And when that happened, more than a small piece of her would die. Even when she'd lived in another town, it would have hurt. But now? She'd be right here to watch his new life unfold, up close and personal.

Well, she'd deal with that when it happened. Right now, she could adjust her needs from a long hot bath to a quick shower and a change of clothes. She felt hot and grungy. If her mom had made plans for dinner guests, they'd have to be postponed another few minutes.

Purse slung over her shoulder, she marched up the sidewalk, flung open the front door, and stood just inside the living room, gaping like a fool. Gracie and Beck sat cross-legged on the floor playing paper dolls.

A rhinestone tiara perched crookedly on his head and a pink feather boa hung around his neck. Gracie wore a pirate hat.

He glanced up, a crooked grin on his face. "Cat got your tongue?"

She opened her mouth and simply closed it without a word.

"Like my new getup?"

Tansy frowned. "What are you doing?"

Gracie answered. "We're playin'."

"I see that, honey." She smiled at her daughter, a smile that died when she met Beck's gaze. "I'm wonderin' why."

"I stopped by to fix a lock on the garage's man door, and your mom asked if I'd mind keeping an eye on Gracie while she ran dinner out to Ms. Hattie."

"Why didn't she tell me? I'd have arranged something else for Gracie."

"Beck's havin' fun, aren't you?"

"I sure am."

"That's not the point," Tansy mumbled.

"Good ears," Beck said, touching his. "I heard that."

"I'm sure you did. How's Ms. Hattie doing?"

"She's getting old, Tansy." Beck's smile disappeared. "We've got her house in decent shape thanks to Jenni Beth, who realized how bad things had gotten. But Ms. Hattie's pride won't let us do much more—except for chasin' the occasional squirrel out of the attic."

"I loved going to the store when Ms. Hattie and her sister ran it."

Beck laughed. "We'd all get ice cream or soda after swimming in the Frog Pond. You? You'd drink tomato juice." He screwed up his face.

She shrugged. "What can I say? I love it."

"And you love *me*, huh, Mama?"

"I do! I love you so much I could just eat you up for dinner."

Gracie laughed, then crawled into Beck's lap to stare into his eyes. "I like you, Beck."

"I like you, too."

She clapped her little hands on his cheeks and patted them. "You're all scratchy." She rubbed her fingers over his stubble.

"I am. Time for a shave."

"I don't have to shave, 'cause I'm a girl."

"That's exactly right." He kissed the top of her head. "So's Mama."

His blue eyes darkened as they found Tansy's. "I'm all too aware of that."

Breathless, she took a step back. "I'm, ah, going to get some water. I'm thirsty."

"Just like your car, huh?" Gracie grinned. "I gave it some water just like you do, Mama."

"What?"

"You put the big straw in it and give it a drink. Grandma gave me a bottle of water yesterday, and I shared it with your car."

Tansy closed her eyes. The mystery of the water in her gas was solved. She'd have to let Tommy know so he didn't worry about it.

Then she heard the chuckle, all male and, despite everything, so sexy. Still…

"Don't you laugh."

"I'm sorry," he said. "It's just—" He totally lost it, gave in to the laughter.

Gracie, unsure what was so funny, joined him.

"You've both lost your minds," Tansy said. "If you hadn't come along last night, I could have been in real trouble."

"But I did, and you weren't." Beck swiped at his eyes, but still, a couple more chuckles escaped. "I really am sorry. It's just—" He broke off, swallowing new laughter.

"You aren't in the least bit sorry."

"I am." He pulled Gracie closer and hid his face in her hair.

"Gracie, Mama's car doesn't drink water," Tansy began, ignoring the still out-of-control Beck. "I only give it a drink at gas stations. Water can make it sick."

The little girl looked crestfallen. "Is our car sick?"

Beck raised innocent-looking eyes to Tansy, but mirth lurked not far below the surface.

Oh boy. "No, but it had a little bit of a tummy ache last night."

She sent Beck a glare any mother or teacher would be proud of, daring him to start laughing again. "So we won't give it any more water, okay? Let me take care of the car."

"Okay, Mama."

Lifting Gracie, Beck set her on her feet and rose agilely from the floor. "You hungry, Tansy?"

"Why?"

"My mom invited us to dinner."

She put a finger to her lips. "Let me get this straight. My mom's feeding Ms. Hattie, and your mom's feeding us."

"Yep."

"Does she know? That you're inviting Gracie and me?"

"Yes."

She wanted to. She couldn't. It would be too familiar. Too much like times long past. Her emotions were too raw, her body too tired to face this tonight. Even more important, she couldn't let this man become essential. If Gracie got too attached and he left, she'd be devastated—so would her mama. "I'm sorry, Beck, I can't."

"I wanna go." Gracie wrapped herself around Tansy's leg.

"Sorry, sweetheart." She rubbed her daughter's back. "Mama's too tired tonight."

Beck gave her a long stare.

"Thanks for watching Gracie. You keep steppin' up, don't you?"

"That's what friends do for each other."

Friends. Could they simply be friends? She'd never felt this need to melt into a friend before, to be held by him. Right now, though, she had no words.

Beck kissed Gracie good-bye and left.

The door clicked shut behind him, and Tansy closed her eyes on the tears that sprung up.

Chapter 8

Tansy fretted.

Lamont Elliot wasn't due to return from his fishing trip for two more days, and the waiting was agony. Beck's dad had talked to Lamont over the phone, and he'd agreed to the sale, but with all this thinking time, she worried Pops might change his mind.

And she was absolutely, one hundred percent sure Beck wasn't done fighting it. Their last few encounters had been civil. More than that. But he'd made his feelings about the house very clear.

To the casual observer, Beck came off as laid-back and easygoing. She knew him better than that casual observer, though, and when he got his teeth into something, he put a bulldog to shame. He'd no doubt argue with his grandpa about the sale, and maybe he'd win. After all, he was an Elliot. His feelings would and should carry a lot of weight.

Still, she'd hold fast to her dreams. Refusing to believe the sale wouldn't go through, she drew up plans in between working on the wedding cakes for Magnolia House's brides while her mom and Gracie did gardening and household chores. The only way to keep her sanity was to stay busy.

<center>~~~</center>

Tansy was trying her best to cajole a pouting Gracie to eat her green beans when the doorbell rang.

"Mom, can you get that?"

"I certainly will." Her mom's heels tapped across the wood floor. "Lamont, how nice to see you! Come in, please. How was the fishing?"

"Absolutely great. Caught one this big."

Her mother chuckled. "I'll just bet you did, and if I ask Earle, he'll back you up and tell me about the one he caught. My guess? It'll be a foot or two bigger than yours."

Lamont's hearty laugh echoed in the house.

"Who's that, Mama?" Wide-eyed, Gracie scooted off her chair and hurried to Tansy's side, clutching the leg of her slacks.

She stood and hitched her daughter up onto one hip. "He's the man who owns that beautiful house we're gonna buy, sweetie."

Strangely shy, Gracie hid her face in her mom's neck as they walked into the living room.

"Mr. Elliot!"

"Tansy, honey. Come here and let an old man give you a hug."

She did just that, Gracie squirming between them.

"And who are you, young lady?"

Peeking at him, she said, "Gracie Bella Forbes. I'm this many years old." She held up four fingers.

Lamont laughed again. "Is that right?"

She nodded bashfully.

"Well, you sure are a cutie. I like that skirt." He pointed at the purple tulle ballerina skirt Gracie had insisted on wearing to dinner.

"Me too." Gracie ran a hand over the skirt and picked up one end to hold out to him, her shyness forgotten. "It's tickly."

The old man rubbed the skirt between his thumb and forefinger. "Does it bother you?"

"Nope, it's my favorite."

"You've got good taste. So does your mama." He met Tansy's eyes. "Heard you're in the market for a house."

Her heart hammered.

Before she could answer, her mother asked, "Would you like some iced tea, Lamont? Coffee?"

"No thanks, Rexanna," he boomed. "Judy had dinner ready when I got home." He patted his stomach. "Afraid I overindulged, but that woman's chicken pot pie is the best there is. On top of that, she had a loaf of homemade bread right out of the oven."

"Your son married one of the best cooks in the Low Country. Tansy, how about you?"

She shook her head. "I'm good."

"I think I'd like a cup of coffee." She reached her arms toward Gracie. "Why don't I take my grandbaby to the kitchen to help and you two can talk?"

"Thanks, Mom."

"You're welcome." The little girl now in her arms, Rexanna turned to Lamont. "Don't be makin' yourself a stranger now. Have a seat."

The big man dropped onto the sofa and nodded toward the other end as Rexanna and Gracie left the room.

Tansy sat down, then blurted, "You know Beck is against this, don't you?"

Oh, sweet Jesus! She could have cut out her own tongue. That was hardly the way to sweet-talk him into selling to her, but there it was. The elephant in the room.

He nodded. "Understood. My wife and I raised our children there. It was a happy home, but it hasn't been since I lost my Elsie. I want it to be happy again." He leaned toward her and laid a worn and gnarled hand on her cheek. "If I'm not misreading those beautiful eyes, I don't think you've had all that much happiness lately, either. We'll see if we can change that. For you *and* the house."

She couldn't stop the tears. "I love you, Mr. Elliot."

He wrapped her in a warm, comforting hug. "I love you, too, sweetheart. I..."

He didn't have to finish. He'd hoped she'd be part of his family—so had she.

"I want you and that sweet little girl to make that house your home. Stanton tells me you've agreed to my price with no quibbling."

"It seemed fair."

"It is fair. Thing is, the family have all settled into their own homes. Nobody jumped at it when I offered it to them."

"Beck would now, just to keep me out of it."

"He might, but since he's already refused once, I'm holdin' him to that. His own little place suits him fine."

She nodded. "He's upset with me, Mr. Elliot. He probably will be with you, too."

He patted her hand. "Don't you worry about my grandson. He'll come around."

"I hurt him."

His eyes grew sad. "You did, sweetie, you certainly did. I can't argue that. Not a single one of us, though, gets to rewrite our history. It is what it is, and we take it from here."

A single tear trickled down her cheek, and he thumbed it away.

"And, Tansy? Call me Pops like you used to."

Sniffing, she nodded. Elsie Elliot had been one lucky woman to have shared her life with this wonderful man.

She thought of Emerson. Would he have wiped away her tear?

She nearly snorted. Hardly. He'd have reminded her she wasn't a pretty crier and that her nose and mascara were running. Then he'd go out and lose a week's salary at one of his illicit backroom gambling clubs and blame it on her.

Beck? During their years together, he'd wiped plenty of her tears. During her father's funeral he'd been a rock and had given her the strength to endure those awful days. Then she'd stabbed him in the back.

She brought herself back to the here and now.

"I'll talk to Kemper and get the legal wheels rolling. That is if you're certain you want to buy the old homestead."

"I do."

He held out a hand, and they shook.

"You've got yourself a home, missy."

"Thank you." She hesitated. "Pops."

She threw her arms around him and savored the moment, then pulled away.

"My guess is it'll take a little time to get all the legal rigmarole out of the way." He dug in his pocket and came out with a key. "Take this. That way if you need some measurements or whatever, you can get inside the house."

"I can't take your key."

"Sure you can." He took her hand, turned it palm up, and dropped the key in it. Curling her fingers over it, he said, "There you go. The house belongs to you now. Take good care of her."

The next couple of weeks veered close to insanity. The bride and groom gushed over the Vegas wedding cake and the Elvis groom's cake. The vintage wedding cake stole everyone's breath, and the bride cried. Before the debris from those weddings had even been cleared, Jenni Beth handed her three more cake orders.

How did they all keep up?

Every time she visited Magnolia House, Tansy caught herself studying the cameras Beck had placed around the estate. Jenni Beth had told her about what happened—or, at least, what she suspected. Why in the world would anyone go through her files? It made no sense.

Then there was her new house! Even with a cash closing, there were reams of paperwork. Kemper Dobson, the Elliot family's attorney since the dawn of time, had handled all their legal needs over the years. Because of that, he was able to expedite things.

Since he'd done a lot of work for her parents over the years, too, Tansy trusted Mr. Dobson and let him take care of everything.

And the key Mr. Elliot had given her? She was close to being ashamed of how many times she'd used it. Sometimes alone, sometimes with her mom or Coralee. Her aunt was working on a sign for her: Tansy's Sweet Dreams.

A few afternoons and early evenings, she'd simply gone inside and sat in the middle of the living room floor or out on the back patio, unable to believe this incredible house belonged to her. At least it would, as soon as she signed on the dotted line and handed over the check — the check funded by her father.

Her chest tightened. She missed her dad with her whole heart. They'd shared a special bond. When she'd received that phone call at college telling her he'd died, she'd lost it.

Her world had never been, would never be, the same.

Enough of that. Her dad would want her to look toward the future rather than back at the past.

Speaking of the past. She'd been so sure she'd hear from Beck, if only to argue with her some more. It wasn't like him to take this lying down, and it made her nervous.

Today she and Gracie had driven to a little antique shop on the outskirts of town. One of the things she'd packed in her SUV and brought with her to Misty Bottoms was her teacup collection. A fragile cup and saucer trimmed in gold, with gorgeous red roses splashed across them, had caught her eye when she and Emerson had been first married.

She'd bought it.

After that, everywhere she went, she added a teacup and saucer to her collection. She'd kept them boxed up in the closet of one of their extra bedrooms. Now? She'd use them to serve her customers. But she'd need more, and that meant hitting all the area shops. She grinned. Tough job, but somebody had to do it.

She and Gracie bought six that day, one with tiny bluebirds darting across the china. Another bloomed with pale-blue forget-me-nots. A black-and-white teapot had come home with them, too. She'd start watching for cups to go with it.

About a mile from the house, Gracie gave in to the yawns and fell asleep. Tansy lifted her eyes to the mirror and smiled at the sight of her daughter, rosy cheeked, head slumped to the right, and hoped happy dreams kept her company.

Tansy had had a whopper of a dream last night, with Beck playing the starring role. When she'd awakened this morning, she'd half expected to find him there, cuddled into her, his arms around her. Instead, she'd been the bed's sole occupant.

Would she sleep alone forever? She hoped not. Even after Emerson, the romance of Magnolia House and her brides wasn't lost on her. She wanted a shot at the dream again.

When they reached her mom's, Tansy carefully carried the still-sleeping child inside. A finger to her lips warned her mom.

After she had Grace tucked in, she found her mom on the back porch, two glasses of iced tea waiting.

"Good trip?"

"The best." She shared what they'd found. "I'll wait till Gracie wakes to bring them inside. Right now I'll take these few minutes to relax with you." She sank onto one of the wicker chairs and rested her feet on the footstool.

"Good, because there's something I want to talk about."

Tansy sat up straighter. "Everything okay?"

"Absolutely." Rexanna sipped her tea. "I'd like to have a welcome-home party for you, honey."

"My comin' back isn't really a cause for celebration, Mom."

"It is to me."

"Who do you intend to invite?"

"I haven't made a list, but I thought we should have all your friends and a few of mine. We'll invite some children for Gracie to play with, too."

"Jenni Beth?" Tansy asked.

"Of course."

"Cole?"

She nodded.

"Cricket and Sam?"

Her mother smiled. "Aren't they the cutest couple?"

"They are. What about Cricket's cousin?"

"Who?"

"Beck."

Her mother started to nod. "Oh. No, I don't suppose that would be a good idea."

"Me, either. But all of Beck's friends would be here?"

"Oh dear."

"Oh dear is right, Mom. We can't have a party. It would be too awkward."

On a reluctant sigh, Rexanna agreed. "I suppose that's true, but it doesn't seem right. I'm so happy to have you back. It feels like we should do something."

"Tell you what." She leaned toward her mother. "Why don't we have a girls' day?"

Her mother threw up her hands. "Perfect. We'll still have fun, but skirt the Beck issue. What do you have in mind?"

"Let's make it Sunday, so no one has to take off work, and since the weather's so beautiful, how about a tea party right here in your backyard?"

"With hats."

"Big, gorgeous hats. We can use my teacups. I'm not sure I have enough pots, though."

"We can round up some, and I'm sure Coralee has a few," her mom said. "Let me worry about that."

She went inside and came back with a small notebook and a pen. Heads together, they fussed with the list.

"Instead of sending invitations, why don't we do phone invites instead? It'll be more personal."

"Agreed. You want to make the calls or should I?" Rexanna asked.

"Why don't we divide them up? It'll go faster that way. You know we'll have a few who want to chat."

"True." Mom took her half and went inside to start calling.

Tansy pulled out her cell. She'd squeeze in a few before Gracie woke. Before she made the first, she closed her eyes for a few seconds, felt the gentle warmth of the autumn day on her face.

She and Gracie were exactly where they needed to be.

Chapter 9

TANSY WENT OUT OF HER WAY TO GIVE BECK A WIDE berth, although since he seemed to be doing the same, it probably wasn't necessary. Kitty had him in to fix some little thing one day when she'd been working on a four-tiered wedding cake, but they'd ignored each other. Same thing when she was in the diner and Dee-Ann called him to take care of a door problem.

Still, Tansy wasn't taking any chances. She and his grandfather were scheduled to sign the house papers the following Wednesday.

She could barely sleep from the excitement.

Gracie, on the other hand, had never slept so well. Tansy had worried herself sick about uprooting her daughter, about tearing her away from everything she knew. She should have done it sooner.

Every day brought new excitement for Gracie and new friends, young and old, into her life. She played in the yard till she was ready to drop. Unlike Beck, Emerson hadn't earned his spot in the family business; he'd simply inherited it. Because of that he hadn't valued it and had often stayed out late, feeding his addiction, then sleeping till noon. Fortunately, he'd worked in the family business, which meant that if he didn't show, the paychecks still rolled in—until even the family gave up on him.

But when he slept all day, she and Gracie had to do

quiet things like reading books or coloring or watching a movie in Gracie's room.

At her mother's, noise was never a consideration. If it was warm enough, they hooked up the sprinkler and played in the water, squealing every time it hit them. If it was too cool for that, they rode bikes or played dolls or hide-and-seek.

Life was good. With the exception of Beck Elliot.

When she'd lived out of town, she could put Beck and her feelings in a little box and shuffle it to the back of her mind. Here, that box had sprung its lock.

Somehow or other, she had to get past it. She couldn't keep crossing the street or checking out quickly without half of what she needed when she spotted him in the grocery store.

Playing hide-and-seek with Gracie in the yard was one thing. Playing hide-from-Beck was another entirely.

Bound and determined to make Tansy's homecoming a happy event, her mother and Gracie hit up every antique shop within driving distance and rounded up more teapots along with a beautiful set of pink Depression glass dishes. They'd use them for the party; then they'd become part of Tansy's Sweet Dreams stock.

The calendar flipped to October, and the Sunday of the get-together couldn't have been more perfect. Sunny and with barely any humidity, the temperature hovered in the midseventies. Coralee showed up early to help with the decorating, bringing a few surprises of her own. In no time, they had the yard looking like a fantasy garden.

They'd set up an adult table and one for the little girls. Her mom had found several vintage tablecloths in pink-flowered cotton that created a festive air all by themselves. Pots of pretty flowers, courtesy of Cricket's Enchanted Florist, dotted the patio area with splashes of color. Coralee had painted several outside canvasses with *Alice in Wonderland* tea-party scenes featuring Tansy's friends and family. She hung the ornately framed paintings along the fence.

"My welcome-home gift for you. When you open Sweet Dreams, they'll look cute hung around the tearoom."

"They're awesome!" Tansy hugged her, then studied the faces on the canvasses. "Coralee, these are magnificent. You've captured everyone perfectly, including their personalities."

"It's a gift, dear."

Tansy threw back her head and laughed. Her aunt did not believe in hiding her light under a basket. No false modesty here.

Kitty brought mini-cakes in chocolate, red velvet, lemon, and white, along with yummy-looking Mason-jar pies. Tansy helped her arrange them on a serving table decorated with teapots filled with pink rosebuds and baby's breath.

"In another week, sweetie, Kitty's Kakes and Bakery will be a thing of the past. It'll be up to you to provide fancy little treats for parties like this."

"I don't want you to leave, though."

"Don't worry. I told you, Harv and I are in no hurry. Before we jump into our next adventure, we're gonna put our feet up and enjoy some quiet do-nothin' time."

"Good for you."

"And who knows? A certain someone might like an old woman's help getting her business off the ground."

"I'd love that, Kitty."

"You let me know when and how I can help. Otherwise, I'll keep my nose to myself."

"Anybody here?" The back gate opened, and Cricket and Jenni Beth peeked into the yard.

"Oh my gosh, you two look beautiful." Tansy hugged them. "Turn. Let me see."

Both did slow, dramatic three-sixties, huge grins on their faces. Cricket wore a flowing vintage dress in sage green with strappy little sandals, while Jenni Beth had chosen a silk sheath with three-quarter-length sleeves in old gold. Both wore the requisite big hat.

"Look at us!" Jenni Beth put her arms around the other two girls' shoulders. "Together we've covered Mother Nature's autumn palette."

Tansy looked down at her own burnt-orange tunic worn over black leggings. "Yes, we have!"

Her mother clicked a picture. "For your Sweet Dreams photo board."

"Photo board?" Jenni Beth asked.

Tansy shrugged. "I thought it might be nice if my customers shared their special moments with others at the shop. Kind of a celebration of life in Misty Bottoms."

"Great idea!" Jenni Beth turned to Tansy's mom and aunt and took in their outfits. "May I just say wow!"

Tansy applauded her friend's tact.

Rexanna wore navy slacks and a lacy white top, the epitome of understated Southern elegance. Coralee, on the other hand, wore a long, loose caftan in a bright blue, red, and orange print with two chunky turquoise necklaces and silver cuff bracelets. Today's shoe choice was a leopard-print wedge sandal.

Cricket held up a bunch of flowers. "Where do you want these?"

"I thought we'd scatter them in those." She pointed to clear bottles hanging from a couple of the trees.

Gracie wrapped her arms around Tansy's leg. "Mama and me stringed them up this mornin'."

"Well, you did a great job!" Cricket held out a hand to her. "Want to help me arrange the flowers in them?"

"Uh-huh."

And they were off.

"She's adorable, Tanz. You must be so proud of her."

"I am, Jenni Beth." She stared at her daughter. "She starts preschool next week."

"And she can't wait, and you're dreading it."

"Yeah." She grinned. "Mom insists it'll be fine. She'll only go three days a week for a while. Give her— or me, more likely—a chance to get used to it."

Jenni Beth held up a platter of finger sandwiches. "Charlotte and Mama made these this morning. We have cucumber and cream cheese, pimento cheese, and bacon and tomato."

"I find myself craving Ms. Charlotte's pimento cheese spread."

"You and me both. She remembered that was your favorite, so she was hell-bent on making it."

"She and your mom are coming, aren't they?"

"They were leavin' a few minutes behind us. I wanted them to ride with us, but they insisted they'd come in Dad's van. I gave up arguin' with my mom a long time ago."

"Got you. She's doin' better, isn't she?"

Jenni Beth nodded. "The wedding business at Magnolia House has been good for her. It keeps her busy and her mind off my brother's death."

"I'm glad." Tansy squeezed her friend's hand. "Let's set those sandwiches over there. We have enough food for an army. Kitty brought dessert, and Mom and I made a fresh fruit bowl, warm and cold pasta salads, and more finger sandwiches. On top of all that, we have chicken salad, egg salad, and asparagus rollups."

Beside the food table was another that held ice-cold lemonade and a box of teas in more varieties than Tansy could count.

The gate swung open. Adorable in their hats and fall outfits, Mrs. Beaumont and Charlotte came in, followed by Cole's mother and… *Oh my gosh, Beck's mama*. Tansy, gaping, glanced toward her mother, who was smiling broadly.

Bringing up the rear was Darlene, Dee-Ann, and Ms. Hattie.

Judy Elliot wasted no time moving in for a hug. "It's so good to see you, Tansy." Pulling slightly away, she said, "I won't lie. I'd hoped that you and my son would be growin' a family by now, but that's between the two of you. I've always loved you, and that hasn't changed."

"Thank you." Tansy's eyes misted.

"I didn't mean to make you cry, sweetie, but I don't want you to feel funny or awkward around me or, for heaven's sake, avoid me. Promise me that won't happen."

She gave her a wobbly smile. "It won't."

"Good." With that, she crossed the yard to Rexanna. Tansy took a deep breath and greeted their other guests.

"Ms. Hattie!" She wrapped the wizened woman in a warm hug. "It's so good to see you."

"Good to see you, too, child. Guess you heard what Jenni Beth, Cole, and Beck did for me."

"I did."

Ms. Hattie, who'd helped nearly everyone in Misty Bottoms at one time or another, had aged. Now, she needed help, and Tansy's friends had pitched in, fixing up her badly-in-need-of-repair home.

"I wish I could have been here to help."

"Well, you're home now, and that's what matters, isn't it?"

"Yes. It is."

Gracie gave a happy shout when she turned from her flower decorating and spotted two towheaded young girls skipping through the yard.

"My sister's granddaughters," Darlene told Tansy. "Fraternal twins, Dixie and Trixie." She rolled her eyes heavenward. "They've been pesterin' me somethin' awful about this. We made their hats yesterday."

"They're darlin'," Rexanna said.

Trixie wore a pink straw hat decorated with a feather boa and pink roses. Dixie had gone with a red cowgirl hat boasting white roses and a peacock feather.

"I have a hat, too." Gracie patted her floppy felt hat with its yellow tulle bow. Daisies sprinkled the wide brim.

The girls dropped in the grass and tried on each other's hats, then, holding hands, ran across the yard to the games.

"I think they're gonna do just fine," Charlotte said.

"It was nice of you to bring the girls, Darlene."

Tansy watched the children. "Gracie has missed her play friends."

Darlene waved a hand. "Don't think a thing of it. I love those two like they were my own. And believe me, their mama is enjoyin' a little free time. My guess? She's up to her neck in a tub full of bubbles right about now."

Quinlyn peeked around the gate. "Am I late?"

"No, you're not!" Tansy made a come-on-in motion.

The yard filled with talk and laughter, and Tansy acknowledged her mother had been right. She needed this. They all needed this.

The kids squealed and laughed as they played ring toss and threw a beanbag at a wooden clown, its mouth wide-open. Cole had sent that earlier as his contribution. The older women drank tea and caught up, while Quinlyn, Cricket, Jenni Beth, and Tansy ate finger sandwiches and talked about her plans.

Home. A slice of heaven.

Tansy lowered her voice. "Jenni Beth, I know you put a ton of work into Magnolia House, and that Cole and Beck helped a lot. Who else did you use?"

"For the actual work?"

Tansy nodded.

Her friend grimaced. "Beck arranged it. Some of the men were his crew; others were friends of his in the business. The guy's got a Rolodex ten inches thick."

"Oh."

"I might be able to go back through my records and pull some names for you."

"No." Tansy shook her head. "I won't ask you to do that. Somehow that seems disloyal, and neither you nor

I would feel good about it. I'll check around town and see who I can find."

"There's a board—oh, shoot." Cricket shut herself down.

"What?"

"There's a board where some of the guys post their business cards, but that's in Elliot's Lumberyard, too."

Tansy sipped her tea. "This will be harder than I realized. When it comes to help and materials, Elliot's Construction and Lumberyard has the town pretty well sewn up."

There'd been a time when that would have been a big plus for her, when Beck would have jumped right in and done whatever was necessary for her. That wasn't going to happen this time.

She allowed herself all of two minutes to brood over that while the chatter continued around her. Then she dusted herself off and joined the debate about which type of shoe they couldn't live without—ballet flats, nude pumps, kitten heels, or stilettos. They finally agreed they needed them all.

"I had the strangest conversation with one of our future grooms the other day," Jenni Beth said.

"What'd he say?" Cricket asked.

"That now Brandy—that's his bride—would be a permanent part of our town's history. I guess my face gave me away because he said, you know, as a Magnolia Bride. It was the way he said it that struck me as odd, but I can't quite put my finger on why."

"Well, then, why don't you put your finger on one of these?" Coralee suggested, holding a tray of the Mason-jar pies. "Time to eat up, ladies."

"What the heck? I'll eat salad all next week." Jenni Beth plucked a lemon meringue off the tray. "Y'all have to have one, too."

Tansy, Cricket, and Quin all picked their favorite.

They talked, laughed, ate, and drank tea and lemonade. Finally, though, the little ones wore down, and everyone wandered off, a few at a time, until at the end of the wonderful day, it was just her and her mother in the kitchen. Tansy stacked the last of the plates in the dishwasher. Her welcome-home party had been awesome.

She'd worried when Judy Elliot showed up. She shouldn't have. Beck's mom was, without a doubt, one of the warmest, most gracious people on earth. Not once had she thrown Tansy's betrayal in her face.

But Judy's son was now at the root of Tansy's problems.

How could she possibly turn the Elliot house into her dream without his cooperation?

The question of the day.

Heck, the question of the rest of her new life.

Chapter 10

IT SEEMED STRANGE TO WAKE UP IN HER CHILDHOOD bedroom. In the soft light, Tansy could almost pretend she was seventeen and hadn't a care in the world other than what she'd wear on her weekend date with Beck.

Almost.

Reality? She wasn't seventeen and her own daughter slept peacefully in the room next door. The three young girls had worn each other out yesterday. She stretched her arms over her head. Then, tossing back the covers, she slid out of their warmth and padded barefoot into the bath. Quietly, she brushed both her teeth and her hair and swiped mascara over her lashes. Returning to her room, she slipped into jeans and a light sweater. This late in the year, the mornings could be a little chilly.

She crept downstairs and scrawled a note for her mom, telling her she'd run over to the new place. If Gracie woke before her grandma, Tansy knew she'd go in to wake her.

Careful to lock up behind herself, she headed for Tommy's Texaco and that first cup of bracing coffee. She hadn't wanted to take a chance on waking either her mother or her daughter with the noise from the single-cup brewer at home.

She swung through the door, breathing in the scent of the fresh-brewed coffee. "Hey, Tommy."

"Hey right back at you, Ms. Tansy. What in the world are you doin' up so early?"

"I couldn't sleep."

"Too much on your mind?"

"Yes, way too much, and right now I need a shot of caffeine."

"You're in luck then. Just made a fresh pot."

"Wonderful." She wandered over and poured a cup, then added a generous dollop of half-and-half and took her first hit. *Mmmm*. The biscuits smelled too good to resist. "I really need one of those ham biscuits, Tommy."

"Wife made them up fresh this mornin', like always." He lifted the cover, took out one of the wrapped biscuits, and handed it to her. "There you go. Can I get ya anything else this mornin'?" She shook her head, took a bite, and sighed with pleasure. "These are the absolute best. Tell Erlene I haven't had a better one for four times the money."

"I'll do that." He frowned. "You don't mind my sayin' so, you look worried."

"I am." She slid onto one of the old stools just inside the door. "My guess is that you know I'm buyin' the old Elliot house."

"Yep."

"And I'm sure you know, too, that Beck is less than happy about that."

"That would be one way of puttin' it."

She swallowed and rolled her eyes. "Right. The house is in great shape. No surprise there, considering it belonged to the Elliots. But for what I need, there's quite a bit of remodeling to do. I want to turn the downstairs into my business and the upstairs into living quarters for Gracie and me."

"Heard that, too."

She gave a mirthless laugh. "I'll bet you did. Here's the thing. I need skilled workmen to make the changes happen. And materials."

"Can't you just..." He trailed off and ran a hand over the coppery stubble on his chin. "The Elliots pretty much have a monopoly on both those things here in Misty Bottoms, don't they?"

"They do. Thus my problem." She popped the last bite of the biscuit in her mouth and wished it had been bigger. Wiping her hands on a paper napkin, she said, "I'm not sure what to do."

"And that's why you're not sleepin'."

"One of the reasons."

"Go see him. Talk to him."

"Who?"

"Why, Beck, of course. Who else would I mean?"

"I don't know. I can't just—"

"Sure you can. He's runnin' a business, ain't he? You're a customer same as anybody else. Either just walk in, bold as brass, and place your order with one of the guys or go in and have a heart-to-heart with Beck. I think he'll see reason."

She sighed. "Oh, if only that were true."

"You've seen *The Godfather*?"

"No."

He stared at her. "You serious?"

"Afraid so. Should I have seen it?"

"Hell yes! Beg pardon. Yeah, you should have.

There's a line in there that's the best ever written. Michael Corleone, you know, Al Pacino?"

Baffled, she shrugged.

Tommy shook his head sadly. "Anyway, he says…" Tommy cleared his throat and deepened his voice. "'It's not personal, Sonny. It's strictly business.' That's what this is, Tansy. You know." He waved a hand back and forth between them. "It's business. What happened between the two of you—you and Beck—that's personal. One shouldn't get in the way of the other."

She sent him a skeptical look.

"Trust me. It'll all work out."

"I sure hope so." She wadded up the wrapper and napkin and tossed them in the wastebasket, refilled her coffee, and gave Tommy a hug. "Thanks."

"Didn't do nothin'."

"You listened to my whinin'."

"It was sharin', not whinin'." He grinned.

"Right."

―――

With food in her stomach and coffee in hand, Tansy felt better. The morning was fabulous, one of those days they write about in the tourist books on Georgia's Low Country.

As she drove through the still-sleeping town, she rolled down her windows, let the fresh air blow her hair into a chaotic tumble, and smiled. The leaves on the trees had begun to turn, and she inhaled deeply. Nothing beat the smell of autumn, unless it was the smell of a baby right after her bath. She loved the four-year-old Gracie, but she missed that baby smell of lotion and powder and sweetness—had hoped to have more babies. One more loss for which she had no one but herself to blame.

And wouldn't it be stupid to spoil this gorgeous day with sorrow for what she didn't have? Instead, she'd celebrate what she did have, and that was a lot! Top of the list? Gracie Bella. Her mother, aunt, friends, and neighbors. A beautiful new home and a soon-to-be-open business.

She drove straight to the empty house at the end of Main and unlocked the door. It creaked as she opened it, but some WD-40 would fix that. Taking off her shoes, she meandered slowly through the rooms, the early morning sun splashing over the hardwood floors and her footsteps echoing in the empty space.

At the door to each room, she stopped, imagined it the way it would be. It nearly took her breath away. She was so close to her dream, so close to starting her new life here in Misty Bottoms with Gracie.

But none of it would happen without Beck's help—or at least his cooperation.

Tommy's advice replayed in her mind, and she knew he was right.

What she couldn't come to grips with was why she'd even think she had the right to ask Beck for help. Hadn't she shot his dreams out of the sky? Why, now, should he help make hers come true?

If this impacted only her, she'd be tempted to give up, but it didn't. She wanted Gracie to grow up here in Misty Bottoms, and that meant it was time to suck it up, pull on her big girl panties, and take care of business.

Tansy marched into Elliot's Lumberyard and practically dared anyone to stop her.

Beck had no legal right to block her from the store. No legal right to keep her from buying whatever she wanted as long as she paid for it.

Of course, what good would a pile of lumber and sheetrock do if she had no one to turn it into walls? She'd worry about that later—no, she wouldn't. She'd worry about that right now.

It was time she remembered who she was, what she was. She was a Southern woman, and Southern women didn't back down from a fight. They rolled up their sleeves and got to work, did whatever needed doing. And right now? That meant having a discussion with Mr. Elliot, the younger.

Oh God. Her heart might give out first.

Jeeters came around the corner, and Tansy swore she read the fight-or-flight argument in his eyes as they darted from one side to the other.

"How are you, Jeeters?"

He swallowed audibly. "I'm fine, Ms. Tansy. You?"

"I'm good. Is Beck in?"

"Umm…" He swallowed again.

His nervousness actually calmed her. "It's all right. I promise we won't kill each other. Is he in his office?"

He gave a quick little nod.

"Thanks." With that, she breezed past him.

She didn't bother to knock.

When she opened the door and stepped in, he jumped from his chair.

Softly closing the door behind her, she leaned against it. "I'm busy, Tansy."

"I'm sure you are. You're workin', and that's what this visit is about." Staring into those beautiful eyes, her courage slipped a notch. She went on quickly before she lost her last shred of nerve. "Here's the deal, Beck. Like it or not, I'm buyin' your grandpa's house. He and I have agreed on it, and I'm just waiting to sign the papers."

He grunted.

"Like Michael Corleone said, this is business. It's not personal." She'd paraphrased, but close enough.

Beck didn't even blink. "Bullshit."

"What?"

"I said bullshit. This thing between you and me?" He laughed derisively. "It's always been personal. For me, anyway. If you need something, one of the guys out front can help you."

"No, they can't. Not with this."

He tossed a pencil onto his desk and dropped into his chair. "This is exactly what I've been tryin' to avoid. I can't stop you from buyin' Pops's place, but I don't have to like it. Despite that, I've gone out of my way to be polite, even invited you to dinner at my folks'. You turned me down. Seems you and me have nothin' more to say to each other."

Ouch.

Those midnight-blue eyes used to look at her as if no other woman existed. Now? Cold and distant. Her mouth was so dry, she wasn't sure she could speak. She reached deep down inside for a new supply of courage and found a few last dregs. "I'm really sorry about the other night. I really was tired."

"Again, bullshit."

Switching tactics, she said, "I haven't seen you around lately."

"No. I've sent one of the guys when Kitty or Darlene or Dee-Ann or whoever the hell calls with some made-up excuse to get me to their place when you're there."

"They're conspiring, aren't they?"

"Bingo."

"I had nothin' to do with that."

"I know. You looked as shell-shocked as I felt when I walked in—time after time."

"I guess they mean well."

He made a noncommittal sound.

"Here's the thing," she said. "I need work done at the house."

"That house is in great shape."

"I agree. But I need some remodeling done."

"What you need is a different house. In a different town."

"That being said." She continued, ignoring his pique. "I thought you might be able to supply the name of some workers or"—she took another deep breath and clenched her hands together till her knuckles turned white—"maybe I could hire your company."

The expression on his face had her searching for a hidey-hole. A trickle of sweat dampened the back of her cotton sweater. But she couldn't back down. She'd never ever be able to do this a second time.

"In addition to workers, I'll need materials. If you won't or can't help me, I'll take my business elsewhere."

When he remained silent, she threw her last argument on the table.

"It doesn't feel right fixin' up an Elliot's house with

someone else's material, but that's what I'll do if I have to. The choice is yours."

He pushed up from his chair, and it crashed against the wall. "Shit! Some choice."

"I know."

"Do you? I'm so mad right now, I can't see straight."

"I live with a four-year-old, Beck. I'm used to tantrums."

She saw in his eyes that she had pushed him too far. But he wouldn't hurt her. Reminding herself of that as he slowly moved toward her, she took a step backward.

"Beck?" Her hand shot out, pressed against his chest.

He shrugged away. "Don't touch me."

"But—"

"Damn it, Tansy! You were my girl." He reached out and pulled her off her feet, his mouth crushing hers in a kiss meant to punish.

Instead, she met it, beat for beat.

What felt like ages later, yet not nearly long enough, he released her as abruptly as he'd begun the kiss.

Barely able to breathe, she stared at him. "You know, you're like a big old bucket of testosterone that's so full it keeps sloppin' over. Do you have a soft side at all?"

"Not anymore. When you're ready to start destroyin' Pops's house, let me know. I'll arrange things for you. Right now, I've got work to do."

Message received, she scooted out the door, her lips and cheeks burning with his heat.

Neither of them had won that round.

$$\sim\!\!\!\sim\!\!\!\sim$$

Beck stood in the doorway and watched her go, watched that sleek body in the worn denims skedaddle out the front door. She used to live in jeans, but she rarely wore them anymore. Too bad, because a pair of jeans had never looked better.

Sighing, he leaned against the jamb and ran an embarrassingly shaky hand through his hair. What the hell had he been thinking to grab her like that, to kiss her till he'd nearly forgotten his own name?

Worse, she'd kissed him back, stoked fires never quite extinguished.

That kiss. It had been so long—too long. God, even in his anger, she'd tasted like a dream.

He'd loved that woman to distraction, and she'd left him with no warning. No chance to talk to her, to try to change her mind. With one tearful phone call, a huge chunk of his life broke off and crumbled. The most important chunk—that softer side she'd wondered about, the part that could trust and was free to love.

His fingers bit into the doorjamb as he tried to shake off the anger and hurt. He scanned the store his grandfather had built. The aisles, cluttered with everything a person could need to build, remodel, or renovate a house, had grown in number over the years as the business expanded. He'd moved their inventory to the computer despite his dad's and Pops's objections, which made it so much easier to keep track of supplies and orders.

A business this size couldn't keep up if they didn't step up. Inch by inch, he'd dragged the company into the twenty-first century.

Day in and day out, he worked hard to keep the business moving ahead, but he often wondered what would have happened if he'd gone to college with Tansy instead of staying here.

Would Tansy and Gracie Bella both be his?

How he wished.

After five solid minutes of starting at the wall, Beck called his grandfather. "You home?"

"Nope, I'm in the lumberyard's parking lot. Came to talk. You got time?"

"Yes, sir, I do."

"Good. I've got coffee and a bag of doughnuts. Don't tell your mother."

Beck chuckled. "I won't."

Before he could clear the top of his desk, Pops walked in and dropped onto one of the chairs. Holding out a coffee and the doughnut bag, he looked around. "This place could stand a good cleanin', son."

"Guess it could." Beck opened the bag and drew out a chocolate-frosted doughnut, then handed the bag back to his grandfather. "I doubt that's what you came to talk about, though."

"No, it's not. We need to talk about Tansy and the house."

"Are you sure you're makin' the right decision, Pops?"

"Sit down, Beck. Let me tell you a story."

Beck sat.

Leaning back in his chair, Pops folded his hands over his stomach. "I loved your grandmother with all my heart. Always did, always will."

"I know."

"Did you know I almost didn't marry the girl?"

"No."

"I went to Atlanta for a few days and, when I came

back, a friend told me Elsie had gone to the Saturday night dance with another man. I was heartbroken."

"NeeNee did that?"

"She did." He took a bite of his doughnut and washed it down with coffee. "When I went to her house and asked her about it, she admitted it straight out. Without waiting to hear any more, I told her we were finished. I wouldn't be by again."

Beck stared incredulously at his grandfather.

"Elsie looked at me with those same midnight-blue eyes you see in the mirror every day and said, 'If that's what you want, fine.' Then she closed the door on me. Left me standin' on the stoop."

"But, Pops, you were in the right. I mean, if she went out with someone else..." Beck twisted his coffee cup in his hands.

"I certainly thought I was right. Thing is, I didn't have all the facts. The man she went with? A cousin. He shipped out for Korea two days after the dance."

"Why didn't NeeNee tell you that?"

"I asked her that very question. She said she shouldn't have had to. That I should have trusted her." Pops reached into the bag for another doughnut. "And she was right. I never made that mistake again."

Mulling over Pops's story, Beck popped the last of his doughnut into his mouth. "I'm not sure exactly what that has to do with Tansy and me, with Tansy and the house. But I suspect you're gonna tell me."

His grandfather leaned forward in his chair, his coffee dangerously close to spilling. "One thing I've learned is that life isn't always what you expect. The trick is to stay open to it, to the possibilities it offers."

"Okay."

"You and Tansy? Untapped possibilities if you pay attention."

With that, he stood and walked out.

Possibilities. Not so very different than opportunities.

Hadn't Tansy just walked in here and offered him one?

Chapter 11

TANSY HAD NO IDEA HOW MUCH GUFF LAMONT Elliot had taken from Beck, but he'd made it happen. She'd closed on her house at the end of Main Street.

Exhilaration surged through her. The phenomenal house was hers, all hers. For the first time ever, she didn't have to answer to anyone and could do exactly as she pleased. She'd sink or soar, but it would be her doing.

Tansy'd left Pops and his old pal Kemper sharing a celebratory glass of bourbon after she'd traded a check for closing papers and a second key. She and Gracie had a home of their own and a brand-new chapter in their life.

Raising the house key to her lips, Tansy kissed it. Then she lifted her eyes to the sky. "Thank you, Dad, for making today possible. You're still taking care of me." Tears blinded her, and she swiped at them. "I'm so sorry you never got to meet Gracie Bella."

A lump in her throat, Tansy slid behind the wheel and rolled down the window. A beautiful rainbow arched across the sky. Her father telling her all would be well?

A sense of peace settled over her, and she didn't doubt for a minute that things would be better.

It was all coming together.

Yesterday, the bank had called to tell her she'd been approved for the renovation and start-up loan. Ethan

Cooper had asked her to come in and sign the papers. Although her nerves had been on high alert over the idea of being responsible for repayment, she felt almost giddy. All by herself, she'd procured the loan. Coastal Plains Savings and Trust had deemed her worthy.

While the gift from her father meant she'd have a far lighter load, she'd still needed the loan.

Jenni Beth was keeping her busy with wedding and party cakes. They had one very special wedding coming up: Cole and Jenni Beth's. They'd begun tossing around ideas for the cake. It had to be her most incredible to date because her best friend deserved no less.

If only Beck could be happy for her. He'd always known what he wanted. Her? She'd gone to college because it had been expected. Then, she'd veered off course and strayed from the path.

This time, she had to get it right.

She started up her SUV, turned onto Old Church Street, and drove to the periwinkle blue railroad car. Flowers bloomed out front and welcomed customers to stop by and browse.

Tansy pulled up to the curb. For starters, she'd buy herself a celebratory bouquet or maybe a plant she could transfer outside when it quit blooming. Kind of a house-warming gift to herself.

As she stepped inside the shop, she breathed deeply, inhaling the heady floral fragrance.

"I did it, Cricket." She waved the papers. "The house is mine!"

"That's fantastic!" Cricket crushed Tansy in a hug.

"I want flowers, lots of flowers. I want a bouquet for my mom to thank her for everything she's done, one for Gracie—it'll be her first—and one for myself for sticking to my guns. And one to take to the cemetery. For my dad." She shut down the tears before they could start again. "This house—oh, Cricket, Gracie and I are going to be so happy there."

"Yes, you will." Cricket hugged her again.

"Am I crazy? I've never worked a day in my life, and now I've bought a big old house and plan to start my own business."

Cricket put a hand on each of Tansy's arms. "I know exactly how you feel. Well, you have a daughter, so that's an added responsibility I didn't have, but when I came into town and bought both a house and this shop? Whew!"

"Yeah, and you've made it."

Cricket smiled. "I have."

"What if I open and no one comes?"

"You sound so much like me it's scary. That was my biggest fear. I'd throw this wonderful grand opening, and no one would show."

"But they did," Tansy said.

"And they will for you, too. I'm so glad you're here."

"Me too." She bit her lip. "I know when you first met me—"

"Forget that. Please." Cricket waved a dismissive hand. "I didn't know you then. What happened between you and Beck is in the past. Come on." She pulled her toward the cooler. "Pick what you want, and I'll make the arrangements especially for you."

Cricket's words echoed in her head. *In the past.*

Forcing her smile back in place, she drooled over the flowers. As they picked through the choices, she asked, "You sell fountains, don't you?"

"I have a couple in stock, but I can order anything you want."

"I'd like to put one outside the dining room window, in full view from inside."

Cricket nodded. "I have one in my backyard and absolutely love it, especially at night. Sam and I spend a lot of evenings curled up in one of the chairs back there, doing nothing, saying nothing. Simply enjoying the magic of the evening and the night sky. For a city boy, he's really come around."

Tansy grinned, glad the two of them had found each other. City and country. So different, yet they melded very well. While they finished remodeling the old house Sam inherited from his aunt, they were living in Cricket's smaller home.

"Why don't you and Gracie come for a visit after work today? I'll show you my fountain and what I've done in the yard. I'm actually going to hate leaving that little house." She sighed. "Lots of great memories there."

"I can only imagine."

The two looked at each other and broke out laughing.

"Frog Pond Lane has been very good to Sam and me."

―⁓―

Tansy stopped by the post office to change her address. 321 Main Street, Misty Bottoms, Georgia. Her face hurt from smiling.

Odette, the postmistress, took her filled-in card. "What's goin' on with your aunt?"

Tansy's smile faltered. "Coralee?"

"You got another?"

"No."

"She's gettin' padded manila envelopes by the dozen. All from guys."

"Seriously?" *Not good, not good, not good*.

"Oh yeah."

Tansy thanked her and left.

Though she was itching to stop by her new house, she drove instead to her aunt's. Halfway down the street, she came to an abrupt stop. One entire side of the house was covered in blue tarps.

By the time she reached Coralee's driveway, her paint-smeared aunt was leaning on the mailbox.

"Tansy, nice to see you! Did you close on your house?"

"This morning!"

"I'm so damn proud of you! I'd give you a hug, but…" She opened her arms wide, showing off the paint splatters.

"Aunt Coralee, are you up to something?"

"Me?" She tapped a vivid purple fingernail to her chest.

"Why is your house tarped?"

"Havin' it fumigated."

Tansy groaned. "You only have one side tarped. To fumigate, you tent the entire house."

"It'll be fine, dear. It's a new process. Did you bring me anything wonderful from that kitchen of yours?"

"I have a few cupcakes. I tried a new recipe this morning while I was waiting to sign the papers."

She grabbed them from the SUV, and she and her aunt sat in lawn chairs and ate them in comfortable silence.

"These are good, sweetheart. You should include them on your menu."

"I think I will." After a beat, she said, "God help me, but I have to ask. What's with all the manila envelopes from guys?"

"That damn Odette! Somebody needs to staple her lips shut."

Tansy winced.

"It's business, Tansy, pure and simple. You're a businesswoman now. You should understand."

A total nonanswer, and all she'd get.

———

She hadn't talked to Beck since…since the kiss. Since their blowout. But she was worried about Coralee, worried enough to risk the wrath of Beck. Today wasn't the day she'd have chosen to bait him again, but it was what it was.

Driving straight to the lumberyard, Tansy said a quick prayer that Beck would be in a better mood today, a little more inclined to play nice—not that she could blame him for last time.

She walked through the front door, smelled the familiar scent of fresh lumber, and stopped for a longing look at a tile she'd love in her new kitchen. It was way, way, way out of her price range.

Reaching Beck's office, she knocked at the open door.

His hair slightly mussed, a pencil tucked behind his ear, he glanced up from the open folder in front of him. "Tansy."

"Beck."

A muscle worked in his jaw. "I'm not gonna apologize."

"I don't expect you to."

"Okay, so what brings you here today?"

"Has Coralee bought any pesticides from you lately?"

He sighed and rubbed his forehead. "Think I've got the beginning of a headache. To answer your question, no, she hasn't."

"Have you driven past her house lately?"

"Yes, I have. Several customers asked me what was going on, so I drove over to see. When I asked her about the tarps, she told me she'd rented them. I offered to help with any problem she might have, and she told me to mind my own business." He spread his hands. "She's *your* aunt."

Tansy dropped into a chair across from him.

"But…" Beck raised one finger. "She bought a lot of paint."

"Paint?" She groaned.

"Yep."

"God-awful colors again?"

"Actually, no, and she bought small amounts of a whole lot of colors."

"I saw some of those colors. She was wearing them on her clothes and face." She chewed on her thumbnail. "What do you think she's up to?"

"I haven't a clue."

"There's more." She filled him in on her trip to the post office and all the padded envelopes her aunt was receiving. "You don't suppose—" Tansy felt the heat rush through her, knew her neck and face had turned red. "Coralee wouldn't be getting some kind of, you know, pictures in them, would she?"

"Pictures?"

"Porno."

Beck laughed. "Sugar, I doubt that very much. Your aunt is a lot of things but into porno? No."

"You're sure?"

"No. I'm not sure of anything anymore." He leaned back in his chair and studied her. When his eyes met hers, they were intent, serious. "Women are a mystery to me, Tansy. Y'all do things that baffle me. Things I don't see comin'."

"Beck—"

"I'm speakin' in generalities, Red. Nothin' personal."

"Hmmm." Then she jumped up. "What's this?" She walked to a framed certificate on the wall, traced her finger over it. "Beck?"

He looked embarrassed. "Figured it didn't hurt to have a college degree."

"But you let me think you hadn't gone. When did you?"

"I took a few night classes in Savannah, finished the rest online." His mouth grew tight. "Does that piece of paper make me good enough for you now?"

"Beck!"

"Don't 'Beck' me."

"You've got everything backward." She spoke quietly.

"What do you mean?"

"I'm the one who's not good enough. It's always been that way."

"Tansy…"

Not trusting her voice, she simply shook her head.

"You know what? Maybe it's time we both take the high road and let bygones be bygones." His voice, hard and impersonal, belied his words. "The Chamber of Commerce meets every second Tuesday of the month in the Coastal Plains' social room. I'll look forward to seeing you there, Tansy."

One hand on the door, she said, "I think I'll leave now."

"You always do. Close the door on your way out, would you?"

So much for the high road, she thought.

She wanted to slam the door, forced herself to close it

softly. Proud of herself, she made it to her vehicle before the first teardrop fell.

Doubts and insecurities bounced around in her mind— about Beck, about her new business. No matter how she swatted at them, they continued to dive-bomb her.

Well, all the more reason for a night out.

Tansy decided to take Cricket up on her offer to check out her backyard and fountain. She and Gracie made a quick stop at their house on Main, though, because Gracie wanted another look at her new room. She and Grandma had been checking out paint samples.

"I like this one." Gracie held up the cotton-candy-pink swatch.

"Okay. Lay it on the windowsill so I buy the right color."

Tansy watched her daughter lay the strip down, carefully straightening it, her tongue on her upper lip in concentration.

"What do you say we visit the Dairy Queen and pick up a container of soft serve to take to Cricket's?"

Gracie clapped. "That's a good idea!"

They'd almost reached the ice cream vendor when Gracie cried out, "I forgot Penny at our new house."

"Are you sure you didn't leave her at Grandma's?"

"No." Tansy heard the beginning of tears in her daughter's voice. "I wanted to show her where she'd be sleeping. I need her, Mama!"

Penny. The raggedy pig was Gracie's favorite stuffed toy.

"How about we get her tomorrow?"

"No, I need her now."

"Okay, okay." Tansy picked up the ice cream, then made a U-turn and headed back to the house.

They hunted high and low, but the pig wasn't in Gracie's room or anywhere else. She thought of someone sneaking into Jenni Beth's carriage house. Had someone been in here? She almost laughed. Stupid. There was nothing here—except a little girl's stuffed pig.

Still, it was time to leave.

"Come on, sweetheart. I'll bet Penny's waiting at Grandma's for us."

"Okay." But Gracie's lashes glistened with tears.

"Let's go see Cricket's garden."

She turned on the DVD player with one of Gracie's favorite movies, and her daughter got lost in it. Penny was forgotten—at least momentarily.

The evening was beautiful. She lowered the windows and let the soft, cool air blow through her hair. Low Country smells filled the car. Green vegetation, flowers from Ms. Esmeralda's garden as they passed, a slight tang of salt from the nearby marshes.

She turned onto Frog Pond Lane. How many hot, lazy summer days had they spent swimming in the pond at the far end of the road? She and Jenni Beth and her brother, Wes. Cole and Beck. Luanna and Les came a lot, too. So did Moose and his girlfriend, who was now his wife and the mother to his two little boys.

Back when they'd all been innocent, before insanity and death had rocked their worlds.

She was glad Cricket and Sam would be settling in his aunt's house. It would be a good place to start their lives together.

When she pulled into the drive, Gracie asked, "Are we here, Mama?"

"Yes, honey, we are."

"I like Cricket, even if she does have a funny name." She giggled. "We found a cricket out in Grandma's yard yesterday." Her expression turned serious as she met her mother's eyes in the rearview mirror. "I watched it hop for a while, but I didn't hurt it."

"Good girl." Her sweet, sensitive child.

When they showed up at Cricket's door, Sam answered, still in uniform, which for him meant a uniform shirt and snug jeans. He'd told her he hadn't worn a full uniform since his rookie days and didn't intend to ever again.

Sheriff Jimmy Don needed the whole I'm-in-charge wardrobe; he didn't.

Hobo, the stray dog Sam had adopted, ripped around a corner and came to a skidding stop. Then, with a doggy grin, he gave Gracie a big, slurping kiss.

Giggling, she threw her arms around him. "I like doggies."

"They grow on you," Sam admitted.

"Does he do tricks?"

Sam reached down and cradled the dog's muzzle. "Hobo, get your ball."

With that, the old dog tore off for the living room.

Gracie wiped at her face, then studied Sam with big eyes. "You gonna shoot somebody?"

"No, ma'am." He knelt down to her height, his hand over his service revolver. "In fact, I'm putting this away right now. Two beautiful women come calling? That's a special day." He nodded toward the bag in her hand. "What have you got there?"

"Dairy Queen!" she shouted. "Mama said we could all have some."

"Sweet! Come on in!" He ushered them inside. "Give me a minute."

As he left the room, Cricket stepped out of the kitchen, drying her hands on a dish towel. "Did I hear you come bearin' gifts?"

Gracie shook her head. "Nope, but we have ice cream."

Tansy had to hand it to Cricket. She covered her laugh very well.

"Guess we should eat this before it melts, huh?" A weaponless, T-shirted Sam headed back toward them. "Why don't you ladies head out to the garden and take a peek while I dish it up?"

Hobo, a ragged green tennis ball in his mouth, nudged Sam's leg. He wrestled it from him and tossed the ball through the open back door. The chase was on.

When they stepped into the backyard, Tansy gasped. The entire yard was fantastic.

Beside her, Gracie took her hand. "It's so pretty, Mama." Her voice was tiny and reverent.

"It is, honey." She stared at Cricket. "You did this all by yourself?"

"No. I'd like to take credit for it, but Mrs. Michaels, the woman who lived here before me, loved flowers and gardening as much as I do. She'd already done a lot of this. I added a few touches." Cricket turned on the white fairy lights.

"Oooohhh." Gracie put a hand over her mouth. "Mama," she whispered. "Do you think fairies live here?"

"They might."

"Do you think they'll come out so I can see them?"

"I don't know."

She turned her big, brown eyes toward Cricket, one small hand patting Hobo's head. "Have you ever seen them?"

"No, but sometimes, at night, when it's really, really quiet, I can hear them."

"I wanna hear them. I can be very, very quiet." Gracie moved to the stone bench and hoisted herself onto its edge.

Sam came out carrying a tray loaded with dishes of ice cream. He eyed the dog. "None for you."

"Cricket said the fairies talk sometimes," Gracie said quietly.

The man didn't bat an eye. "They sure do."

"Have you heard them, too?" Her eyes couldn't have grown any bigger.

The big, bad former New York City detective nodded solemnly, and Tansy understood perfectly why Cricket had fallen head over heels in love with him.

They ate and chatted. Hobo, worn out from all the excitement, snored at Sam's feet. Pretty soon, Gracie laid her head in Tansy's lap and, within minutes, she, too, fell asleep.

"Looks like we won't hear any fairies tonight," Sam said.

"No." Tansy brushed the hair back from her daughter's face. "But I'll bet she dreams of them."

How had she ever thought she was in control of anything? After that peaceful interlude in Cricket's garden, everything had snowballed till Tansy didn't know which

end was up. The beautiful house she'd bought just a
week before now looked more like a construction site
than a home.

This was temporary, she reminded herself, and would
pass. And when it did? Excitement bubbled up inside
her. When it did, she'd have her dream!

In the meantime, she had an unpleasant task she
needed to take care of. She'd rather eat fried gator, but
good manners and a good upbringing demanded she
stop by the lumberyard to thank Beck.

The two of them still had a hard time playing nice,
but despite how he felt about her plans for his grandfather's place—her house now—he'd sent his crew to do
the work and made sure materials got ordered on time.
She understood how much that had cost him.

As she made her way down the crowded aisles, she
smoothed her black pencil skirt. She'd paired the just-
above-the-knee skirt with a black tank top and a single
button blazer in a soft melon color. Low black pumps
and a silver-and-black beaded necklace completed
her ensemble. She hadn't worn the outfit for him, she
assured herself. She'd worn it for her. Because she felt
good in it. Because it gave her enough confidence to
enter the beast's lair again.

Her last trip here hadn't ended as badly as the first—
nope, she wouldn't think about that first encounter.
About the kiss or the heat that had burst into flames.
That kiss had kept her awake every night since
it happened.

Did it keep Beck awake?

Of course it didn't. It meant nothing to him. He'd used
it to punish her, to remind her of what she'd discarded.

Well, he'd done a damn fine job. She remembered. Oh boy, did she ever!

The sad truth? She'd never forgotten.

She'd been forced to give him up because of a stupid, rash impulse, but she'd learned from that mistake and had vowed never to make it again. Unfortunately, so had Beck. Their chance at a happy ever after had evaporated.

All of which made these trips to his office so darned hard.

Rather than barging in, she knocked on his closed door and waited this time.

"What?"

She winced at the gruff greeting. "It's me. Tansy. May I come in?"

She heard footsteps; then he threw the door open.

"If you greet all your customers like that, I'm surprised anyone shops here."

He stepped aside and waved her in. "Sorry. I was in the middle of something. What can I do for you?"

The formality hurt worse than his anger. He was busy, though. She looked past him at the cluttered desk. Then she smiled and pointed to the container of red gummy candy.

"Swedish fish?"

"Cole buys them for me at some little candy store in Savannah." He lifted the lid and nudged the jar toward her. "Go ahead. Indulge. It's good for the soul." His eyes met and held hers.

She cocked her head, aware they weren't talking entirely about Swedish fish. If only she dared.

But that wasn't why she'd come, and truth? She *didn't* dare.

"No thanks." She shook her head. "I won't keep you long. I stopped by to thank you. Even though you don't agree with what I'm doing, you've stepped up and I appreciate it. Without your help, I'm not sure any of this would be happening. I'm grateful, Beck."

"You're wrong, Tansy. I don't have a problem with your plans. It's the location."

"Touché." She toyed with her jacket button. "Still, thank you."

"Anything else you need?"

"For the house?"

The room went totally still except for the ticking of the wall clock. Tansy was certain Beck could hear her heart racing.

"Yeah," he finally said. "For the house."

"No."

The meeting, as short as it had been, had given her a doozy of a headache. What she wouldn't give for a good masseuse. Her muscles were so tense she could have bounced a quarter off any one of them.

Since no massage loomed in her future, she'd work off her nerves.

Pulling into her drive, she grabbed the duffel bag that held her work clothes. There was still a lot to finish up, so she'd pitch in wherever she could.

She walked inside, and Charlie nodded toward the dining room. "Is that what you've been hunting?"

There sat Penny the Pig. "Thank you! Gracie has been driving me crazy looking for the thing. Where did you find it?"

"Out in the backyard. Right under Gracie's bedroom window. My guess is she fell out."

She nodded. "I'd better add screens to my to-do list."

"I think the Elliots had them. Maybe stored somewhere?"

"I'll check. Thanks." She held up the filthy stuffed animal. "I think Penny needs a good bath."

"Yeah, she got rained on a couple times."

She ran upstairs and changed her clothes, then worked like a dog, sanding, painting, and even using the nail gun without too much damage. When the workers left and things quieted down, she fixed a cup of coffee and put together a new, much smaller list of things she still needed for the house, including those screens.

Time to call it a day.

Grabbing Penny, she headed out the door.

Halfway to the preschool, Tansy remembered her mother's monthly card game with the girls was tonight at the Brysons'. Maybe she and Gracie should eat out before they headed home. She wasn't sure she had the energy to fix even mac and cheese. Hell-bent on driving Beck from her mind, she'd attacked the renovations full force, and now her body was crying foul.

The instant she opened the school's door, though, and saw her daughter, all that slipped away.

"Mama!" Gracie threw herself into Tansy's arms.

Tansy reached into her huge purse and brought out the dirty stuffed pig.

"Penny! You found her, Mama?"

"Charlie found her playing outside in the backyard. We'll have to be careful about the windows upstairs. I think maybe she fell out. But she showed up today. Guess she missed you."

"I missed her, too." Gracie gave the stuffed pig a big kiss and hugged her tightly.

They gathered up her sweater, backpack, and her day's drawings and stepped out into the late afternoon.

"I thought we'd eat out tonight. Where do you want to go, sweetie?"

"Ms. Dee-Ann's. She makes me grilled cheese samiches when Grandma and I go there."

"Sandwich," Tansy corrected, stressing the *d* sound.

"That what I said. Samich." Gracie twirled on the tips of her toes. "Can we go there?"

"To the diner?"

"Uh-huh."

"Works for me."

After parking on Main Street, Tansy looked down at her faded jeans and pale blue sweater. Shouldn't she change out of her work clothes before they went in to Dee-Ann's? What she really wanted to do was grab a bite with Gracie, then go home and soak in the tub for about an hour with a glass of wine. And that's exactly what she was going to do.

Gracie, on the other hand, had on a cute, little long-sleeved tunic top and leggings in a pretty shade of green. Tansy's mom's doing.

She also had bare feet when Tansy opened the back door.

"What happened to your shoes, baby?"

"I took them off."

"Why?"

"I don't know."

"Well, put them back on, and we'll go get that grilled cheese."

"'Kay, Mama."

—⁓—

Beck had spent an endless day putting out one fire after another, and Tansy's visit hadn't helped. She set him on edge and made him want things he couldn't have. He'd snapped and snarled his way through the morning. After that, he'd locked his office door and immersed himself in paperwork, hoping it might clear his head.

It hadn't.

Time to head home.

He'd skipped lunch and was ravenous! But he didn't want to go home and play pick and lose with his refrigerator, nor did he want to barge in on his parents. He'd stop in town and pick something up, then take it home to eat while he caught the Falcons game he'd recorded over the weekend but still hadn't found time to watch. Maybe he'd hit Dee-Ann's for a burger and a piece of her pecan pie. Nobody made it better—except maybe his mother, but since he wasn't going to his parents' tonight, he'd settle for the next best thing and be perfectly happy.

His fingers had already curled around the doorknob when he spotted them. Gracie Bella and Tansy sat in one of the left-hand booths, coloring. Gracie had practically crawled into Tansy's lap, her upper body wormed under her mom's arm.

Gracie's tongue stuck out between those Cupid-bow lips as she concentrated, a raggedy stuffed pig on the table beside her. Tansy said something to her, and the little girl put a hand over her mouth and giggled.

Redhead and brunette. Curly hair and straight. At first blush, mother and daughter looked nothing alike. Until they raised their heads and a person saw that square jaw

and porcelain skin. The sharp mind and inquisitive eyes.
Times two.

They hadn't seen him yet.

So, a quick change of plans. He'd pick up something
at the BiLo deli.

He dropped his hand, started to turn, and wondered
what the hell he was doing.

Over the course of their comings and goings, he and
Tansy were bound to run into each other. He couldn't
keep turning tail every time they did. His grandfather's
story popped into mind. Possibilities.

Sweat popped out on his brow.

Mustering up the courage to walk in, he felt a hand
drop on his shoulder.

Sam, looking very official in his uniform shirt and
wearing his MBPD ball cap, a gun holstered on his hip,
stood behind him.

"You going in?"

Beck nodded.

Sam tipped his head toward Tansy's booth. "You
want company?"

"Yeah, I do. As pathetic as that is."

"Thought you might. Gonna cost you a piece of pie
and a cup of coffee, though."

Beck narrowed his eyes. "You still on duty?"

"For another"—Sam checked his watch—"fifteen
minutes. Then I get to go home to that sexy little cousin
of yours."

"I don't even want to think about that." He took off
his dark glasses and slid them into his shirt pocket. "Pie
and coffee doesn't come under the heading of bribing an
officer of the law, does it?"

"Nope. Just two pals who will soon be related sitting down over a meal—or, in my case, dessert."

"Actually, I was gonna do take-out."

"Can't now." He jerked his head toward Tansy. "It'll look like you're on the run."

"You're right." Beck tugged the door and that damn bell jangled overhead. Tansy looked up, met his eyes, and quickly bent her head over the coloring book.

Gracie snuggled closer. "I'm hungry, Mama."

"Our food's comin', honey. Give Dee-Ann time to fix it."

"'Kay." That little tongue came out again, her red crayon busy.

"How 'bout we sit over there?" Beck tipped his head toward the far side of the diner.

"That's good." He held up a finger. "One minute."

Sam strode across the room to say hello to Tansy and her daughter.

While they talked, Dee-Ann came out with dinner for the table next to them, and Sam said his good-byes and joined Beck.

Beck, already seated in the booth, stared at him. "Why'd you do that?"

"Because I like her." Sam's brow rose. "Despite the history between you two, I'm impressed with the way she's tackled all this. Can't be easy, with a kid and all."

"No, I don't suppose it is."

"Beck!" Gracie scrambled out of the booth and flew across the room. "I didn't see you."

"Well, I saw you! Thought you were gonna stand me up!"

"Huh?"

"Never mind." He scooped her in his arms and gave her a big cheek smooch.

She laughed and kissed him back. "Your face is scratchy!"

"Yeah, it is."

Over the little girl's head, Beck saw Tansy watching, her eyes sad. He'd like to go over there and lay a hot one on her, but that wasn't in the cards.

"What are you up to, sweetie?"

"Waitin' for Dee-Ann to make me a grilled cheese samich."

"Oooh, she makes the best."

"Uh-huh. What's she makin' you?"

"I'm not sure yet."

"'Cause you just got here?"

"Yep."

"Wanna come sit with me and Mama?" She looked at Sam. "You can come too." To Beck she said, "We went to Sam's house last night. He's got fairies in his garden. I wanted to hear them talk but I fell asleep."

"You did?"

She nodded. "But Mama said maybe we could go back."

"You're welcome anytime, Gracie," Sam said.

"Okay. I gotta go now. I don't want Mama to be lonely."

"Take good care of her," Beck said.

"I will."

With that, she took off across the room toward her mother.

"Take a good hard look at Tansy," Sam said.

"I saw her when we came in."

"I know you did. But I want you to look again. Is that the same relaxed woman you spotted before you opened the door and walked in? Be honest, at least with yourself."

Beck studied her. No, she wasn't relaxed anymore. Her forehead was creased with worry, her body rigid. Tension radiated from her.

When he'd stood outside looking in, she and Gracie had been having fun. They'd been carefree. Now Tansy looked brittle enough to break in two. Did he do that to her?

Of course he did. And it made him feel like hell. Beating up on an underdog didn't do much for him and never had.

He'd always thought himself the victim in this whole scenario. Maybe, just maybe, there'd been two victims.

His gaze strayed from Tansy to Gracie Bella. Make that three.

"Maybe I ought to leave."

"Maybe you ought to make peace with the situation."

Dee-Ann took their orders, then sailed off to the back to nag the cook.

Luanna, who'd graduated with Tansy, carried her and Gracie's food to them. The little girl instantly rose to her knees so she could reach.

Beck watched as Tansy cut her daughter's sandwich into quarters, then put a dollop of ketchup on the plate for her french fries. As the little girl dug into her meal, Tansy dipped a fork into the side dressing and took a small bite of her salad.

"Why's she eatin' that?"

"What? The salad?"

"Yeah. She's thin as a willow branch. She needs food. Protein."

"She needs somebody to take care of her. My guess is that ex-husband of hers didn't."

———

Luanna slid his burger in front of him and set a huge piece of cherry pie by Sam. "There you go, boys. Need anything else?"

"Maybe a refill on my coffee, Luanna."

"Sure thing, Sam. You okay, Beck?"

Beck bit back his answer. He was so far from okay, he didn't figure he'd ever get there again.

His problem.

"Everything's great, sugar. Thanks."

He looked up to find Sam watching him.

"You lie really well."

He told Sam, in no uncertain terms, what he could do.

Sam threw back his head and laughed. "Might be interesting to give that a try."

Across the room, Gracie giggled again, and Beck's gaze drifted back to the pair. Cute little girl, beautiful mama.

It was killing him to stay away from the construction, to let someone else's hands reshape the old house. And he couldn't stay away from Tansy. Sick puppy that it made him, he had to spend some time with her.

Tomorrow was booked. Day after, he'd strap on his tool belt and head over to 321 Main Street.

Chapter 12

TWO DAYS LATER, IMPATIENCE NIPPED AT TANSY. She'd made a few changes and a couple additions to her original design, so the project was taking a little longer than first planned. The house was still far from livable, and that drove her crazy. She wanted so badly to settle in, to wake up in the morning in her *own* home, the first she'd ever really had.

The house where she and Emerson had lived had never been hers. His parents had picked it out and paid for it. Their mistake? The deed had been in Emerson's name only. And one night that deed had gone into the pot—and Emerson had lost.

The new owner had allowed Tansy a few months to move out.

Emerson's parents had enrolled him in another rehab—and blamed her for their son's addiction. As long as she left quietly—and with no financial responsibility on their part either for her or their granddaughter—their attitude was one of "don't let the door hit you in the butt."

They enabled their son's destructive behavior.

And all that was totally and completely behind her.

The house on Main? All hers! She couldn't wait to decorate it for autumn. She wanted to use fall flowers and leaves on the tables in her bakery, to set pots of mums in bronze and rust on the porch steps. To carve pumpkins and hand out candy to trick-or-treaters. To take Gracie around the neighborhood with her own bag.

For the first time since she'd lost her father, Tansy felt truly alive.

Now she was champing at the bit to move into 321 Main.

Last night, she'd started to pack up her and Gracie's bags, certain they could deal with the tail end of the construction. Her mother had walked in halfway through the first duffle. She'd marched her into the kitchen and, over a steaming cup of coffee, told her in no uncertain terms that she would not be moving her granddaughter into a work zone.

She'd unpacked the duffle.

This morning, she felt ready to pack it again.

Her phone rang. "Hello?"

"Tansy? This is Greta Polinsky. I hope I'm not calling too early."

"No, not at all. You caught me with my sketch pad. I'm working on the cake for your big day."

Tansy could hear the bride's excitement through the phone. This one was a little different than their usual. In celebration of their fiftieth anniversary, she and her husband had decided to renew their vows at Magnolia House.

"That's what I wanted to talk about." She chuckled. "Obviously. I want something truly decadent. The decision to wear the wedding gown I wore all those years ago meant some serious dieting. I'm so tired of lettuce and grilled chicken I could scream, but my dress fits again. Your cake will put an end to all these weeks of deprivation so I want to do it right. Huge sugar rush!"

"Then let's do it!"

"I stopped by Lyda Mae's pottery shop the other day, and she said you make a deep dark chocolate cake with Italian meringue buttercream that's out of this world."

"I do."

"And that's what we're saying to that cake. We do—want it."

"I'll make a sampler for you."

"No need. If Lyda Mae says it's what I want, it's what I want. She and I have been best friends since high school. Now Lem? Can't trust his taste. If it's free, it's perfect."

They laughed.

"Are you still in for the different-shaped layers, Greta? Round, square, round?"

"You bet. Can you make gold frosting?"

"I can."

Slipping into the kitchen for another cup of coffee, Tansy assured Greta that the second fifty years with Ron would be even better than the first fifty and that this wedding cake would wow everybody.

When they hung up, she slipped on her shoes, poured her coffee into a to-go cup, and drove to her new home. The place was a beehive of activity.

Not a single member of Beck's crew was a slacker, and the guys had been working flat-out every single day. Beck had stayed away, though, putting Charlie Pearce, his finish carpenter, in charge. Tansy sincerely doubted a person could find a better carpenter in all of Georgia. His work at Magnolia House had been nothing short of fabulous.

More important, Charlie and her dad had been friends, so it felt a little like having her dad be part of all this.

There was a small space tucked beneath the attic stairs in the room she'd chosen for her bedroom, and she'd puzzled over what to do with it. "What do you think, Charlie?"

A fist cocked on his hip, he studied it. "If it were me, I'd turn the nook into a reading area. It'll hold a chaise, a small table, and a lamp." He gestured to the small wall area. "Hang a bunch of different-shaped mirrors above the chaise. That'll make it feel larger. I can build a few shelves there for you, too, if you want. If you take after your daddy, you've got your nose stuck in a book half the night."

"He loved to read." She'd almost forgotten that.

"He and I did a lot of book swapping." Charlie scratched his head, a couple gray hairs standing on end. "In fact, I still have a couple of his. I'll bring them tomorrow. You might want to put them here. A piece of him."

Another poignant moment that tugged at her heartstrings till she thought they'd snap. There'd been a lot of them since she'd returned home.

Charlie pretended not to notice her quick tears. Instead, he took inventory of the room. "I know somebody's not too happy about it, but buyin' this house was a smart move on your part."

Downstairs, the front door opened and closed.

"Anybody home?"

"Beck?" she whispered. "Why would he be here?"

"Gotta be a problem." Charlie stuck his head out the door. "Up here, Boss. Be right down."

"Don't bother. I'll come up."

And he did, bounding up the stairs two at a time.

"What's wrong?"

"Nothin'. Thought I should stop by, make sure every-thing's okay."

She grinned. "Liar, liar. You couldn't stay away."

"Hey, you know what they say about curiosity and that cat." He leaned against the doorjamb. "The place is lookin' good. Your guys did a great job with the living room trim, Charlie. Speakin' of guys, where's the rest of the crew?"

"They're out back staining the dining room trim. That way we don't have to worry about construction dust."

Beck nodded, all the while studying the room. "What are you plannin' to do in here?"

"Tansy's gonna use this for her bedroom."

When Beck's heated gaze flicked to her, Tansy blushed.

Charlie, seemingly unaware of the temperature spike, explained the reading niche idea.

Good thing, she thought, because she couldn't get past the fact that Beck had shown up today.

But, then, he was the boss. No doubt he needed to check on his crew.

"You always were a reader, Tansy. This'll be a good spot to curl up after Gracie's asleep."

Mutely, she nodded.

"Cat got your tongue?"

When she just shook her head, he laughed.

"Tell you what, Charlie, why don't you head down-stairs and keep those guys moving? I'll build some shelves and finish this area." His eyes burned into hers. "Seems only right for an Elliot to leave his mark some-where on this reno."

"Beck—"

He held up a hand. "That wasn't a slap. Sorry if it

came off that way. It was an observation, a realization I finally came to."

Charlie slipped out of the room.

"Let me run downstairs and grab a sawhorse and a few tools. If you don't mind helpin', we can bang this out in no time."

"Sure."

Within minutes, he was back, a sawhorse in one hand, a saw in the other, and a worn, leather tool belt tossed over his shoulder.

"Those clothes okay to work in?" His gaze swept the length of her.

"Yeah, I'm good. These jeans and T-shirt have seen more work the last few weeks than I'd have thought possible."

Half an hour later, sawdust in her hair and the pungent scent of freshly cut wood in the air, Tansy couldn't wipe the grin off her face. If anyone had suggested this morning that she and Beck would work—amicably—side by side today building shelves in her bedroom, she'd have told him he was crazy.

But here they were.

"What's your color scheme in here?"

"I don't know. I can't seem to pull the trigger on that decision."

"You'll need to. Soon." He slid his hammer into the tool belt. "Somethin' you need to know, Tanz. Jenni Beth had another break-in. And before you ask, she didn't set the alarm I put in or turn on the camera, so…"

"What's goin' on, Beck?"

"Damned if I know, but you need to lock up here. Every time you leave."

She nodded. "Does Sam have any ideas?"

"That's the hell of it. Nothing is missing."

"Jenni Beth's sure?"

"Yeah. Sam figures whoever was there got spooked because a couple files, both dealing with upcoming weddings, were dropped on the floor." Beck rubbed the side of his neck. "While we're at it, I should probably apologize for—"

"Nothing," Tansy interrupted. "I'd feel the same way in your place."

He rested a hip against the wall. "Remember the time we snuck up here?"

"You kissed me." Her heart skipped a beat.

"Yeah, I did. With the whole family downstairs."

"Do you think they knew?" she asked.

"Absolutely."

"Really?"

"I saw your face. So did they. Your eyes, your flushed cheeks."

She laughed. "Stop!"

"What do you say we try it again—with my whole crew downstairs?"

"I'd say it would be a dumb thing to do." She could barely breathe, and, of its own volition, one hand reached out, rested on the side of his face.

"Yeah, you're right." His arm shot out and his hand snaked around her waist, drew her to him. Those blue, blue eyes of his, heavy-lidded now, shot heat through her. Then his lips were on hers. She met him beat for beat, their tongues tangling, dancing. There was no world other than him, right here, right now.

His callused hand crept beneath her T-shirt; his thumb brushed over her breast.

"Hey, Boss!"

They pulled apart, both breathing raggedly.

"Yeah, Charlie?"

"Can you come down here a minute?"

"Sure thing." He drew her against him. "Let me hold you for a few seconds more before you tell me that shouldn't have happened."

"Actually, I had no intention of saying that."

He drew back and looked down at her. "Seriously?"

"Seriously."

"Well, damn, we really are makin' some progress here. I should have come by before."

She smiled. "Maybe you should have."

Tool belt hanging low, Beck headed down to see what Charlie wanted—and left Tansy wanting a whole lot more.

~~~

The next morning, true to his word, Charlie showed up with the promised books tucked inside brown wrapping paper.

"One of those will make good readin' for Gracie when she's old enough."

She took the package and gave him a quick peck on the cheek. "Thanks."

Carrying them upstairs, she stowed the package on her new shelves. Beck's shelves. She had to hand it to the man. He'd wanted to leave his mark on the house, and he had—in her bedroom. She didn't know if she'd ever walk in here and not remember yesterday's kisses, ever look at the shelves or remove a book from them without thinking of him.

And speak of the devil. He showed up just before noon with lunch for his crew and a BLT, without the lettuce, for Tansy.

"You remembered." Their fingers touched and lingered as she took the sandwich.

"I remember everything about you, Tansy."

He grabbed his own sandwich, a couple of Cokes, and herded her out the back door, away from the guys. "It's quieter out here. Listen. Can you hear the birds?"

She did. They calmed her—usually. With Beck lounging beside her on the back porch steps, close enough their hips touched, she felt far from calm. Supercharged and overheated, but not calm.

He surprised her. She'd always said he never met a stranger, that he could strike up a conversation with anyone. But today, she realized all over again what an easy conversationalist he was and how well-rounded. He could talk about anything.

Was he ready to sideline the animosity? Could they find a middle road?

The bigger question—could her heart survive if he simply wanted to be friends? Because the truth was she didn't want to be friends with Beck. She wanted more.

Yeah, and people in hell wanted ice water.

Still, if she had only herself to think of, she'd be tempted to give it a shot. But she was a mother now, and Gracie liked Beck way too much for her to take a risk. If she brought him into their lives and things didn't work out, Gracie would be heartbroken. Again. Worse, Gracie's trust in men would further erode.

So she'd enjoy now. The sunshine, the feel of him beside her. The easy conversation.

Halfway through lunch, he reached into his shirt pocket. "Almost forgot. I brought a couple paint swatches you might like for your bedroom."

He handed them to her, and she lost the ability to speak. The chips were the same pale lavender and forest green they'd argued over for her bedroom in high school.

"Beck." She tipped her chin to look at him.

"I told you, sugar. I haven't forgotten anything."

She wanted to cry. Instead, she said, "My bedroom at Mom's is still this lavender."

He arched a brow. "And you're plannin' on slappin' it on the outside of this house."

"No, I'm not." Taken aback, she took another look at the swatches and sighed. "I hadn't realized... Okay, same color family, maybe, but different shades."

He grunted. "In case you're gettin' tired of the same old, same old, I brought a few more." He slid several more chips from his pocket. "And if you don't like any of these, I have a gazillion more to choose from. Now"—he wadded up his sandwich paper—"I need to get inside and put those slackers back to work."

"Thanks for lunch. I enjoyed it."

"Me too. I'll give the guys a hand with the kitchen cabinets; then I'm heading out to Ms. Hattie's. She needs a new hot water heater. Hers isn't very efficient."

"You're a good man, Beck."

"Try to remember that."

And he was gone.

⁂

Later, after the men left for the day and the house was once again quiet, Tansy unwrapped the books Charlie had brought. Right there on top was a dog-eared copy of *Where the Red Fern Grows*. Somewhere in her mother's attic, there was an equally worn copy in which her dad had scrawled, *To my Tansy. Love you, Daddy*.

She placed a hand over her heart and stared at the ceiling. *Whew!*

She dropped onto the bare wood floor and paged through the book. Oh, the memories. When she was in sixth grade, she and her dad sat on the front porch and read the story together, a chapter a night. And, oh boy, had she cried buckets at the ending.

After she'd settled down a bit, her dad took her into the kitchen and fixed them both chocolate marshmallow sundaes. With whipped cream. She'd eaten hers and pretended to be okay, but when she went to bed that night, she'd cried a few more tears for young Billy and Little Ann and Old Dan.

Charlie was right, though. Gracie should read this book, with its message of such unconditional love. She hugged it to her chest, and even though he'd already gone home, she said, "Oh, Charlie, thank you."

She'd dig through the boxes at her mom's to find the copy her dad had given her. In a few years, she and Gracie would sit on the big front porch and read the tearjerker. They'd both cry, then she'd take Gracie inside and fix her a chocolate marshmallow sundae. And, no doubt, Gracie would cry a little more when she went to bed that night. So would she.

Tansy's mind drifted back to the book's theme. Unconditional love. She wanted that. Had had it with Beck and thrown it away. How could she have been so stupid?

Why'd he really come by yesterday and today? And those kisses yesterday! Whew! The one in his office had been fueled by anger. The one they'd shared after he'd found her stranded on the side of the road? Frustration, maybe. But yesterday's? Pure, unadulterated heat! Beck threw her off balance; he kept her awake at night.

—⁓—

She spent the next day poring over catalogs, chatting on the phone with vendors, and watching the front door for Beck. Disappointment about swallowed her whole when he didn't show.

While Kitty's bakery was wonderful, Tansy wanted more. Great pastries, cookies, and cakes, yes, but when her customers stopped by for coffee and a doughnut, she wanted them to enjoy their time at Sweet Dreams. She wanted them to feel free to sit and visit, to search the web, and post their special memories on her photo board.

And, yes, she admitted, she had her heart set on giving the ladies of Misty Bottoms a nice place to meet with friends while they savored tea from her collection of china or a cup of coffee made with her fancy new espresso machine.

At the same time, she had to rein herself in. Because she loved soft colors and froufrou, it would be easy to go so over-the-top feminine that she'd lose the male population and that would be a disaster. The men of Misty Bottoms had to feel welcome here, too. Maybe she'd buy some heavy mugs with big finger holes. She smiled at the idea of families stopping in on Saturday mornings or after soccer and Little League games for hot chocolate and doughnuts.

Even more, she loved catering weddings and parties. Anniversaries, birthdays, graduations, new babies — she'd be a part of them all. Right now, though, she bordered on exhaustion. Her back ached from sitting hunched over too long, and she put her hands on it and stretched.

Her mom and Gracie had left earlier for Savannah to take in a *Disney on Ice* production. Gracie, dressed as Elsa from *Frozen*, had left the house higher than a kite. Tansy wished her mother lots of luck, although Gracie's high spirits didn't seem to faze Rexanna in the least. The two enjoyed each other, another bonus to being back in Misty Bottoms.

She shut down her computer, turned off the lights, and closed the door.

Tonight, she found herself free as a bird, a rare occurrence.

One thing was for sure. She definitely didn't intend to cook. The evening was gorgeous, so she decided to walk down Main to Dee-Ann's and pick up a burger and fries to-go. An added bonus to her new address.

When she walked in, Lem Gilmore sat at one of the tables, devouring a piece of apple pie.

Leaning toward Dee-Ann, Tansy asked, "So who's paying for Lem's treats now that Sam's wised up to his tricks?"

Dee-Ann smiled and shrugged. "Until some new sucker comes to town, Lem's diggin' into his own pocket. The old coot sure had Sam bamboozled." She sighed. "Our new deputy has a heart of gold. Cricket's one lucky lady."

"She is that," Tansy agreed.

When her take-out order was ready, Dee-Ann set it on the counter. "You enjoy that now. You need to eat more. You're too skinny."

Tansy rolled her eyes.

When she arrived back at her new house, she carried dinner around back and spread it out on the picnic table Cole had found for her. For about two seconds, she considered turning on her iPod but decided nature's sounds fit her mood.

The evening temperature had dropped, and birds flew from tree to tree, chirping and chattering to each other. Very little traffic passed the house, and Tansy felt as though she was in the middle of some enchanted forest. She'd forgotten how much she loved being outdoors, doing simple things.

A squirrel raced up the side of one of the large oaks, no doubt storing food for winter. She popped the last fry in her mouth and scooped the wrapper into the bag. Wadding it up, she tossed it in the construction Dumpster off to the side of the house.

Tonight would be the perfect time to weed the front flower bed. She was quickly losing the light but still had enough time to make a nice dent in the job. Ruthlessly, she pulled the weeds that threatened her late-blooming roses and the bold chrysanthemums in gold, bronze, and fiery orange she'd planted a few days ago.

Tansy heard his truck before she saw him. Her heart thumped in her chest far faster than her work warranted.

"Want some help?"

Tansy tugged at her ear, certain she'd heard wrong. She stood, tossing weeds onto the building pile. "What did you say?"

Beck opened his door and got out.

Sexy. That single word rumbled through her brain and blocked all other thought. In faded jeans, a black T-shirt, and dark glasses, the man screamed sex.

"Tansy?"

"Yeah." She wet her lips, forced herself to focus on his words.

"I offered to help pull some weeds." He rubbed the back of his neck. "I've been doin' a lot of thinkin'. We've made some progress, you and me, and, well, guess it's time I put the past behind me. Like you've done."

Ah, a gloved punch this time. Even wrapped in silk, a blow was still a blow. Even so…

"I've got plenty of weeds, and another pair of hands would be more than welcome."

He knelt and tore into the task. "Where's Gracie?"

Her head snapped up. Even though dusk was falling, he still wore his dark glasses, making it impossible to see his eyes.

"She and Mom drove to Savannah. *Disney on Ice.*"

"So you're alone?" His voice took on a slightly husky tone.

"I am."

Sliding his sunglasses to the top of his head, he breathed deeply. "How about we call a truce? At least a temporary one."

"Don't want to make any long-term commitment, huh?"

"No, that would be you who can't do that."

"Ouch." She made a face. "Below the belt, Beck. Didn't you just call a truce?"

"You didn't accept yet."

"Jeez, you didn't give me time!" On a sigh, she stuck out her hand. "Truce."

Instead of shaking it, he kissed the back of it.

An explosion of desire ripped through her. She gasped and drew her hand away.

His gaze locked on her. "What's wrong?"

As if he didn't know. "My hands are dirty. I forgot my gloves."

Get it together, she ordered herself. This man was off-limits.

He made her nervous. He made her want things she couldn't have, things she'd once had and walked away from. Worse, he made her dream of him, of them.

He made her feel like a lovesick teenager again.

Without a word, Beck turned back to his truck, giving her a great view of that incredible denim-clad butt as he rooted around in a box. When he came back, he held two pairs of gardening gloves. He offered one to her and pulled on the second pair. "Always prepared."

"It helps to own a store that sells them."

"There is that."

They worked side by side as dusk deepened, their weed pile growing.

"If we're gonna both be livin' in Misty Bottoms, we need to be easier with each other." Standing, he stretched his arms above his head. "Walk with me. I want to take a look out back."

He pulled off his gloves, then hers, and tossed them onto the front porch steps.

When he took her hand, she had a moment of déjà vu. How many times had she and Beck walked in this yard at twilight?

They strolled slowly, a slight breeze teasing her with his warm, masculine scent.

When he laced his fingers with hers, pure joy zinged through her. And need. The kind of need she hadn't felt since—well, since the last time she and Beck had been together.

"Cricket said you plan to put a fountain outside the dining room window. I'm not sure why we didn't think to do that sooner."

He stopped, and she realized they'd made their way to their favorite oak tree.

"Still can't see the house from here," he said. "Which means no one can see us, right?"

Her stomach did a free fall to her toes. She opened her mouth to agree, closed it as he, in one smooth move, had her backed against the tree. His body pressed full-length along hers, his heat nearly singeing her. She found it next to impossible to breathe.

"Beck."

"Tansy?" His head lowered. His lips drew closer and touched hers lightly. Tingles cascaded through her entire body. "Is this okay?"

"Oh, yes." The words came out of their own volition.

"I've missed you, Tansy. Missed this. Missed us."

One hand settled at her waist, while the fingers of his other hand toyed with the bottom on her blouse.

Her breathing grew ragged. "You've got really great hands, Beck, but you're awfully slow."

"I can be." One button slipped through the hole. "Jenni Beth mentioned you're havin' a class reunion." His lips slid down her neck and raised goose bumps.

"Mmm-hmmm."

"Let me take you."

"What?"

"I want to take you to the reunion. Promise you'll go with me."

He kissed her again, and her knees buckled.

"Tansy?"

"What?" Her lashes fluttered.

"I want to go with you. Take me."

"Take you?" She thought she'd died or was dreaming. Beck Elliot wanted her to *take him*?

"To your reunion."

"Oh, sure."

"Then it's a date. No reneging."

"No." She shook her head, then lifted her mouth to his.

Threading her fingers through his hair, she drew him closer. One kiss, one touch led to another. The intervening years slipped away, his touch, his taste, familiar yet new. The feel of him on her bare skin was nearly more than she could take, and she groaned when he moved away.

How had her blouse come half undone?

A tiny voice in the back of her brain scolded her.

Tansy shushed it. Beck was a man; she was a woman. She hadn't signed on to be a nun, yet it had been years, literally, since she'd slept with a man. With *this* man.

"Why?" The single word slipped out.

"Why?" Beck echoed.

"Yes, why are you doing this?"

He stepped back and clasped his hands on the top of his head. She was right to question his motives since he didn't have the sense to do it himself. "I'm sorry. I hadn't planned this."

"And yet it's happened twice in the last couple days."

He nodded, feeling like a heel. Like a horny heel.

Tansy's lips were swollen, those incredible turquoise eyes passion filled. He wanted to toss her to the ground. Take her right here. He needed her so badly he hurt like a son of a bitch.

But if they rushed into this, he'd lose her again. If there was the slightest possibility for them, it had to be built on a solid foundation. He had to move slowly or he'd scare her away.

With unsteady hands, he straightened her clothes and buttoned her blouse. Slowly. The backs of his fingers brushed against her skin.

"Best I go. You sleep well now, sugar." He kept his tone, his words light, but inside? He called himself every name in the book. He'd screwed up.

Even in the darkening night, he could see the sadness in her eyes. "You tell me to sleep well? After this?"

He held up his hands in surrender.

"I'm confused." Pinching the bridge of her nose, she closed her eyes.

"Understood. I didn't stop here tonight with the intention of carting you off to bed. I saw you out front working, and I stopped to help. Period."

"I believe you. And I'm sorry, too. I...I guess I got caught up in the moment. You... I... It felt so right."

"Sugar, you're killin' me here." He dropped his forehead to hers.

"If it makes you feel any better," she said, "I'm suffering, too, but I have to think about Gracie. When Emerson moved out of the house, she asked me if she was the reason her daddy didn't want us anymore. She likes you,

Beck. Really likes you. If we"—she flicked her hand—
"you know, and then it didn't work, she might—"

He caught her hand. "I understand. We'll go slow."

She swore her heart tripped. "I don't think we can
go at all."

Those huge eyes of hers, full of emotion he couldn't
quite read, met and held his. And that was when he
knew he had to walk away. For tonight anyway. Tansy
had a hell of a lot on her plate and was vulnerable
right now.

With another heartfelt sigh, he leaned forward, gave
her one last, very thorough kiss. "Lock up when you get
to your mom's."

He walked through the near dark to his pickup. Time
he went home to an ice-cold shower.

He and Tansy? The very definition of star-crossed
lovers.

Tansy waited till she heard Beck's truck door close, then
walked around to the front yard. Arms wrapped around
her waist, she stood and watched his taillights grow
smaller and smaller until they disappeared in the night.
It was almost as though he'd never been here.

But he had been.

Oh, yes, he surely had been.

Every inch of her body sizzled.

Dropping onto the dew-kissed grass, she called herself every kind of fool. She had the entire night to herself, and she'd sent Beck home. Who would have known
if he'd stayed? Would it really have hurt anyone? What
was wrong with her?

Maybe tomorrow morning she'd call old Doc Hawkins and have him take an X-ray of her head. See if she still had a brain.

Except that, deep down, she knew the bigger mistake would have been sleeping with him. A one-night stand wouldn't be enough for her. And anything more than that? Couldn't and wouldn't happen.

Chapter 13

CURIOUS FRIENDS AND TOWNSPEOPLE STOPPED BY to chat and check out the changes at the old Elliot place. Both the grapevine and goodwill would be crucial to her business's success, so every single time the door swung open, Tansy made sure her visitor got the nickel tour.

She knew, too, that more than a little of the curiosity had to do with the fact that Beck's crew was doing the work. Misty Bottomers loved their gossip, and she and Beck had provided plenty of fodder in the past. A lot of her drop-ins wanted to see if the pot was being stirred between the two of them again.

Whew! If anyone caught a whiff of what had gone on the other night under the oak... Definite stirring!

As she stepped from the kitchen, the door opened and Lamont Elliot walked in. She watched nervously as his gaze traveled over the rooms, taking in the changes, watching the workmen who all stopped long enough to acknowledge him.

"What do you think?" she asked.

"I love it!" he boomed. "Exactly what this old place needed—new life and new energy."

Tansy breathed a sigh of relief. "I'm so glad. I know it's different, but—"

"It needed to be. Can't do what you want and not make any changes." He waved a hand at her. "Show me around."

She did.

"My grandson's doing right by the place, isn't he?" Pride filled his voice.

"Yes. I'm so glad Beck agreed to do this remodel."

"Why wouldn't he?"

"Well, because—um, he—"

Lamont laughed and chucked her under the chin. "Tellin' you, girlie, that's water under the bridge."

Maybe, maybe not.

When he left, he promised to return for opening day.

She watched him lumber down the sidewalk of what used to be his home and blinked back tears when the old man turned to look out over the backyard, no doubt remembering his life here, his family playing and relaxing in that yard. His Elsie.

Now, he'd entrusted the house to her, and she swore she'd do right by it.

Cricket popped in. "Have two minutes?"

"Absolutely." She snagged a couple bottles of water from her mini fridge. "Let's sit at the picnic table."

With sunshine bathing them, Cricket pulled out her phone. "Wanted to show you the flowers Lacy Hampton picked out for her bridal bouquet. Thought you could use them when you design the wedding cake. She's coming in next week for a consult." Cricket scrolled through photos. "Her colors are emerald and melon. Very dramatic. I'll use Juliet garden roses, sweet peas, and white lilacs for her nosegay with lots of greenery to pull in the emerald. Jenni Beth's decided on melon for the table linens. For the tall centerpieces, I thought I'd include some vines."

"Different." Tansy nodded. "I like that. She's planning on around a hundred and twenty guests, so I'll do a four-tier, fourteen-inch-wide cake. Fresh flowers might be better than sugar ones since Lacy's trying to keep the cost down. It won't be as labor-intensive, so the fresh will actually be more cost-effective. Let me grab my notepad."

As she walked in the back, the front door opened. It was Cole.

"Look what I found." He pulled out his phone and brought up photos of a vintage pink fridge he'd found at Dinky's, a friend's architectural salvage place.

"What do you think? I know you're buying Kitty's industrial fridge for your supplies, but I thought maybe you could use this one behind the counter."

"Yes, yes, yes! I can stock it with creamers, milk, and butters for my customers. Besides looking awesome, it'll save hundreds of steps a day." She grimaced. "He won't sell it before you get back to him, will he?"

"Nope."

"You sound awfully sure."

"I am." He laughed. "I already bought it. It was made for Sweet Dreams."

She threw her arms around his neck. "You're the best!"

"I am." He hugged her back just as the back door opened. "Hey, Cricket."

"Hey, yourself. Jenni Beth told me you were on a buying trip, and I walk in and find you getting all snuggly with Tansy."

"I *was* on a buying trip, and Tansy threw herself at me."

Laughing, Tansy smacked him on the arm.

"I could take it back."

"Not if your life means anything to you, you won't."

He threw his hands up in surrender. "I stopped by to show this to Tansy." He held up his phone.

Cricket took a peek and grinned. "Oh my gosh! It's perfect."

"Exactly my words," Cole said. "And I need to hit the road again. Don't suppose you could spare a coffee for a friend?"

"For you? Anything." Tansy moved to her new machine and brewed him a cup.

"You girls locking up at night and when you're gone?" Cole asked Cricket and Tansy.

Both of them nodded.

"You heard that Jenni Beth had an uninvited visitor a couple of times at Magnolia House?"

"I don't understand that." Cricket stuffed her hands into the pockets of her loose cotton pants.

"Me, either." Cole turned to Tansy. "Have you seen Beck? I thought with his guys here…"

A hot blush raced over her chest, up her neck and face.

"Um, not lately, no."

Cole narrowed his eyes, and Cricket tilted her head thoughtfully.

"Somethin' goin' on? Problem?"

"Absolutely not." She handed him the coffee, then crossed her fingers behind her back.

He sipped his coffee. "Excellent brew. I'll pick up that fridge in a couple days."

"Thank you, Cole." She clasped her hands together. "I can't wait to get it in here!"

He threw her a wink and gave Cricket a jaunty salute. The new bell Tansy had hung over the front door tinkled merrily as he left.

"Is it my imagination, or did I detect an undercurrent just now?"

Tansy opened her mouth, then closed it. Too many ears. One of Beck's men worked with a tile cutter while another installed those tiles as a backsplash for her work counter. "Let's go outside."

"Good. I brought plants and seeds for the garden. They're in my Chevy."

The second the door shut behind them, Cricket asked, "So what's up?"

"Can you keep a secret?"

Cricket nodded.

"You can't share this with anybody! Not even Sam."

Cricket crossed her heart over her vintage sweater.

"I'm a mess. Things have thawed a little between Beck and me, but…" She spilled her guts.

Cricket whistled. "Oh boy."

"Oh boy is right. Beck and I have all this stuff to deal with. He took a step forward the other night, and I messed it up. Then again, maybe it's best we don't… you know."

Cricket nodded. "Do you still love him?"

"It doesn't matter." Her throat tightened. "There isn't going to be any Disney happy ending for us, Cricket."

"I wouldn't be too sure about that."

"I am. I screwed up. I hurt him. I was engaged to him and married someone else!" She rubbed her hands over her face. "The chemistry's still there, but I destroyed his trust. Without that, we can't possibly have a future. Sleeping with him isn't enough. And then there's Gracie…"

She threw her hands into the air. "I don't want to talk about this anymore."

"Fair enough." Cricket gave her a one-armed hug, then started toward her vehicle. "Come look at the pretty plants I brought you."

———∽∾∿———

The next afternoon, Sam pulled up in his old truck with Jimmy Don riding shotgun. Tansy's fountain had come in, and Cricket had tapped the two of them to deliver it. After they'd grunted and groaned and placed it where Tansy said, she'd run inside to peek out the dining room window. A couple more trips inside and some adjustments by the guys, and the fountain sat in exactly the right spot.

Cricket showed up several hours later. She'd closed Enchanted Florist and, along with Sam and Hobo, went to work plumbing the fountain. When Tansy offered to help, they'd kicked her out. Battling guilt, she left them hard at work while she went home to spend the evening with her daughter.

By the time she walked through the door the next morning, water cascaded from the newly installed fountain and, grinning, she rushed to open the window. Like an idiot, she just stood there, listening to the soft splash.

Charlie Pearce, tool belt low on his hips, rounded the corner from the kitchen. "Like it?"

"I love it. I love the whole house! Thank you for what you've done here, Charlie." Without thinking, she kissed him full on the lips. "Don't tell Martha I did that, but isn't this house fantastic?"

"It surely is." His eyes twinkled. "As for the other? My lips are sealed, sweetheart. If an old man can't get a kiss from a pretty young thing every once in a while, what good is livin'?"

She laughed and threw herself into the day's work.

The week went from busy to busier.

Light fixtures came down; others went up.

Tansy hated that she chose her work outfits a little more carefully and bothered with makeup on the slim chance Beck would come by. When he didn't, she told herself it was for the best. The two of them together was tinder to fire.

The built-in wall cabinets and arched nooks Lamont had installed in the dining room for his bride would be repainted a pale, pale pink and used for both storage and display of for-sale items. They'd look fantastic with her new pink refrigerator, and her refinished hardwood floors shone like a new penny.

On Thursday, Kitty's bakery closed after over four decades, a bittersweet moment for the whole town. Much of the citizenry of Misty Bottoms had been weaned on her pastries, and her final day found the shop bursting at the seams. But new was always exciting and everybody looked forward to the Sweet Dreams opening.

"The king is dead; long live this king," Tansy mumbled. "I hope I can live up to the town's expectations."

Had she bitten off more than she could chew? She prayed not. Jenni Beth had two degrees to back her up, one in business and one in events planning. Cricket had worked in a flower shop before opening her own.

Tansy grimaced. She'd taken some cake decorating classes and practiced in her kitchen, and here she was opening her own business. The biggest difference between herself and her friends? Cole had Jenni Beth's back, and even before Sam came to town, Beck was there for Cricket. Both women had men who supported them, while she was on her own—with a child to support and care for.

Well, it was what it was. She reached in her pocket for an antacid.

———

A delivery truck backed into her drive, and Tansy ran outside to meet it.

The equipment from Kitty's had arrived. The Elliots' family kitchen had already been dismantled and what she couldn't use upstairs in her new kitchen had been donated to Habitat for Humanity in Savannah. Beck's crew had upgraded the electricity and plumbing to handle the industrial appliances.

Charlie moved up behind her. "You look like a kid in a candy store, Ms. Tansy."

"I feel like one."

"My men will hook these up before they go home today."

"Thank you." Shame on her for feeling sorry for herself. She had an entire town—minus one—rooting for her.

Yet even that one had helped her weed her front flower bed. His men worked on her house, and he'd handled the ordering, the delivery of supplies, and built shelves for her bedroom.

Reluctant or not, didn't he, in his own way, have her back?

She'd take a page out of Scarlett's book and think about that another day.

Right now, the house was really coming together. She ran a hand over the stainless-steel double convection oven. How many cakes had Kitty baked in this old workhorse? Like all of the equipment, it was far from new, and realistically, some would need to be replaced before long. For now, though, Tansy could live with them.

True to his word, Charlie's crew had everything up and running before they left. Just in time, too, because in four short days, she had to deliver another wedding cake for a Magnolia House bride…and no longer had Kitty's kitchen to use.

The bride and groom had decided on the perfect cake for their fall wedding. London would carry a simple bouquet of vibrant orange calla lilies and gold roses with fall foliage woven in. For their cake, Tansy would fashion a three-tiered lemon sponge creation with white buttercream scrollwork. The labor-intensive part was the scattering of orange and yellow fondant leaves. Each one had to be formed by hand along with the fondant acorns and minipumpkins. She'd have a lot of time invested, but this would be a cake she could be proud of. *Would* be proud of.

Around and above her, the sounds of late-day hammering and buzz saws provided the soundtrack for her dream. Over it all, another sound reached her ears as she knelt to finish painting the living room baseboard.

She peeked out the window and nearly swooned. Her new display case. Oh! Carefully, she set down her brush and placed the lid securely on the can. Wiping her hands on paint-stained jeans, she rushed to the door, then stopped as a pickup pulled in behind the delivery van.

Jeeters hopped out. And Beck.

Her stomach did a rather shaky cartwheel.

She hadn't seen Beck since, well, since he'd stopped to help her weed. Okay, that wasn't entirely true. He'd been at the store a couple times when she'd run in to pick up something or to place a new order.

They'd spoken a mumbled hello, a how-are-you kind of thing that strangers or barely acquainted people did. Inside, though, heat had licked through her. From the quickly banked expression in his eyes, she was almost certain that same flame burned inside him.

On the off chance he'd stop by, she'd actually made a practice of being the last to leave in the evenings. And how stupid was that? She was a grown woman, not some love-struck adolescent—although, to be honest, around Beck, she reverted to a moon-eyed teen. If she caught either Cricket or Jenni Beth acting so addle-headed she'd be tempted to give her a kick in the butt.

"Jeeters mixed your exterior paint today." Beck lifted two cans from the back of his truck. "You do know we painted this house seven months ago."

She chewed her lower lip. "I do, but I really have my heart set on different colors."

He lifted the cans higher. "Purple and green? Haven't we had this discussion?"

"Imagine and Julep," she said stubbornly. "Look at the cans. Those are the colors."

Beck rolled his eyes. "Semantics."

"I'll leave the gingerbread white and use the julep sparingly."

"I sure as hell hope so. Still, purple?"

"Pale lavender. Imagine. She'll look like one of San Francisco's beautiful painted ladies."

"You're forgettin' something."

"What?"

"We're in Misty Bottoms, not San Francisco."

"Doesn't matter. If I leave it white, it'll still be the Elliot homestead. I need people to look at it and see Sweet Dreams."

He snorted. "This is Misty Bottoms, sugar. It'll be, 'Hey, let's go to Sweet Dreams. You know, the old Elliot homestead.'"

Because he was right, she said nothing.

When he handed the first can to her, he stepped close and defiantly invaded her personal space. Her fingers curled around the bail, and his fingers curled over hers. Their eyes met.

"You and me? We have some unfinished business, sugar."

Her heart went from near zero to sixty.

"What? Nothin' to say?"

She shook her head.

"Good." He turned back to his truck to get the rest of the paint.

Then he and Jeeters, with help from some of the other guys, unloaded her new display case. Stainless steel and glass with a pristine white top. She couldn't wait to load it full of cupcakes and cakes, cookies and doughnuts.

"Jeez, what is this made of?" Jeeters complained.

"I'm sorry. It's heavy, but it'll last forever. When I'm open, you have a month of free doughnuts."

"Honest?"

"Honest."

"I'm already payin' you, Jeeters."

"I know, but she offered."

"Only because you're whinin' like a baby."

"Boys, play nice."

Beck scowled at her, and Jeeters laughed.

"What? You want free doughnuts, too?"

"Doughnuts weren't quite what I was thinkin' of, sugar." Jeeters snorted.

"Coffee, then," she said. "And that's my final offer."

"We'll see about that."

She led them to where the dining room wall had once stood. "Right here. It'll separate the sales area from the dining space."

As they muscled it into place, she sighed. "It's gorgeous."

"Yeah, it is." Beck moved toward the door. Hand on the knob, he turned. "Absolutely beautiful."

But he wasn't looking at the case. His eyes ran over her, making her painfully aware of her paint-splattered jeans with a hole in the knee, the oversized plaid shirt, and her wild hair. Why hadn't he come on one of the days she'd looked nice? Self-conscious, she reached up to smooth the tangled mass, then remembered too late she still had paint on her hands.

Beck laughed. "Nice look, Red. My guess? You saved a ton on highlighting."

Then he was gone.

~

That evening after dinner, when dishes were finished and Gracie tucked in for the night, Tansy gave in to her need for solitude.

"Think I'll take a long bubble bath, Mom."

"Good for you." With a gentle hand, Rexanna brushed a paint-streaked strand of hair from Tansy's face. "You were awfully quiet at dinner."

"I'm so tired. It's been a crazy few weeks."

"It has. A lot going on and a lot of changes. I think there's more, though."

Tansy squirmed. Her mother always had seen right through her lies and half-truths. She guessed that, at least, hadn't changed. "Nothing some quiet time won't take care of."

"A bubble bath should do the trick, then. Take a good book and a glass of wine in with you."

"I will."

"And don't worry about Gracie. I'll keep an ear open in case she wakes and needs anything."

"Thank you." She gave her mom a quick cheek kiss.

Twenty minutes later, Tansy realized that while she was turning the pages of her favorite author's new book, she hadn't absorbed a single word. Her mind kept wandering to Beck. To those kisses beneath the old oak. To memories.

She was confused. Every two seconds she changed her mind about what to do, what she wanted.

Run. Fast. Away from Beck.

Run. Fast. *To* Beck.

Did he think she'd been teasing him, leading him on? But he'd started it, and damn it, they hadn't finished it!

She slapped at the water, spraying droplets on her book. Closing it, she tossed it across the room. Another sip of wine, and she leaned her head against the back of the tub, her eyes drifting shut.

What if they had finished it? If they'd gone inside? How would she feel tonight if they'd—

"Tansy!" Her mother's voice came through the door.

"What?" Instantly alert at her tone, Tansy straightened.

"Everything okay? You didn't answer the first couple times I called. You scared me."

"Sorry, Mom. Guess I was woolgathering."

"Let me know if you need anything."

"I will. Sorry again for scaring you."

As her footsteps faded, Tansy thought about what she'd told her mother. *Sorry*. That's exactly how she'd feel if she and Beck had finished what he'd started. But, then, didn't she feel sorry anyway? And frustrated to boot!

God, she missed him. Missed what they'd had.

A tear trickled down her cheek and dripped from her chin. A second, then a third followed.

She *was* tired. Tired of floating aimlessly. Tired of being alone. Even when she'd been married, she'd been alone except for Gracie. She and Emerson had never been a couple, never shared dreams or set goals, never shared love.

She and Beck had.

When the sobs racked her, she turned on the water to cover the sound and simply let the tears flow. Her life was a mess. Beck didn't like her anymore, her daddy was gone, and she was all but broke.

She cried and cried, afraid that, now she'd let them loose, the tears would never stop. Placing a cool washcloth over her eyes, she laid back and cried her heart out. Finally, feeling wrung out, she watched the water swirl down the drain.

A glance at her mother's quirky little jeweled elephant clock told her it was time to call it a night. That
morning alarm would go off all too soon. But when she
caught sight of herself in the mirror, she winced. Her
red and swollen eyes would give her away if her mom
saw her.

She'd have to be sure she didn't.

Intent on sneaking to her room, she wrapped herself
in a thick terry robe and tiptoed from the steam-filled
bath. Her mother stood at the end of the hallway, but
whatever she'd been going to say never came. Instead,
she simply opened her arms.

Tansy rushed into them, fighting back the tears that
threatened to start again.

Rexanna hugged her tightly.

"It's damned hard to lose our men, isn't it?" she
whispered into her daughter's hair.

"It's not Emerson," she choked out.

"I know. I've always known."

Tansy nodded wordlessly and lost the battle. She
gave in to fresh tears that mingled with her mother's as
they cried together. For her dad. For Beck. For lost love
and dreams.

Hiccupping, Tansy finally managed a soft, "How do
you do it, Mom?"

"One day at a time, honey. One day at a time."

Chapter 14

THE HOUSE WAS SO CLOSE TO BEING FINISHED. She'd promised her mother she wouldn't move Gracie into a construction zone, but patience wasn't one of her strong suits.

His hammer hanging loosely from one hand, Charlie promised, "We'll have it done by next Wednesday."

"You sure?"

"Positive."

"Okay."

He must have heard the doubt in her voice because he added, "I've figured in a contingency day just in case something unexpected comes up. Wednesday is D-Day. Done Day. You and that little girl of yours can count on it."

"Thanks, Charlie. I'll call the moving company and have my things brought from storage on Thursday, then talk to Cole about the pieces I bought in Savannah."

She handed him a warm cranberry-walnut chocolate cookie. "I'm experimenting. What do you think?"

Charlie took a bite and grinned. "This one's a keeper."

Cookie in hand, he headed off to finish the front bath.

"I wouldn't mind one of those," a sexy voice said from behind her.

"Beck!"

"You look nice this mornin', Tansy."

She snorted as heat rose to her face. "Thank you.

Since I don't have to paint today, I took a chance and wore my new top." With a grimace, she glanced down at the faded, old sweatshirt.

He stepped closer. "Isn't that the sweatshirt you bought when we went to Myrtle Beach your senior year?"

"It is. I left it at Mom's on one of my visits home from college. When I found it last weekend, I thought, why not wear it."

"Remember the Putt-Putt golf course there?"

"I do. I beat you four out of five games."

He laughed. "I let you win. Figured I'd be the real winner in the long run." He waggled his brows.

Her blush deepened, the curse of a redhead. "It was a fun weekend."

"Yeah, it was. So what are you feedin' Charlie?"

"Cranberry-walnut chocolate cookies. Warm from the oven."

"Sounds good. Got another?"

"I do. But"—she held up a finger—"I also have cinnamon roll sugar cookies."

"With cream cheese frosting?"

She nodded.

"You used to leave those in my locker at school."

"For your before-football-practice snack."

He sobered. "I liked to think you baked a lot of love into those cookies."

"I did, Beck."

"Did you bake lots of it in today's cookies?"

She tugged at her sweatshirt's neck.

"Unfair question. I rescind it and will ask another instead. Can I have one of each?"

"Yes," she whispered. "You can."

"In exchange, I'll help Charlie with that bath."

Popping the last bite of cookie into his mouth, he headed off to work. After her nerves settled, still very aware of Beck in the house, she ran a mental check on what would be coming from storage.

Most were personal items—clothes, pictures, that kind of thing. Emerson's parents intended to sell the furniture and pretty much everything else, including their wedding gifts. Just as well. A clean break. The problem, though? She had this big house and very little to put in it. But with Cole's help and a quick trip to Traditions, his shop in Savannah, she'd found enough to furnish the downstairs, along with the basics for their apartment upstairs.

Her décor would be simple and understated. In other words, nearly bare. Still, it would be *her* nearly bare home, and that counted for a lot.

She stood in the center of the former living room, now the dining area, and listened as Charlie and Beck worked in the bath. Sunlight streamed through the windows. Soon, she'd hang some drapes or, maybe, lace curtains. She didn't want to block the sun or the view. She wanted people to drive or walk by and be drawn in by the cozy look of the place, and she wanted her customers to look out and enjoy the spectacular yard and gardens.

Stepping onto the front porch, a sense of satisfaction filled her. A fall wreath her mother'd made graced the front door. Yesterday, Tansy had picked up several flower baskets and ferns from Cricket. She'd hung them from the overhang and set out four mismatched rockers she'd bought at an antique mall outside of town and painted the same minty green as the window trim. For the final touch, she interspersed a couple small tables among the rockers. Battered, flea market, galvanized metal buckets filled with colorful mums and silvery dusty miller paraded up the stairs.

She walked across the lawn, then turned and studied her work.

Perfect. With the broad overhead fans rotating slowly, the veranda welcomed people to come sit. To enjoy a pastry and a cup of coffee.

Every single day, she loved this house more. How had Lamont brought himself to sell it?

Beck stepped out onto the porch. "The downstairs bath's good to go. Charlie's headed up to finish the plumbing in your apartment, and I'm off to hang new shelves in Dee-Ann's pantry." He walked to where she stood. "The cookies were great, Tanz. You'll do well in your new venture."

He leaned toward her, and she held her breath. Then, just as abruptly, he stepped away and, with an over-the-shoulder wave, hopped into his truck and drove away.

Eyes closed, she lifted her face, felt the sun's warmth. Maybe they'd eventually be okay, but it sure didn't feel like it right now.

In the meantime, she had too much to do and too much to be grateful for to feel sorry for herself.

Back inside, she strolled though the rooms, surveying them with a critical eye. Imagining them filled with furniture and customers, her heart swelled near to bursting.

Right now, though, she had a wedding cake to finish before tomorrow. All the fondant acorns and pumpkins were completed and nearly half the colorful leaves. The lemon sponge cake layers were waiting.

Time to roll up her sleeves.

―⁓―

Saturday morning arrived, and Tansy woke again at the crack of dawn. Smiling, she placed a hand over her stomach, hoping to still the butterflies. Today's bride was a local, so this could very well be a make-or-break event. Friends would judge her. Was the cake heavy enough? Light enough? Too crumbly? Decorated well enough?

Whew, nerves on steroids.

Her mom had offered to watch Gracie today and, for that, Tansy sent a silent thank-you to her still-sleeping parent. Tansy had delivered and set up the first couple cakes she'd made for Magnolia House weddings, then slipped out before the festivities began. Today, she'd stay to help with the entire affair, which added a whole new layer of nerves.

Dressing extra carefully, she slid into a pair of flats and slipped her heels into a bag for later. She caught a glimpse of herself in the mirror and grinned. It had been a while, quite a while, since she'd gotten all dolled up. Today definitely called for it, though. Today was her coming-out.

She'd chosen a maroon, lightweight wool dress. Subtle, it would let her blend into the background since she was, technically, the help, although she'd been invited as a guest, too. The dark color would also play into the bride's autumn color scheme.

Kitty, bless her, had agreed to help transport the cake and set it up. What with the remodeling and everything else, she'd cut it far too close and hadn't finished the cake till late last night.

The leaves had been real buggers, but today? Every second that had gone into them had been time well spent.

---∿∿---

"Oh, Tansy!" Kitty walked into the kitchen an hour and a half later, a look of absolute rapture on her face. She circled the table. "This puts anything I've ever made to shame."

"It does not. I've seen your cakes."

"I don't have your touch, Tansy." She splayed her hands on her hips. "Things work out the way they're supposed to."

"Most of the time."

"Sometimes, honey, we have to be patient."

Tansy bit her lip. Was Kitty still talking about the cake and her new business, or had she traveled to more personal roads? Best not to ask.

Instead, she tipped her head in the direction of the dining room. "Come on. Let's put my new espresso machine to work. We've got time for a cup before we hit the day running."

"Sounds good to me." Kitty stepped into the display area and ran a hand over the stainless steel counter.

Moving to the window, she checked out the backyard. "Cricket's been here, hasn't she? And the front porch…so warm and friendly. It made me want to sit down and try out one of those rockers. Chat with my neighbors while I sipped some of your fancy coffee."

"Thank you. And, yes, Cricket's performed her magic. She's an absolute genius with anything green. Although…" She paused. "I did the porch myself."

"Well done to both of you."

Tansy wrapped an arm around the older woman's waist. "I love my fountain."

Kitty nodded. "And the roses. They're lovely."

"They are." Tansy sighed deeply and swiped at the single tear that escaped. "I'm so happy."

"I can see that," she said dryly. "Now, where's that coffee you promised?"

———

Cricket was already at Magnolia House when they pulled up in front. Busily wrapping ivy around stand-alone white pillars, she barely paused when Tansy and Kitty got out of the SUV. She'd placed the pillars so the rose garden, still in bloom, formed a backdrop for today's happy couple.

"Jenni Beth is around here somewhere," she muttered absentmindedly.

"We have the cake."

"Oh!" Cricket jumped up, greenery scattering around her. "I want to see!"

Tansy laughed. "Not yet. Give me time to set it up, then I'll unveil it."

"Don't forget to come get me."

She chuckled. "I won't."

When she stepped into the kitchen, Kitty right behind her, she was surprised to see Beck at the counter, drinking coffee and chatting with Charlotte.

"Hey, Kitty. Tansy. You need help draggin' stuff in?"

"Stuff?" She went for playfully indignant. "Are you referring to my cake?"

He shrugged. "Guess so."

"You'd better watch out, boy, or she'll cuff your ears, and I'll help her. You're talkin' about a work of art." Charlotte drew herself up.

Beck rolled his eyes, and Charlotte nailed him with *the look*. "You'll be wantin' to move, too, 'cause she's gonna need this counter for her things."

"Things is better than stuff?"

"Yes." Charlotte, Kitty, and Tansy spoke in unison.

"Guess that's unanimous. Set your *things* down, Tansy, and we'll go get the rest of your *things*."

Walking beside her to her SUV, he put a hand at her waist and leaned in to sniff her neck. "You smell good."

"Like lemon cake and frosting?"

"Nope. Like hot, sexy woman."

"Beck—"

"Just sayin'." He opened the vehicle's back door. "What needs taken in?"

"Everything you see."

His brows arched. "All this for one cake?"

"One very special wedding cake."

"Right." He dragged out the word. "The work of art."

In no time at all, they'd hauled everything inside, and she shooed both Beck and a very reluctant Charlotte out of the kitchen. Jenni Beth had invested in a wheeled table for her bridal cakes, and Tansy set a cut crystal plate in the middle of it, then carefully placed her first cake layer.

She'd finished all the scrollwork and intricate patterns at her own shop. Now, she only had to insert the dowels for strength, set the layers and pipe around them, then place the decorations and topper. Surprisingly enough, her hands were steady.

Within half an hour, she stood back. "What do you think, Kitty?"

"I think the bride's gonna cry when she sees it, and every single woman in attendance today will be knocking on your door askin' you to make her cake when the time comes."

"Thank you."

"I didn't do anything."

"Oh, yes, you did."

The kitchen door squeaked open and Charlotte's head peered around. "Are you done yet?" Then her eyes widened. "Oh, honey, that is just the prettiest thing I've ever seen."

———

Since the cake was ready to roll, literally, and had been duly admired by all, Tansy moved it to the reception area, which consisted today of the old plantation home's living and dining rooms. Most of the furniture had been moved out, and small round tables had been covered in pale yellow linen. The bridal table sat in front of the fireplace that Cricket had decorated for fall, turning it into an autumn wonderland and promising some incredible photos.

Jenni Beth hustled around putting the final touches on the room, and Cricket finished her decorations. Both stopped to check out the cake again.

"That is phenomenal, Tansy." Jenni Beth walked to her, burnt-orange candles in hand.

"I have to say the same about what the two of you have done." Tansy turned a full three-sixty to take in the entire area. "Cricket, you used real pumpkins for the vases on the table! Clever girl."

The pumpkins held orange calla lilies, gold-colored roses, and burgundy mums along with vivid maple leaves and deep-red berries.

"Thank you." Cricket bowed. "I scooped out the pumpkins and rinsed them with a bit of bleach water. Easy-peasy."

Several fall leaves in hand, Cricket linked arms with Jenni Beth and Tansy. "We are awesome, aren't we? And we clean up pretty darned good, too."

"We do. When we're finished here, we'll raise a toast to the very first wedding we've all been here for." Jenni Beth grinned.

"Why wait? Why don't we raise that toast right now?" Cricket headed toward a table filled with flutes and champagne. She popped a cork and splashed a little into each glass.

Today, her chopped, pale-blond hair was held back from one ear with a glittery barrette. She wore an incredible vintage olive-green silk dress that Tansy coveted. Jenni Beth, her long golden hair flowing down her back, looked polished and tailored in a chocolate-brown suit.

Crossing the room in her sparkly shoes, Cricket handed them each a glass. Before they could toast, though, Beck stuck his head in the room, whipping his phone from a pocket. "Might never again get a chance to shoot three women this gorgeous."

Tansy faltered, but when the other two, their arms around each other, raised their glasses and smiled at Beck, she joined them. One flash, then a second.

"Gotcha." He dropped the phone into his pocket and

disappeared for all of two seconds. Peering around the doorjamb, he said, "Um, Tansy? Thought I'd remind you that you owe me a dance."

"I do not."

"Yes, you do. You danced with Angus Duckworth during our song at the prom."

Outraged, she gaped at him. "You remember that?"

"I told you. I remember everything about you, sugar." His voice deepened, and she felt its rumble in the pit of her stomach.

"Jenni Beth needed a break," Tansy protested. "Her toes couldn't take anymore."

"I really did, Beck." Jenni Beth chuckled. "She did me a huge favor."

"I have no problem with that. Damn shame Cole bailed on you and you had to go with Angus, but the fact remains, she owes me a dance, and I mean to collect." With that, he was gone.

Cricket sipped her champagne, her big eyes the color of a winter storm studying the other two. "You girls have interesting pasts."

"The problem with the past," Tansy mumbled, "is that it doesn't always stay there."

―⁓―

The wedding went off without a hitch. Sitting in a folding chair toward the back, Tansy marveled at both the simplicity and the elegance. She understood both were the result of long hours spent by Jenni Beth and her bride in the planning stages and even longer hours by Jenni Beth after all the meetings. Every single detail had been tended to superbly.

Resplendent in an A-line chiffon gown with a sweet-heart neckline and beaded waistband, the bride, on the arm of her groom, turned to face the guests. Her black hair hung in long waves, a crystal headband its only adornment. The groom, in his black tux, wore an ear-to-ear grin. Halfway through their recessional walk, he swept his surprised bride off her feet and, laughing, carried her the rest of the way to the cheers and applause of family and friends.

That, Tansy thought, *is what a wedding should be— absolute unadulterated bliss*. She said a quick prayer that today's couple would always be this happy. Then she slipped unnoticed into the house to help prepare for the onslaught of guests into the reception area.

After one final check on the cake, Tansy pitched in. Although, to give Jenni Beth her due once again, she'd hired staff that knew exactly what to do.

A couple hours later, the sun set and the wedding party and their guests moved outdoors to dance beneath the stars. Tall patio heaters had been placed throughout the table areas. In addition to providing a touch of wel-come warmth, their glow added to the romance of the candles and a full moon.

That same warm glow filled Tansy. Her friend had hit a home run, and she couldn't have been happier for her. And that she, herself, had played a part in the celebration, and would again, many times over? Thrilling. She caught a glimpse of Jenni Beth, Cole's arm wrapped around her, their heads bent close as they talked. At the next table over, Cricket and Sam held hands and chatted with Lem Gilmore and his wife, Lyda Mae.

Two by two, like Noah's Ark. Everyone in pairs.
Except her.

She scanned the yard and the portable dance floor.
No Beck.

Guess he didn't want that dance after all.

Weddings made Beck nervous. They put crazy thoughts
into every female's head. He'd tried to catch Tansy for
their dance, but every time he'd checked, she'd been
busy. Time to chalk it up to a lost cause—for now.

Deciding to say good night to Charlotte, he checked
in the living room first, thinking that even though Jenni
Beth had told her not to, she might be in there fussing
and cleaning up. The room was empty.

Turning, he bumped smack into Missy Frampton.

"Hi, Beck. You've been busy lately."

"Lot goin' on, Missy."

"When you get a free night, why don't you give me
a call?"

He thought about a redhead with turquoise eyes. "I'm
not sure that's a good idea."

She stepped closer and wrapped her arms around his
neck. "I can make you forget her, Beck."

Before he could extricate himself, he heard footsteps
coming their way, moving toward them. High heels. He
knew that gait.

"Whoops, excuse me." Tansy's voice could have
sliced steel. Without another word, she turned and
walked out.

By the time he'd freed himself from Missy, who'd had way too much champagne, Tansy was nowhere in sight. Jenni Beth said Tansy had pleaded a miserable headache and had gone home.

Disgusted, Beck shook his head and left. He wouldn't be getting his dance tonight.

Chapter 15

MONDAY MORNING DAWNED GRAY AND FOGGY. A velvet morning in Misty Bottoms.

Wasn't velvet supposed to be soft and cuddly, though? Tansy wondered. Apparently, this morning had missed that memo because it definitely felt prickly and tense. Saturday night and yesterday had dragged, had felt like an entire week of long days—because of Beck and self-doubt. Had she overreacted? Probably. Her emotions were riding too close to the surface for comfort, and this particular roller coaster was wearing her out.

Even though she hadn't officially opened, several tables were filled with the workers. She'd begun practicing on them, making up items she hoped to serve and brewing her fancy coffees for them. Kind of a soft opening. The guys had become her guinea pigs. *Very satisfied ones*, she thought smugly.

It would take more than that, though, to improve her mood.

Missy Frampton? Seriously?

Jimmy Don, hand resting lightly on his sidearm, stepped in out of the fog.

Without even asking, she handed him coffee. "Morning, Sheriff. Anything else?"

"Nah. I'd love one of those apple fritters, but if the missus found out, she'd skin me alive. Thinks I need to lose a couple pounds." He laid a hand on his ample belly and grimaced. "Heck, she's probably right."

"I have some low-fat, reduced-sugar lemon bars I made fresh this morning."

When his nose wrinkled, she laughed. "Tell you what. Try one. You might be pleasantly surprised."

"Your feelings won't be hurt if I don't like it?"

"Not at all." She moved behind the counter and plated one. "Here you go."

Lem Gilmore and his wife came through the door, and Tansy smiled at them.

"Saw some cars out front. Thought we'd wander in and see what's goin' on."

"Hopin' to catch a free pastry's more like it," the sheriff muttered.

Lem ignored Jimmy Don's comment and pulled out a chair for his wife, but Tansy knew he wouldn't be pulling out his wallet. He plunked himself down across from the sheriff. "What've you got there?"

Jimmy Don licked his fork. "One of the best lemon bars I've ever tasted."

Turning her back to the dining area, Tansy smiled slowly.

"Bring me one of those, too," Lem said. "You want one, Lyda Mae?"

"No, I'll just nip a bite of yours."

Tansy had their drinks made and their pastries ready to go when the bell over the door jingled again. A welcome on her lips, she turned and nearly dropped her tray.

Hurt and betrayal flared, made her want to throw Lem and Lyda Mae's order across the room.

Beck, bold as brass, came through the door.

Ignoring him, she served Lem and his wife. "There you go. If you need anything else, let me know."

Wishing she had an antacid, she swiped her hands over her apron and took a calming breath. It didn't help a bit.

"What can I do for you this mornin'?"

Looking around the room, he asked, "What are you guys doin'? You're supposed to be workin'. And you." He pointed a finger at Tansy. "You're not supposed to be open yet. I'm not payin' these men to sit around drinkin' coffee and eatin' doughnuts." He spied Jimmy Don. "Although guess it's natural for you, huh?"

Before Jimmy Don could get into the middle of what was her and Beck's fray, Tansy said, "They're helping me. Taste testing my new recipes."

"Whatever. That's not what I came for. We need to talk."

Her chin came up. "Fine. Go right ahead."

Beck glanced over his shoulder at their audience, all of them gone quiet now. "Ah, I think we might want a little more privacy for this."

"Sure." She whipped off her apron. "Why don't we step onto the back porch?" Then she raised her voice. "If y'all will excuse me one moment." She held up a finger. "I'll be right back."

"These aren't paying customers."

"Still…"

Tansy maintained the smiling face and calm till they were out of view, then she stomped out to the porch. Instead of holding the door for Beck, she let go of it and heard him swear as he put out a hand to keep it from hitting him in the face.

She rounded on him. "What do you want? My blessing for you and Missy? Fine. You've got it." Damn. Hot tears burned at the back of her eyes, but she swore she'd give up her grandma's pearls before she let him see her cry. Again.

"Blessing?" Beck looked like he'd been sucker punched. "Hell no, I don't want your blessing! Missy and I went out exactly two times!" He raised two fingers to press his point home. "And no sex! Ever."

"It doesn't matter." Tansy managed to keep her own voice steady and quiet, though her emotions nearly drowned her.

"Yeah, I think it does. You promised me a dance. Instead, you ran away."

"I didn't run away."

"You sure as hell didn't have a headache."

"Okay, you're right. I didn't. And you can be with whomever you choose, but, darn it, seeing you with Missy—it hurt."

"You want to talk about hurt? How 'bout hearin' your fiancée is marryin' someone else? How 'bout spendin' four years thinking about her in bed with another man?"

"He never touched me, not once, after we were married."

"What?"

"I said—"

"I heard you."

"I need to get back to my customers."

Beck's hand shot out to take hers. "Not yet. And they're not your customers. They're guys who are supposed to workin'. Most of them anyway. Knowin' this town, everybody will help themselves to whatever they need."

Gathering her courage, she met his eyes. "Maybe I should have asked this before now, Beck. I made an assumption, so I'll put the question to you now. Anyone sharin' your bed?"

"Hell no! You think I'd have kissed you like I did if I was seein' somebody else?" He held her gaze. "You?"

She shook her head.

"I want *you* in my bed, Tansy."

The air left her. "Beck."

"I want you in my bed."

"That's a big step."

"Yeah, it is. One I don't take lightly. Never did."

He moved in to kiss her.

She wanted this so badly, but at the last second she raised a hand and placed it flat on his chest. "Uh-uh. Lips that kissed Missy Frampton's Saturday night don't kiss mine Monday mornin'."

"Emotion brings out the Misty Bottoms in you, Tansy. That drawl gets heavier and those *g*'s slide away like snow in an avalanche."

"And you're changin'—changing the subject."

One side of his lips turned up into a sexy smile. "I didn't kiss Missy. Even if I had, I've brushed since then. Several times. Flossed, too."

"This isn't funny, Beck."

"I know. Yesterday was miserable." He crooked a finger. "Kiss me, Tansy."

Her eyes moved to his lips. Oh God, they were so sexy, so hot!

"I'm not sure that's a good idea."

"Come on."

He crooked that finger again, such a sexy motion, and her heart stuttered. "You're crazy, Beck Elliot."

"Probably."

By now, he'd drawn her against him. She felt his body heat, smelled that totally masculine scent that was his alone. Her knees went weak even as her resolve faded.

She kissed him, the merest touch of lips.

He cupped the back of her head, deepened the kiss till her toes curled and her legs turned to rubber.

Gasping, she pulled back. His mouth turned up in that grin that was part naughty boy, part little boy.

"I'm sorry about Saturday night. I had no idea she was in the living room. I went there looking for Charlotte." As he spoke, he dropped tiny kisses along her jaw, the scruff on his chin sending shivers along her spine. His head dipped lower, and he kissed the curve of her chin, her neck.

She stepped away. "I need to go inside."

His hand snaked out, drew her back. "Before you do, I'd like to hear more about that bombshell you dropped. You owe me that much."

She stared down at the strappy sandals she'd slipped into that morning. He was right; she did.

Beck placed a fingertip beneath her chin and tilted her face up till their eyes met. "He didn't touch you all these years?"

"No. We had sex one time." The injustice of it ripped through her. "Once!"

"And you got pregnant."

She nodded, clasping and unclasping her hands until he took them in his large ones.

"Oh, Tansy." He rested his forehead on hers. "We're a disaster zone, aren't we?"

"I am," she whispered. "Not you, Beck. Never you. You're solid and steady. You always do the right thing. It was me. I screwed up."

"Circumstances played a big role. You got hit with

the equivalent of a perfect storm when your dad died. Too much, too fast. I didn't realize how badly you were takin' on water, and I should have. I'm sorry."

"You didn't do anything to be sorry for, Beck. All that rests right here." She tapped her shoulders and decided to risk it all. "Think we might be able to work through this?"

"I honestly don't know."

Automatically reaching into her pocket for an antacid before she remembered there were none there, she saw his eyes follow her movement and withdrew her hand. Licking her dry lips, she now read a totally different expression in those bedroom eyes.

"I feel like I'm on a roller coaster, Beck. Or in one of those little cups that go 'round and 'round and make me dizzy and sick."

"I make you dizzy and sick?"

"No, not sick," she said quickly. "But dizzy. Definitely dizzy."

"That's a start. When you're ready to forgive yourself and move on, you know where to find me. I have to get to work."

"Me too. I have a lot of people inside."

He left without even a cheek kiss.

A mockingbird called from her bird feeder. She laughed derisively. Even the birds mocked her. And why not?

It was about time she discovered who she was, way down deep. She leaned on the porch railing and rested her chin in the palm of her hand. "Who are you, Tansy Calhoun Forbes?"

Until she knew the answer to that question, it wasn't fair to either Beck or herself to get involved.

Chapter 16

TANSY'S HEART SWELLED WITH GRATITUDE. HER and Gracie's first night in their new home. They'd celebrate birthdays here. They'd decorate for Halloween, Christmas, and the Fourth of July. Gracie's prom date would pick her up at the beautiful, carved front door.

The movers had shown up yesterday with their furniture, and Tansy had spent the entire day arranging it exactly the way she wanted. She'd chosen what she wanted and where she wanted it. She'd decided on the colors for the walls—and it was heaven.

Gracie had spent yesterday morning at Grandma's, but after dropping the little girl off at preschool, Rexanna stopped by and helped Tansy unpack and get organized.

After they'd finished, her mom had gone home and started dinner, while Tansy picked up Gracie. In the short time they'd been with her mother, they'd spilled out of their rooms and had stuff strewn everywhere. It had taken over an hour to gather all of her and Gracie's things.

Moving out had been harder than Tansy had anticipated. Always best friends in addition to being mother and daughter, she and her mom had stayed up until the wee hours talking about the future and reminiscing about the past.

But tonight, Tansy and her own daughter would sleep at 321 Main Street.

It felt strange. But it felt right.

Life might not have turned out quite the way she'd once thought it would, but darned if she wasn't feeling lucky. Very, very lucky.

"Honey, why don't we go downstairs? Mama needs to do some things down there."

"To get the shop ready?"

"Yes."

"'Kay."

They puttered in the kitchen for a bit, then, while she entered the last of her equipment inventory into the computer, Gracie wandered off toward the front of the house.

"Don't go outside."

"I won't, Mama."

Pop! Snap!

Tansy peeked around the corner. Gracie sat in the middle of what had been the Elliots' living room playing with strips of leftover bubble wrap. As each bubble burst, she giggled. It didn't take much to entertain Gracie.

The wrap had come off two precious pictures she'd taken from her former house. One was of Gracie on her first birthday, the other the last picture she had of her parents and herself. Less than a month and a half after the photo had been taken, her dad was gone. No warning and no time to prepare or say good-bye. It sucked.

She moved into the pantry to survey the supplies she had and decide what she still needed. Sitting at the small table, she cross-referenced those lists with her ordered-but-not-yet-arrived one. Lists were her lifeblood.

When she'd dealt with that, she wiggled the knob

to make sure the front door was locked. Carefully, she stepped over the strip of green bubble wrap that formed a small carpet in front of the door.

"Gracie?"

"I'm here, Mama." Her daughter peeked around the kitchen door, another strip of plastic in one hand, a roll of tape in the other.

"Were you outside?"

"Just for a minute."

"I told you not to go out."

Studying her feet, Gracie said, "I didn't go off the porch."

Tansy sighed. "What are you doing?"

"'Tectin' us."

"'Tectin' us?"

"Yeah." She held up the plastic. "I heard Grandma telling Aunt Coralee that somebody broked into Jenni Beth's. If a bad man tries to get in our house, he'll step on this and we'll know to run and hide."

Tansy didn't know whether to laugh or cry. Kids didn't get to stay kids long enough, but in her own innocent way, Gracie had decided to 'tect them. The only thing that needed 'tectin' was Tansy's heart, and she doubted a little bubble wrap would do much good there. On the other hand, Gracie was right. Someone *had* broken into Jenni Beth's.

Evening settled around them, and outside the kitchen window, Tansy saw an occasional firefly dart through the yard. With the cooler weather, she'd opened the windows to let in the soft Georgia breeze.

"I'm hungry." Holding her threadbare Penny the Pig, Gracie rested a foot on the bottom rung of one of the ladder-back chairs Tansy'd picked up for a song.

"Me too. I made a celebration dinner, our very first in our new home."

"What'd you make?"

"Mac and cheese." She knelt to remove it from the oven and heard Gracie's happy cheering behind her.

"My favorite!"

"I know." She set the hot casserole on a trivet. "I'll dish up. Why don't you wash your hands while it cools? Your milk's already poured."

Twisting a long, dark lock of hair around her finger, Gracie asked, "Since we're cele—celebring, can we have soda instead of milk?"

Tansy turned to see her daughter's best *please, please, please* expression. As hard as it was to refuse this child, soda this late would mean very little sleep for either of them. "Not tonight." She gave her a pat on the bottom. "Now go on. And use soap."

Halfway through dinner, popping and snapping exploded, sharp as a round of gunshots.

Tansy let out an involuntary little squeak.

A gruff male voice cut through the darkness. "What the hell?"

More popping and snapping.

"It's the bad man. He's here." Gracie scampered from her chair and all but crawled up Tansy's leg to get to her lap. Her dark-brown eyes huge, she wrapped her arms around her mother's neck.

More movement outside was followed by more sharp pops.

"Tansy?"

Beck Elliot.

Making soothing noises and bouncing a scared little girl on her hip, Tansy moved toward the door.

"Don't go, Mommy! He'll hurt us!" Gracie buried her head in her mom's neck.

"Where do you get these ideas, Gracie Bella? Nobody's going to hurt us."

"I saw it on TV."

"On TV?"

"With Daddy. The bad man had a knife."

"Oh, for—" One more black mark in Emerson's column.

"Tansy!" Beck banged on the back door. "Everything okay?"

"Yes," she called. "I'm comin'."

She threw open the door, Gracie cowering against her.

"Why in the hell do you have bubble wrap taped all over the porch floor? 'Bout gave me a heart attack." He winced. "Sorry. Bad choice of words."

"It's okay."

Then he noticed Gracie curled into Tansy. "What's wrong? Is she sick? Can I help?"

She shook her head. "No. Gracie put the bubble wrap there. To protect us from the bad man."

"The—" He frowned. "I'm not a bad man."

"She doesn't know that. After all, you did breach the perimeter and—" She pointed at the green plastic. "You set off the early warnin' system."

His chin drooped to his chest. "I scared her."

"Yeah."

Gracie opened her eyes. "Beck?"

"Hey, sweet Gracie. I'm sorry I scared you."

"That's okay. Wanna color?"

"We're eating, sweetheart," Tansy reminded her.

Beck held up a casserole dish. "My mom sent this and insisted I bring it over. Tonight. She's a meddler, Tansy. What can I say?"

"Why don't you set it on the counter?"

She held the door open wider for him and was instantly sorry. The moment he stepped inside, the kitchen grew smaller, and she found it hard to breathe. This man did things to her system. He always had and, God help her, he probably always would.

He stepped closer.

"Beck?"

"Yeah?"

"How come you know my mama?"

Beck caught Tansy's eyes. "Your mama and I used to be good friends. We went to school together."

Used to be.

"Did you fight with her?"

Tansy read the indecision in his eyes, saw a flicker of—what? Pain?

"I gotta be real truthful with you here, Gracie Bella, 'cause that's what my mama taught me to do. Your mama can be really stubborn, so, yeah, we got in a few arguments. She likes to have her way."

"She does!" Gracie nodded. "Like when I want soda? She says, 'Milk today. Maybe you can have soda tomorrow.' But then tomorrow?" The little girl shook her head sadly. "She says milk today—"

"Maybe you can have soda tomorrow?" Beck added.

"Yeah. How'd you know that?"

"She used to tell me that a lot, too. Maybe tomorrow." His gaze locked on Tansy again, and she felt heat flood her face. They were absolutely not talking about soda anymore.

Gracie pulled away from her mother and scrambled to her feet. "You like soda, too?"

Beck laughed. "Yeah, I do."

She released a long, pity-me sigh. "I have to drink milk."

"Milk is actually good for pretty little girls."

"It is?"

"Yep."

"Want some mac and cheese? Mommy made lots. We've got more chairs, too." She slid one out and patted it.

Tansy felt like she'd hopped a runaway freight train. How had this gone from Beck being the bad man to her daughter inviting him to dinner?

Before he could answer, Gracie walked to the counter and stood on tiptoe to look in the dish Beck brought. "What's in here?"

"That's the best banana puddin' you'll ever taste."

"My grandma's banana puddin' is the bestest."

He rolled his eyes. "Then this is the second best."

"'Kay." She turned to her mom. "Can we have banana puddin' for dessert, Mama?"

"Sure." Tansy's manners got the better of her. "Would you like some mac and cheese, Beck?"

She knew that he knew she'd rather have bitten off her tongue than ask. It had to be pretty clear, even to him, that she didn't want him there tonight.

Still—and maybe because of that—he said, "I'd love some. I haven't had dinner yet, and I have it on great authority that you make a mean mac and cheese."

He winked at Gracie and she giggled.

"Does he have to drink milk, too, Mama?"

When she opened her mouth, more than a little flustered, Beck piped up. "You know what? I'd love a glass of ice-cold milk."

The time for Gracie to go to bed had long since come and gone. Tansy had procrastinated, but Beck and Gracie, their heads practically bumping, sat at the cleared table coloring Princess Aurora and her friends. His curly blond hair contrasted with Gracie's straight, dark hair.

It made her want things that could never be.

Why wouldn't he go home?

"Beck, I'm sorry, but I need to get Gracie off to bed."

"No problem. I'll wait on the porch while you get her settled."

Now the man was being obtuse. On purpose. Frowning but not wanting to argue in front of Gracie, Tansy scooped up her daughter and turned, fully intending to leave him sitting there.

"Will you tuck me in, Beck?"

Tansy stopped halfway to the stairs. Gracie raised her head from her mom's shoulder and looked up at her.

"I want him to," she whispered.

"Tansy?" Beck looked to her for guidance.

"Sure. That would be great. But he can't stay."

"I know, Mama."

Beck followed them up the stairs, with a suddenly shy Gracie smiling at him over her mother's shoulder. As they hit the landing, he blinked. He hadn't been up here since early in the renovations, leaving that to Charlie and the crew. He hadn't wanted to see her private area, hadn't wanted to imagine her here.

Now, he had to hand it to her. She'd done a bang-up job designing the space. She'd opened two of the rooms totally and gotten rid of the hall to provide more family space.

He didn't see the polished, expensive furniture he'd expected or the fancy bric-a-brac. Instead, the place was homey and comfortable. He found it restful.

She'd kept everything bright and fresh. The two sofas were slipcovered in white cotton. Throw pillows in bright colors and designs had been tossed haphazardly on them. A very solid-looking wood plank coffee table sat between the sofas on a multicolored rug. A black-and-white ottoman provided additional seating. A dresser painted sunshine yellow sat against the far wall, a mirror resting on it. Nothing was new.

It matched the kitchen she'd had his men install—simple and basic. She'd left the beadboard in place and run white cabinets along two of the walls. Stainless-steel appliances, good quality black quartz countertops, and a splash of red finished the room.

"If you'll give us a few minutes, Beck, I'll help her into her pj's."

"Works for me." When she disappeared, he walked over to the bookcase tucked under a window. He loved to see what people read. Tansy's shelves surprised him. They held one of the most eclectic mixes he'd ever seen.

Cake decorating, wedding planning, and recipe books. Those didn't surprise him. Furniture restoration, flea market finds, and decorating on a dime. Those *did* surprise him.

Mysteries, romances, civil war history, and Dr. Seuss filled the remaining shelves. What had she put on the shelves in her bedroom?

Beck turned and examined the room again. Where were all the expensive things he'd expected? All the sleek wood, the crystal baubles, the high-end furniture and art?

The question nagged at him.

One and one weren't adding up to two, and unless he was very mistaken, something was off.

She'd done the remodel on a shoestring budget, and even then, she'd borrowed from the bank to pay for the changes and the equipment and supplies to get her new business up and running. He wasn't supposed to know that, but they lived in a small town. If anybody in Misty Bottoms believed they had secrets, they'd be sorely mistaken.

And that included him. Since Tansy had returned, the number of pitying looks and hand pats he'd received had him nearly running for the hills. He'd guess some were actually upset he hadn't broken down in an inconsolable heap now that his ex-girlfriend and former fiancée had returned. No doubt more than one citizen hoped for a splashy confrontation or breakdown.

Neither was gonna happen.

At Saturday's wedding, he'd felt like a specimen under glass. He could only imagine how Tansy felt, but she'd kept it together. Until Missy Frampton, anyway.

Best to ignore all the busybodies and their gossip, because sooner or later, somebody else would screw up or win the lottery and take him and Tansy off the front page.

—— ⁓ ——

"Beck?"

"Yeah." He turned to see Tansy watching him.

"Gracie Bella's ready for you." Her forehead creased. "Are you sure you want to do this?"

"It's good, sugar. Your little girl's a real sweetheart. It won't be any hardship at all to tuck her in."

"Okay, then."

He followed her down the now-much-shorter hallway.

At Gracie's bedroom, his hand involuntarily tightened around the jamb. There were the bunk beds his grandfather had built. How many times had he and Cole, or he and Wes, or, heck, all three of them bunked down in this room?

And now Tansy's little girl would sleep here.

The room looked the same but different. Gone were the blue and green walls. Tansy had painted them the color of cotton candy, then whitewashed over that. The bedcovers? More girly pink.

Even the ladder to the top bunk had been painted pink.

A paper chain, like the ones they used to make in school at Christmas time, stretched over her dresser. A little lamp, with its flowery shade, shed a pale light over the room.

A man would have to guard both his testosterone and his man card if he spent much time in here.

He knelt beside the bed and tucked the covers around her. Then, leaning close, breathing in her little-girl scent, he whispered in her ear.

She giggled and wrapped her arms around him, hugging him tightly.

He hugged her right back and dropped a soft, little kiss on her cheek.

~~~

Tansy's heart hiccupped watching Beck's blond head bent over her daughter's dark one. But when he stood, she managed a wobbly smile.

"'Night, sweetheart. Pleasant dreams."

"You too, Mama."

Gracie's eyes had already closed, dark lashes fanning over her cheeks by the time Tansy pulled the door partially shut.

She walked ahead of Beck and straight down the stairs, expecting him to leave.

He didn't.

"Why don't you come outside for a bit? It's a nice night."

"Beck, I still have lots to do."

"It's late. It'll wait till morning. Besides, I won't stay but another minute."

On a sigh, she followed him out the back door, onto the wide porch. He was right. The night was soft and moonlit, perfect for back-porch sitting. Should she offer him something to drink besides milk?

She didn't, out of self-preservation. If he stayed much longer, she'd break down in tears. Being around him like this and not being able to touch, to taste, was unbearable. She didn't want to be friends with him.

But she'd try.

She settled in a rocker while he dropped onto the old porch swing that had been his grandfather's.

"Once the bakery opens, Gracie and I will eat

upstairs," Tansy said. "We ate in the kitchen tonight so I could finish some computer inventory and check my supply list."

"It makes sense, and it's your house to do with as you want."

That had to hurt like a sore tooth...or had he finally come to terms with her ownership of the Elliot homestead?

She wished she'd poured them some tea. Her mouth was Sahara dry. "I know you didn't want me here, Beck, not in Misty Bottoms or in your grandfather's home, but—"

He glanced toward the house, the open windows. "Let's not talk about that right now. Gracie might not be asleep. Little ears..." He shrugged.

"Thank you."

"She's a beautiful child, Tansy. She's done nothin' wrong."

Tansy winced at the implication. She *had* done something wrong.

She forced herself to put the thought away as they sat together enjoying the night sounds, the smell of jasmine and late roses from the backyard. She found herself relaxing for the first time all day.

She saw his smile in the soft light of the moon. "What?"

"You need to do this more often, Tanz. Take time for yourself. And I need to go home. Get some sleep."

Pushing himself from the swing, he said, "Thanks for dinner."

"You're very welcome." Even to her own ears, she sounded like a prim, old-maid schoolteacher.

Oh, well. For all practical purposes, she was an old maid.

He stepped into the darkness and headed for his truck and home.

Letting his mother badger him into bringing the pudding over tonight had been one thing. Staying? Another matter entirely. But when Gracie asked him to stay for dinner and pulled out a chair for him? How could anyone say no to that child?

Then he'd compounded his error by sitting in the dark with Tansy. He swiped the bead of sweat off his forehead. Stupid times ten!

The moonlight had shifted across her face as it dodged in and out of the clouds, and he'd tried to read her expressions, as ever changing as that silver beam of light.

He'd let nostalgia get the best of him, had allowed himself to get wrapped up in the pretty picture of home and family tonight. But Gracie wasn't his, and neither was Tansy. Maybe he should have that tattooed on his forehead.

Chapter 17

Beck kept promising to put some distance between himself and Tansy, yet here he stood on her front porch. Again.

Why?

Hell, his crew had done the work here, hadn't they? What kind of a boss would he be if he didn't check it out before he sent her a final bill? He'd always done that before and didn't intend to stop now.

A rueful, half laugh escaped. Maybe somewhere in the great state of Georgia he could find some sucker who'd actually believe that BS.

That damned moth-candle syndrome. That's what it was. Tansy drew him to her, and even knowing the consequences, he couldn't resist.

He raised a hand to knock but stopped, trying to decide on the best approach.

It turned out he shouldn't have sweat it. While he flip-flopped between excuses for showing up, the woman herself came around the side yard, a smile on her face.

"I thought I heard your truck." She climbed the stairs and opened the door. "Come on in."

He stepped inside to a whole new world. He hadn't seen this room last night. Two miniature tables, one painted a soft pink, the other a delicate lavender, brought a sparkle of sunshine to the corner where his grandmother's hutch had stood. Dainty lace tablecloths covered them, and both had been arranged with child-sized tea sets.

Despite himself, Beck grinned. What little girl wouldn't be in seventh heaven here? And, while the little girls entertained themselves, mamas could drink tea and gossip with their own girlfriends.

The rest of the room was waiting for her touch. Furniture and boxes were strewn haphazardly over it.

Oh, yeah. Tansy knew what she was doing. But the house was no longer Pops and Grandma Elsie's.

"You've been busy."

"I have, and you're out and about early," she said.

"So are you." He nodded toward the roses she held.

"Tomorrow's my grand opening, and that makes me both ecstatic and queasy. There's still so much to do before Sweet Dreams opens its doors."

She looked one step away from panic. Lots to do and not enough time, and now he'd shown up at her door. Since his reason for coming was nebulous even to him, it could wait.

"It looks good to me, Tanz."

"Do you mean that, Beck?"

"I do. I won't keep you. Just stopped by to make sure my guys got everything done."

"Charlie and his crew went way above and beyond for me."

"If you don't mind, I'll do a quick inspection, then leave you to it. From what I saw last night, the upstairs looks good, so we won't worry about that today. This floor is top priority."

Without waiting for an answer, he took off for the

kitchen, even though he'd seen it last night. Charlie had already done a final check on both floors, but what the hey? He'd needed to see her again, and how pathetic was that?

"You want coffee?" Tansy called to him.

"Nope, already had one. Thanks."

———

Ten minutes later, Tansy stood by the front window, once again watching Beck's taillights. She seemed to have developed a new hobby. This morning's visit surprised her. She could have sworn Charlie'd already done an inspection.

Not her worry. The guys would work that out. But she'd think of Beck today and that male essence that was his alone.

Enough. She scrubbed her hands over her face. She had the last bit of inventory to unpack, the last of the tables to arrange, and pastries to bake. How would she get it done?

Her mother had picked up Gracie earlier and, God bless her, had brought breakfast. Now, here she was alone.

First things first. She made herself a fresh cappuccino with her new espresso machine. The coffeemaker was so beautiful it made her want to weep. Actually, the entire shop did.

Hers. All hers.

The grin that split her face should probably be illegal. Carrying her caffeine-laden drink to a table by the bay window, she started a list. Within the first sixty seconds, she'd hit number twelve and her grin disappeared.

The front door opened and in walked Jenni Beth and Cricket.

"Got more of that fancy coffee, Tanz?" Jenni Beth, her long, blond hair pulled back in a ponytail, wore jeans as old as Tansy's own and a long-sleeved blouse.

"I want one, too," Cricket said.

Sam called her his little pixie, and Tansy could see why. Her short, blond hair looked like a cyclone had hit it, and it suited her perfectly. She wore a pair of dark-green cargo pants and a baggy sweatshirt. Emerald-green crystals sparkled at her ears.

"What are you doin'?" Jenni Beth peered over her shoulder.

"Makin' a list of the day's have-to-dos."

Reading over Tansy's shoulder, Cricket whistled. "Good thing we showed up, huh?"

"What?"

"Do your magic with that fancy machine. After we savor every last drop, we'll split up this list and get it done."

"You've come to help?"

Jenni Beth nodded. "I don't have anything pressing today, and Darlene's sister is watching the flower shop. So we're all yours."

She went misty-eyed and Jenni Beth shook her head. "Uh-uh. No tears. I have a vested interest here. I have a wedding coming up, and I need another cake. One of yours. After last Saturday's, your name's on every bride's lips!"

"It went well, didn't it? Your planning and Magnolia House, Cricket's magnificent flowers, and my cake."

The other two nodded.

"And soon? I'll make my best friend's wedding

cake!" She did a little happy dance on her way to the espresso machine. "Remember how we talked into the wee hours of the night when we had sleepovers? About what we'd wear, how we'd fix our hair, our flowers."

"I do. It was Cole then, and it's Cole now."

Tansy and Cricket both sighed.

Tansy placed a steaming cup of rich, dark coffee in front of each of them, along with a creamer. "You're lucky, Jenni Beth."

"Don't I know it! I did everything in my power to chase the man off, but he stuck." She ran a finger over the diamond on her finger.

Tansy grinned. "I'm so happy for both of you."

"Are we making it harder on you?" Jenni Beth asked quietly.

"No." Tansy shook her head. "Absolutely not. I can't wait to dig into your wedding."

"We're keepin' it small."

"That's what you say *now*, wedding planner."

"We are!" Jenni Beth sent Tansy another appraising look.

"Look. Let's address the elephant in the room and have done with it," Tansy said. "This...thing with Beck. It's my mess. He loved me, and I walked away from him. With no warning, no explanation, I married Emerson. But now, thank God, that's behind me."

"Can we just call your ex 'the butthead' from now on?" Cricket asked.

Tansy smiled. "Works for me." She sobered. "Except when Gracie's around."

Both nodded.

"I could talk to Beck," Cricket began.

"No. I hurt him. Badly. First by betraying him, then by buying this house. We're makin' some progress, but where we go from here has to be his decision."

"He never got over you," Jenni Beth said.

Tansy finished her coffee. "He should have moved on, should have married and had children of his own. He's always wanted a big family."

"He's dated—a lot. And came close once."

"But he never made the leap."

"It would have broken your heart if he had."

"But he'd be happy."

As she carried their cups to the dishwasher, she had to admit that the idea of Beck married to someone else nearly killed her—and that probably hadn't helped her own marriage any.

Although it really wouldn't have mattered.

If she'd loved Emer—the butthead, it would have hurt when she'd left him. It hadn't. Still, she'd tried to make the marriage work for Gracie's sake. His gambling and lying made it impossible, and now the marriage was over and she had a new life, wonderful friends, and a future.

Albeit without Beck.

She sighed and reached for her ever-present antacids. She'd have to stop popping these things. Soon.

Cricket turned the list so she could read it easier. "All right if I unpack the cups and saucers?"

"You bet."

"I'll do the first three items on the list," Jenni Beth volunteered. "Why don't you start baking? That's something Cricket and I can't do. But we'll be here to taste test for you."

"Tough job," Cricket said, "but somebody's got to do it, right?"

Tansy nodded, then flicked back the lace panel at the window. Beck's Ram pickup drove past slowly.

The other two crowded in behind her, elbowing each other for room.

His eyes, shaded by dark glasses, seemed to bore right through Tansy. Then he hit the gas and disappeared.

"Does he do that often?" Cricket asked.

She nodded.

"Seems my cousin is interested. Very interested."

Tansy shrugged. "Maybe he's heading to a job."

"Driving that slowly?" Jenni Beth asked.

"He stopped in for a few minutes this morning."

"Really?"

"He's curious. After all, this was his grandpa's house, and his crew did the remodel."

Jenni Beth's hands went to her hips. "Are you stickin' up for him?"

"No! I'm just sayin'—"

Cricket shook her head. "Why was he so stubborn about you and this house?"

"Because he's an Elliot," Tansy replied.

Cricket's mouth opened. "So am I. Well, my mama is."

Jenni Beth simply looked at Cricket.

"I'm not stubborn," Cricket argued.

"Seriously? You sent Sam back to New York."

"That was different. Entirely."

Jenni Beth arched a brow, then picked up the list. "Everyone understand their jobs?"

"Yes."

"Yeah."

In no time, the girls had supplies and inventory unloaded and put away, tables polished, and fresh flowers on each. Lace doilies under glass decorated the tables, and the enticing smell of vanilla and chocolate floated through the rooms.

Jenni Beth slipped into the kitchen to watch Tansy decorate the latest batch of cupcakes. After the sixth or seventh one, she wrapped an arm around her friend's waist. "Sweet Dreams is exactly that, Tanz. Wipe that frosting off your hands and come look."

She did. The display cases, lined with paper doilies, waited for her creations. Wall shelves held teas and fragile-looking cup and saucers for sale. Stacks of sturdy coffee cups in all the colors of the rainbow had *Sweet Dreams* splashed on the side of them. Some would be used to serve coffee, while others would be sold as souvenirs or gifts.

Easy chairs sat in pairs around small tables. Slipcovered dining room chairs had been placed around larger tables, and the chandeliers sparkled. And in the middle of it all? Two of the best friends a girl could ever have.

A huge chalkboard hung on the wall, and Cricket, after consulting her several times, had written tomorrow's selections on it. Jenni Beth had helped her hang the bulletin board by the front door. Tansy intended to leave notices and business cards on it, along with photos of her customers' special moments. She wanted Sweet Dreams to belong to Misty Bottomers. Wanted it to be a place where her customers felt welcome and at home. Prayed it would be a place they visited often.

She reached into her pocket and pulled out the photo

her mother had taken at the tea party as well as the one Beck had taken of them toasting each other at the wedding.

Tansy tacked them on the board. "Sweet Dreams's first special memories."

Tansy took one last look around the first floor. Miraculously, everything was finished.

Jenni Beth and Cricket had left half an hour ago. As soon as the last batch of brownies came out of the oven, she was leaving, too. Time to go to her mom's to pick up Gracie. Her mom had offered to fix dinner for the three of them, and Tansy hadn't put up any fuss. She was tired.

Her palms grew sweaty thinking about tomorrow.

Her mom would swing by early, take Gracie to pre-school, then come back to help.

Her cell rang.

"Hello?"

"Hear you're opening your new business tomorrow."

Her knees went weak, and she sank into the closest chair. Butthead. She grabbed her water bottle and took a sip while her mind raced.

"Tansy?"

"I'm busy. Is there something you want?"

"Yeah. I've changed my mind. I want our daughter."

The blood rushed from her head.

Oh God!

"I don't understand." Her lips would barely move, barely form the words.

The front door opened, and her gaze flew to it. She hadn't locked up when the girls left, and for one awful second, she thought it was Emerson come for her daughter.

It was Beck.

She stared at him silently.

"What's wrong?"

In a few giant strides, he crossed to her.

"Who's that?" Emerson asked.

She shook her head. "No one." Her eyes met Beck's. "A friend."

She thought she'd either throw up or pass out.

"Is Gracie okay?" Beck asked quietly.

She nodded.

"Your mom?"

She nodded again, fighting back tears now.

He took the phone from her nerveless fingers. "Who is this?"

"I might ask the same."

"What's goin' on? Tansy looks like hell."

A smarmy laugh answered him. "Nothing new there. This is her husband."

Beck saw red. "I believe you mean ex-husband, don't you?"

"You sleepin' with my wife?"

"What do you want, Forbes?"

"My daughter."

Beck's head snapped around to Tansy. No wonder she looked like death warmed over.

"Put my wife back on the phone."

"Your *ex*-wife." He handed the phone to Tansy and started to move away. He should leave. But, God, she looked so fragile. So incredibly beautiful and so, so wounded. From what he'd heard, Forbes had never filled the role of dad while he'd lived with Gracie. What kind of a game was he playing?

"The divorce papers are very clear, Emerson. I have full custody of Gracie Bella. You're out of my life and hers." She listened another minute, then said, "Try it. You won't win." She powered off the phone, threw it onto the table, and buried her head in her hands. Her shoulders shook with her weeping.

Her tears ripped through Beck. No way in hell could he leave. Not now.

"Tansy—"

"Go away. Please. Just leave me alone."

For several seconds, he stood, torn by indecision. He looked at the door, then back at her.

"Hell," he growled. "I'm not leavin' you." Placing a finger beneath her chin, he tipped her tear-drenched face till their eyes met. "It'll be okay."

"He wants to take my baby." Her voice broke.

"He won't." He dropped to one knee and drew her to him, held her while she cried. Rubbing her back, he pushed that incredible, fiery hair away from her face.

When she still didn't stop, he stood, scooping her into his arms. Then he sat back on the chair and simply hugged her close.

"Go ahead, sugar. Get it out. When you're done, we'll talk about what we need to do."

"Not we. Me." She sniffled. "He doesn't love her."

"Where is she now?"

"Gracie? With my mom. I'm supposed to be there for dinner."

The sun had gone down. Beck pulled his cell from his pocket and texted Rexanna.

Tansy will be a little late.

His phone buzzed.

Should I put Gracie to bed?

He thumbed back a quick Yes.

Her response came quickly. Have fun!

Oh, if she only knew.

On second thought, it was better she didn't.

Finally, Tansy went quiet. Beck was almost afraid to breathe. Had she fallen asleep? He felt like a wet dishcloth that had been wrung out, then wadded up and thrown away. A sucker for tears under any circumstances, these killed him. They'd torn their way from her.

Streetlights came on outside the window.

He laid a hand on her cheek. "Sweetheart, look at me."

She did. Her eyes were red and tears clung to her eyelashes. His stomach twisted. This woman had no idea the power she held over him. One look, one word, and he wanted to hand her the world.

Except she didn't want it from him.

"What am I going to do, Beck? I don't have the money to fight the kind of lawyers his parents can hire."

"Did you spend your settlement?"

"Settlement?" She gave a watery laugh. "Oh, Beck, there was no settlement. I walked away with the clothes on my back and Gracie. Very little else. No money at all."

His brain went on hold. Had he been so wrong all this time? Yet hadn't he wondered? Little things hadn't added up, had nagged at him, yet he'd brushed them away along with his mother's words. "I don't understand."

"Emerson has a gambling problem. Despite several

rehab stints, he lost everything we had. I'm so ashamed."
Another tear trickled down her cheek.

"Why are *you* ashamed?"

"I couldn't fix it."

And there was the girl he'd fallen in love with, the one who wanted to take care of the world.

"Gracie was nothing but a liability to Emerson. Neither he nor his parents even asked for visitation rights. Until now." Her face crumpled again.

"The divorce is final, isn't it?"

"Yes. Months ago."

"So what's he up to?"

"I don't know. He might want money. His parents have pretty much cut him off, and he doesn't have access to his trust fund."

"He'd use his own daughter to extort money from you?"

"In a heartbeat."

"Let me call Kemper Dobson. I'll put him on this."

Tansy laid her hand on his arm. "Beck, I can't afford a lawyer."

"Do you have a choice?"

"No."

"Then let's get Kemper's take."

"Why would you get involved in this?"

Their eyes met. "Let's just say for old time's sake."

She sat quietly while he talked to the family's long-time attorney.

When he hung up, she asked, "What did he say?"

"He wants you to stop by tomorrow. He understands you'll have a really busy day, so any time that works for you."

She nodded.

"After you talk, he'll call the prick and remind him he's already signed off on custody. He'll let him know that if he asks for anything, it'll smack of extortion. Kemper will be subtle, but he'll get his point across." He rubbed his stomach. "Let's talk about this over dinner. I'm so hungry I could eat a bear."

Her nose wrinkled.

"Okay, bear's off the menu. How about pizza?"

"Gracie—"

"I sent your mom a text. Gracie's had dinner and is spending the night there."

"Thank you."

He took her hand in his, shocked at how cold it felt. "I could almost feel sorry for the jerk. He'll never experience the joy Gracie would have brought him."

"You're a good man, Beck Elliot."

"Damn right, Tansy Calhoun." He pulled her to her feet. "Time for dinner."

She scrubbed at her face and ran a hand over her hair. "I can't go anywhere looking like this."

"No, I don't suppose you feel much like kickin' up your heels. Don't worry. I've got it covered."

Hitting the number for Mama's Pizza and Wings, he ordered a pizza to go. Putting a hand over the receiver, he asked, "Do you still eat pepperoni and jalapeños? You pop antacids like candy."

Her face flamed. "Yes, I do. To both."

"All right." He finished the order, then said, "Grab a sweater. We're eatin' al fresco tonight."

Chapter 18

TANSY'S HEAD HURT FROM CRYING. SHE HATED THAT Beck had witnessed her meltdown but was, at the same time, grateful for him. Emerson's call had chilled her to the bone. Gracie was hers, not his.

This had nothing to do with him wanting his daughter. It was either about money or his ego. He'd lost everything, while she'd landed on her feet.

She closed the door to her beautiful shop and locked up, her heart heavy. Beck took her hand, and anger, pain, and regret folded together. Unlike a soufflé, though, so light and airy, these ingredients produced something vile—emotions that ate her up, had her stomach in knots.

Beck's truck sat beneath the streetlight, but it wasn't the big Dodge Ram he usually drove. Nope. He'd come in his '65 Chevy short-bed stepside pickup. He'd bought the truck while he was in high school, working at the family's lumberyard. As always, the thing was polished to within an inch of its life.

"You still have it." Tansy ran a hand along the truck bed. "I thought you would've sold it by now."

"Nope. She's mine. When I fall in love with somethin', it's forever."

"Beck..."

"Forget I said that."

As if. Her hand trailed over the side of the truck

and moved lower on the fender, right above the back tire. The dent was still there, and she felt a tug on her heart. Her dad had put it there. She and Beck had missed curfew. By a lot.

When they'd pulled in, Dad stood on the porch beneath the light, shifting the ball back and forth between hands. The minute she opened her door and stepped out, he winged the baseball at the truck's side, and Beck took off like a shot.

"You left me there to face Dad alone."

"Yeah, and I'm real sorry about that."

She studied him. "No, you're not."

"You're right. I'm not." He chuckled. "My life would have ended right then and there if I'd stayed. Your dad was pissed! I'd never guessed he had an arm like that. I did feel bad leaving you to face him alone, though."

"Right."

He opened the truck door and took her hand to help her up. Then he went 'round to the driver's side, got in, and started his baby. He said nothing more. No doubt he was as lost in the past as she was.

Sealed inside the small space with him, with darkness closing around them, the truck felt intimate, and her senses went into overdrive. She ran a hand over the smooth leather of the seat. Classical music played on the radio. That side of Beck always surprised her. He'd never seemed the Beethoven type to her. Over and above all that, though, was the smell. The inside of the truck smelled of leather and Beck.

She sighed.

"It'll be okay, Tansy, trust me."

She nodded.

"When we get to Mama's Pizza and Wings, you can wait in the truck."

"By al fresco, did you mean eating in your truck with the windows down?"

"Nah." He shook his head.

"I'm not going to your house."

"Understood." His voice was tight.

She raised her hand. "I'm sor—"

"Do not apologize again. I'm warnin' you."

"Fine." Her hand jumped into her lap to join the other.

He reached out and swallowed one of her hands in his big one. "And don't wring your hands. I'm not the big bad wolf here—or the monster."

They rode in silence the rest of the way. When the neon sign for the pizza restaurant came into sight, her hand was still tucked firmly inside Beck's. She'd missed that, the small contact with another person.

Her eyes misted, and she blinked rapidly. There must be an awful lot of pollen in the air because her eyes seemed to be watering constantly since she'd hit the Misty Bottoms town limit.

⸙

Beck hurried inside, afraid to take too long. Tansy was a whole bunch of squirrelly tonight. If the pizza wasn't ready, he was liable to go out to an empty truck.

"Hey, Hannah. My order ready?"

"Let me check." The brunette headed into the kitchen and came back with his food. "Anything else?"

"Yeah. How about a couple sweet teas?"

"Sure thing."

"See you traded the green and blue streaks in your hair for pink ones."

"You like them?"

"Yeah, strangely enough, I do. They suit you."

The young waitress smiled shyly and handed him his drinks.

He paid, then headed out the door. Tansy spotted him and reached out the window for their teas.

"The pizza smells delicious. I didn't realize how hungry I was till I rolled down my window."

"Then let's go. We're five minutes from our destination." He drove down to the river and grabbed a blanket from the back. "Thought we could eat under the stars."

"Thank you."

"No thanks needed. You've had a big day and a tough evening. Time to shut it down." He turned the key to accessories and fiddled with the radio. A quiet country song floated into the night air. "Why don't you get the drinks? I've got the pizza and napkins."

They ate cross-legged on a blanket he had stashed behind his seat. From the size of her, Beck didn't figure Tansy had been eating all that well, so when she reached for a second piece, he nearly did a fist pump.

She polished it off, then wiped her hands on one of the paper napkins. "I can't eat another bite."

"Me, either."

He lay back on the blanket and drew her down beside him. Her head rested on his chest, and he wrapped an arm around her. The night was alive with sound as the river flowed softly past and cicadas serenaded them.

How many nights had he lain in bed imagining

exactly this but knowing it would never be? He'd had his chance, and it had slipped through his fingers.

Yet here they were.

His fingers stroked her arm, and he wished she weren't wearing that sweater he'd told her to grab. The black cashmere was soft, but Tansy's bare skin? Infinitely better.

He kissed the top of her head and when she sighed, he nearly came undone.

His hand found hers, and they laced fingers. Overhead, more and more stars twinkled. He recognized the Big Dipper with the North Star at the end of its handle. Moonlight reflected in the water, and a gentle breeze rustled the leaves overhead.

He could lie there forever.

Yet the past nagged him. Tonight was a time out of time, and tomorrow all the problems between them would return. If only he could understand why she'd left him. He wanted so badly to ask her, but she'd suffered too much tonight already. He refused to add to it...

But then immediately, on a resigned sigh, he thought, *Yeah, I will.* The dark added a slightly anonymous touch, almost as if he were wearing a mask. She wouldn't be able to see his face. See the hurt.

"You broke my heart, Tansy." His voice sounded rusty.

"I know."

"Why'd you do it?"

"It's complicated."

"Okay." He nodded. "I might not be one of those college boys you're used to, but try me. Maybe I can understand."

"I didn't mean it that way, Beck. I've never thought of you as—"

"Dumb?"

She gasped. "Don't you dare talk about yourself that way!" She pinched his arm.

"Ouch! Jeez, Tansy, that hurt!"

"Good! Look at what you've accomplished. What you've done."

"Yeah." He hated the derisive tone in his voice but was helpless to change it. "I took over a business my dad and grandfather built. Whoopee."

Tansy came up on her elbow and invaded his personal space. "You're seriously pissing me off, Beck Elliot. Besides, *if* it mattered to me—which it doesn't—you have a college degree." Then she flopped onto her back. "Are you still mad at me?" She spoke so quietly he could barely hear her.

"Honestly?"

"Yes."

"Actually, I'm madder. You left me for a jerk who's willing to use his own child as leverage. That's about as low as it gets, yet you chose him. I don't understand."

"I—"

"No." He rolled onto his side to face her. "As much as I want to know, not tonight. I shouldn't have brought it up. It's too important, and right now I'm upset. And you? You're… Well, let's just say you're more than a little worked up, too. My bad."

He raised her hand to his lips and gently kissed the tips of her fingers, then dropped her hand and, in one smooth motion, rose to his feet.

After she, too, stood, he wadded the blanket into a ball and picked up the cardboard pizza box. She grabbed what was left of their iced teas, and together, they walked back to the truck.

"Un-Break My Heart" by Toni Braxton came on the radio, and he groaned out loud.

Again, very, very bad timing.

Tansy stopped. She raised her face to the sky, the moon glinting off that incredible mass of red hair and those sharp cheekbones.

Beck swore and punched the off button.

———

When they pulled up in front of her house, Beck hopped out and hurried around to open her door.

"Thank you."

He didn't take her hand this time, didn't help her out. Today had been the biggest roller-coaster ride of her life. She'd had the best time with Jenni Beth and Cricket, and her new business opened tomorrow.

Then Emerson and Beck had happened.

Emerson? All bad. No way in hell would she let him have Gracie. He might be her daughter's biological father, but that was the beginning and end of his involvement. He'd never have married her if it hadn't been for that damnable text his mother'd found.

And Beck? His role in the day was almost impossible to categorize. Up, down, up, down. She hated that it would end on a down, but she'd grown used to disappointments. She'd survive.

She stepped onto the porch and turned to thank him again. Instead, she gave a surprised yelp. The man was so close she actually grazed his nose with her forehead.

"You shouldn't be alone tonight."

Her heart thudded. "Beck—"

"I know you. The minute I'm out the door, you'll make

yourself sick worryin' about that phone call. Besides, I wouldn't put it past the jerk to call again tonight. I'm stayin', Tansy Elizabeth. I'll sleep on the couch."

Her mind went blank.

"If you don't have an extra blanket, I'll run out to the truck and shake off the one we used earlier."

"I have plenty of blankets, but Gracie—"

"Your mom has that under control."

She fumbled with the keys. After three tries, he took them from her and opened the door.

Stepping inside, he flicked on the lights, then stood in place, looking around. "You've done a lot today. I was too afraid you were going to pass out on me earlier to notice much else." He moved into the sales area.

"Your grandfather stopped in again yesterday."

Beck grunted.

"He likes what I've done here. He says your grand-mother would approve, too, that she'd like all the people enjoying the house again."

Hands stuffed in his pockets, Beck met her gaze with expressionless eyes. "I need to be up early, and so do you. It's best we hit the sack."

Her mouth went dry; her heart bumped into high gear. She blew out a breath. "Do you want anything? Something to drink?"

"Nope. Just your couch and a pillow."

He followed her up the stairs, and she tried not to think about spending the night under the same roof as this man, the only man who could set her on fire with a single touch.

"Do you want to sleep in Gracie's room?"

"Nah, too many memories there. Besides, it's all girlie."

"I doubt you'd lose any man points for spending a single night there."

"The couch will be fine."

She gathered a pillow and blanket. When she walked into the living room, he sat on the edge of her couch, his boots and socks off, his shirt hanging over the back of one of her dining room chairs.

How long could a person survive without breathing, she wondered, because she was in serious trouble. He quite literally took her breath away. Without a word, she handed him the bedding and scurried down the hallway to the safety of her own bedroom.

Beck heard the snick of her door, then listened for a lock to turn. It never came. If she had any idea how badly he wanted her, she'd triple lock that door and push a dresser in front of it to boot.

He slipped out of his jeans. Then, one blanket beneath him, another over him, he stretched out on the comfy sofa. He had to give Tansy points. She'd made great choices with her furniture. It was a little on the feminine side, but something a guy could live with.

He thought of the old emerald-green sofa in his own house. It needed to be replaced but, boy, he loved that thing. He'd spent a lot of Sunday afternoons on it with pizza and beer, watching football, NASCAR, baseball, hockey, you name it. And the rickety white coffee table was perfect for putting up your feet. Its plastic top cleaned easily and wore like iron. His decor was comfortable and practical. No muss, no fuss.

More than one woman he'd dated had made noises

about redecorating the place, and that generally marked the end of the relationship. It meant they smelled more than an occasional date, more than a tumble once in a while.

He didn't want long-term. He didn't do long-term. Not anymore.

With Tansy, he'd thought future. Marriage. Kids.

Since her? Not in the cards.

He closed his eyes. A mistake.

His imagination kicked in. Not much more than twenty, thirty feet separated them as Tansy uncovered all that perfect, pale skin, that incredible body. What did she wear to bed? Jeez, did she wear *anything* to bed? Did she still sleep on her stomach, one foot hanging out of the covers?

An even bigger question: If he opened her bedroom door right now, would she welcome him or kick his ass out? He half rose, then dropped back onto the sofa. He'd promised to sleep on the couch, so he would.

Would Emerson really try to take Gracie, or had that been idle talk?

Why hadn't Tansy come to him when she'd found out she was pregnant? He'd have married her and loved both her and Gracie.

Life flat-out sucked sometimes.

Reaching up, he switched off the table lamp. This room, or half of it anyway, had been his grandparents' bedroom. So much had changed.

Time would tell what it meant.

He heard water running, then silence.

For a long, long time, he laid in the dark, listening.

Chapter 19

THE PHONE RANG. STARTLED, BECK THREW BACK THE blanket and sat up. Sunlight streamed in through the open drapes. For the space of about thirty seconds, he couldn't remember where he was. Then it hit him.

He'd spent the night with Tansy.

Well, not *with* Tansy, but...

The phone rang again.

All rumpled and sleepy, Tansy stumbled up the hall, ready to pounce on the offending instrument.

He beat her to it, grinning at her openmouthed expression.

"You can't answer my phone," she hissed.

"Fine." He handed her the receiver.

"Hello?" She sent Beck a warning look. "Hi, Mom. Yes, everything's fine." She listened. "Uh-huh. Yes, I was with Beck. Thanks for watching Gracie. What did we do? We, uh, had dinner and talked for a while."

"Tell her what happened," Beck said.

"*Shhh!*"

He realized she regretted the sound instantly.

"Yes, Mom. He's here, but—yes, I'll put him on." She held the receiver to her chest. "Do not get cute. Tell her the truth."

"All of it?"

"Yes! No! Don't tell her about—" She shrugged. "You know."

"Hello, Mrs. Calhoun. How are you this mornin'?"

"Do either of you need me over there?" Rexanna asked. "Either of you need an ambulance? The EMT?"

"No, ma'am, we're both fine."

"It's early, very early, so the question needs to be asked. Did you spend the night with my daughter?"

"I did, but Tansy slept in her room, and I spent the night on the couch."

"Why?"

He almost swallowed his tongue. "Why?"

"A simple question."

He rubbed at his cheek and realized he badly needed a shave. "Why did I spend the night, or why did I sleep on the couch?"

Tansy groaned and stomped her foot. Then she waved her hand across her throat in the "cut" motion. "Give me the phone."

He shook his head.

"I'm guessin' the answer to the second question is that my daughter wouldn't have it any other way. So why did you spend the night?"

"You and your daughter need to have a long talk. That jerk she was married to called last night."

"What did he want?" The genteel Southern woman disappeared, and a mama bear reared her ferocious head.

Beck took note and decided Rexanna Calhoun wasn't anyone he'd want to tangle with. "That's something the two of you need to discuss. In person. I'm leavin' for work now. You won't be long?"

"No. An hour at most. Tell Tansy I have a change of clothes for Gracie. I'll feed her and drop her off at preschool and still be there in plenty of time to help with the opening."

"I will. Listen, when you drop Gracie off, you might want to remind Lucinda to only let her go with you or Tansy."

"This is about Emerson's call."

"Yes. You have a good day."

"Not so fast, Beck. I'm only going to say this once, so listen carefully. My daughter has been through a lot. Don't you add to her hurt."

"No, ma'am. That's not my intention." He hung up and turned to face an upset Tansy.

"Out." She pointed to the stairway. "Now."

"Don't I even get a cup of coffee?"

She arched one brow.

"Hey, it's not my fault she knew I was here. You're the one who shushed me."

With a sigh, she dropped onto the sofa, automatically folding one of the blankets he'd used.

"Tansy, you're not a little girl anymore. For heaven's sake, you were married. You have a child. Your mother isn't harboring the idea that you're still a virgin."

"It doesn't matter. She'll think we slept together."

"I told her we didn't."

"That doesn't mean she believed you."

Was there even a shred of logic in that? Sighing, he ran his fingers through his hair. He needed a trim almost as bad as he needed that shave.

"And you shouldn't have mentioned Emerson's call."

"She needs to know. Look—"

"No, you look. Today's a big day for me. It's my grand opening. My dream! This matters. A lot! I still have no idea why you felt you needed to stay over because Emerson isn't the type to come banging on my door in the middle of the night, insisting I let him in." She held his gaze. "He doesn't care enough to do that."

"You were too upset to be alone. Emerson might not care, but I do."

With that, he picked up his work boots and his keys. Ignoring Tansy's startled expression, he walked downstairs and let himself out.

———

"Why did Beck really stay the night?" Her mother slapped herself on the forehead. "Never mind. Don't answer that. I think the answer falls under TMI."

"No, it doesn't. He did sleep on the couch, Mom."

"That's what he told me, but—"

"Why?" Kitty stuck her head into the dining room.

Oh, jeez. Maybe she should just text the whole town. "Why?"

"You heard me. You have that beautiful man here overnight while Gracie is gone, and you make him sleep on the couch? What's wrong with you?"

"Seriously?"

"Yes, seriously."

"It's complicated." She raised a hand to her forehead. "And that's exactly what I said to Beck last night and offended him. Emerson called."

"And that's another thing. What did he want?"

Her lower lip trembled despite her best intention. "He's taking me back to court. He wants custody of Gracie."

"Over my dead body," her mother said.

"Mine, too." Kitty stepped into the front area. "The

man has caused enough hurt. What would he do with that child?"

"I don't know." Hot tears burned at the back of Tansy's eyes, and she blinked them away.

"You listen to me." Her mother put her hands on her daughter's shoulders. "You're not alone anymore. You have family and friends to stand with you."

She nodded. "Kemper Dobson is already working on it."

"There you go." Kitty applauded with flour-covered hands. "Now put that away for now. Don't let that jerk spoil today for you…and that's an order."

"Yes, ma'am." She snapped a sharp salute.

Even though Emerson's call nagged at the back of her mind, the grand opening went better than she could have imagined. In her wildest dreams, she hadn't expected the outpouring of love and good wishes showered on her…and she'd never needed it more.

From the time they opened the doors, people—singly, in couples, and in groups—filed through. They ate, drank coffee and tea, talked, and laughed. Tansy didn't fool herself into believing this kind of traffic would continue. Right now she was a bit of a novelty. People wanted to check out the new shop, take a peek at the Elliot residence after the remodel, and catch a glimpse of the girl who'd left town, married rich, and came crawling back.

She understood all that.

Still, her pastries were darned good. So was her tea and coffee. And the house? She hugged herself. 321 Main Street looked magnificent.

Jenni Beth and Cole dropped by with both sets of parents.

"This place is crazy." Cole laughed. "It reminds me a little bit of the bar scene in *Star Wars*. A little bit of everything. Looks like your aunt Coralee and the new Baptist minister are havin' themselves a heated discussion."

Tansy nodded. Her aunt had outdone herself today. Her red hair, as untamed as ever, clashed with the pink peasant blouse worn over black-and-white plaid pants. Black Converse tennis shoes completed her outfit.

"Where do you think she finds her clothes?" Jenni Beth asked.

"I have no idea, but the place should be shut down." Tansy topped off their coffee. "I had a nibble on an engagement party at Magnolia House this morning. Eugenie Pryce came in sporting a brand-new engagement ring. Blake proposed last night. She's going to give you a call."

"She'll make a beautiful bride," Jenni Beth said. "I'll see if we can't talk her into having the wedding there, too."

Tansy crossed to her aunt. "More coffee?"

"I think I've had enough." She took Tansy's hand. "Your father would be so proud of you, honey. I wish he were here today."

"Me too."

"I love you, sweetheart." Her aunt kissed her cheek. "Now go take care of your other customers."

Cricket closed the Enchanted Florist for lunch, and she and Sam stopped in. Ms. Hattie and Tansy's second-grade teacher wandered in around two for a spot of tea.

Friends from school asked about the class reunion

they had planned for next month. Since they hadn't met for their five year and didn't want to wait till ten, their always-unique class had decided to throw a seven-and-a-half-year reunion.

When Sawyer Liddell, the sole reporter for the *Bottoms' Daily*, came in to take a few photos and do a quick interview, she noticed Sam giving him the stink eye. She caught, too, the little swat Cricket landed on her fiancé's arm. There was some kind of history there, she thought, as Sam slipped his hand over Cricket's, making it very clear that Cricket was his. *Interesting*. She'd have to talk her friend into spilling the beans.

Beck's mom and dad, along with his grandfather, stopped in for doughnuts and coffee, and Tansy gave them a quick tour of the upstairs and down. When Judy Elliot gave her a huge hug, Tansy wondered if she knew where her son had spent the night.

Probably not.

But then, it didn't really matter, did it? It had been totally innocent. Just another case of Sir Galahad protecting the damsel in distress.

"You've done a good thing here, honey. I'm proud of you." Judy hugged her again.

Judy's son, however, was a no-show. But he did send flowers—a huge, happy bouquet of sunflowers, soft yellow roses, and lavender sweet pea.

At one, he sent a text asking if she'd seen the lawyer.

Appointment at four, she texted back.

For the next few days, Tansy kept so busy she didn't know which end was up. With the lawyer's help, she prayed her problem with Emerson was under control. As far as the shop went, her mother and Kitty both pitched in when they could. Still, the responsibility rested on her shoulders, and she worked harder than the others put together.

A glance at the clock showed it was closing time. At last. She flipped the sign in the window to "Closed," turned off the coffee machine, and breathed a sigh of relief. After the lunch rush, she'd sent her helpers home.

Right now, she wanted to soak both her feet and her body in a nice, hot bath.

First, though, her daughter, who sat at the kitchen table coloring, needed food.

While she was deciding what to fix for dinner, the phone rang.

Emerson.

Chapter 20

"HOW'S YOUR NEW BUSINESS GOING?"

Just the sound of Emerson's voice sent Tansy into a nosedive. "Very well."

"Glad to hear it."

She went on full alert.

"Guess you won't mind lending me a hundred thousand then, will you?"

"Excuse me?"

"Do that, and I won't press the custody thing."

Her heart hit the floor.

"Mama, is that Daddy? Can I talk to him?" Gracie Bella reached for the phone.

"I don't want to talk to her, Tansy. I don't have time for her nonsense."

Gracie had been close enough to hear Emerson's words, and her lip trembled.

Tansy wrapped an arm around her and drew her close. "It's okay, baby."

"When can you get me that money?"

"Where are you?" Tansy asked.

"In rehab."

"You have a phone in rehab?"

"My roomie smuggled one in."

Gracie had moved from upset to full-cry mode.

"Good-bye, Emerson. Don't call again. There's nothing here for you."

His tone turned whiny. "Look, I owe some guys, nasty guys. If you don't help me out—"

Shaking, she hung up and held her daughter close, making little comforting sounds.

Behind her, Beck cleared his throat.

When she spun around, eyes wide, he held up a hand. "I didn't mean to eavesdrop, but the back door was open."

Gracie reached for him, and he took her from Tansy, cupped the back of her head when she snuggled in close. Over her head, he met Tansy's eyes.

"If he's in rehab, the judge won't override the custody ruling."

"Are you sure?"

"Positive. I'll talk to Kemper again." He stepped closer and drew her into his and Gracie's circle.

For several minutes, the three stood silently.

"I can't drag you into this, Beck. It's my mess."

"And I'm a friend who wants to help."

She nodded, a few tears of her own escaping.

"Don't cry, Mama." Gracie kissed her.

"It's okay, baby." Tansy took her daughter from Beck and set her on her feet.

"You're white as a sheet," Beck said. "You're not gonna pass out, are you?"

"No."

"Would you mind if I had Sam give him a call?"

"What good would that do?"

"Sam's the law. People tend to back off when the law gets involved."

She nodded. "If he can find out where Emerson is, I'm fine with that."

"Good." Beck nodded at the dish he'd abandoned by

her door. "Mom sent another casserole over. I came up with a hundred and one reasons why bringing it to you wasn't a good idea, but Judy Elliot simply wears a body out. The woman shot down every single reason I threw at her." He looked at her, at Gracie. "Thank God my mom's so stubborn."

"I'll call and thank her." Tansy picked up the casserole. "It's still warm." Lifting the cover, she smiled. "Your mom's scalloped potatoes and ham. Why don't you have a plate with us?"

"That's probably not a good idea."

She laid a hand on her daughter's head. "Gracie, Beck's staying for dinner again. Isn't that nice?"

"Oooh, that's playin' dirty."

She smiled, a dimple winking in her right cheek. "Yes, it is. I'll let you set the table."

"Will you read me a bedtime story, Beck?" Gracie asked.

"I sure will."

"'Kay." She patted his cheek.

She popped an M&M in her mouth while Tansy popped another antacid.

Him? He could use a beer. But that would have to wait.

―――

After Gracie'd been tucked into bed, Tansy started making noises about it being late. In other words, it was time for him to leave—except he wasn't ready yet.

"Why don't we have another cup of coffee and talk a bit?" he said. "Sit. I'll fix the coffee."

In the kitchen, he fumbled with the fancy machine she'd bought for her own use, but he finally managed to get the job done. Carrying their cups into the living room, he read the unease in those gorgeous, turquoise eyes.

He handed her the coffee, then took a chair across from her. After his first sip, he decided he'd done a pretty darned good job and took a second. Then he set his cup on the end table. "I know you're tired, and you want me gone. It's been one hell of a night for you, and you have to be up early tomorrow. That said, I think it's past time we clear the air. Past time for me to hear what happened to derail us."

"I tried to tell you a few nights ago."

"I know. I wasn't ready."

"And you are now?"

He took a deep breath. Exhaled. "I think so."

She nibbled at her fingernail, then raised her eyes to the ceiling. "This is hard. I imagined this talk so many times. And now I'm not sure where to start."

"Anywhere works."

"Okay." She met his gaze. "First, though, I need you to know I loved you with all my heart."

He felt the punch. *Loved*. Past tense. But he sucked it up.

"After Dad died, I fell apart. I lost him, and I lost my way. When I returned to school after his funeral, I was a disaster. I didn't care about anything. I cut classes and quit studying. Some friends asked me to go to a bar with them one Friday night, and I had way too much to drink." She raised a hand. "I'm not makin' any excuses. Just telling you what happened."

"Understood."

Her fingers raked through her curls. "Emerson came in with a couple of his buddies. One of the girls knew him and asked the guys to join us." She lifted vulnerable eyes to his. "You don't really want a blow-by-blow account, do you?"

He didn't, but he said, "If that's what it takes."

"Eventually we paired up. You know how that goes. I ended up with Emerson. He didn't know about my dad, so I could just leave that for a while, get away from the hurt and unhappiness. He offered a few hours respite."

"Okay."

"Then it all snowballed. He ordered drink after drink after drink. And with the mood I was in, I drank them as fast as they came. Afterward, I wondered if he'd been drinking, too, or if I was flying solo. Anyway, we ended up at his place, and I found myself pregnant."

For the first time, he understood. "He took advantage of you."

"Maybe. And maybe I took advantage of him. Does the why matter anymore?"

"I should say no. A bigger man probably would. But, yes, it does. You were hurting and vulnerable. I can see how it happened. For the first time, I can see that."

And he did. Tansy couldn't hold her alcohol. Two drinks and she was under the table. She must have been practically comatose when Emerson… No, he wouldn't go there.

"Why didn't you come home?" he asked. "We'd have taken care of you."

"Carrying another man's baby?"

"How do you know she's not mine?" There. He'd said it out loud, the question that haunted him. How many nights had he lain awake wondering exactly that?

"She isn't, Beck. She's Emerson's."

"You're a hundred percent certain?"

She nodded. "I wish it were different, but I could never have lied to you about that or claimed she was yours when she wasn't. I couldn't come back to Misty Bottoms and face you with what I'd done. I knew you wouldn't want me anymore."

"I'd have taken you back, taken care of you."

"Maybe. Then again, you've had four, almost five years to live with this. Neither you nor I can know for sure how you'd have acted then."

"You had other options."

"I wouldn't consider abortion."

"No, I wouldn't expect you to," he said quickly. "But you didn't need to marry Forbes."

She made a sound of frustration. "I made the mistake of sending him the news in a text. I thought it would be easier than face to face." She grimaced. "I barely knew him, Beck, which makes all this worse. His mother, who is a termagant of the first order, saw the text, and insisted no Forbes grandchild would grow up illegitimate."

Beck pinched the bridge of his nose.

"She demanded we get married, and two weeks later, we did. I had no fight left, Beck. I'd lost my dad and betrayed you. I was so depressed..."

He nodded.

"The wedding was very small," she said. "The two of us, his parents, and my mother—who, by the way, cried through the entire service and dinner afterward. And believe me when I tell you they weren't happy tears."

"She had a lot coming at her pretty fast, too."

"I know. She wanted me to come home to raise my child—without Emerson."

"I always did like your mother."

A small, reluctant smile teased the corners of Tansy's lips.

"You never loved him?"

She shook her head.

"Was your marriage ever good?"

"No. He resented me and resented Gracie. I was supposed to be a one-night stand."

A tic started in Beck's cheek. "Yet you stayed."

"I did. Gracie means the world to me. There was no way I'd risk his family taking her away from me. If that meant I had to stay..." She shrugged.

"So why did you finally leave?"

"It's ironic, really. I stayed for Gracie, and I left for Gracie."

His eyes narrowed. "Don't think I'm followin' you."

"Emerson gambled, and, one night, he threw the house in the pot at a poker game. We'd already received our eviction notice."

Sick to his stomach, Beck sat silently, his hands fisted, while she continued.

"I could live without the house. It never felt like mine anyway." She looked around her new living room. "This already feels more like home than the house I lived in for nearly five years."

"And?"

"Two men showed up at the house one morning. They were there to collect my jewelry."

"What?"

"Again, to cover a gambling debt. I looked at them and thought of Gracie asleep upstairs. How far would they go to collect what her father owed? And I knew I had to get Gracie far away."

Beck made a low, guttural noise. "God, I'm so sorry, sugar. You shouldn't have had to go through that."

"It was a choice I made. Gracie didn't have any option. The day those men showed up, I phoned a lawyer and started divorce proceedings."

"You did the right thing."

"I should have done it sooner. There are going to be times when it's tough sledding, but Gracie and I are far better off on our own here in Misty Bottoms." Her eyes met Beck's. "Gracie's laughing again. She's laughing, Beck. She's running and playing and being a four-year-old. There's no more fighting. No more hate."

The last of the wall around Beck's heart crumbled.

Chapter 21

SAM STOOD OUTSIDE TANSY'S DOOR SUNDAY afternoon. Her hands busy with a pile of freshly laundered tea towels, she nudged the screen open with her elbow. "Come on in."

"I understand your mom and Gracie are fixing dinner for you tonight."

She frowned. "Yes, they are. Why?"

"You're alone and can talk?"

"Yes."

He stepped inside and waited while she set her stack of towels on the table. "Kemper and I took a ride to Atlanta yesterday."

Slowly, she nodded. "Is that where Emerson is?"

"Yeah. His folks are footing the bill for an expensive country-club-type rehab." He leaned against her counter, his arms and feet crossed. "You won't have any more custody problems. Your ex signed off on any and all claims to Gracie." He handed her an envelope.

Relief bubbled up inside her, made her light-headed.

"He won't be bothering you for money, either. Kemper and I both laid down the law. We made it crystal clear that any more attempts to extort money from you will land him in jail."

She could barely speak, her voice thick with emotion. "I can't thank either of you enough."

"Thank Beck. He's the one who orchestrated this."

She nodded. "I will. Would you like some coffee? Iced tea?"

"No, I need to get home. Cricket's attempting lasagna. The woman's hell on wheels when it comes to flowers, but in the kitchen… Let's say she has her moments. The woman makes a mean pancake."

"Sam, if I can ever do anything…"

"Believe me, this was my pleasure. Men who don't do right by their families are on my short list." He gave her a quick hug and headed to his car.

She'd have to make it her business to find out what his favorite dessert was and see to it he had it at least once a week. Weak kneed, she dropped onto a chair. Emerson wouldn't bother her or Gracie ever again. What a gift! Beck had quietly taken care of the matter.

Pulling out her phone, she hit his number.

Why was he so good to her after she'd hurt him so badly?

After a lot of deliberation, Tansy decided to close at two during the week and four on Saturdays. That gave her time to get the shop cleaned up and the next day's baking started before she picked up Gracie from preschool. Her mom would watch Gracie on Saturdays.

Kitty, though, had other ideas. After only a week, she decided she wasn't ready for full retirement. "Can I run the shop on Saturdays?"

"Did my mother put you up to this?"

"Nope. My husband and I talked and decided that for the health of our marriage, we can't be joined at the hip 24-7. That might work for some, but not us. The weekends will be busy for you, doing things with Gracie, catching up on the housework. Besides, Magnolia Brides is growing by leaps and bounds. If you want to take care of that side of the business, you're gonna need someone to handle the shop on weekends."

"Are you sure?"

"Totally." Kitty walked over to the display of cake toppers. "These are wonderful, but you need time to put them to use. I'm offering that. By the time hubby and I decide to pull up stakes and move to Charleston, you can have someone else trained. In the meantime, it'll be good for both of us."

When Tansy still hesitated, Kitty said, "I'm not gonna encroach on your business." She waved a hand. "This… what you've done here…is nothin' like my bakery. Kitty's Kakes was a hit-and-run kind of place. Sweet Dreams is a destination."

"I'm not worried about that, Kitty. If you're really willin' to pitch in, it would mean the world to me."

"There you go. We're both a little happier now, aren't we?"

⁓

Beck drove through the sleepy little town and headed down Main. A late-evening emergency plumbing call had turned into a nightmare, but he'd finally managed to get it fixed. The Foleys were once again dry.

Rubbing his eyes, he groused. He was the boss; he should have delegated the job to one of his guys. But since most of them had families and plans for tonight, he'd taken the call himself.

A big yawn escaped. One twenty-nine a.m. Jeez

Louise, tomorrow would start before he even got to bed. On top of that, he was driving in the wrong direction, away from his house and toward Tansy's.

He couldn't stop thinking about her. He needed his Tansy fix. Pathetic. But even being on the same street would help.

And how juvenile was that?

She'd be sleeping—alone in that big king-sized bed.

Maybe he should call Rachel or Lucinda. Unfortunately, it was auburn curls and sea-blue eyes that danced in his head. He didn't want anybody but Tansy.

He was in deep doo-doo.

When he reached her house, a light shone at the back of her shop. He pulled to the curb, hoping she'd step onto the back porch so he could catch a glimpse of her.

Did this make him a voyeur? Probably. Still, he didn't put the truck into drive.

When she didn't make an appearance, he turned the radio to a soft rock station. Would she turn off the lights and head upstairs to bed?

He wanted to talk to her. Just talk. But if he knocked on her door at this time of night, he'd scare her...or wake Gracie.

A minute stretched to two, then five, and still the lights remained on.

Time to call it a night.

Instead of driving away, though, he found himself outside the truck, quietly closing the door. Peepers serenaded him from the backyard. The hoot of a solitary owl echoed in the night. Above, the moon played hide and seek in the clouds.

He walked around to the back door. A kitchen window

was open, and he heard strains of Rascal Flatts's "What Hurts the Most."

How many times had he and Tansy listened to this song while they'd parked in his old truck? How many times had they danced to it?

Now the lyrics haunted him.

What hurt the most…never knowing what could have been.

He peered through the old door's window. Tansy, in a short little nightshirt, had her back to him, those hips of hers moving slow and sexy in time to the music. She'd pulled her hair up in a messy little bundle. A few auburn tendrils escaped to brush over that ivory skin, skin he wanted to kiss.

With his forearm, he wiped a bead of sweat from his brow.

Before he could change his mind, he rapped on the windowpane, then swore when he heard her small shriek. When she grabbed the rolling pin and held it out like a sword, he couldn't help the quick laugh.

A wild-eyed Tansy, makeshift weapon in hand, tiptoed to one side of the door and peered out, straight into his eyes. "Beck!"

"Really? A rolling pin?"

She shrugged and unlocked the door. "Couldn't sleep?" she asked.

"Got a house call. The Foleys' youngest boy tried to flush a toy car down the toilet, so it was Beck to the rescue."

Laughing, she asked, "All's good now?"

"Yep." He sniffed the air. "Sure smells good in here. What are you baking at—" He glanced at his watch. "At a quarter till two? And why?"

"My brain refused to shut down, and I couldn't sleep." She picked up a plate. "I decided to play around a bit. With fall in the air, I wanted to do something a little different to fit the season. Tonight's featured dessert? Apple cookies with caramel frosting. Want one?"

"You don't need to ask me twice." He scooped up one. "Got any milk?"

"Ice cold. For my hero. I haven't had a chance to thank you in person for helping me with the custody thing." She moved to the fridge, removed the milk, then reached into the cabinet for a glass. Her nightshirt rode up, and Beck about swallowed his tongue.

"And that view alone is thanks enough."

"Argh." She pulled at her shirt. "Why are you here, Beck?"

"Huh?" He blinked, fighting to focus. "I don't know."

She poured two glasses of milk and carried them to the table.

Beck took one bite and groaned. "These are decadent. You'll make a fortune off them."

"I hope so." She smiled and broke off a small bite.

"Tell me that's not all you're gonna eat."

"I bake for a living. If I ate everything I made, I'd weigh a ton."

"You have more self-control than me." He could have bitten off his tongue at the innuendo. Instead, he took another bite of cookie. "So what are you thinkin' so hard about that you can't sleep?"

Tansy hesitated. It was late and her guard was down, but she found herself wanting to share with Beck. Like old times. She missed that.

"I'm afraid."

"Of what?" His eyes darted around the room. "Of being here alone?"

She pinched the bridge of her nose. "I'm afraid I'll never know who Tansy Calhoun Forbes is. I've never been on my own. Never had to stand on my own two feet before."

"You're doin' a hell of a job of it right now."

"Am I?"

"How can you even ask that?"

"Could I have made this work without my mom? Without Jenni Beth. Without you, Cricket, Cole, Sam, Kitty…"

"Sugar, you're a strong woman. You're capable of doin' whatever you set your mind to."

"But who *am* I?"

"Shoot, Tansy, does anybody really know who they are? Deep down at the core? I don't know. I think we're constantly changin'. Evolvin'. A lot like that onion you use in your breakfast quiche." He nodded toward one on her counter. "Layer on top of layer. We change because of situations that pop up. Because of people who come into—or come *back* into—our lives."

His eyes darkened. "I've missed you, Tanz. You were my lover, yes. The woman I loved and wanted to marry. But you were also my best friend. I miss my friend. How 'bout we start there? By being friends again."

Her fingers crumbled the cookie on her plate as a bubble burst in her chest. "Oh, Beck, I can't count the times over the last few years when I've thought, 'Wait till I tell Beck.'"

He reached for her hand and she took his, felt the strength there. "Friends?"

"Friends," she answered.

"You know, I never did get my dance at the wedding." He drew her up and led her toward the door. "The stars are out tonight."

As if in a trance, she followed him across the kitchen floor.

He knelt beside a pair of pink, rhinestone-covered flip-flops. Lifting her foot, he slid the sandal onto it, then repeated it with the other.

Tansy could barely breathe.

"Gracie—"

"Is asleep. The window's open. You'll hear her if she needs you."

She nodded. Her fingers laced through his, they slipped outside into the soft night air. Fireflies twinkled.

"You know," he said, "when I was little, the rule was that when the fireflies came out to play, I went inside. To bed. Despite that, they're magical."

The radio still played inside, the music drifting out to them.

Grass, damp with dew, tickled her toes.

And then Beck drew her in, and she forgot everything but his touch. His lips dropped tiny kisses along her neck, and her knees turned to mush. Those same lips moved to her ear, and she nearly moaned.

The kitchen light shone onto the yard and created shadows.

As they danced, she realized they could have been the only two people in the universe. At that moment, her world began and ended right there in Beck's arms, his work-callused hands strong and steady.

One song ended and another began.

He spun her out, and she laughed. When he pulled her close again, she sighed.

"I'm not sure friends is gonna cut it for very long," he whispered into her hair.

"Oh, Beck, if it were only me… I want you. So badly. But Gracie's already lost her father. I can't make another mistake."

"Believe it or not, I understand, sugar."

"Do you?"

"Yes. I'd be a liar if I said I won't keep trying, though."

He stepped away, and she shivered. The night air had cooled, or maybe she simply hadn't noticed it before.

"Time we both found our beds, friend. Morning's gonna come, ready or not, and we both have work." He dropped a featherlight kiss on her cheek. "Go inside. I'll wait till you're in. Lock up."

She couldn't find her voice, so she simply nodded.

Once inside, she turned the lock and knew she'd dream of Beck tonight.

Chapter 22

SATURDAY MORNING. *AHHH.* TANSY CURLED HER TOES into the sheets and stretched. Guilt tried to creep in, but she shoved it away. From downstairs, she heard the whir of the coffee machine. Customers ate her pastries and drank her coffee, yet upstairs, she lollygagged in bed. Could anything be more indulgent?

A glance at the clock warned her she couldn't lie in bed long, though. Today's schedule was jam-packed. From the second her feet touched the floor, she'd be on the go. She needed to wake Gracie and get her dressed and fed, then drop her off at Grandma's. After that, she'd drive to Magnolia House to meet their next bride, who was coming in to finalize her plans.

Sweet Dreams hadn't opened yet when they'd ironed out the other details, so the cake selection was still up in the air. After studying pictures of the flowers, the dresses for both the bride and her attendants, and the colors for the groom and his groomsmen, Tansy had put together several designs. She hoped the bride would jump on one of them.

———

They met in Jenni Beth's office. The plantation's former carriage house was everything a wedding planner's office should be—romantic and feminine, but not so over the top that a soon-to-be groom would feel uncomfortable.

Before a bride even stepped inside, the century-and-a-half-old bricks, the red French doors, and the white metal buckets of bright flowers welcomed her. Inside, ivory walls, a whimsical cherub-and-crystal chandelier, and a gorgeous fireplace added to the ambience. White sheers at the windows ushered in the sunshine, while love seats and overstuffed chairs gave the space a cozy feeling.

Jenni Beth had a bottle of champagne chilling, and Cricket fussed with a small bouquet of flowers in the center of the small table where they'd sit. After the meeting, she'd offer the bouquet to the bride to take home. Tansy's contribution was a small red velvet cake decorated in the bride's colors.

Her phone buzzed, and she plucked it from her pocket. A text. From Beck.

Checking to see how my new friend is doing.

She smiled and texted back.

I'm great. Waiting for a bride. You?

A minute later he sent his answer.

Happy! Thinking about my friend.

She felt herself blush.

Cricket nudged her. "My guess is those messages aren't from Gracie or your mom."

"You'd be right." Without saying more, she grinned and dropped the phone into her purse.

The sound of a car coming down the lane snapped them all to attention.

"And she's here," Jenni Beth said as she hit the power button for the small stereo system. Classical music, the volume so low it was a mere whisper, rained down from ceiling speakers.

Car doors opened and closed.

"We're on." A smile on her face, Jenni Beth moved to the door. "Sara, good morning. Mrs. Lowell, what a beautiful dress. How are you today?"

"Wonderful," the mother of the bride answered. "I know this is Sara's day, but I'm every bit as excited as she is. Her father and I eloped, so I missed all this." She hugged her daughter. "Thank heavens she and Jayden didn't choose that route."

Tansy watched and listened as Jenni Beth led the bride through the seemingly endless checklist.

When the discussion turned to flowers, the bride hesitated. "I'm rethinking the table centerpieces."

"That's fine. If something doesn't feel quite right, trust your intuition. It won't lead you wrong."

"Thanks." Sara swiveled to face Cricket. "I asked for plain white vases, but that's not what I want. Not really. Because everything else is so simple, I think I'd like something a little bit…I don't know…*more* for the centerpieces."

Cricket held up a finger, then thumbed through her phone and brought up a picture. "How about something like this?"

Their bride grinned. "That's exactly right! How did you know?" Hopping up, Sara hugged her. "Oh, y'all are so wonderful!"

"Are those soup tureens?" Tansy asked.

Cricket nodded. "Antique ones. I can get them for a song. Well, maybe not with my voice." She laughed. "But since we're using low arrangements to keep from obstructing the guests' view, I think these will be stunning."

"Now the cake," Tansy said.

Mrs. Lowell popped the last bite of the red velvet dessert into her mouth and washed it down with champagne. Pointing her fork at the empty plate, she said, "This was delightful! I've never had better."

"Thank you. This is what you said you were thinking of, Sara, but I have lots to choose from if this doesn't work."

Their bride shook her head. "This is definitely what I want. With cream cheese frosting."

"Wonderful. Your colors are black and white with a touch of red. Here's what I had in mind." Tansy slid a page toward her.

"Oh, Sara!" Mrs. Lowell laid a hand on her daughter's arm.

"I love it!" Sara smiled at Tansy. "This is so incredibly perfect."

"If I remember correctly, you're not using a topper."

"We're not. But this… Wow!"

Cricket and Jenni Beth leaned forward to get a closer look.

"She's right. This *is* perfect," Jenni Beth said. "It's formal but with a touch of playfulness."

"I'll frost the layers in white, then scroll pipe the black," Tansy explained. "This design uses what's called C-scrolls. On each layer, we'll add a few small clusters of chocolate-dipped strawberries, then build a tower of them at the top."

"Sold!" The bride beamed. "Jayden will love this."

In no time, the three stood at the carriage house's red French doors and waved good-bye as the bride and her ecstatic mother drove down the oak-lined lane. Tansy glanced up at the security camera. What a shame Jenni Beth had to install it.

"Sara's wedding's going to be beautiful," Cricket said.

The other two nodded.

"It helped that she knew what she wanted," Jenni Beth added.

"How about yours?" Tansy turned to her friend.

"What do you mean?"

"Will it be beautiful?"

"Of course!"

Tansy shook her head. "No, it won't. Not if you don't make some decisions pretty soon."

"I know."

"Are you in a hurry, Tansy?" Cricket asked.

"Nope. Gracie's with my mom, and they were talking sleepover when I left."

"Good. Got another bottle of that champagne?" Cricket asked.

Jenni Beth laughed. "As a matter of fact, I do."

"And that's what we're aiming for. To get you to say 'I do' to Cole."

"Let's do it then." Jenni Beth tapped her head. "I've got so many ideas running around in here. Actually…" She walked over to a closet and slid out a poster board and a notebook. "I have pictures."

"Oh!" The girls oohed and aahed over her choices, discarding a few, giving a thumbs-up to most.

"I have a suggestion." Cricket cleared her throat. "It's only an idea, so if you don't like it, please, please, please say so."

"Okay."

"This would be for the table centerpieces." She waggled her brow. "Hot topic today, right?"

"Yeah. I'm so glad Sara spoke up."

"Me too. A bride shouldn't settle. So here's my idea." She tipped her head from side to side. "Actually, Cole and I have this idea."

"You and Cole?" Jenni Beth looked surprised.

"Mmm-hmmm. We've already started working on it, but like I said, if you don't like it, it's a no-go."

"My curiosity's piqued," Jenni Beth said. "What have you two been up to?"

"Inquiring minds want to know," Tansy added.

"All right, here's the deal. During one of Cole's buying trips, he found this incredible white vase with bird wings raised on the vase itself, and a bird's neck and head coming out from it. Almost like a handle, but not."

"It sounds beautiful." Jenni Beth smiled.

"It is, believe me. He gave it to me for my shop, but I couldn't bring myself to sell it. So I put it away. Then he came to me with another incredible all-white pitcher thinking it might make a good vase, along with a fantastic white watering can."

"Which you put away, too." Tansy nodded. She thought she saw where this was headed.

"I did. I also have one with a white bas-relief flower and free-formed leaves that extend past it, a white vase with a flat surface partway up the side so it looks as though it's leaning, and a free-form one that looks a little like a white paper bag. Some are very simple, others extremely intricate."

"But they're all white."

"Yes, and every single one is different."

"We'd put one on each table." Jenni Beth smiled. "They'd be a piece of Cole."

Cricket nodded. "The man's nothing short of a genius when it comes to salvaging. I have twenty now. If that's not enough, we'll send him out searching for more."

"Now I know how Sara felt when she saw those soup tureens," Jenni Beth said. "This adds such a personal touch. Thank you, Cricket."

"Thank Cole."

"Oh, I will, but if you hadn't thought to save them…"

"I'm really good, too, aren't I?" She laughed.

"Yeah, but don't sprain that arm pattin' yourself on the back," Tansy warned.

"I want pale, pale blue tablecloths and blue and white flowers."

"Can do." Cricket made some notes. "I'll pull together some ideas for you and do a few sketches."

"Can we actually pull this off? I mean, if we're all in the wedding party, who will take care of the actual work? We can prepare the cake and flowers beforehand, but that still leaves a lot to do," Tansy worried.

"Everybody's offered to pitch in. Duffy's offered to close the pub that day, and he, Binnie, and his cook will work, along with Luanna from Dee-Ann's. A couple of her friends have worked other weddings for me, and they've agreed to help. Jeremy Stuckey and his mom will pitch in, too." Jenni Beth pointed at her computer. "I've got a whole list—and a lot to be thankful for."

"We all do." Cricket pulled the others in for a group hug.

A rap sounded on the door just before it opened. "Can I get in on this?"

Tansy's heart fluttered. Beck.

Jenni Beth stiffened as she looked from him to Tansy.

To put her friend at ease, Tansy said, "Hi, Beck. I didn't expect to see you here today."

"I was looking for Cole."

"He's in the main house," Jenni Beth said. "Probably in the kitchen with Charlotte, trying to talk her out of a few more cookies. Honestly, he's the biggest kid I've ever seen."

"Okay, I'll check there for him." He winked at Tansy and left.

A quizzical expression on her face, Jenni Beth turned toward Tansy. "Do I detect a thaw in the air?"

"Maybe. We're talking." Tansy's face grew warm, a telltale sign her face was beet red. That darned pale skin gave her away every time.

"Talking? Nothing more?"

"I wonder what he needs with Cole," Tansy offered.

"Ooohh, good deflection, pal. I'll let it go. For now. But we will get back to this discussion later. The guys are working on something for Veterans Day."

Beck had a lot going on, Tansy mused, and yet he'd taken time to send her a text, to ask how she was doing. Her heart smiled.

The wedding business was thriving, and on Wednesday afternoon, Tansy headed back to Magnolia House. A new soon-to-be bride had scheduled an appointment with the three of them.

Cricket stepped out of the Enchanted Florist's door as Tansy pulled up.

"You sure you don't mind driving?" she asked as she slid in.

"Not at all." Tansy nodded at the center console. "The one in the front cup holder is yours. Iced coffee, cream and sugar."

"You are the best!" She fastened her seat belt, then picked up her cup and took a drink.

On the way, they chatted about business, weddings, and Gracie.

"How are things between you and Beck?"

Instead of answering, Tansy asked, "How are things with you and Sam?"

Cricket laughed. "That good, huh?"

"Probably not."

They reached Jenni Beth's only five minutes before the eager bride.

"I know I'm early, but I'm so excited I couldn't wait! *We* couldn't wait!" She pointed at her mother, who stood behind her, glowing.

"That's understandable, Brianna." Ever the gracious hostess, Jenni Beth ushered them inside and offered refreshments. "I see you've brought a few ideas with you."

Tansy eyed the huge bundle of books and notebooks and mentally congratulated Jenni Beth on her ability for understatement.

"I did." She pulled a couple onto her lap.

Her mother sent a prayerful look their way. "She's been plannin' for this day since she was four years old.

Heaven help us. I don't know how we'll ever wade through all this." She waved a hand at the pile of materials her daughter'd brought along.

Brianna leafed through one of the bridal magazines. Sticky notes marked dozens of pages. Dress after dress, floral arrangements, cakes, and themes. After a few minutes, all of it started to run together.

"Do you want to see my notebook? I have more ideas in it."

Tansy held up a hand. "Maybe we can narrow it down a little before we look at anymore."

"Narrow it down?"

"Yes. How big will the wedding be?"

"Right around two hundred guests."

Jenni Beth nodded. "Inside or out?"

"I'm not sure." The bride looked nervous.

"That's all right." Jenni Beth patted her hand. "Do you want formal or something a little more casual?"

"Formal. Definitely formal."

"Okay. Good." She jotted it down. "How about favorite colors?"

"That's easy. Red and black."

Jenni Beth nodded. "So when we look at the ideas you've brought, we might want to start eliminating some. For instance…" She flipped to pictures of a barn wedding. "If you want formal, this probably won't work."

Brianna stared at it for a few seconds without saying anything.

"Do you see yourself getting married in a barn?"

"No."

"All right, then." She pulled the sticky note from the page.

Tansy swore Brianna's mother heaved a sigh of relief.

They went through a couple more magazines, eliminating most of the marked pages.

"You like red and black. Is that what you want for your attendants' dresses?"

"Definitely."

Tansy thought about Sara. She'd used black and white with a touch of red. It would be interesting to see how two brides came up with totally different uses of the same color…or, rather, how Jenni Beth did.

"For your flowers?" Cricket asked.

"The same colors."

"Any favorite flower?" She opened up a notebook of her own, turned to a section that fit the color theme, then pointed out the ones that were formal, talking all the time about tweaks they might make, changes that would personalize them for Brianna.

"I'll take care of your bouquet, your attendants' flowers, roses for the flower girl to spread, the boutonnières for the guys, and corsages for the moms." Cricket smiled at Brianna's mother. "And, of course, the centerpieces for your reception. I can do the rehearsal dinner, too, if you want."

"Y'all are as wonderful as everybody told me." The bride got teary, and her mother gave her a big hug and a hanky.

Cricket, Tansy, and Jenni Beth listened intently to the bride's wishes, made suggestions, and took pages of notes. An hour later, they had a pretty good handle on things.

They helped Brianna and her mother lug the mountain of magazines and notes to their car, then waved them

off. As the Lexus rounded the bend in the drive, Jenni
Beth lifted her hand for a high five. "We're awesome!"

"Oh, yeah," Cricket agreed.

"Anyone want a glass of champagne?" Jenni Beth
headed back inside and reached for the bottle.

Tansy held up a crystal flute. She looked at her
friends, at the incredible office Jenni Beth had created,
and thought about the businesses they'd embarked on.
The business she was now part of. How lucky could any
woman be?

She tapped her glass to the others'. "All three of
us left Misty Bottoms for one reason or another. Now
we've all returned, and thank God for that. To friends
and coming home."

After she dropped Cricket off, Tansy drove through
town. Halfway down Main, she slowed, her heart in
her throat.

Oh my gosh! Could there be a more incredible sight?
Misty Bottoms' founding fathers had had the foresight
to create a wide Main Street with a small, parklike green
area in the center. The Ladies' Garden Club of Misty
Bottoms took care of the actual flowers and plants, but
others often pitched in and helped with some of the
other chores.

Right now, a sweaty trio was hard at work scraping
and painting a wooden bench and pergola. Mums and
red-leafed bushes provided a backdrop. Sam, Cole,
and Beck chatted while they restored the wood to a
pristine condition.

She pulled into a parking space and reached into the

backseat for three bottles of water. Since Gracie always seemed to get thirsty halfway to nowhere, she'd taken to carrying a cooler.

Sliding out of her car, the skirt of her ivory, short-sleeved cowl-necked sweater dress rode up, and she tugged it down. When she closed the vehicle's door, the men looked up and Cole gave a wolf whistle.

She laughed. "I'm not gonna tell Jenni Beth about that."

He chuckled. "That's probably a good idea."

"What are you three up to?"

"We're getting the park ready for Veterans Day. Or helping, anyway."

"Is something big planned?"

Cole nodded and pointed to an area to the right of them. "We're adding to the War Memorial."

Her forehead creased in a frown. "Why?"

"There's nothing to mark those who have died in the Middle East while servin' their country."

Jenni Beth's brother. "Wes?"

Cole nodded. "We're adding another marker and hoping like hell we'll only have two names to engrave on it."

"Two?"

"Yeah. Lem and Lyda Mae lost a niece in the war. She's from Rincon, but since they don't have anything like this, Lem asked if we'd include her."

"That's as it should be."

"Lem chipped in on the cost of the monument. We told him he didn't need to, that we had it covered, but he insisted."

"Jenni Beth said you were working on something. Does she know what it is?"

"She does. We discussed it with her and her parents before we committed to it. The granite marker will be here next week. We'll keep it covered till Veterans Day. There'll be a short program and, at the end of it, Jenni Beth and her parents, along with Lem and Lyda Mae, will unveil the marker."

"It's a good thing y'all are doing here," she said.

"Believe it or not, this was Sam's idea."

"The Yankee," she said.

Sam grinned. "The Yankee."

"You know, I have to keep bumping up my evaluation on just how lucky Cricket is. You're quite a guy, Sam DeLuca."

He blushed beneath his deep tan.

Tansy held out the waters. "Anybody need a cold drink?"

"Oh, yeah." Sam took two, and handed one to Cole.

Beck walked toward her, more than a little swagger in his stride. When he took the offered bottle, his hand lingered over hers.

"Let's head over to the big oak, take a break in the shade."

She fell into step beside him.

When they stopped, he tugged her onto a bench. Heat flared, both between them and in his eyes. Maybe she'd been wrong about the temperature. Suddenly very, very hot, Tansy tugged at the neck on her dress.

"Nice outfit," he said. "That ivory sets off your hair and eyes. Hugs those curves of yours real nice, too." His gaze dropped lower. "Those high-heeled leather boots are sexy as hell. Makes a man drool."

"Beck—"

"Just sayin', sugar. No need to get nervous about it, although the way you look right now tempts me to get you out on the dance floor again."

Her heart lodged in her throat. "We weren't on a dance floor the other night."

"We weren't, were we? Just you and me beneath a pretty moon with the grass under our feet and the smell of roses in the air."

She swore the temperature spiked another ten degrees.

"Hey! You intend on giving us a hand here?" Sam called.

"Yeah, yeah, I'm comin'." Beck's grin disappeared. He reached out toward her, then caught sight of his hands and drew them back. "I'm too dirty to touch you. Where have you been? Surely you don't wear that when you're bakin'."

"No." She grabbed his water and took a drink, then handed it back to him. "I've been at Magnolia House. We booked another wedding!"

His smile was proud. "That's great, sugar. Any bride lucky enough to have you three workin' on her wedding is in for a real treat."

"Thank you."

"I mean it, Tanz." His eyes darkened. "Come out with me."

"What?"

"I know I've been pretty surly, but I'd like to have dinner with you."

"Are you askin' me out on a date, Beck Elliot?"

He grinned. "I believe I am, Tansy Calhoun."

Her maiden name. She didn't correct him. "When?"

"How about this weekend? Friday night. Word is

Kitty's coverin' the shop on Saturdays, so we can stay out past your curfew without you losin' too much sleep."

"I'd like that."

"Good. Wear somethin' fancy. We'll head toward Savannah. I know a great restaurant halfway there, away from the eyes and ears of Misty Bottomers."

She wanted to cry, and how stupid was that? Beck was asking her on an actual date. Period. If she broke out in tears, he'd probably run away—and she wouldn't blame him. Still… Might they have a second chance?

If those kisses he'd laid on her in the backyard had been any indication, the chemistry between them was still there. Tenfold. She practically floated to her car. She had a date with Beck!

Breathe, she told herself. *Breathe. In, out, in, out.*

And the day just kept getting better and better!

She picked up Gracie and headed home.

"What do you want for dinner tonight, baby?"

"Pizza!"

"You sure?"

"Uh-huh." She bobbed her head up and down, her dark curls bouncing. "I like pizza."

"How about I order one from Mama's?"

"'Kay."

She hit the restaurant's number on her contact list, half-ashamed it was there. But the days at the bakery were long, and she couldn't always find the energy to cook. Did that make her a bad mother? Probably. On the nights she did fix a meal, she worked hard to make it nutritious yet still palatable to a four-year-old's taste, a sometimes-tough balancing act.

Inside half an hour, the inside of her car smelled like tomatoes and garlic and warm crust. Tansy's stomach made a little growling noise.

Gracie giggled. "Are you hungry, Mama?"

"Yes, I am. You?"

"Uh-huh. We had peanut butter samiches and potato chips at school today. Ms. Lucinda cut the crust off for me."

"Did you thank Ms. Lucinda?"

"Yep. I like her. She's nice, and she smells good."

Tansy said a prayer of thanks. Her little girl had adapted so well. All that worrying she'd done had been for naught.

Then she thought of Beck and how her situation with him might affect Gracie. Would her worrying there be for naught, too? A conundrum.

Dinner was a casual meal at the counter with both of them drinking milk.

After they finished eating, Tansy gave Gracie her bath, then lay beside her in bed while she read one of their favorite stories. The little girl yawned hugely at the end of it, and Tansy gave her a hug and a kiss.

"'Night, baby."

"'Night, Mama. I love you."

"I love you more."

Gracie giggled, and Tansy dropped another kiss on the tip of her nose.

She'd closed her eyes before Tansy even had the light turned off. She left the door open a crack so she could hear her daughter if she woke. Tonight would be an early one for her, too. Four o'clock came way too quickly.

Maybe she'd take a quick bath herself. It might help her sleep. It might also give her a little time to think about her upcoming date with Beck. A slow smile spread over her face as tiny little bubbles of pleasure spread through her.

It had been so long.

She hadn't expected to ever feel this way again.

If she was smart, though, she wouldn't get her hopes up too high.

But she already had, hadn't she?

Chapter 23

THE WEEK FLEW BY. BECK COULDN'T REMEMBER when he'd worked so hard or been so tired at the end of a workweek. He swore every single household in Misty Bottoms had run into some sort of repair or remodel crisis in the past five days.

But Friday night had finally arrived, and he had a date with fiery-haired Tansy Calhoun. After he'd thought about it a little more, he'd called her with a change of plans. The fancy restaurant hadn't felt right. He wanted something a little more—them.

Time would tell if he'd made the right decision.

He swung into her drive, then hopped out. Sprinting up her porch stairs, he bounced his truck keys in his hand.

When she opened the door, he nearly swallowed his tongue. The woman was exquisite. Soft light shimmered behind her, creating a halo effect. All those beautiful auburn curls had been piled high, exposing a long, sexy neck. He wanted to bury his face in it, drop kisses along its length. And those eyes—the color of the Caribbean Sea on a sunny day—sparkled.

"Beck?"

"You take my breath away, Tansy. I'm rarely at a loss for words, but right now? Truth be told, they fail me."

She laughed, a sweet, tinkling sound, and he felt it sizzle through his heart and head straight south. Tonight might turn out to be the biggest test of willpower he'd ever faced, and darned if he didn't mean to enjoy every minute of it.

"Dinner and roller-skating, right?" She had one hand on the doorknob.

"Right. You don't mind the change of plans?"

"Not at all. In fact," she said, "this sounds like more fun."

"We'll catch that fancy dinner another night." He waited for her reaction to the mention of another date, braced for her to remind him this was a one-shot deal.

She didn't, and he exhaled.

He cocked his head. "God, you're gorgeous."

"Thank you." She dipped a half curtsy.

"Every man who sees you tonight is gonna hate my guts 'cause I'm with you and he's not."

"Go on!" She mock punched him on the arm. "You are so full of it."

"The only thing I'm full of is gratitude you agreed to comin' out with me tonight."

"Remind yourself of that when you're picking me up off the rink floor. I haven't skated since—well, since the last time you and I went."

"It'll come back to you."

"That's what they all say."

He wanted to kiss her. Instead, he held out his hand. When she took it, he felt like he'd won the lottery. Tansy Calhoun and he had a Friday night date to go skating.

She'd worn a pair of jeans that had to have been made just for her. They hugged her in ways that almost brought him to tears. With them, she'd worn a light-weight, mocha-colored cotton sweater. On her feet? Nothing sensible there. Mile-high heels.

He swallowed.

"It's Flashback Friday, so Mason will make good use of his old disco ball tonight. We'll be skatin' to music from the fifties all the way through the nineties. Nothing new tonight."

"Some of us will be skating," she reminded him. "Some might be warmin' the bench."

"I don't think so."

She stepped outside, locking up behind her.

He'd brought the '65 Chevy and watched the grin spread over her face when she saw it.

"Our truck."

"Yeah."

When he looked her way again, she was blushing. "I didn't mean that the way it sounded."

"What?"

"Our truck. I mean, it's your truck. I have no right—"

"Tansy?"

"Yes?"

"Put it away. Our history. Our problems. Tonight's for fun. You and me." His voice grew raspy. "Let's see if we have any kind of chance, if maybe we can't start over."

Her bottom lip trembled, and he fought against the urge to wrap her in his arms. Tonight would be an important night, and he needed to keep his hands to himself. The chemistry had always been there between them, so strong it was almost overwhelming. That had never been their problem.

He'd wanted her years ago, and he still wanted her.

These past years, he'd denied it was anything more than that.

It was time to stop lying to himself.

On the outskirts of town, Beck turned into the parking lot. *Barney's* flashed in orange neon.

When they walked into the building, it was like stepping back in time.

"It hasn't changed a bit." Tansy took hold of Beck's arm. "I can't believe it!"

"Two years ago, they sanded and redid the original maple floors, the same ones Barney laid when he opened this place in 1948. The family's darned proud of these floors."

"They should be."

While Beck paid their admission, Tansy checked out everything. It looked the same, right down to the gaudy neon signs by the snack bar menu.

"Are we eating here?"

He nodded, and she squealed in delight. "Oh, Beck, this is the best date!"

"I was hopin' you'd feel that way."

"I can't tell you how happy I am you changed your mind about tonight. This is exactly what I needed."

"Me too." He shook his head. "It's been a rough week."

"You can say that again!"

"It's been a—"

She snatched one of the plastic-coated menus and swatted him with it.

"Where do you want to sit?"

She studied the worn, plastic chairs and the faux-wood tabletops. "Our table's empty."

"Let's do it."

As one, they moved to the far corner table.

When their waitress showed up, they agreed they should have adult meals. He ordered chicken nuggets, tater tots, and a chocolate malt. Tansy laughed, then ordered a corn dog, tater tots, and a root beer float.

Just like old times.

Almost.

They chatted about their week. Beck told her about the shelves he'd put in for Darlene at Quilty Pleasures, and she told him about the frosted sugar cookies she and Gracie had delivered to Ms. Hattie earlier in the week.

"It's nice to be back, Beck. I've missed all this, missed the sense of community."

"And me?" He reached for her hand.

"And you."

"This probably isn't the best place for this discussion, but…" Beck played with his straw paper, then wadded it into a tiny ball. "Can I ask you something?"

"Sure, as long as I have the prerogative of answering or not after I hear the question."

"Fair enough."

He stared at the table so long, Tansy thought maybe he'd changed his mind.

"What happened? I mean, I know you already told me, but I still don't get it. You were pregnant, but how'd that happen, Tanz?"

Her gaze flew to his, and for a single, awful second, she thought she'd laugh. She choked it back. "I think you know how it happens, Beck."

A muscle in his jaw ticked, and his blue eyes darkened. "That's not what I meant, and you know it."

"Sorry." She threw up her hands. "We've already talked about this, Beck."

"I know. I understand that, but still…"

Pushing aside the paper tray of tater tots, she said, "While I was here in Misty Bottoms, right after Dad died, I had a lot of support. Once I went back to school, that all fell away, and I couldn't cope with it by myself."

"I'd have come if you'd called. If you'd told me you needed me."

"I almost did. I can't tell you how many times I started to."

"But you didn't."

She shook her head.

He reached across and placed a finger beneath her chin, tipped her face so he looked directly into her eyes. She'd never seen such intensity in his.

"Did Forbes rape you?"

The pain on his face was almost more than she could bear. She barely recognized his voice, the anger so strong, his emotions barely in check.

"No." Her chest and throat grew so tight she could barely draw breath. "He didn't. But I was…let's say past rational thought."

"You don't drink, Tanz. One glass of wine sends you over the edge."

"Believe me, I had way more than one that night, and at the time, I didn't care. I just wanted to forget." She braced herself. "We had sex. I won't say we made love because we didn't. I barely remember anything from the time I got in his car."

"Sugar, in my book, takin' advantage of someone who's that far gone is tantamount to rape."

"I didn't say no, Beck—not that I remember, anyway.

I can't begin to tell you how much I hated myself afterward. I loved you, had promised myself to you, then slept with another man. I was unfaithful." A tear spilled over, and Beck leaned in to wipe it away.

God, how could he be so gentle when she'd been so awful?

Reaching into her pocket, she thumbed out a Tums and popped it into her mouth. "To say I'm sorry is so pathetically inadequate. I ruined our lives, the life we'd planned together." She held up a finger. "One stupid night of irresponsibility! But I have Gracie Bella."

"Yes, you do, and she's extraordinary."

She blew out her breath. "Can we talk about something else?"

"We can." He popped his last tater tot into his mouth. "You gonna eat the rest of yours?"

"No, I'm full."

He pulled the red-and-white paper tray toward him and finished hers off, too. She watched, finding her equilibrium again. Done with their meal, they pushed back their chairs.

"I need to rent skates. Mine are probably in Mom's attic, but I didn't have time to dig them out."

"I figured that." He cupped her elbow and led her to the rental counter where Aiden, Barney's son, was working.

"Boy," Aiden said, "I know it's Flashback Friday, but seeing the two of you standing here? That really is a flashback."

"Yeah, it is, isn't it?" Beck looked slightly uncomfortable. Did he think she'd bolt? Or was he thinking of bolting?

"I need a size seven, Aiden."

"Sure thing, Tansy." He moved to the wall of wooden

shelves and grabbed a pair of beat-up white skates. Setting them on the counter, he said, "There you go."

A few minutes later, skates on and laces tied, Tansy stood, wobbled, and nearly fell. Beck reached out and, taking her hand, led her onto the skating rink.

"Leave me here at the railing. I need a little time to get the feel of it again."

"You sure?"

"Positive."

She watched as he effortlessly glided away, then turned, skating backward, to smile at her. What a show-off! Very slowly, she freed her grip from the railing. Two feet away from it, she went down.

Getting to her feet, she tried again, having more trouble than she'd anticipated. Finally, though, she managed to skate around the entire rink, staying fairly close to the padded wall.

Beck, looking hot in his jeans and dark gray Henley shirt, skated up beside her, hooked an arm around her, and pulled her close. When she let out a quick squeal, he rested his chin on top of her head and dropped a kiss on it.

"Hold on to me. I won't let you fall."

She had an idea there was a double meaning in those words and took comfort in them. Hope filled her chest. Could she and Beck find their way back to each other?

"It's all about trust, isn't it?" she asked.

He nodded. "For both of us. We'll take it slow."

Neither was talking about roller-skating.

—◦◦◦—

Laughing and holding hands, they stepped outside. The temperature had dipped while they'd been skating, and

Tansy shivered as a gust of wind hit her. When Beck drew her closer, she rested her head on his shoulder.

Even though it had hit seventy-three today, the weather forecast called for a drop into the high fifties overnight. With the breeze off the water, it felt nippy. All the shops were decked out with colorful autumn leaves, acorns, haystacks, and goblins. Fall had definitely arrived.

Beck started the truck and cranked up the heater. "Do we need to stop by your mom's to pick up Gracie?"

"No. She said she'd take Gracie back to our house and put her to bed after they finished dinner."

"So no sleepover for me tonight." He kept his tone light, but still, he understood the words were a risk. He held his breath, waiting to see how she'd react.

"I'm sorry, Beck, but no." She bit her bottom lip, and he swallowed his groan. "I can't believe I'm asking this, but would you *like* a sleepover? Not tonight," she added quickly, "but soon?"

"Sugar, I thought you'd never ask."

"Is it too soon to be thinking about that?"

He laughed. "Too soon?" He pulled her hand into his lap. "What do you think?"

———

Halfway to Tansy's, he turned left and drove down the old store road that ran parallel to the railroad tracks. Back when they'd been kids, the store had been kind of a hangout for them. Years ago, it was the mail drop and post office. A big metal arm hung near the platform so the train could slow down and pick up and drop off bags of mail.

Now, it was all done in town by truck, the mystery gone.

The store had always been well stocked with candy, soda, and ice cream. After swimming at Frog Pond, they'd ride their bikes there for a treat. Summer days had been so easy then, Beck realized, with nothing to worry about except what to do the next day or whose house to play at that night.

After the store closed, the road had become a favorite make-out spot. He figured it should work every bit as well now as it had when they'd been in high school.

"Beck?"

"Hmm?"

"What are you doing?"

He sent her a sideways glance. "You really are out of practice, aren't you?"

"Ha-ha! Seriously, though, my mom's waiting at home."

"Wasn't she always?"

"You're right. She was. Sitting in the living room, watching the clock. Right beside my dad."

Beck brought the truck to a stop under some tall pines and tuned the radio to a slow-song kind of station. "Once we hit your house, our date's over. My chance to kiss you is gone. I'm not quite ready for that, sugar." He unsnapped his seat belt, reached over, and undid hers. Then he slid the seat back and reached for her.

"I'm beginning to understand why you brought the '65 instead of your new truck."

"Bench seats. Gotta love 'em." He lowered his head, their lips nearly touching. His eyes met hers and held.

"Beck."

"Tansy." His lips dropped to hers, nipping, tasting,

teasing. He thought he might die from the wanting, the anticipation, and realized he was playing with fire. "You're killin' me, Tansy." He groaned. "I want you so damn bad."

Her fingers fisted in his hair. "Kiss me. Please."

"Just you and me, Tansy. I want you." He punctuated his words with a long, drawn-out kiss. "You want me." Another kiss followed by another.

"I do! Tonight. Now, Beck," she whispered breathlessly.

His hands roamed to her breasts, then wandered still lower till she was squirming beneath him with pleasure.

Whoop, whoop. A siren cut through the night air.

"If that's Sam, he's a dead man." Beck pulled Tansy's sweater down and straightened her clothes as well as he could.

By the time the flashlight streaked across them, he was fairly certain Jimmy Don wouldn't get a free peep show.

"What the hell are you doin', Jimmy Don? This your idea of a joke?"

"No, sir. Saw your truck on the side of the road and thought you might have run into some trouble."

"If you'd wipe that silly-ass grin off your face, you'd sound a lot more convincing. And if you weren't wearin' that uniform and that wide-brimmed trooper's hat, I'd show you what I think of this sudden concern of yours."

"You threatenin' me, Beck?"

"Nope. Just statin' a fact." He squinted at the sheriff. "Anybody ever tell you that hat makes you look like Boss Hogg from *Dukes of Hazzard*?"

Jimmy Don's smile faded. "Ought to write you a ticket."

"For what? Insultin' you?"

The sheriff craned his neck to peek around him at Tansy.

"She's legal, Sheriff."

"And willing," she added.

Both men whipped around, surprised. She simply grinned at them.

"Jimmy Don, my mom's babysitting. Beck and I went out to dinner and roller-skated for a while. We're adults and wanted a little adult time before he drops me off." She checked her watch. "I still have an hour before my curfew, so we thought we'd do a little neckin'. Can you blame us? I mean, you're going home to your wife. Beck and I? We're sleepin' alone."

Red crept up Jimmy Don's cheeks. "Sorry, Tansy. I was just havin' a little fun, that's all. Didn't mean no harm."

Beck scowled at him, and the sheriff flicked off his flashlight.

"You two behave yourselves." With that, he hiked back to his car and took off.

"Doing a little neckin'?" Beck turned to her. "I can't believe you, Ms. Straitlaced, would tell him that."

She shrugged. "He was startin' to annoy me."

Beck threw back his head and laughed. "I love it!" Then he started to slide toward her, but she held up a hand to stop him.

"I think we'd better leave this tonight."

"Why?"

"Why? Because I, for one, don't know how much more necking I can take without falling off the edge."

He nuzzled that neck. "So we fall together," he whispered into her skin.

"That's what I'm afraid of." She pulled away. "Home, Mr. Elliot."

He blew out a huge breath. "I'm gonna kill Jimmy Don."

Her laugh was soft in the night air. "And I'll swear under oath I never heard you say that."

Chapter 24

TWO DAYS LATER, TANSY BROKE THE PROMISE SHE'D made to herself to give her and Beck some breathing room. Gathering her courage, and before she could change her mind, she invited him to dinner.

He said yes.

She'd been pretty sure he would, but a date out was a lot different than an invitation to spend the night with her and a four-year-old. To eat, she mentally corrected herself, not to spend the night.

The rest of the day, she was rattled.

Darlene stopped by to pick up a sour cream raisin pie she'd ordered. "What's wrong, Tansy? You look a little frazzled."

"Nothing's wrong."

"You answered that question a little too fast, I think. Anything I can help with?"

"Not really." She puffed out a breath. "I invited Beck over for dinner."

"Ah."

"Yeah, ah. With Gracie and me."

"What are you fixin'?"

"Since I'm working today and the air's just that touch nippy, it has to be something easy and warm. I think I'll make Swiss steak with noodles since mashed potatoes will take more time than I'll have."

"He'll like that. Do you put tomatoes in yours?"

"No, but onions, lots of onions." She pointed over her shoulder. "That pumpkin spice cake with honey frosting is dessert."

"Sounds to me like everything's under control." Darlene patted Tansy's hand. "Stop fretting, and enjoy that handsome young man."

Tansy decided to do exactly that.

~~~

Beck showed up right on time, his hair still damp from his shower and wearing jeans and a long-sleeved T-shirt.

"Come on in," she called through an upstairs window when he knocked at the back door. "It's unlocked."

As he trotted up the stairs to their living quarters, he raised his chin and sniffed the air. "If this meal tastes half as good as it smells, I'm in heaven."

Spotting the cake on the counter, he swiped a finger through the frosting and popped it into his mouth.

Laughing, Tansy swatted him. "Stay out of that. You can have a piece if you clean your plate."

Gracie leaned into him and wrapped an arm around his leg. "That's what she tells me all the time." She sighed.

"That's 'cause you're a growin' girl. You need fuel for that body so you can grow up as pretty as your mama."

"Okay." Twirling, she headed to the table. "Since Beck's here, Mama, can we eat now? I'm hungry."

"Me too," Beck chimed in.

"Go wash up while I finish here," she said.

Both of them left for the powder room, Beck tossing a wink and a wicked grin over his shoulder. Tansy's stomach did a funny little dance.

Oh boy.

She watched Beck and her daughter over dinner, their heads bent close as he cut up her meat. She'd offered, but Gracie had wanted Beck to do it. And she wanted Beck to put the gravy on her noodles and mash her carrots for her. Seemed her daughter had a thing for Mr. Elliot, too.

She'd worried about having him at the house. About it confusing Gracie. It seemed she'd worried needlessly.

About the food, too, because Beck did, indeed, clean his plate.

"Tanz, that was incredible." He patted his stomach. "That steak was some of the most tender I've ever eaten."

"Thank you, kind sir."

"No, thank you. Are we gonna have that cake now?" He eyed it.

"Absolutely."

She cut generous pieces, and Gracie talked about her day at preschool while they ate.

Beck pointed at a picture on the fridge. "You do that?"

Gracie nodded. "Mama said she might put it in a frame."

"That would be a smart thing to do. Tell you what. Next time you're in the mood, why don't you make a picture for me? I'll hang it in my office."

"You will?"

"I sure will." He glanced down at his plate. "Looks like my cake is all gone. How about yours?"

Gracie nodded.

"Why don't the two of you go into the living room and relax?" Tansy suggested.

"You're not comin'?"

"As soon as I clean up here."

"As soon as *we* clean up," he said.

"You're company."

"No, I'm Beck, and my mother taught me to help out."

He cleared the table, while she put away leftovers and loaded the dishwasher.

The kitchen tidied up, Tansy said, "I'll make us some coffee."

"Sounds good. And speakin' of good, that cake was fantastic."

When she walked in carrying their mugs, she found Gracie curled up in Beck's lap, listening to her favorite story. Her heart did a little twist as she leaned against the wall. The two of them looked good together. Emerson never held Gracie or let her cuddle with him, afraid she might get something on his expensive clothing.

There'd never been any question about his priorities. It was all about him, about appearances and his comfort. She could almost feel sorry for what he'd missed out on. Almost.

————

Beck finished the book, his arm tightening around Gracie as he leaned forward and laid it on the coffee table. He sniffed her hair. "You smell good, Gracie Bella."

"My mama puts lotion on me."

"Ah, I see. Do you think that's why she smells good, too?"

"Uh-huh." Gracie looked up at him with those expressive eyes as she twisted the bow on her T-shirt. "My daddy doesn't like me."

The words left Beck totally vulnerable.

Gracie sat very still in his lap, her eyes never leaving his.

He fought for the right words. Kissing the top of the girl's head, he said, "That can't be true, sweetheart. How could anyone not love you?"

She shook her head, her long hair swinging side to side. "He told me so. Lots and lots of times." She reached up and put one hand on either side of his face. "I wish you were my daddy."

He heard a small sound and looked up to see Tansy in the doorway.

"Wait! I forgotted." Gracie jumped off his lap and skirted around Tansy. Crouching, she rooted around in her backpack. Pulling out a small piece of crumpled red paper, she ran back to Beck. "Teacher said to give this to our daddy. I don't have one anymore, so I'll give it to you."

Jeez, could she stick that knife in any deeper? He unfolded the paper, skimmed it, and glanced up at Tansy.

"What is it?"

"An invitation to the preschool's father/daughter luncheon tomorrow."

The color leeched from her face, and she sank into a chair, setting the coffee cups on a side table. "Oh, sweetie." She drew her daughter to her. "Why didn't you tell me? Beck can't—"

For a heartbeat, he couldn't string three words together. Then he blurted, "Yes, Beck can," he said. "If it's okay with you."

"Please, Mama, please." Gracie twined her arms around Tansy's neck. "I want Beck to go with me."

"Are you sure?" Tansy raised stricken eyes to his.

"I am."

"But you have to work."

"Nothin' needs done that won't wait. This is important, sugar."

Gracie looked from one to the other with basset-hound eyes. It would take a stronger man than he was to say no to that face. How could a person ever deny her anything?

"I think it would be wonderful." The smile Tansy sent his way did crazy things to him. "Gracie, honey, why don't you tell Beck good night? It's time for bed."

"Will you come for my school party tomorrow?"

"I will."

Gracie patted his cheek. "Will you come for dinner again?"

He looked to Tansy for help. What did he say? The tenacious child was laying him bare. The daughter wanted him here, but did her mother? He hoped so, but with Tansy...

"We'll see." A nonanswer, but the best he could do.

Gracie's grin was his reward. She crawled back up into his lap, pulled his head toward hers, and gave him a big, sloppy kiss.

He kissed her back, then lifted her off his lap. "'Night, sugar."

"'Night, Beck."

As she left the room, one hand in Tansy's, she turned and blew him another kiss.

He caught it and closed his fist, holding it tightly.

Then he slipped quietly out of the house.

Tansy gave Beck megapoints when he showed up with flowers in hand for his date the next morning. Gracie had wanted to wait and go to school with him at ten thirty.

Good sport that he was, he'd agreed, without a second's hesitation, to pick her up.

Gracie was over the moon, her young voice high with excitement. "Look, Mama! Look what Beck brought me! Will you put one in my hair?"

"I can do that." She mouthed her thanks to Beck, who waited patiently while she wove one of the small pink roses into Gracie's French braid.

"You couldn't have chosen better, Beck."

"I figured little girls and pink—they kind of go together. Besides, Cricket told me that was Gracie's favorite color. And after seeing her room, it just made sense."

The color was a perfect match for the lacy dress she'd chosen, and earlier that morning, Tansy had quickly painted her nails in a pale, pale pink. Gracie had even worn a pair of stick-on earrings because she swore Beck would like them.

And Beck? He was dressed in khakis and a button-down shirt the exact blue of his eyes. His hair, a tad shorter than he'd worn it in high school, still curled at the ends. Tansy loved that dark-blond hair.

"You owe me a cup of coffee," he said.

"I do. You left without yours last night."

"I thought it might be for the best."

She nodded slowly. "You were probably right."

A few minutes later, Tansy stood at the front door of her bakery and watched as Beck and Gracie walked, hand in hand, to his truck. She waited on the front porch while he fiddled with Gracie's car seat, then gave a final wave as they pulled out, her heart pinching more than a little at the sight. Her high school sweetheart and former fiancé with her little girl.

A grin spread across her face. She wondered if Beck, after he'd gone home last night, had wondered what the heck he'd gotten himself into—or wondered that now, with Gracie no doubt chattering a mile a minute.

Then another thought wiped the grin right off her face. What might Gracie Bella tell Beck? There were no secrets as far as her daughter was concerned, and Beck might learn more than Tansy wanted him to know. Oh, well. Nothing for it now.

Since she was between the breakfast rush and the lunch bunch, she had no customers in the shop. Her baking finished, Tansy made herself a cappuccino and sat at the little table that overlooked the back garden and its pretty fountain. High up in the oak, a bird sang happily. Another waded in the new birdbath she'd added. Lush green grass spread out to the tree line.

Her heart raced with hope, and she felt lighter than she had in way too long.

Coming home the past few years had been hell. Every time she crossed the city limits, dread filled her at the idea she might run into Beck, followed by a fast, heartfelt prayer that she would. She'd hoped he wouldn't catch sight of her but dressed carefully in case he did.

And the few times they'd bumped into each other... Whew! That time in Jenni Beth's office, he'd made no bones about his feelings. She'd left that day and driven to the river to cry her heart out before returning to her mother's for Gracie and the drive home.

Now? This morning? Beck had taken her little girl to

a father/daughter party at school. Her woman's heart, her mother's heart nearly burst with emotion.

—⁓—

Beck opened Gracie's door and reached in to lift her out.

"Your hair's curly like my mommy's." She reached out to touch it, then pulled a couple curls till they stretched out.

He laughed. "Yes, it is."

"But it's not the same color."

"No. Your mommy's is prettier."

With all the innocence of the young, she nodded. "It looks like fire sometimes."

"It does." And it matched the fire inside, he thought. The fire that was returning with each day.

When he walked through the door, Lucinda, the preschool teacher, did a double take.

"Beck! What are you doing here?" Then she saw who he was with. "Gracie, don't you look pretty." Her gaze went back to Beck, and she tipped her head toward the little girl. "Does this mean you and Tansy…"

"It means I came to a party with my favorite girl."

"He's gonna be my daddy."

"For today," Beck amended quickly.

"Yeah." Gracie did a pirouette on her shiny, new patent leathers. "He bringed me flowers. See?"

She did another turn to show off the rose in her hair.

"That's beautiful, honey."

Lucinda's attention moved back to him, but when she opened her mouth to ask what he was sure would be another question about him and Tansy, he beat her to the punch. "Where do you want us to sit? I see you've got other daddies comin' in. Don't want to tie you up."

"You could."

He knew he blushed.

She laughed and pointed to a table on the right side of the room. "Gracie, why don't you show Beck where your table is?"

Singing in her high, little voice, Gracie took his hand and led him across the room, then pulled out a chair for him. A tiny chair. A teeny-tiny chair. He perched on it cautiously, praying the spindly little legs would hold his weight. Gracie knelt on hers, talking a mile a minute, pointing out the weather chart she'd helped with yesterday, the finger painting she'd done, the class's ant farm.

With his knees practically around his ears, he listened to her chatter and realized how refreshing it was to see life through a child's eyes.

Other dads started taking their seats, too, sitting uncomfortably in the small chairs. He and a couple others made some small talk while they waited.

Trick-or-treating was coming up soon. If he was really lucky, maybe he could convince Tansy to let him tag along with her and Gracie. Christmas and Santa must be insanely fun. He looked around at the other dads in the room and felt like an imposter. He wasn't Gracie's daddy; he wasn't anybody's daddy.

As he watched, the sweet little girl beside him broke her cookie in two.

"You want half, Daddy Beck?"

He stared, dumbfounded. *Daddy Beck?* Where had that come from? He should tell her not to call him that.

"Mama made them. They're really good."

He couldn't do it, couldn't burst whatever bubble she was blowing. Not now. Not here. She might cry, and then what would he do?

Instead, he took a deep breath and accepted the offered cookie. "Thank you, Gracie Bella."

"You're welcome." Then she looked up at him with those big, brown eyes and stabbed him dead center in the heart. "Will you be my daddy?"

Leaning into him, she wrapped those little hands around his arm.

What could he say? Instead of answering, he leaned down and kissed that beautiful dark hair.

When he straightened, he met Lucinda's gaze. A sad little half smile played on her lips. The two of them had gone out a couple times, but there'd been no chemistry, no buzz. Not for him, anyway. He had a sneaking suspicion she'd wanted it to work badly.

He was sorry for that. He knew how it felt to want and not be able to have.

They ate cupcakes and more cookies and drank lemonade. Then it was entertainment time. Gracie had a small solo in a cute song about five little ducks that left one by one, then all returned. She and the others acted it out with a lot of waddling and quacking and hiding behind the bookcase, and he enjoyed every second of it.

When the program ended, Beck stood. He had to go to work. Gracie, who was staying for the rest of the afternoon, walked him to the door.

"Thanks, Daddy Beck." She suddenly turned shy, looking down and tapping the tip of his shoe with hers.

He knelt and placed a finger under her chin. "I had a great time, Gracie. Thanks for invitin' me. And your mama's cookies?" He leaned closer to whisper, "They were the best ones!"

She grinned and threw her arms around his neck. Tansy's little girl was a definite keeper.

He left the classroom with a smile on his face and a small photo of him and Gracie at their table, tapping their cups together and grinning at each other as if they shared a special secret. Maybe he'd stop in at the bakery and show it to Tansy. He really should give it to her, but he was probably going to be selfish and keep it. Maybe he'd make a copy for her. Later.

Right now, though, he needed to see her. After spending the better part of the day with Gracie, he found himself wanting to talk to her mama. Badly.

He wanted to kiss her mama, too. Naughty thoughts about what else he'd like to do to and with Gracie's mama chased one another through his brain. Oh yeah, he had it bad.

Chapter 25

According to the clock on the front of Coastal Savings and Loans, it was half past twelve and Beck was hungry. The cookies he'd shared with Gracie had been good, but they weren't enough. He stopped at the Dairy Queen and picked up a burger and fries along with the news that Shorty Boudreaux's oldest daughter had received a letter of acceptance from the University of Georgia.

Dominic, at the new wine and cheese shop, knew his inventory, but he was less than handy when it came to tools. The doors on his wine cooler needed to be adjusted, and he'd called Beck yesterday afternoon. Even dressed the way he was, he figured he could handle that.

While he tightened the last of the screws, he remembered his dad had planned to spend some time at the lumberyard today, and that assuaged some of his guilt for taking the morning off. Actually, it sopped up enough that instead of driving to the family business, he found his truck headed toward Sweet Dreams...and an even sweeter Tansy.

"Thought you closed at two," Beck said walking in, the overhead bell jingling.

"I do." Tansy stood behind the counter wearing a frilly, pale-green apron and rearranging cookies on a doily-covered plate.

"It's a quarter after."

"Really?" She glanced over her shoulder at the clock. Brushing back a curl that had fallen over her forehead, she shook her head. "Where did the day go?"

Beck flipped the sign on the door to read "Closed" and turned the lock.

Untying the apron, she stepped from behind the counter. He didn't give her time to remove the apron or ask how the school party went before he took her mouth with his. When her lips parted, his tongue darted in, tasting her, devouring her. In an instant, his pulse had spiked, and he was breathing hard.

When they broke apart, Beck swore he must be having a heart attack. He leaned into her, his chin resting on top of her head.

"I don't deserve this, Beck. None of it."

"That's bull." Remembering the photo in his shirt pocket, he took a step backward and pulled out the picture of him and Gracie. "How about this? Pretty cute, huh?"

She took it from him and dropped right onto the floor. "What are we doing, Beck?"

Uncertain what was going on in her head, he went for honest. "Damned if I know, but I don't want it to stop."

Tansy swiped at tears with the hem of the apron she'd never taken off.

"You cryin'?"

She nodded and sniffled. "Yes."

He lowered himself to the floor and pulled her into his lap. "You're gonna get that pretty dress dirty."

"I don't care."

"Take a deep breath, sugar."

She did. Then she laid her hand on the side of his face. "Better," she whispered. "Let's go upstairs."

Every inch of him went on full alert. "Are you sure?"

She nodded.

He swallowed. "Do you mean what I think you mean?"

"Well, I'm not a mind reader, so I guess I can't answer that with one hundred percent certainty, but if you're thinking I want you to take me to bed, then, yes, it does."

He kissed her again, right there on the dining room floor, where anyone who might have been wandering by hoping for a chocolate-covered doughnut or a sugar cookie could see them.

More nervous than he could have imagined, he stood and scooped her up. Starting for the stairs, he stopped midstep.

"Sugar, I don't have any protection with me. Didn't think I'd need any, seeing as how I was spendin' the day at preschool."

"It's okay. I'm on birth control."

"Thought you said—"

"Emerson hasn't touched me, Beck, not since that night. But he was unpredictable. As much as I love my daughter, I didn't want to bring another child of his into this world."

"Good enough." His face tightened. "How 'bout we don't speak his name anymore? I don't want to think about him."

"Me either." She pulled his head toward her and kissed him till he thought he'd burst from wanting.

Upstairs, he headed for her bedroom. His first impression was cozy, comfortable with a little sass thrown in.

The room fit her. Then it and everything else faded into insignificance when she removed her apron, her eyes on his.

Her shoes, high-heeled and very sexy, went next, and he was almost sorry to see them go. When she reached over her shoulder for her dress zipper, he shook his head.

"Uh-uh. That's my job."

Slowly, he turned her. He skimmed his fingers along the nape of her neck, brushed away her curls, and lowered his lips. One kiss after another along her neck and shoulders had goose bumps racing over her beautiful porcelain skin.

His fingers trailed over that same skin till he reached the zipper. He lowered it a couple inches, his lips and tongue worshipping her. Another slow inch, then another. When he uncovered the scrap of black lace she wore for a bra, he smiled and wondered if he'd find more of that black lace as he traveled farther south.

He did.

Driving them both crazy, his fingers traced over her hips, the dimples in her backside, up the curve of her spine. Then he slid the dress over her shoulders, and it puddled at her feet.

He turned her to face him, took in the passion-filled Caribbean-Sea eyes, the red, red lips, the tiny pieces of black lace. It had been so long—so very, very long since he'd been allowed to touch her like this.

And now, thanks to answered prayers, she would be his again. He could run his hands and lips wherever he pleased. He could pleasure her again.

"I've changed," she whispered. "Having a baby—"

"Made you even more beautiful." His hands and lips

moved to her breasts and worshipped them. Sliding his fingers to her back, he released the clasp of her bra. One strap at a time, he slowly slipped it off and drank in the sight of her.

Palms on his chest, she said, "No more till I get rid of this." She started unbuttoning his shirt, but her fingers trembled. "I'm all thumbs, Beck. I can't believe how nervous I am. I feel like a teenager all over again."

"Good. That makes two of us."

Grabbing the tail of his shirt, he brought it up and over his head and gave it a toss.

She ran her hands over his chest, over those incredible, toned abs. "You're beautiful, Beck. You were gorgeous before. Now? Whew!"

"Sweetheart, believe me when I say the feeling's mutual."

His own fingers clumsy, he made quick work of the rest of his clothes, then followed her down to the bed.

"I want to make this good for you, sweetheart. Special. But it's been so long. I don't know—"

"It's already special, Beck. Take me. Please."

And he did.

His hands, his mouth explored every inch of her. He thrilled to her soft sighs, to her cries of pleasure. And when her fingers trailed over his skin, he nearly came undone.

He'd dreamed of this, of having her here under him again.

When he entered her, Beck understood this Tansy was, in so many ways, the same young girl he'd loved when they'd been a couple. Except for that one night, no other man had touched her.

Her body had changed, become a woman's, but inside, she was still his girl.

Familiar yet so new. So incredible.

Afterward, they lay wrapped in each other's arms, their breathing ragged. He traced his finger over her bare hip.

"Let's take a shower." He stood and pulled her up.

When she grabbed the sheet to cover herself, he tugged it from her hands.

"Uh-uh. Don't hide from me. I love lookin' at you, sugar."

In the bathroom, Beck spied the old claw-foot tub she'd had reglazed and contemplated taking a long, lazy bath with her.

"I thought you'd probably get rid of the tub."

"No way. It's one of the best things about this house. I love to fill it full of bubbles after Gracie's gone to bed and spend an hour relaxing and reading."

"And that image will keep me awake for weeks," he growled.

She laughed.

"But right now..." He wrapped an arm around her waist, turned on the water, and pulled her into the shower with him.

She gasped as the still-cold water hit her.

"It'll warm up in here. Trust me."

Chapter 26

THE NEXT AFTERNOON, A KNOCK SOUNDED AT Tansy's back door, and her heart kicked into overdrive. She'd hoped—and feared—Beck might stop by last night after work. Her head and her heart were at odds, so when he hadn't shown up, she'd told herself it was for the best.

She hadn't believed herself for a second.

Up to her elbows in bread dough, she called out, "Door's open. Come on in." Surprised when Jenni Beth walked in, she said, "I didn't expect you today. Give me a second, and I'll set this aside to rise, then grab us some coffee."

"Finish that. I can get the coffee."

Jenni Beth turned her back, but not before Tansy caught the expression on her face. "What's wrong?"

"Who said anything was wrong?"

"Come on! One look at you and anybody'd think your dog died."

"Zeke's fine."

While Tansy covered the bowl of dough and washed her hands, Jenni Beth carried two steaming cups of coffee to the table. She dropped into one of the sturdy chairs.

"Somebody broke in again."

"No! Did you call Jimmy Don or Sam?"

"Not yet."

"Why not?"

Jenni Beth wet her lips. "The camera was on." She hesitated. "Tansy, it's Coralee."

"What?" Tansy felt the blood drain from her face.

"I'm so sorry, Tanz."

"*You're* sorry? Why should you be sorry? She's my aunt."

"Exactly. And that's why I haven't contacted Sam. Have you seen Coralee lately?"

"She's stopped by a couple times this past week." Tansy shook her head. "This has something to do with that damn tarp."

"Want to pay her a visit?"

"Absolutely. Do you think I should call my mom?"

"It might not be a bad idea to have her with us."

Tansy dropped her head in her hands. "My aunt. A burglar."

"I don't think she took anything."

"But she broke into your office! Aren't you angry?"

Jenni Beth shrugged. "She's Coralee."

Tansy laughed humorlessly. "And doesn't that say it all?" She picked up her cell and hit speed dial. "Mom, I have a favor to ask."

Half an hour later, the three women pulled up in front of Coralee Calhoun's house. As they opened their doors, a corner of the tarp flipped up and her aunt stepped out.

Tansy studied the blue tarp more carefully and realized it didn't actually lay flat against the side of the house. Something propped it up and kept it from touching.

"What's up?" Coralee asked. "Did I forget we'd made a date?"

"Nope." Tansy took in the old sneakers, the faded jeans, and hot-pink tank top. Her aunt's fire-red hair was pulled back in a messy ponytail. She noted, too, that everything was smeared with paint. "We thought we'd run out to Magnolia House."

"Oh?" Just the tiniest flicker of nerves skittered across Coralee's face. "Doesn't make much sense with Jenni Beth right here."

Tansy shrugged. "Probably not. Especially since you were just at her place last night."

Her aunt's mouth dropped open.

"Coralee! How could you?" Rexanna stepped toward her. "I am so embarrassed! And your brother, if he were still here with us, would be horrified."

"I don't think so. I didn't—"

"Coralee, Beck installed a security camera," Jenni Beth said. "You did break in last night."

"It was for a good cause." Never one to back down, Coralee all but dared them to argue with her.

"Good cause or not, you broke the law," her sister-in-law said.

"Does it have something to do with this?" Tansy pointed to the tarp.

"That's none of your business."

Ignoring her aunt's protests, Tansy and Jenni Beth moved to the tarp, one on each side. They gave a couple hard tugs, and it dropped to the grass.

Flabbergasted, they both stepped back. An incredible mural covered the entire side of Coralee's house. In the center stood Magnolia House with its sweeping front porch, columns, and gardens. Roses bloomed gloriously and moss-draped oaks lined the drive. Magnolia House brides wandered over the grounds, each painted in meticulous detail right down to the delicate lace on their gowns, the jewels in their hair, and the vibrant flowers in their bouquets.

"There's Stella, our first Magnolia bride, on her Harley. She and Bear were so happy, and I was about dying from nerves." Jenni Beth pointed to another woman. "Here's Holly, our Victorian bride, and, look. Our Virginia bride with her sprig of dogwood. And Katie. She made a beautiful bride."

"Good memories, aren't they?" Coralee asked.

Jenni Beth nodded.

Tansy, though, wasn't about to be mollified. "Why?"

"Why what?"

"Why'd you break into her office?"

"I told you. It was for a good cause. I needed names. Addresses and phone numbers." She shuffled her sneakered feet.

"Why, Auntie?"

"Your dad's heart attack was so unexpected, so devastating. None of us suspected he had a heart problem. Do you know that one percent of babies are born with congenital heart defects? Fortunately, most can be easily fixed. There's a group in Atlanta that's involved in research to help the others. I've been donating in Roger's name. So far, I've sent them twelve hundred and fifty dollars."

"Where's the money coming from?"

"Jenni Beth's files. I've contacted the grooms and explained what I'm doing. For a contribution of fifty dollars, I add their bride to the mural."

"Why didn't you tell us?"

"You'd have said no."

"We wouldn't have," Jenni Beth assured her. "This is incredible."

"You're not painted in yet, honey, but I saved this spot right in the center for you." She pointed to a spot on the front lawn. "I've seen pictures of your dress." Her face turned red, but she rushed on. "I didn't want to jump the gun, though, in case Cole happened to catch sight of this before your wedding day. I'd hate to ruin the surprise for him when he sees you walkin' toward him on your big day."

"Thank you." Jenni Beth kissed Coralee's cheek.

"You still have to answer to the law," Rexanna said. "You broke into Jenni Beth's office and went through confidential records."

"Pshaw! Jenni Beth isn't going to press charges. Are you, honey?"

Jenni Beth looked at Tansy, then at her friend's mother. "Sam needs to know our culprit's been caught."

"Culprit?" Coralee pulled herself up to her full five-foot-four height.

"You like burglar better?" Tansy asked.

"No, I do not."

"Then culprit you are."

Sam dropped his chin to his chest. "I can't believe this." Then he lifted his head and grabbed a large key ring off his desk.

"What's that?" Coralee asked.

"The keys to the jail cells. You'll come along nicely, won't you? You won't make me handcuff you?"

Coralee's eyes went saucer wide. Her gaze darted from him to her niece to her sister-in-law. Finally, she turned to Jenni Beth. "You're gonna lock me up?"

"Not up to her, Coralee," Sam said. "You broke the law."

Panic crawled up Tansy's throat. She hadn't actually expected Sam to lock up her aunt!

"You have a lawyer?" Sam asked.

"Oh dear." Coralee dropped onto a chair. "Rexanna, explain it was for a good cause."

"It was, Sam. She was raisin' money for children with heart problems."

Jenni Beth jumped in. "If you lock up Tansy's aunt, Cricket's going to be awfully mad at you, Sam."

"It's my job." His back to Coralee, he winked. "I suppose if she promises to never ever do this again…"

"I promise!" Coralee blurted.

"And promises to never paint her house some ungodly color…"

"I won't."

"What do you say, Jenni Beth? You were the injured party." Sam tucked a thumb in his belt, the key ring dangling from his other hand.

Jenni Beth faced Tansy's aunt. "Coralee, what you did was wrong. I worried about my family's safety and the confidentiality of my brides and grooms. From here on in, if you need something, you come to me and ask. Understood?"

Coralee nodded.

"I need to hear you say it."

Tansy studied her friend with new respect. She'd expected her to simply fold, but she read a fierce riot act.

"I won't break into your office again. I promise. If there's something I want to know, I'll ask." She hesitated. "Could you give me your grooms' names as they book, so I can contact them about the mural?"

"I think we can work something out," Jenni Beth said.

"So we're good here?" Sam asked.

They all nodded.

"Go on then," he said. "I've got work to do."

Tansy's aunt beat them all out the door.

———

Tansy knew she shouldn't bother Beck at work, but she needed to see him. It was as simple as that. She gave one quick rap on his office door and opened it. "You got a minute?"

He nodded, and she stepped inside, closing the door behind her.

Beck rested a hip on the edge of his desk. "I heard about Coralee's side business, and I know you're upset about it. How can I help?"

Tansy shrugged.

But she did know. By loving her warts, crazy aunts, and all. By loving her through temper tantrums, crying jags, and self-doubt.

He crooked his finger in a come-here gesture.

Barely breathing, she did just that.

When she reached his desk, he pulled her to him. She felt every muscle, every inch of his body, felt his desire.

His mouth crashed down on hers. Gone were the soft, teasing kisses. Today's were hot and demanding, and she made a small sound of pleasure. He slanted his mouth and changed position to take still more. He kissed her like his life depended on it.

Tansy felt light-headed. She'd missed this so badly.

It had always been Beck.

His hand strayed beneath her blouse, his fingers trailing over her skin to the underside of her breasts. Despite her loveless, sexless life these past years, she'd never quit wearing sexy underwear, and she'd never been happier about that than right now. Today she'd chosen red lace.

As Beck undid her buttons, the lace peeked through and he smiled. "Nice."

"I like it."

"Matching panties?"

"For you to find out!"

"You're killin' me, sugar."

Chapter 27

How could it be Halloween already?

Tansy slid a pan of cookies into the oven and set the timer, her head all but bursting with things that needed done.

Sweet Dreams looked good—darned good. Gossamer spiderwebs covered the windows and the corners of her display cases. Decorations hung from the ceiling. Candy-corn-colored vases held bright fall foliage, and her display case overflowed with Halloween cookies and cakes.

A white-frosted cake with a black spiderweb and spiders piped over the top and sides sat front and center in the case. Cupcakes with meringue ghosts and witches' hats made from mini-waffle cones kept company with others decorated as jack-o'-lanterns.

Her drink of the day? The Witch's Brew, a special blend of coffee spiced with cinnamon and just a touch of pumpkin. The pièce de résistance, though, was the fire that crackled and popped in the big stone fireplace. Cinnamon brooms rested on the hearth and carved pumpkins decorated the mantel.

And her little girl was celebrating the day with friends. Gracie, or rather Pippi Longstocking, had barely looked back today when Tansy took her to preschool. She'd made cupcakes with orange, yellow, and white swirls of icing on them, then stuck a candy corn on each. They were cute and easy for the kids to eat.

Gracie's costume had taken longer this morning than Tansy had planned. Thanks to a wire hanger, Tansy'd finally managed to transform Gracie's long hair into braids that stuck straight out. A patched denim jumper; a pair of mismatched, striped knee-high stockings; and a few eyeliner freckles, and Gracie had been delighted. She carried her stuffed horse, calling him Old Man, since that's what Pippi called hers.

Tonight, they'd change costumes for trick-or-treating, and Tansy could barely wait.

But before any of that could happen, she had a wedding. Kitty and her mom had offered to handle the shop so she could spend the day at Magnolia House.

"You're sure you'll be okay?" Tansy asked as she got ready to leave.

"Better than okay," her mother assured her. "I've waited for weeks to do this. I love Halloween! You can be anyone or anything you want, and here, I'll get to see everyone's costumes."

"So true," Kitty said. "It's one of my favorite holidays."

The two women had shown up that morning dressed as Lucy and Ricky Ricardo. Tansy studied them again, shaking her head. They looked good; they looked like longtime friends set to enjoy themselves.

Charlotte sat at the table, savoring a cup of coffee and watching Tansy assemble the cake. "That's a little different, but it's mighty pretty. Your bride's gonna love it."

Though the Halloween theme had seemed bizarre originally, under Jenni Beth's guidance, it had actually turned out to be tasteful. Not a zombie or a skull in sight. The bride's gown was stunning, a ballroom style with a sweetheart neckline and layers upon layers of ruffles on the voluminous skirt. As a nod to Halloween, the gown was black.

Tansy had frosted the top layer of the three-tiered cake in deep purple accented with black, lacy scroll-work. The center section was black-and-white striped, while a silhouetted haunted house scene made from black fondant banded the bottom layer. On the top, a black-caped groom held the bride in his arms.

The cake turned out striking, and the bride's happy tears made every minute spent on its construction worthwhile.

Cricket had created the bride's bouquet using deep-purple roses, white lilies, and black feathers. Jenni Beth picked up the theme with black, white, and a softer shade of purple for the reception.

The wedding went off without a hitch.

The next one? Jenni Beth and Cole's!

Before they left for the day, Jenni Beth hauled out her own wedding file, and they went through the checklist one more time.

"We're all set?"

"Unless you change your mind about something," Tansy said.

"I won't."

Cricket laughed. "That's what they all say."

—∽∾∽—

When Tansy finally dragged her tired body home, she found the entire shop, kitchen, and display area spic-and-span and shining. On top of that, the heady aroma of her mother's meatloaf drifted down to her. She could have wept!

She'd barely hit the top step before Gracie ran to her, hugging her and filling her in on her day.

"I'm so glad you had fun, sweetheart."

"I did. And Beck's gonna take us trick-or-treating tonight."

Tansy's mouth dropped open.

Her mother jumped in. "Before anyone goes trick-or-treating, Gracie, your mother's taking a nice, long shower, after which the three of us will sit down and eat a good dinner." She looked at Tansy. "Maybe it will help dilute her sugar high. Then I'll clean up the kitchen while the two of you slip into your costumes."

Tansy hugged her mom. "You're the very best mother in the whole wide world."

"I am." She laughed. "Now go get that shower. We're starving."

Tansy started toward her bedroom. "About Beck—"

"He called and said he'd be over at six. That way you can hit the houses you want and make it back in time for the ghouls and goblins who'll show up at the door for their treats."

"But—"

"Take your shower."

—————

Beck arrived at a quarter to six.

"Well, if it isn't Ms. Bo Peep and her sheep." He

grinned and made a twirling motion with his finger. They pirouetted for him. "These have to be two of the best costumes ever."

"Thank you." Tansy curtsied, and with an impish grin, Grace baaed at him like a good little sheep.

Tansy had gone all out. As Little Bo Peep, she wore a big-brimmed bonnet and a long, pale-blue dress that laced up the front. Her shepherd's crook was covered in blue ribbon. Gracie made an adorable sheep in her one-piece fuzzy, white pajamas. Tansy had sewed a pink belly and a fluffy tail on them and made her daughter a woolly, white tie-on hat with big, floppy ears decorated with pale-blue ribbons.

"I can't believe you're in costume, too, Beck."

"Your mom told me your plans, so I figured why not come as a shepherd?"

He looked good in his white shirt, knickers, and suspenders. A fedora with ribbon trim perched on his head. Judy had to have helped him put it together.

"I have a request," he said.

"Okay." She drew out the word, not sure where he might be headed.

"If you have any feelings for me whatsoever, we'll stop by Mom and Dad's. I got orders, so please don't make me look bad."

She laughed. "I wouldn't think of it."

—✺—

Together, they hit Grandma Rexanna's, Kitty's, Jenni Beth and her parents', Beck's parents, Cricket and Sam's, and a couple of Gracie's new friends' houses. They even stopped at Lem and Lyda Mae's. Back in town, they visited Dee-Ann at the diner and Quinlyn at the Realtor's office. Darlene was dressed as Snow White and Moonshine and Mint Julep as Happy and Doc. They let Bo Peep and her lamb take a picture with them.

Then they drove to Coralee's. She'd placed flood-lights on the side of her house so the mural could be seen night and day.

"It's pretty incredible," Beck admitted.

Tansy's aunt, dressed as Mae West, leaned against the jamb in a come-on-in-boys pose. "I'm wonderin' when I'm gonna be able to add my niece to it."

"Excuse me?" Beck asked.

"You heard me, boy. When are you gonna make an honest woman out of Tansy here, so I can add her to the Magnolia brides?"

"Oh my God! Coralee!" Tansy's mouth dropped open. "Have you lost every last one of your filters?"

"Maybe. Maybe not. Seems a fair question to me. After all—"

Tansy put her hands over Gracie's ears and refused to meet Beck's gaze. "I don't think we need to be havin' this conversation right now."

"Fine. Come get some candy then." She held out a dish. "Think I've got something special in here for you, Lamb Chop." Digging into her pocket, she produced a hair ribbon decorated with spiders.

At the sheep's delighted urging, Little Bo Peep attached the ribbon to her pet's ear. They all exchanged hugs with Mae West, then headed for home.

"I apologize for my aunt, Beck."

"Why? You can apologize for things you do, but why

would you feel you have to apologize for what some-body else says or does?"

"Because..." Tansy waved her shepherd's crook. "Because she's my aunt. And she was out of line."

"Was she?" He sent her a sideways glance that nearly melted her bonnet.

Would undoing the laces on her dress help her breathe?

Gracie, digging through her bag of goodies, piped up. "I gots two peanut butter cups, Beck. Do you want one?"

"Not right now, sugar. Think I'll save dessert for a little later."

His gaze held on Tansy, her eyes, her lips, her... halfway-unlaced bodice.

"The light turned green," Tansy stuttered.

His lips curved into the sexiest damn smile she'd ever seen. "Oh, yeah? I've got a green light?"

"Behave!"

He started singing a Dierks Bentley tune. "Come a little closer, baby...where we can work it out."

"You sing good, Beck," Gracie chirped from the backseat.

"Thank you. I think your mama likes it, too."

"What am I goin' to do with you, Beck?"

"I've got a couple ideas."

Her cheeks flooded with heat.

When they pulled into her drive, they were greeted by lit jack-o'-lanterns that grinned wickedly from the porch stairs. Lifting Gracie from the truck, Beck said, "Those look great, kid. You and Mama do them?"

"Uh-huh." Her arms around his neck, Gracie put her mouth to his ear and whispered, "I wished you could have helped, but Mama said you were busy."

He looked toward Tansy but couldn't read her. She might still be ruminating over her aunt's question. Talk about being put on the spot. Thing was, he hadn't been horrified by Coralee's none-too-subtle suggestion.

"I'll help next year."

"Okay." She kissed him, then wriggled down and ran inside with her mother to get the trick-or-treat candy.

The street was soon flooded with ghosts and monsters, ballerinas and princesses, pirates and hobos. Even the Pillsbury Doughboy paid a visit.

In between kids, Beck asked, "No remorse about, ah, the, ah, nap I took here the other day?"

"I have to take naps, too," Gracie said. "Ms. Lucinda makes us."

Beck shot a sideways glance at Tansy, who wasn't even bothering to hide her smile. "You don't like naps?"

She shrugged, her little sheep's nose wrinkling. "Sometimes they're okay."

"My nap the other day was phenomenal."

Ms. Bo Peep blushed, and he laughed.

"What's phe...phomen... What's that word mean?"

He met Tansy's eyes. "Phenomenal means that something you want really, really badly finally happens, and it's better than you could ever have imagined."

Tansy sucked in her breath and broke eye contact. Then she reached for Gracie's goodies. "You probably shouldn't eat any more candy, honey. You don't want to get a tummy ache."

"One more?"

"One more."

With a fierce determination, Gracie dug through her

candy and came out with a full-size peanut butter cup. "This one."

"That's pretty big."

"You said one more."

Tansy gave in.

By a quarter after eight, their visitors had trickled away to nothing, and Beck blew out the pumpkins. Snuggling the sleeping sheep, he carried Gracie inside and upstairs.

Torn between waking her and letting her sleep in what was essentially pajamas but was also her costume, Tansy opted to simply remove Gracie's shoes and hat. She wiped as much makeup from her daughter's face as she could, then dropped a kiss on her cheek.

Beck watched from the doorway. "You're a good mother, Tansy."

"She should have had a bath."

"Nah, it's one day out of the year. It's allowed."

Then he turned off the overhead, took Tansy's hand, and led her into the living room. "I know you're bushed, too. You've had a very long, very busy day, so I'm not gonna stay. But before I go, I really need this."

He kissed her, long and deep, then simply held her close for several moments, drinking her in.

"Okay, Ms. Bo Peep, walk me out and lock up behind me. Then crawl into bed and get some sleep."

"I wish—"

"What?" Beck prompted.

She shook her head.

At the door, he asked for one more kiss to tide him over. "Consider it my treat."

Chapter 28

OCTOBER SLIPPED QUIETLY INTO NOVEMBER.

Tansy'd taken down the Halloween witches and goblins and replaced them with red, white, and blue for Veterans Day. Normally, she'd have stuck with the whole fall thing because Thanksgiving was quickly creeping up on them. But because the town had planned such a big event this year to honor their veterans, it seemed only right to play it up in Sweet Dreams, too.

Since Veterans Day landed in the middle of the week, they'd decided to hold the unveiling ceremony at six, after most were done with work. It turned out to be a spectacular chamber-of-commerce day: the weather couldn't have been more perfect, all the shops flew the Stars and Stripes proudly, and red, white, and blue balloons bobbed from light poles up and down the street.

After a small parade featuring the county's veterans along with some from neighboring counties, everybody converged at the grassy park area dedicated to honoring those who'd paid the ultimate price for their country.

The high school band played the national anthem, and everyone sang along. Sawyer Liddell moved among the crowd, snapping pictures for tomorrow's newspaper. When the post chaplain of the local American Legion moved to the podium, the crowd hushed. Somewhere toward the back of the group, a baby cried, then even it stilled as though understanding the solemnity of the occasion.

Jenni Beth, her parents, Lem and Lyda Mae, along with their niece's parents and brothers moved to the front. The chaplain spoke about the courage and valor of the men and women who put their lives on the line and about Wes Beaumont and Melissa Gilmore.

Then he stepped back, saluted, and signaled for the parents to come forward.

The two sets of parents, the Beaumonts and the Gilmores, moved slowly to either side of the granite marker. Together they lifted the cover to unveil the monument, tears filling all four sets of eyes as their children's names were revealed.

Mrs. Beaumont addressed the crowd. "I want to thank y'all for coming out this evenin' to honor Wes and Melissa and all the others who have fought for our freedom." She reached out to hold hands with Mrs. Gilmore. "This is a moment we will never forget."

The parents in the crowd nodded and held their children a little more tightly.

The band played a final song, and people began dispersing, most of them back to their homes for dinner and bed.

After Jenni Beth dried her tears and saw her parents off, she stood arm in arm with Cricket and Tansy. Beck, Cole, and Sam stood off to one side.

"I can't begin to tell you what this means to me and my parents." A few more tears leaked, and Cole wrapped his arms around her from the back. She sighed and leaned into him. "I know it means every bit as much to Melissa's family."

Then she looked up and down the street. "The town looks good, doesn't it?"

"It does," Sam said.

"Misty Bottoms is comin' back to life."

Tansy had to agree. A few short months ago, the street looked like a ghost town. Empty buildings nearly outweighed the barely-making-it businesses. Since the opening of Magnolia Brides, new shops had opened in the now-bustling town.

"*You* did it, Jenni Beth," she said. "You had a dream, and you made it come true."

"With your help."

Cricket shook her head. "You took the leap first. Without your dream, I doubt the Enchanted Florist would have made it. I know for sure it wouldn't be blooming the way it is."

The others groaned.

"Okay, okay." Cricket grinned. "Bad pun."

"A really bad pun," Beck said.

"You know what we need to do now?" Jenni Beth's eyes sparkled.

Tansy checked down the street, where her mother waited with Gracie. "I need to rescue my mother. She has plans tonight."

"Okay, but give me one minute before you get her. We need to decide on decorations for our class reunion."

"Thanksgiving and Christmas are coming," Tansy moaned.

Cricket shook her head. "I'm not involved in this. I graduated from Blue Ridge, remember?"

"That doesn't mean you can't help. We'll need

flowers." Tansy threaded her arm through Cricket's. "You're an honorary class member."

"Oh, no. I've got plenty on my plate with the weddings coming up. Including yours," she reminded Jenni Beth.

"Actually, I've been thinking about this in all my downtime." Tansy laughed and rolled her eyes. "I think we should recreate the senior prom."

"Perfect! Tanz, you're a genius."

"I am, aren't I? There're a lot of pictures floatin' around to pull from."

"Get Gracie, then come over to our place," Cricket said. "We'll have an impromptu wiener roast. What do you say?"

"Sounds good to me," Sam said. "I think we've even cleaned once or twice this month."

Cricket elbowed him. "Ha-ha!"

———✺———

An hour later, Gracie curled up in Beck's lap. Marshmallow coated her bottom lip from the s'more she'd just devoured. The talk circled back to last-minute wedding plans for Cole and Jenni Beth.

"I honestly think we're ready to go," Cricket said.

"We'd better be because ready or not, Cole and I are getting married Saturday! Three days from now!" Jenni Beth dropped a long, hot kiss on her fiancé.

He sent her a smoldering look. "I, for one, am totally ready!"

"Bet you are," Beck said.

"Can I have a kitty or a puppy, Mama?"

Tansy shot Beck a glare.

He threw his hands up. "I didn't say anything about a pet. I swear. I'm an innocent man."

"Maddie brought her puppy to school for show-and-tell."

"See?" Beck said. "Not my fault."

Tansy shot him a look, then addressed Gracie. "We've talked about this before, baby. We can't have an animal right now, not with the bakery downstairs. The health department would have a conniption."

"What's a 'niption?"

Sam laughed and leaned over to tweak her nose. "It's what you'd have if I stole that cute little nose of yours."

Her hand flew up to cover her nose. "It means somebody without a nose? I don't want to be a 'niption. How could I breathe?"

Everybody laughed.

"Now you've done it, Sam." Cricket punched his shoulder.

Sam blew out a huge breath. "Very literal, this child of yours, Tansy."

"Sometimes." She leaned toward her daughter. "He was using that as an example, sweetheart. A conniption is when somebody gets mad or angry."

"Like my daddy when I played and he wanted to watch TV?"

Everybody went quiet.

Beck's eyes met Tansy's. She looked shattered.

"Or," he jumped in, "the way you'd get if I started to tickle you, and I wouldn't stop." He moved his hand to the little girl's stomach and gave her a tickle.

She giggled, then laid a hand on his cheek. "But I wouldn't have a 'niption, Daddy Beck, 'cause you'd stop if I wanted you to."

Slowly, he became aware of the silence, like being in a vacuum-packed canister.

No one said a word, but all eyes were trained on him and Gracie.

"What?" he asked.

Cricket swiped at a tear. He turned toward Jenni Beth and saw her do the same. *Well, shit!*

"Daddy Beck?" Jenni Beth asked quietly.

"It's…a long story."

"He went to school with me. For daddy/daughter day," Gracie said. She twisted a button on his shirt. "Daddy Beck."

"I…" Tansy, wide-eyed, held her hands out, palms up.

"I think it's beautiful," Cricket said. "And I love you for doin' that, Daddy Beck."

"Me too." Gracie rested her head on Beck's shoulder. "So can I, Mama?"

"Can you what?"

"Have a kitty or a doggy?"

Everybody laughed.

"Oh, she's good," Cole said. "Very good."

Gracie smiled.

Sam grinned. "She's gonna wrap some poor sucker around that little finger and have him dancing to her tune."

"But I want a puppy."

"I know you do, honey. Maybe someday, but not now."

The sweet little girl looked like she was about to transform into something ugly.

"Tell you what," Beck said. "I've got a couple animals at my place. The cat's about to have a litter…um, babies…any day now. Why don't you pick one out, name it, but leave it with me? You don't want to take it away from its mama, do you?"

"No, but—"

"Anytime you want, you can come play with it. At my house."

"Beck—" Tansy said.

Gracie, however, threw her arms around Daddy Beck and hugged him hard.

Tansy nailed Beck with the evil eye over her daughter's head.

"What? It's a good solution."

"You can't give in to her all the time."

"I don't. Thing is, she's her mama's daughter, and that's pretty darned powerful."

By the time they were ready to leave, Gracie had fallen asleep. Since they'd ridden together to Sam and Cricket's, Beck drove them back to where they'd left Tansy's SUV and carried Gracie to the car.

As they walked side by side along the sidewalk, greeting friends and neighbors who were still out, Beck cleared his throat. "About the Daddy Beck thing. I didn't... I honestly don't know where it came from. She just said it. While we were at school. I would never—"

Tansy rubbed a hand down his back. "I know. Gracie, well, she gets these ideas. If you don't want her to call you that, I'll talk to her."

"No!" he said quickly. "I don't have a problem with it. I'm good with Daddy Beck if you are."

"She goes through phases, and this one shouldn't last too long, Beck. She'll move on to something else."

He sure as heck hoped not. He liked being Daddy Beck.

Chapter 29

EVEN THOUGH SHE'D BARELY SLEPT A WINK, A SLOW smile curved Tansy's lips. Her best friends were getting married today!

There hadn't been so much as a hiccup during last night's rehearsal and dinner, and the bachelorette party she and Cricket had thrown for Jenni Beth had been perfection. Afterward, Beck had stopped by and stayed most of the night. Again. Her body still hummed from his touch. He was an addiction, and she hoped she never found the cure.

They'd fretted over how they'd pull today day off. Could Jenni Beth be both the wedding planner and the bride? Would Cricket be able to handle the flowers and all that entailed and still be a bridesmaid? And could Tansy create and set up the cake while serving as maid of honor?

Cole, as usual, rode to their rescue. He hired a complete staff from Savannah for the day, including a set-up/take-down crew, a five-star caterer, servers, bartenders, and a DJ. Many of them had worked with Jenni Beth at Chateau Rouge and jumped at the chance to help. Since they were a known quantity, the bride happily turned over the reins.

Yawning and stretching, Tansy fumbled for her slippers. Moving to the window, she stared out at the picture-perfect wedding day. Autumn kissed the leaves and the air, and in just a few hours, Cole would kiss his new bride.

A tiny jolt of envy buzzed through Tansy. Wasn't this what every bride dreamed of, what she should have had on her wedding day? Instead, when she'd gotten married, a reluctant Emerson had mumbled his vows. There'd been no passionate kiss to seal the deal. No honeymoon. No real marriage.

Staring out past the tree line where the fog was just beginning to lift, she thought about her marriage. Both of them had gotten a raw deal. To him, she'd been a one-night stand, nothing more, and instead, he'd ended up with a wife and child. They'd both caved to pressure. Standing there, she saw things from a new perspective. His gambling aside, they were never meant to be. The realization both humbled and freed her. The divorce hadn't been her fault; she hadn't failed.

Today's bride and groom? They loved and cherished each other and were entering this union with eyes and hearts wide-open. Jenni Beth and Cole's marriage would last forever, and she couldn't be happier.

Nor could she be late. Even with the help they'd hired, there was a lot to do! Yet she took a moment to fantasize what it would be like if today were her wedding day and Beck waited at the other end of the aisle.

Whew!

After a quick shower, she wakened Gracie and practically force-fed her breakfast. It would be a long day, and she prayed her daughter would be able to handle it.

"Do I get to wear my princess dress today, Mama?"

"You sure do, sweetheart."

"Are you gonna wear yours?"

"I am."

The gowns Jenni Beth had picked for her and Cricket were a dream and absolutely spot-on for an autumn wedding.

————◦◦◦————

After hours of hair and makeup sessions, manis and pedis, a few champagne toasts, and more than a few tears in Magnolia House's second floor bridal suite, it was time. Since the wedding would be held in the same rose garden Cole had worked so hard to restore for his bride, they moved downstairs.

Peeking around the corner of the house, Tansy heard the guests talking quietly to each other while music played softly in the background. A few high clouds drifted by in the bluebird sky, and the scent of roses perfumed the air.

Tansy turned to her friend, who gripped her dad's hand as if her life depended on it. "Are you ready?"

"More than," Jenni Beth replied.

"Then let's get this done."

She signaled the DJ to start the processional music.

Crouching, Tansy smoothed Gracie's hair, gave her several last-minute reminders, and straightened the pink bow on her white satin and tulle floor-length dress. Then she handed her a basket of pink rose petals.

"Remember, when you're done, go to Grandma."

"I will, Mama."

"Okay, wait your turn. I'll tell you when to go." She turned to Cullen Jansen, his stocky four-year-old body tucked into a miniature gray tuxedo.

"You have your pillow?"

"Uh-huh, and I'm 'posed to hold it this way." He held up the pillow, letters-side out. "Cole told me. So did my daddy."

Tansy gave him a thumbs-up.

The music began, and Cricket stepped out, sparkling in her champagne-colored, floor-length chiffon dress and carrying a simple bouquet of shell-pink cabbage roses, to walk to where the groom, Beck, and Sam stood beside the minister.

The guys looked fantastic in gray tuxedoes with white shirts. Even though Jenni Beth had gone with pink as her pop of color, Cole had nixed that for him and his guys. No pink bow ties, no pink pocket hankies or cummerbunds. He did give in, though, on the boutonnieres. They were pink roses.

"Okay, Cullen, your turn."

The little boy solemnly started up the aisle. As he got closer, the guests started to laugh, and he did, too, though Tansy figured he hadn't a clue why. The pillow he carried read "Here comes your girl, Cole!" The ring was tied beneath the words with a pretty pink bow.

When Cole caught sight of it, he rubbed his hands together. "I can't wait!"

The guests laughed.

"Okay, sweetie." Tansy gave her daughter a little nudge.

As if she'd been born to it, Gracie Bella sailed down the aisle, smiling at everyone and scattering her petals.

When Tansy stepped out in her copper-colored, floor-length chiffon halter-neck dress, a quick glance assured her Gracie was safely with Grandma. Her attention shifted to Beck, and their gazes held. Her breathing quickened; her heart raced. Beck Elliot, stunningly handsome in his gray tux and looking oh so male, set off a longing in her that would never be satisfied.

What if they'd walked down the aisle years ago, as they'd planned?

She nearly stumbled from the heat in those dark-blue eyes. Steadying herself, smile in place, she reached the altar and took her place beside Cricket.

The music changed, and Jenni Beth, on the arm of her father, started down the rose-strewn aisle looking like a dream in a strapless satin organza creation, classic and elegant with its court train. She wore her blond hair straight with a blusher veil that flowed from appliquéd lace and crystal flowers. It showcased her gown's corseted, lace-up back. She carried a cascade bouquet of old-fashioned pink cabbage roses and ivy.

Tansy glanced at Cole, who wore an awestruck expression. She'd never seen a prouder, happier groom and seriously doubted Jenni Beth's feet, encased in the most incredible sequined shoes, ever once touched the carpet of pink roses Gracie had sprinkled.

Mr. Beaumont's voice shook with emotion as he gave his daughter away.

When Cole and Jenni Beth exchanged their vows, Tansy doubted there was a dry eye in the house. If ever there were two people meant for each other, it was them.

And then it was time for the walk back down the aisle. Beck offered his arm, his eyes so intense Tansy thought she'd melt. Somehow, her legs didn't give way and her feet didn't trip. When they reached the receiving line, Beck dropped a quick, unexpected kiss on her lips, right there in front of everyone.

"More later," he promised. Then, as if the world

hadn't just tipped on its axis, he put on his best smile and greeted the guests.

Flustered, she shook hands and made small talk, but later she had no idea what she'd said. Beck was a constant surprise; he kept her off center.

Then they were off for formal photos while the guests trickled inside to wait for the newlyweds.

After that, they joined the reception. Tansy cried when Jenni Beth and Cole took the dance floor for their first time as husband and wife. Later, after the eating, the toasting, and all the well-wishing, the real dancing started.

Beck crouched in front of Gracie Bella and held out a hand. "May I have this dance?"

Gracie giggled. "I don't know how to dance, Daddy Beck."

"Then I'll teach you." Taking her hand, he walked her onto the dance floor.

Gracie stopped a couple times to look over her shoulder at her mama.

Beck motioned for Gracie to put her feet on his. When she did, he took her hands and led her into a waltz. Even over the music, Tansy could hear her daughter's delighted laughter as they glided across the dance floor.

Then he scooped the little girl into his arms, and they finished the dance.

When he escorted her back to the table, he pulled out her chair. "Okay if I dance with your mama now?"

Gracie nodded, a grin still on her face. "Go ahead, Mama. Daddy Beck will teach you how."

"I'm sure he will."

As she moved into his arms, she realized again how

well she and Beck fit together. His heart beat steady and strong as she laid her head on his chest. One dance became two, then three. Someone announced it was time to cut the cake, and she drew away.

"I need to—"

He shook his head. "Cole has someone to do that."

"I know, but I'd like to watch Jenni Beth and Cole cut their piece. Make sure it's okay."

"You know the cake's gonna be better than okay." He toyed with a curl beside her ear. "You made it."

She rolled her eyes, and he laughed.

Beck took her hand, rounded up Gracie, and set her on his shoulders. Together they watched the bride and groom feed each other, then invite everyone else to enjoy.

"The cake's amazing, Tanz."

"It is, isn't it? And where has my modesty gone?"

"Has nothin' to do with modesty. It's about truth."

"A lot of love went into that cake."

She was proud of the four-tiered cake with its white-on-white scrollwork and delicate, pastel-pink, sugar-paste magnolias. Jenni Beth had insisted nothing else would do for her Magnolia House wedding.

Rexanna came up behind Tansy. "Honey, a certain little girl is all tuckered out."

"I know." She looked toward Gracie who was all but asleep on her feet. "I'll take her home now."

"No. You stay. I haven't had her all too myself in a while now. Time for a sleepover." She looked across the room where Beck stood talking to Ms. Hattie. "If you want to sleep in tomorrow, I'm fine with that, too."

"Mom—"

"Whatever. I'm just sayin'."

Beck caught her mother before she left. He leaned down and kissed Gracie, then gave her mom one, too.

Tansy smiled.

"It about makes your heart burst out of your chest, doesn't it?" Cricket asked as she dropped into the chair beside Tansy. "Do your feet hurt as bad as mine?"

"If yours hurt any worse, you'd be crawling."

Beck made his way back, and Cricket stood.

"Don't run away," he said.

"Three's a crowd."

All too soon, they stood in the drive, tossing rose petals and waving the newlyweds off to their honeymoon.

Beck nuzzled her neck. "I'm hungry."

"I know you ate. I watched you."

"I did, but I'm hungry again. For food and you, and not necessarily in that order."

"I have leftover spaghetti."

"And an empty house."

"Yes." She smiled. "And an empty house."

They left her car in the parking lot.

"We'll pick it up in the morning."

Since he'd driven his '65 with the bench seat, she cuddled into him on the drive to her house. At the town's only red light, he kissed her, setting her on fire.

"God, Tansy, I'm not sure I can make it another block. I want you."

"I want you right back, Beck Elliot."

By the time they hit her door, clothes were already flying.

Halfway up the stairs, he pinned her against the wall, and they made hot, frantic love.

Leaning into her, he steadied her while they caught their breath. Then, kissing her, he scooped her up and carried her to bed where they made love again and again.

They didn't get to the spaghetti till after midnight, but Beck didn't complain.

Chapter 30

WHILE JENNI BETH AND COLE WERE AWAY ON THEIR honeymoon, the mice probably should have played, but they didn't. The class reunion loomed far too close. Tansy couldn't help but wonder what they'd been thinking when they chose the date.

A small committee had been meeting at Dee-Ann's every week for the past month and a half, and this week was no different. Jenni Beth had given strict instructions they weren't to wait for her return to wrap up the plans.

Tansy took a bite of the BLT she'd ordered, sans lettuce.

"Angus Duckworth is comin'," Luanna announced. "His RSVP came today."

"You're kidding."

"Nope."

"That should be interesting." Tansy laid down her sandwich. "Jenni Beth's substitute prom date. Has anybody seen Angus since graduation?"

Nobody had.

"He practically pulverized Jenni Beth's feet," Moose said. "I'm no dancer, but compared to him? I'm a regular Patrick Swayze."

Luanna snorted. "Seriously? You do know Patrick's dead?"

"Not to my wife. She still watches *Dirty Dancing* once a month."

Tansy sighed. "One of my favorite movies."

"Angus's wife's name is Bertha."

"Bertha Duckworth?" Quinlyn asked. "Try saying that without a lisp."

"Not kidding. Angus and Bertha."

A lot of eye rolling followed.

"They sound like a matched pair," Moose said.

Since Cricket would be taking care of the flowers, Tansy had cajoled her into joining their meetings, wanting her to be involved in the process right from the beginning. Besides, it would be a great way for Cricket to get to know some of the townspeople she hadn't met yet. It was working like a charm. Any outsider looking in would have no idea she wasn't one of the class.

Cricket drew the line, though, at attending the reunion. "I'll help wherever I'm needed, but I graduated from Blue Ridge's Fannin County High School. Go Rebels!"

"Fine." Tansy's mind went back to Angus Duckworth. Did Jenni Beth know he'd married a Bertha?

Stepping out of Duffy's Pub, Beck rubbed the back of his neck. A rare afternoon off. His dad and grandpa were both at the lumberyard, and he and his crew had finished their project early. He'd sent them home and stopped by for a late lunch.

What he really wanted was Tansy.

He stopped by Darlene's Quilty Pleasures, then ducked into Tommy's to fill his tank and chew the fat for a bit. Maybe he'd go home and grab a shower. He could check the TV schedule for tonight, then decide what to do. Earlier, he'd had a half-baked plan, but now he was having second thoughts.

Unlocking his front door, he stepped in and looked around. The house had too many bedrooms and too many baths for one man. What had he been thinking when he built it?

That it wouldn't be too big for a family.

Had he unconsciously designed it with Tansy in mind? Secretly hoped that someday she and Gracie would live here with him, that he and Tansy would make children together and fill the house to overflowing, turn it into a home?

He flicked on the shower in the master bath.

After the water grew tepid, he threw on some clean clothes and figured he'd better feed the cat. He hadn't seen her this morning before he left or this afternoon, either. Usually she was waiting on the porch to greet him.

A mental alarm went off. Had she had her kittens?

He walked outside, calling her name. "Allie! Hey, Allie Cat, where are you?"

Halfway across the yard, he heard something. He tipped his head and listened.

A soft mewling.

He followed the sound to some holly bushes where he found her curled up, feeding five tiny kittens.

"Honey, why'd you do this all by yourself? Why didn't you let me know?" He dropped to the ground beside her, and her raspy tongue flicked out to lick his fingers.

She needed food and water. The usually well-groomed cat looked like she'd been through a war. He talked to her awhile longer before getting to his feet. He'd pad his laundry basket with some old towels, then gather Allie Cat and her kittens in it to carry them back to the house.

On his way through the yard, he decided he'd make a call, too.

—∿∿∿—

Tansy dried the last of her baking pans and slid it into the rack. Placing a hand at the small of her back, she leaned into it. It had been a long day, and she still had so much to do. On top of that, she hadn't set anything out for dinner. Maybe she'd pick up some pulled pork sandwiches at Fat Baby's Barbecue.

The phone rang, and she checked caller ID. Beck.

Her heart kicked in her chest, then settled into a Kentucky Derby–winning pace. The man made her feel like a teen again, complete with the soaring ecstasy and the plummeting angst. Lately, she'd been wallowing in the angst section of the bleachers. She hadn't seen or heard from him, other than a couple texts, since the wedding four days ago—well, since the morning after the wedding.

And she'd lay naked on an anthill before she'd let on she'd even noticed.

Answering, she forced out a cheerful, "Hey, Beck."

"Back at you, beautiful."

Her toes curled inside the sensible clogs she'd stuffed her feet into that morning. He sounded masculine, carefree, and vibrant. Even over the phone, he made her feel alive.

"Have a good day?" he asked.

A curl fell over her forehead, and she blew at it. "I've had a tiring day that started before dawn. But, yes, it's been good."

Silence.

"Beck? You still there?"

"Yeah. I was gonna ask if you and Gracie wanted to come over tonight for pizza, some popcorn, and a movie."

"And you've changed your mind? You've decided not to ask us?"

"I'd love to have you, but you sound beat. If you want a rain check, I'll understand."

She debated with herself. Did she stick with her original plans, as pathetic as they were, or pack up Gracie and head over to Beck's? Have dinner alone or with a hunk?

She bit back the laugh that bubbled up. "What movie are we watching?"

"*Pocahontas*."

"The Disney version?"

"Yep."

"You have that?"

He chuckled. "No. I threw myself on Darlene's good graces this morning, and she borrowed a copy from Dixie and Trixie when she ran home for lunch."

"Ahhh."

"So what do you say? Yea or nay? Am I gonna spend the evening alone or with two gorgeous ladies?"

Now it was her turn to laugh. "You drive a hard bargain."

"Hard enough?"

"Yes, hard enough. We'd love to come."

"I have a surprise for Gracie."

"What is it?"

He snorted. "I'm not tellin' you. You'd tell her, then it wouldn't be a surprise."

"I can keep a secret."

"Maybe."

"But you're not going to tell me."

"Nope. You'll have to wait."

They ironed out the details, and Tansy did a little happy dance when she hung up. Tonight she'd spend some time with Beck. Even better? He'd invited Gracie to be part of their evening.

Tansy went to the window and stared out over her incredible backyard. Beck made her happy, and that scared her.

⁓⁓

Two and a half hours later, Tansy strapped a hyper Gracie in her car seat. Five minutes later, she asked for the fifteenth time how much farther it was to Beck's house.

"Baby, we're almost there. Please don't ask me again, okay?"

"'Kay." She stayed quiet for all of three seconds. "Does Daddy Beck have any kids at his house?"

Jealousy, raw and unexpected, burned its way through Tansy. How would she feel if he did have a child or two with another woman? Awful. Beyond awful.

Yet he'd accepted Gracie with no fuss. He hadn't said anything hurtful to her or her child. Just the opposite. Once in a while, she saw naked longing in Beck's eyes when he watched her little girl. Did he wish he really were Daddy Beck?

They'd talked about having children—once upon a time. Before she'd screwed up. Did he still want kids, want to be a daddy? He was so good with Gracie.

"Mama?"

"What, sweetie?"

She sighed. "You're not payin' 'tention. Does Daddy Beck have more kids?" she repeated.

"No, he doesn't."

"Just me?"

Tansy opened her mouth, then closed it again. How could she answer that? Her daughter had fallen in love with Beck. And her daughter's mama? She was afraid she had, too. Or more honestly, she'd never fallen out of love with him.

Oh, what a tangled web she'd spun. Could Beck ever truly trust her again?

"Mama—"

"Yes, it'll be just you there, honey."

"'Kay."

That worked. An answer that really wasn't an answer. She turned into his drive.

Opening the back door, she released Gracie from her seat, then reached into the back for the baker's box of goodies she'd brought for dessert. She'd tried a new recipe this afternoon. Once again, Beck could be her guinea pig.

———

Smiling, he met them at the door.

Curious, Tansy stepped inside. She had no idea what she'd expected, but this wasn't it.

"Aren't you the tidy one?" Surprised, she turned to him.

"I have to confess to a cleaning marathon. Well, not exactly a blitz, but almost. The middle's clean, but don't look too close. I ran the vacuum, swiped a dust cloth over most everything, and hid my clutter." He grinned, looking like a young boy trying hard to hide a multitude of sins…and badly wanting praise.

"You shouldn't have admitted that, Beck. Let me believe this is how you keep house."

"I can't lie to you, Tanz."

All the air left the room, and she suddenly felt breathless. No, he wouldn't lie, and he wouldn't cheat. He never had.

Gracie broke the tense moment by throwing herself on the emerald-green sofa. "This is pretty, Daddy Beck. I like it."

"Good." He ruffled her hair. "This is where we're gonna sit to watch our movie."

"After we eat pizza," she shouted.

"You bet. Hungry?"

She bobbed her head up and down. Tansy had pulled her long, dark hair into a ponytail, but strands of the baby-fine hair had come loose and curled around her face.

A quiet mewling came from another room.

Gracie instantly stilled, and her bouncing stopped. "What's that?"

"That's a surprise."

The little girl squealed. "I love 'prises. Don't I, Mama?"

"You do." Tansy had a sneaking suspicion about this surprise. She gave Beck a look that held a touch of censure.

He held up a hand. "It's okay. I've got it figured out."

Gracie looked like a racehorse at the starting gate. "Can I go see?"

He nodded and started out of the room behind her.

"Beck, we can't—"

"I know. Trust me."

There was that word again. *Trust*. It came hard and,

from the look on Beck's face, his demand covered several situations on multiple levels.

Hadn't she fought the trust battle on the way here? Hadn't Beck won? Still…

In the next second, all worry disappeared when Gracie's delighted cries reached her.

"Mama! Mama! Come look. Hurry!"

She did.

There in the corner of the kitchen, in a laundry basket turned on its side, was a mother cat and her five newborn babies. Tiny, high-pitched cries came from the kittens as they crawled and scrambled blindly over each other.

Gracie knelt beside the box, her mouth open in amazement.

"Can I touch?"

Beck got on his knees beside her and took her hand in his. "Very gently."

He guided her hand to a kitten and stroked it with one of her fingers.

"He's so soft," she whispered, turning her face up to Beck's. A world of wonder shone on it.

"He is."

She watched a small, black, fuzzy ball crawl over the others, his tiny feet slipping and sliding.

"Why's he walkin' on the other ones? Doesn't it hurt them?"

"They all do that, sugar, to keep warm. Little kitties are cold, so they cuddle up together." He shot Tansy a meaningful look, and her temperature spiked. Oh, yeah, she desperately wanted to cuddle with this man who was such a puzzle—brisk and curt at times, incredibly tender and gentle at others.

"Why aren't they looking at us? They all have their eyes closed. Like this." Gracie scrunched her eyes shut, mimicking the babies.

"Baby kittens can't see or hear till they're about four days old, so they keep their eyes closed."

"Oh." She closed her own and stood, hands out in front of her. Feeling her way, she walked around the kitchen till she bumped, laughing, into a chair. "When will they open their eyes?"

"It'll be a few days. They were just born today."

"Today's their birthday?" Gracie's voice rose another octave.

He nodded.

"Can we have a party?"

"We are. That's why you're here. Why we're havin' pizza, popcorn, and a movie."

"*Pocahontas.*" She looked serious now.

"Right. You like that movie?"

She nodded, setting her ponytail swinging.

Tansy watched the exchange with interest. Beck was handling this really well, so much better than Gracie's biological father would have. This, she realized, was what a real father did. He shared the miracles of the world with his child.

Daddy Beck was earning himself a big fat A plus.

"What do you think, Mama?" Beck asked playfully. "You like the kittens?"

"They're adorable."

"So here's the thing, kiddo." Beck sat and drew Gracie onto his lap. "You get first choice. Which one would you like for your very own?"

When Tansy opened her mouth to protest, he shook

his head. "Remember, though, sweetie, it has to stay here. You can come over to play with it anytime you want. But no badgering your mom to take it home with you and no tears. Deal?"

Gracie, full of disbelief that she could actually have one, nodded vigorously.

"Can it come to visit me if it wants to?"

Oh, Tansy thought, her daughter was no dummy, and she knew how to work all the angles.

"We'll see. Right now, though, she's way too little to leave her mama." He grinned at Tansy and raised a brow, asking without words how he'd done.

She gave him a thumbs-up and mouthed, "Thank you."

"You're welcome." His eyes burned into her, so hot, so sexy that she felt it to her core. The man was supercharged. He made her tingly whenever she was near him.

"You want to pick now, or do you want to think about it?"

She crawled off his lap and lay down on the floor to study the kittens again.

"That one." She pointed to a tricolored calico. Three of the five were solid orange, the last all black.

"You sure?"

Gracie nodded. "That's Bitty."

"Bitty?" Tansy knelt and studied the calico.

"Uh-huh. 'Cause he's itty bitty."

"She," Beck said.

"Bitty's a girl?" Gracie asked.

"Yep. Almost all calicos are."

"And she's really mine?"

"All yours."

She threw her arms around his neck, nearly strangling him. "Thank you, Daddy Beck."

He buried his face in her hair. "You're welcome, sweetie. Now, didn't you say you're hungry?"

"Yes." She pulled away, dancing around the room. "I'm starved, huh, Mama?"

"Always. Wash your hands."

"Where?"

"Down the hall, on the left." He held up her left hand. "This is your left. Why don't you go with her, Tanz? I'll pull things together here."

She nodded and followed a dancing, chattering four-year-old with her left hand held high. No doubt about it. Christmas had come early this year.

~~~

They ate pizza and drank ice-cold milk seated around Beck's big oak table. Gracie rubbed her stomach. "I'm full."

"After three pieces? I don't doubt it." She looked at Beck. "Want to wait on dessert?"

"Yeah. I'll brew a pot of coffee in a bit, and we can eat your experiment while Pocahontas does her thing. Maybe I can even find a birthday candle around here to celebrate the kittens' birthday."

"Goodie!" Gracie bounced up and down in her chair.

Within ten minutes, the dishwasher was loaded, leftovers stowed in the fridge, and the kitchen put to rights. Gracie's hands and face were cleaned, all traces of tomato sauce removed. At Beck's insistence, all three of them curled up together on the couch, Tansy on one side of him, Gracie on the other. She managed to sneak beneath his arm so that she cuddled into his side. They decided the popcorn would have to wait, since they'd overindulged on the pizza.

Oh, this would be easy to get used to, Tansy thought. *Danger here.*

———

The movie started and Beck winced. A musical? Hell, he'd thought it was a cartoon. Well, he'd get through it. The girls were enjoying it, both of them singing along with the songs. Apparently they'd seen it more than once.

As they settled into the story of John Smith and Pocahontas, Beck asked, "It's a romance?"

"Yes," Tansy sighed.

"Okay, I can do romance."

She looked at him, her eyes half-shuttered. "Yes, you can."

His body reacted instantly. "Behave yourself," he growled.

"Sssshhh. I can't hear the animals," Gracie complained.

Chastised by a four-year-old. Beck grinned. He couldn't remember a better evening.

Halfway through the movie, Gracie shifted so that her head lay in Beck's lap. A tug so strong it hurt yanked at his heart. He wanted this. He wanted Gracie and, dear God, how he wanted her mama.

Fight as he might, the feeling wouldn't go away. Somewhere along the way, he'd given his heart to Tansy and her daughter. But then maybe it hadn't been his to give. He wasn't sure Tansy had ever returned it to him. His heart had been hers for years.

If he told her, what would she do? Toss it back at him again?

"We should go."

Tansy's quiet words brought him back to the present. "What?"

"Gracie's sound asleep."

She was. He reached down and brushed a strand of hair from her face.

"God, she's beautiful, Tanz."

"She is, isn't she? I love her so much it hurts."

He nodded, up close and intimate with that feeling. Did Tansy guess how he felt about her?

"Stay awhile longer. Let me put her to bed in a spare room. I'm not ready for the night to end. Heck, we didn't have our popcorn or dessert yet."

"I don't know. I—"

He leaned into her and kissed her. One hand came up to wrap around the back of her neck and pull her closer still. The low hum she made set off fireworks inside him.

"Don't go, sugar. Stay with me."

"A little longer, but that's all."

He nodded and stood, cradling Gracie in his arms, her head on his shoulder. Leading the way upstairs, he stopped at one of the rooms.

Tansy stood a moment, drinking in the sight of Beck and her daughter, then moved past him and turned down the bed. "You surprise me, Beck. Your house isn't at all what I'd expected."

"What? You expected black leather? Beer cans strewn over the coffee table? Underwear in the middle of the living room floor?" When she said nothing, he shook his head in mock disbelief. "You did. That's exactly what you expected."

"I wouldn't say exactly. Since Gracie was coming over, I figured you'd pick up your underwear." She chuckled. "I'm sorry."

He laid Gracie down and pulled the covers over her, then dropped a light kiss on her forehead.

And that's when Tansy raised the white flag.

The last doubt evaporated. This man was unbelievable. So hot, so sexy, and so good with her daughter. The daughter who should have been his.

He straightened, and the gleam in his eyes was enough to have her backing up.

"Beck." She held out a hand and laid it on his chest. "What are you doin'?"

"Oh, honey, if you don't know by now..."

How someone so large, so muscular could move with such speed and grace amazed her. He was like a cheetah, able to go from absolute stillness to full speed in the blink of an eye. Before she had time to escape, he scooped her up in his arms.

She laughed. Why put up even a token protest? This was exactly where she wanted to be.

"Beck—"

"Tansy—"

They laughed, and he kissed the tip of her nose.

"I'm tired," he said. "How about you?"

Heart in her throat, she nodded.

"Do we have to worry about her wakin' up? Being scared in a new place?"

"No. Once that child falls asleep, she's out for the night."

"Good to know. What about her mama?"

"Her mama sleeps well, too."

"Sleeping's not quite what I have in mind."

"Thank God," she breathed.

His room was at the far end of the hallway, and he stumbled into it, still holding her tight.

"I feel like Scarlett O'Hara."

"Really? Can't say I've read *Gone with the Wind*, but I've caught the scene you're talkin' about in the movie. Mom loves it. My guess is that Rhett Butler made Scarlett a pretty happy woman that night."

"He did."

"I want to do the same for you."

It was a good thing he was carrying her because her legs wouldn't have held her.

A lamp was on low beside the bed, which looked the size of an ocean, covered in a splash of sunshine yellow. The walls were navy blue, the furniture white. The room was sparse save for the pile of books on his dresser.

Beck lowered her to the bed, following her down, and she quit thinking. His weight pinned her. She should have felt confined, claustrophobic, but she didn't. Instead, she felt oh so good.

She ran her hands over his back.

"Take off your shirt," she whispered.

He did. One yank, and he flung it across the room.

Muscles rippled beneath her fingers as she played them over his skin. He worked right alongside his men, lugging, hauling, and hammering, and his body was proof of that. This body had been earned—not in some pricey gym, but by sweaty, honest hard work.

She traced the line of muscles on his back and felt the ones in his arms. *Ooh la la!* She'd struck the mother lode.

Thoroughly satisfied, she drifted off to sleep, Beck spooning against her, a smile on both their lips.

Sometime later, she felt the dip of the mattress, then a chill as Beck slipped from bed. She heard a drawer open and close, the rustle of him slipping into pants. The bedroom door quietly opened and snicked closed.

He was gone; he hadn't wanted to spend the entire night with her.

Hurt jabbed at her and brought tears to her eyes.

Why?

A few hours later, a wide-awake Gracie crawled into bed with her, and Tansy said a silent prayer of thanks that, after Beck left the room, she'd scooped his T-shirt off the floor and slid into it. Then she added another quick thanks that Kitty was opening the bakery today.

"Morning, Mama. Where's Daddy Beck?"

"I don't know," she mumbled, turning to cuddle her daughter.

And then there he was, leaning against the doorjamb, sweats riding low on his hips, all sleep tousled and sexy.

Her mouth watered, and she nearly whimpered.

"I let your mama have my room. I slept in the one by you."

"Because your room's bigger and she's a guest?"

Beck's eyes met Tansy's, a smile in those beautiful blue pools, and he winked.

"Yep." Totally at ease, he sat on the edge of the bed and smoothed her hair with his big hand.

And she understood. He'd gotten up in the middle of the night for her. For her daughter. The tumblers in her heart rattled, rolled, and opened. She loved this man. And she always would.

Beck picked up a giggling Gracie and slung her under one arm. She giggled louder. Leaning toward Tansy, he said, "There's a new toothbrush in the bathroom if you want it. Should be a comb and fresh towels, too, if you'd like to take a quick shower."

When she made to protest, he shook his head.

"Gracie and I'll be fine. We need to go check on those kittens."

Gracie gave an ear-splitting scream of delight. "The kitties! Let's go see the kitties, Daddy Beck! I want to say good morning to Bitty."

Beck threw her another wink, and he and her daughter left the room.

She heard them laughing and chattering the whole way down the stairs. She lay on her back, breathing deeply.

Everything had changed. Her entire world had shifted, and she absolutely loved where she was right now—where she and Beck were.

———

After she'd showered and dressed in last night's clothes, she sneaked down the stairs. Peeking into the kitchen, she spotted Gracie sprawled on the floor watching the new kittens and their mother. Beck stood at the counter mixing batter. From the smell of it, a fresh pot of coffee was brewing.

How did he do it? Make it all look so easy, so ordinary?

He couldn't be used to waking up to a litter of baby kittens, a four-year-old girl, and her mother. Yet he was totally unruffled. No chaos, no confusion. The man was rock steady.

Yet the passion was there. Oh yes. Over and over last night, he'd shown her that. And he had a temper, too. Hadn't she witnessed that these last few years? Yet he'd never deliberately or unfairly hurt her, though she couldn't have blamed him if he had.

Leaving them there, she walked back into the living room. She took a few minutes to study the books and pictures and other memorabilia that spread over the bookcase behind Beck's sofa. Very eclectic. Books about birds, motorcycles, woodworking, and the meaning of dreams mixed with fiction by Michael Connelly, James Lee Burke, and Robert B. Parker.

And while his walls were white, the man certainly wasn't afraid of color. The green sofa dominated the room with its bright throw cushions. A large, white chair had a navy afghan tossed over the back and a multicolored cushion. The white coffee table showcased a rather large red model airplane. And his artwork? Bold and intense.

What could have been a stark room felt like the inside of a box of Gracie's crayons. Tansy liked it.

She liked Beck.

Chapter 31

THANKSGIVING ALREADY! HOW COULD THAT BE? TANSY stared at the calendar, then at the desserts on her counter. Since she'd driven into Misty Bottoms, life had been a fast-moving bullet train.

Today, though, everything would slow, just a bit, while they all took time to be thankful for the blessings in their lives. It was a family day.

Cole and Jenni Beth, back from their honeymoon, were celebrating with their families at the Brysons' farmhouse. Cricket and Sam had driven to Blue Ridge Wednesday afternoon to spend the day with her folks. They'd fly to New York City in December for Christmas with Sam's family.

Thanks to Beck's mom, Tansy, Gracie, and Rexanna would be part of a large family get-together, too. Judy had asked them to share dinner. Counting Lamont and Stanton, there'd be at least seven of them, which would make a nice table.

She'd been to Thanksgiving at Beck's before, but today she was nervous. So much had changed since her last meal with the Elliots. After trying on and discarding half a dozen outfits, she finally settled on one.

"You ready, honey?" she asked Gracie. "Let's go pick up Grandma."

When Beck saw the three generations of Calhoun females walking toward the house, he tucked his hands in his slacks pockets and simply enjoyed the view. Smiles on their faces, covered dishes in their hands, they chatted a mile a minute.

Tansy was happy again, and for that, he was truly thankful.

Him? He felt better than he had since she'd left for college after her father's funeral.

He opened the door and welcomed them to his parents' home, and the energy level inside quadrupled.

Three-quarters of an hour later, Beck wandered into the kitchen as the women put together the last few dishes. Standing in the doorway, he watched their synchronized dance as they finished the meal. Even Gracie was busily arranging cherry tomatoes and carrot sticks on a platter.

Why even bother with veggies today? He'd asked his mother that question every holiday and always got the same answer. *Because.*

Well, he didn't intend to chew on a carrot stick— *because* there were too many other really great dishes. His mom would probably end up making a vegetable soup with them in a couple days.

Finished, Gracie hopped off her stool.

Beck smiled. His family and Tansy's. Blended. It felt right on a deep, deep level. This was what he'd always wanted, had been sure he'd lost.

His mom and Rexanna stood at the kitchen counter, cups of coffee in hand as they waited for the oven timer. Tansy fussed with the table settings. Gracie Bella, an arm wrapped around her mama's knee, wore a sweet, little dark-green dress with tiny burnt-orange leaves embroidered on the skirt. Lace-edged white socks and shiny patent leather shoes completed her outfit.

Her mama? She wore a short, winter-white lace skirt and a cable knit sweater in the same color. A gold and maroon scarf hid most of her slender throat, and she wore another pair of those damn sexy high heels that about brought him to his knees. The woman was spectacular and didn't seem to realize it.

Pulling out a chair from the kitchen table, he turned it and straddled it.

Tansy's mouth went dry at the simple act. Male. So very, very male.

"Anything I can do to help?" he asked.

"Nope, we've got it all under control," his mother gave her son the eye. "As usual, you waited long enough to ask."

He grinned. "Love you, Mom."

"I know. And my cornbread dressing doesn't hurt, does it?"

"Nope." He hopped off the chair, dropped a quick kiss on her cheek, then swung Gracie up in the air. She squealed.

"Give me a kiss, and I'll put you down. Not until."

Laughing, she wrapped her little arms around his neck and gave him a quick kiss.

He set her on her feet and started toward Tansy. The look in his eyes warned her, but she had nowhere to go. Without a word, he pulled her in for a very unchaste kiss.

Her face flamed, and he chuckled. "You've got flour on your cheek, Tanz."

The kitchen had gone silent.

Totally ignoring it, he opened the fridge and grabbed beers for him, his dad, and Pops. "I'll be watchin' the football game if y'all need anything."

———

"I'll say the blessing if y'all don't mind." Pops covered the usual, then added, "Thanks for the years me and mine had with my Elsie, and for the years Rexanna and Tansy shared with Roger. We're truly blessed to have had them in our lives and are remembering them today."

Tansy reached under the table for her mother's hand and gave it a gentle squeeze.

Voice gruff, Lamont's gaze fell on Gracie. "Your turn, little girl. What are you thankful for?"

Gracie Bella faced him, her expression earnest. "Can I say two things?"

"You sure can, sweetie."

"My mama." Gracie lifted her face to smile at Tansy, who dropped a kiss on the top of her head.

"Thank you, baby. I love you."

"I love you, too."

"And?" Lamont said. "What's your second thing?"

The little girl smiled shyly. "Daddy Beck."

Beck's heart did a grinding lurch, and darn if his eyes didn't feel damp. *Suck it up*, he told himself. He didn't dare look at his mother and could only imagine what she must be thinking right about now.

Instead, he focused on the child beside him. "Thank you, Gracie." He took a deep breath and cleared his throat. "I'm gonna jump the line here. I have two things myself."

"It's okay 'cause I had two," Gracie said. "Your grandpa won't care, will you?"

She turned to Lamont.

"Nope, I sure don't. I figure that makes us doubly blessed."

"Uh-huh," she agreed. "Go ahead, Daddy Beck."

He couldn't stop his grin. She could be a bossy little thing. "First of all, I'm thankful for Gracie Bella."

She beamed at him.

"And her mama."

Tansy choked on the sip of water she'd just taken.

He found her gaze and held it. "I love you, Tansy Calhoun."

Her mouth dropped open.

Good, he thought. About time he had the upper hand. The table around them was silent for all of two seconds. Then it erupted.

"Beck—"

He held up a hand. "Not open for discussion, Tanz. You and me. Later." He swiveled toward the end of the table. "Dad? What about you?"

He thought he'd passed the ball quite nicely, and thank God his father didn't fumble it. As though nothing out of the ordinary had happened, Stanton snatched it out of the air and ran with it. Later, though, Beck knew there'd be hell to pay. He'd caught Tansy flat-footed with his declaration. He hadn't meant to do it today or in front of everyone. But it felt right, and he didn't regret it for an instant.

The rest of dinner flew by, with everyone talking, laughing, and eating way too much turkey, sweet potato casserole, and corn pudding. The table fairly groaned under the weight of the food.

Beck noticed a layer of nerves in Tansy. He'd thrown

her off her stride, yet by the end of the meal, she had her feet back under her.

After the women cleared the table, his mom started a fresh pot of coffee and Tansy put the finishing touches on the desserts she'd brought. When she walked into the dining room carrying her caramel apple crisp in one hand and a cranberry upside-down cake in the other, Lamont grinned.

Behind her, Rexanna held a tray with her daughter's sweet potato cupcakes, the maple marshmallow frosting swirled high.

"Now, that's what I call dessert." Pops shot a sideways glance at his grandson and jerked a thumb at Tansy. "A smart man would find a way to keep this one second time around."

Tansy blushed.

"Unless you scare her away before I get a chance, Pops."

"How much of a chance do you need, boy? I figured there'd be little Elliots running around in that house again. Old men are seldom wrong, especially this old man."

"Dad, leave the kids alone," Beck's father said.

"Leave them alone? They need a nudge."

"They do not. Now cut it out, you two." His mom swatted the tops of both his dad's and his grandpa's heads and had them ducking. She held up the coffeepot. "Anybody?"

Black Friday wasn't quite the event in Misty Bottoms that it was elsewhere, but the local shopkeepers all ran specials and business was brisker than normal as everyone got in the Christmas spirit. Overnight, the fall and Thanksgiving windows and decor morphed into Christmas ones.

Tansy fed and caffeinated the shoppers as they rushed in and out, many of them placing dessert orders for parties and dinners coming up in December. She'd need to hire some extra help. Kitty had a couple ladies who'd pitched in once in a while, so she'd give them a call. Later.

First, though, she had to make it through today and this weekend. Again, she wondered why they'd ever thought this timing was good for their class reunion.

Dumb question and one she knew the answer to. They'd figured with so many out-of-town classmates visiting families for Thanksgiving, they'd have a better showing. And, she admitted, it had worked. The last list of attendees showed nearly eighty percent of their class coming.

She and Beck hadn't had a chance to talk last night, and she had so many questions after that bomb he'd dropped at dinner yesterday. They'd have to wait, she thought, as she drew Jimmy Don's coffee and plated a scone for one of Darlene's nieces.

~~~

Saturday evening, Tansy stood in front of her closet debating with herself. What the heck. Call her crazy! Slowly, she drew out her newly dry-cleaned high-school prom dress. Pale, pale blue and ultra feminine, the dress was sweet and sexy at the same time.

The high-neck halter top had beautiful beaded appliqués, and the back dipped low with two crisscross straps. The layered chiffon skirt floated around her and made dancing fun.

She'd felt like a princess when she'd worn it before and prayed she would again tonight. She'd need the extra confidence for what she had planned.

While her mother fed Gracie, Tansy zipped her dress, then opened her jewelry box. Reaching inside, she drew out the delicate gold chain. Beck's Misty Bottoms high school ring still hung from it. The night he'd slid the ring on her finger, she'd curled her palm so as not to lose the too-big ring. The next day at school, she'd proudly worn it around her neck.

Tonight, at the high school reunion, she'd wear it again.

More than anything, she wanted to be Beck's again, and tonight she'd tell him that. There were no rules that said she had to wait for him, were there? Couldn't she take the lead? And if he turned her down, well, she'd change his mind.

Hadn't he kissed her in his mother's kitchen in front of everyone, then told her right in the middle of Thanksgiving dinner, with everyone listening, that he loved her? Of course, in typical Beck fashion, he'd then refused to talk about it.

Tonight, they would.

The time they'd managed to shoehorn in since she'd been back in town had been magical. Far too magical to be denied.

—~~~—

When she opened the door, Beck stood there, his eyes running the length of her.

"Your prom dress."

She nodded.

"I'll be the envy of every man there tonight."

She laughed. "I doubt that." She held out the floor-length chiffon skirt. "A little over the top, maybe, but I thought—"

He leaned in and kissed her. "It's perfect." Then he raised his class ring, warm from her body, from where it nestled between her breasts. His fingers skimmed over her soft skin. "You kept it."

"It means the world to me."

He nodded, not trusting his voice. After a few seconds, he brought his other hand from behind his back. "For you."

Her mouth dropped open. "A wrist corsage. It's exactly like the one you gave me the night of the prom. How'd you manage this?"

"I took our prom photo to Cricket. That girl's good." He tipped his head. "Don't you go cryin' on me."

She sniffed. "You kept our prom picture?"

"I did."

"Me too." She pulled it from her clutch. "Yesterday at dinner, when you said—"

"Later." He swiped a finger down her nose, then nodded toward the wrist corsage. "Too sloppy sentimental?"

"Not on your life."

"Good." He drew her in and kissed her again. His forehead resting on hers, he said, "I needed that."

"Me too."

"Is Gracie still awake?"

"I am, I am!" Gracie bounced into the room, her grandmother right behind her. "Daddy Beck!"

He scooped her up one armed.

Tansy held up her hand. "Look, Mom, what Beck gave me."

Nostalgia swept over Rexanna's face.

"I still have the original in a box in your attic, Mom. I couldn't bring myself to throw it away."

"Let me smell," Gracie demanded, burying her nose in the flowers.

"Here, try this." Beck picked up the smaller box he'd set on the end table. In it was a smaller version of the wrist corsage.

"For me?" The little girl squealed with delight. "Mama, Daddy Beck brought me one, too. It's just like yours." Her tiny fingers worked to open the box.

Beck bent down and helped her. Removing the flowers, he slid the corsage over her wrist.

She lifted it to her nose and inhaled deeply. Arms outstretched, she launched herself at him, wrapping her arms around his neck. "I love you, Daddy Beck."

"I love you, too, sweetie." Over her head, he met Tansy's fabulous turquoise eyes. Oh, yeah. These two females had him wrapped around their little fingers.

And didn't that make him one heck of a lucky guy?

―◦◦―

They walked into the gym to Daughtry's "It's Not Over."

The lyrics grabbed him. Tansy's hand in his was soft and warm, and she held his heart in it. When she started toward where Jenni Beth sat with Cole, he stopped her.

"Uh-uh. Not yet." He pulled her into his arms and swung her onto the dance floor, singing along with the song about second chances.

Her body fit against his perfectly, and he drew her closer still, nuzzling her neck.

When the song ended, he wondered if he should excuse himself for a minute. The woman got to him, and with one look, everyone in the room would know.

She went on tiptoe and brushed a kiss that held promises over his lips. "We aren't over, are we, Beck?"

"Not on your life." He tightened his hand at her waist, and they walked over to join Cole and Jenni Beth who were sitting with Luanna and her husband.

"Watchin' you two out there, a person'd think you were the newlyweds," Cole teased.

Beck just grinned.

"You wore your prom dress! No wonder you wouldn't tell me what you were wearin'," Jenni Beth said.

"I had another dress ready in case I chickened out."

"I'm glad you didn't. You look beautiful," Beck said.

"And look." She held up her wrist. "An exact copy of my prom corsage."

Jenni Beth's mouth dropped open. "You knew she was wearing her prom dress?"

"Not a clue."

"Whoa, that's kind of scary," Cole said. "You do know you're makin' the rest of us look bad, bro."

Beck shrugged.

The doors to the gym opened again, and a movie-star gorgeous couple entered.

Beck whistled softly, and Tansy elbow-poked him in the ribs.

"I was lookin' at his suit," Beck said defensively.

"Right." Tansy gave the couple another assessing gaze. "Although, that suit's an Armani. By itself, it's a couple thousand dollars. The shirt, tie, shoes… That's one well-decked-out guy."

"Who do we know that would dress like that? Who *could* dress like that?" Jenni Beth asked.

Cole shook his head. "Beats me. Bet he gets mani-pedis. And look at his hair. It's manicured to an inch of its life."

"Maybe she's the class member," Tansy said.

"No, I'd remember her." Beck jerked away in time to avoid Tansy's elbow this time.

"Well, that little black dress she's wearing isn't off the rack, believe me," Jenni Beth noted. "It's a Stella McCartney."

Tansy studied the exotic woman with her black hair and deep tan. The figure-hugging dress with its wide V-neck showed acres of cleavage. And the shoes! She'd die for those shoes.

The two wended their way through the dancers and headed straight for their table.

"Jenni Beth, long time no see."

Tansy almost swallowed her tongue. She recognized that voice, and from the stunned look on Jenni Beth's face, so did she.

"Angus? Angus Duckworth?" Tansy's voice cracked.

"Hey, Tansy. How are you?" He extended a hand, shook hers, then turned back to Jenni Beth. "Heard you and Cole here tied the knot. Finally got it done, huh?"

"We did." Jenni Beth still looked shell-shocked.

"This is my wife, Bertha. Bertha, this is Jenni Beth Beaumont. Well, Jenni Beth Bryson now. Jenni Beth and I went to the senior prom together."

Cole hooked a finger in his collar and looked

decidedly uncomfortable. Tansy didn't wonder, since everybody at the table knew Jenni Beth had gone with Angus because Cole had stood her up at the last minute for Misty Bottoms' head cheerleader.

"It's so good to meet you all." Bertha extended a perfectly manicured hand that sparkled with diamonds.

If any woman could look less like a Bertha, Tansy couldn't begin to imagine it.

"You remember Luanna and Les Connors?" Tansy asked, motioning to the couple.

"I do. How are you, Luanna?" Angus kissed the back of her hand, and she blushed.

"I'm good. Still waitin' tables at Dee-Ann's."

"They serve the best burgers in town."

"They do."

"Would you like to sit with us?" Beck slid out a chair and shot Cole a wicked grin.

"We'd love to." Angus seated his wife, then sat beside her. "So, tell me. What's new in town? I haven't been back since graduation."

⌁⌁⌁

After dinner was finished and cleared, the room started to thin out as couples and groups drifted off. A lot of their classmates stayed, though, to talk over another drink and to dance.

Beck excused himself and went up to talk to the band. When he returned to the table, he held out his hand to Tansy. "Dance with me, sugar."

He took her in his arms as the song started. Lonestar. "Let's Be Us Again."

"Beck."

She drew back, but he shook his head and tucked her into him.

"Don't say anything. Just listen to the words, sugar, and let me hold you."

Baby, baby, what would I do? Can't imagine life without you.

He sang the words softly, his breath tickling her skin. Her heart raced. Did she dare hope he'd been telling the truth yesterday?

When the song ended, Beck dropped to one knee right there in the middle of the dance floor. Tansy stared at him.

Around them, the other couples on the dance floor stilled, and the band went quiet. Everyone who'd been talking quit.

"I really can't imagine life without you, Tansy. Let's be us again."

Nervous, Tansy did a quick scan of the room. Yep, everybody's attention was trained on them, and more than a few cameras were snapping.

"Beck," she whispered. "What are you doing? Get up. You're crazy."

"Crazy in love with you, Tansy Calhoun." Without hesitation, he reached into his pocket. "I already did this once, but I'm gonna risk it again. This time I hope it takes."

"Beck—"

"Tansy Calhoun, I love you." He took her cold hand in his. "I've loved you for years, and I promise to love you for all the years of my life to come. I love you and Gracie Bella and all the rest of the kids I hope we'll have. Say you'll marry me, sugar. Put me out of my misery and tell me you want to spend the rest of your life with me. Marry me."

Angus shouted, "Tell him yes, Tansy, and let us get on with the party."

She laughed and threw her arms around his neck. "Yes! Oh, yes, Beck. I love you and always have." She grinned. "I was going to propose to you tonight."

"You were?"

"Yeah. I've been workin' on building up my courage, and I've got to say, I'm not sorry you beat me to it. It's nerve-wracking." She laid a hand on the side of his handsome face. "But I am sorry I wasted so many years, Beck. That I caused you so much hurt."

"All in the past now. This, right here, is the beginning of our future." He slid the ring on her finger and laughed when she got misty-eyed. "You cry when you're sad, you cry when you're happy. What am I gonna do with you?"

"Love me."

"I do."

He looked toward the band and nodded.

The band switched to a new song. Dierks Bentley's "Come a Little Closer."

She laughed. Life with Beck would be quite a ride.

"I might not have been the first to walk you down the aisle, sweetheart," he murmured into her ear, "but I was your first love, and I'll be your last. I'm more than good with that. It's time to get married, so I can kiss you anytime I want!"

She wrapped her fingers around the back of his neck and pulled him in for a kiss full of heat and promise.

Coming back to Misty Bottoms had been a big move. But this? This was truly coming home.

Epilogue

A WISP OF PALE PINK DISAPPEARED AROUND THE corner. Molly Stiles, Jenni Beth's former roommate from Savannah, seemed to be everywhere.

A friend of the bride, Molly had been beside herself about attending today's Magnolia House wedding. The petite whirlwind had come a day early and worked her butt off alongside Cricket, Jenni Beth, and Tansy preparing for today.

Molly's face could be showcased in the dictionary beside *sweet Southern belle*, but after sweating beside her yesterday, Tansy decided the term *steel magnolia* probably fit her better. Appearances absolutely could be deceiving.

Femininity personified, a dimple in her chin, and even covered in heavy *glisten*, she smelled like a rose garden. And her dress? It about made Tansy's heart stop beating. What she wouldn't give to have a dress like that—and in that pale pink.

With her auburn hair, it would never happen. But Molly, with all that long, dark hair and those soulful, brown eyes, looked like an angel in it. One of Victoria Secret's angels, true, but an angel nonetheless.

Tansy wasn't the only one to notice. The groomsmen were keeping an eye on Molly, too, especially the tallest of the three brothers. While Brant Wylder kept an eye on Molly, nearly every female on the property was keeping her eyes on him. He was a handsome devil!

"Focus, Tansy, focus," she reminded herself. Today's wedding would put all three of them over the top, financially, for the month. Angela Deardon, a friend of Cole's from Savannah, wanted only the best for her wedding, and since Daddy could afford it, that's exactly what she'd get.

Angela had not one but two of the most incredible wedding gowns Tansy had ever seen. A mermaid-style lace gown covered in enough crystals to blind a person, paired with an eight-foot long, tulle veil, would be worn for the ceremony. For the reception, the bride wanted to dance unencumbered and had chosen a tea-length, lace-overlay gown with a sweetheart neckline and incredible silk organza flowers at the waistline.

Cricket had created a not-to-be-believed bridal bouquet from pink peonies and lavender orchids. Banks of the same flowed over the tables as centerpieces and decorated the living room's huge fireplace, where Angela and her groom would speak their vows.

And the cake? All modesty aside, Tansy knew it was the most magnificent she'd ever created. Maybe the most magnificent ever created in Georgia. Heck, in the eastern United States. In the entire free world! She chuckled and moved to check on the six-tiered cake one last time. Angie had wanted every layer a different flavor. Red velvet, pink champagne, salted caramel chocolate, carrot cake, hummingbird, and basic white. All great choices that made this cake a lot of fun to put together. Edible pink peonies and lavender orchids spilled from the cake's top, down the side, and around the bottom.

"A masterpiece." Beck wrapped his arms around her from the back and kissed her neck.

"The cake is great, isn't it?"

"The cake? Yeah, it is. I was talkin' about you, though." He chuckled, and goose bumps raced down her spine.

She turned in his arms and gave him a quick kiss but stepped back when he moved to deepen it.

"I'm working." She tapped the end of his nose with her fingertip. "Later."

She loved the way those incredible blue eyes deepened with want for her. "I love you."

"Love you more."

Jenni Beth stuck her head around the corner and crooked a finger. "Come here, Tanz. Molly wants a minute." She glanced at her watch. "And that's about all we have to spare."

Cricket, looking quirky yet elegant in a vintage flapper dress she'd found on their last trip to Savannah, sauntered into the room, a spray of orchids in hand. "You called?" She held up her phone.

"I did. Quick."

When they entered the library, Molly paced in front of the large window.

"Hey," she drawled with a quick little wave. "I know y'all are busy. This'll only take a sec." She drew in a huge breath, then slowly released it. Her eyes met Jenni Beth's, who gave her a little nod.

She clasped and unclasped her hands. "I want to move to Misty Bottoms." The words came out in such a rush that Tansy blinked.

"More than that, I want to open a bridal shop. Y'all are doin' such a fantastic job here, and I'd love it if you'd let me join you. You have all the bases covered, except for that all-important dress. I want to provide that for your brides."

"I've already given her my blessings," Jenni Beth said.

Cricket and Tansy shot a look at each other, then grinned hugely.

"Welcome to Misty Bottoms and Magnolia Brides," Tansy said.

"I'll second the welcome," Cricket added.

"Just like that?" Molly asked.

"Just like that."

The four hugged.

"Speakin' of welcoming, have y'all seen the grooms-men?" Molly asked.

"You mean the Wylder brothers?" Cricket fanned herself. "When they're all in the same room, I'm amazed it doesn't spontaneously combust. All that sexiness." She held out her hand, her engagement ring glittering. "And I'm speakin' from the vantage point of a woman very much in love. If I were single? Well, call me a puddle and mop me up."

The others laughed.

Tansy had to agree. "I can guarantee that more than one woman out there is havin' a few 'Wylder' thoughts."

—⁓—

Three and a half hours later, the knot had been tied, the dances danced, food eaten, and champagne bottles emptied.

Jenni Beth efficiently rounded up the single women for the bouquet toss.

Tansy noted that two of the Wylder brothers sat at the bar watching the goings-on with amusement. The third leaned lazily against a tree, a cocktail in hand.

All the single women swarmed close to the bride—except Molly, Tansy noted. Their new partner was doing her best to escape the melee.

Leaning against her own fiancé, his arms wrapped around her middle, Tansy noticed that Brant Wylder was watching Molly as she frantically threaded her way towards the edge of the throng of women, their hands in the air, each hoping to snag the bride's flowers.

He threw back his head and laughed as the beautiful bouquet hit Molly squarely on the forehead. Startled, she reached up and grabbed it in self-defense. Panicked, she stared up, straight into the incredibly green eyes of Brant Wylder.

Those sexy lips of his turned up at the corners, and he winked.

Tansy swore bolts of electricity sizzled between the two. Her hand slid into Beck's. "I think our Molly might be in for some exciting trouble."

"Oh yeah."

Beck's lips covered hers, and Tansy settled in for a little trouble of her own.

About the Author

Lynnette Austin loves Starbucks, peppermint patties, and long rides with the top down and the music cranked up! One of the great things about writing is that daydreaming is not only permissible but encouraged. She grew up in Pennsylvania, moved to New York, then to Wyoming, and presently divides her time between Florida's beaches and Georgia's mountains. She's been a finalist in RWA's Golden Heart Contest, PASIC's Book of Your Heart Contest, and Georgia Romance Writers' Maggie Contest. Having grown up in a small town, that's where her heart takes her—to those quirky small towns where everybody knows everybody…and all their business, for better or worse. Visit Lynnette at www.authorlynnetteaustin.com.

Saving Jake

Blessings, Georgia

by Sharon Sala

New York Times and *USA Today* Bestselling Author

There is always *hope*

After eight years in the Marines, Jacob Lorde returns to Blessings, Georgia, with no plans other than to hole up in his empty house and heal what's left of his soul. But with a charming next door neighbor and a town full of friendly people, keeping to himself is easier said than done.

as long as you can come *home*

Laurel Payne understands far too well what Jake is going through, after witnessing her late husband experience similar problems. She's in no hurry to jump into another relationship with a complicated guy, but their attraction is undeniable—and perhaps exactly what both of them need.

Praise for *I'll Stand By You*:

"An amazing story by a true storyteller." —*RT Book Reviews*

"Sala hooks you from the first page." —*Fresh Fiction*

For more Sharon Sala, visit:

www.sourcebooks.com

Sweet Southern Bad Boy

Harmony Homecomings

by Michele Summers

He's got something she wants

When Katie McKnight gets lost location-scouting for her father's TV studio, she stumbles upon the perfect setting for their angsty new teen vampire series—a remote barn house unfortunately occupied by a grouchy, disheveled, and incredibly sexy man who instantly mistakes her for the new nanny. Should Katie tell him the truth, or get her foot in the door?

She's got everything he needs

Bestselling author Vance Kerner doesn't just have writer's block—he's been run ragged ever since he was saddled with caring for his brother's three kids, an adopted kitten, and a runaway mutt. The last thing he needs is a teen drama defiling his property, but with fascinating and unconventional Katie underfoot charming the entire Kerner household, Vance is finding it harder and harder to say no.

Praise for Michele Summers:

"Will keep you hooked from the beginning to the end." —*Harlequin Junkies* for *Not so New in Town*

"Emotion and off-the-charts sexual tension."
—*RT Book Reviews* for *Find My Way Home*

For more Michele Summers, visit:

www.sourcebooks.com

This Is Our Song

The Shaughnessy Brothers

by Samantha Chase

New York Times and *USA Today* Bestselling Author

———

She knows him by reputation

Riley Shaughnessy knew that to stand out in his large family, he'd have to go big. Making a name for himself as a musician wasn't easy, but he followed his dreams to rock-star success. But the relentless expectations of fans is not helping the slump he's in now. So of course the person who attracts him is the woman who is not impressed by fame.

Which gives Riley Shaughnessy a lot to prove

Entertainment reporter Savannah Daly is completely unfazed by pretty-boy rock stars. She's just here to get her interview and write her story. But spending an entire month with the Shaughnessys is going to show Savannah a side of Riley she never could have guessed.

———

Praise for *Always My Girl*:

"Another winner in a series that is true
to life." —*RT Book Reviews*, 4 Stars

"Delightful, superbly written… Vivid descriptions
and endearing yet flawed characters add vibrancy."
—*Publishers Weekly* Starred Review

For more Samantha Chase, visit:

www.sourcebooks.com

One More Kiss

Shaughnessy: Band on the Run

by Samantha Chase

New York Times and *USA Today* Bestselling Author

———

Matt Reed is hiding

…from his fans

…from his past

…from a failure too painful to contemplate

Most of all, Matt is hiding from himself.

Vivienne Forrester is a woman who gives her all

…to her friends and family

…to her online food blog

…to the man she loves

Vivienne will try anything and everything to coax Matt out of his self-imposed exile. But for this to work, Matt is going to have to meet her halfway…

———

Praise for *I'll Be There*:

"A fun, flirty, sweet story filled with romance and character growth and a perfect happily ever after."
—Carly Phillips, *New York Times* bestselling author

For more Samantha Chase, visit:

www.sourcebooks.com

The Best Laid Wedding Plans

Magnolia Brides

by Lynnette Austin

Magnolia Brides

———

Some Dreams Are Worth Whatever It Takes

Jenni Beth Beaumont has a dream. She leaves her career as a wedding planner in Savannah for the small Southern hometown whose glory days are long past. She is determined to breathe new life not only into her family's once beautiful antebellum mansion, but also into the town itself. And so she sets out to create a premier wedding destination the likes of which this small town can't even begin to envision, and few want.

But Cole Bryson can...and it's not at all what he had in mind when he set his sights on the crumbling Magnolia House. Cole and Jenni Beth also have a past, one that she does not want to repeat. But she needs Cole's help to make her dream a reality, and Cole can't help himself when it comes to Jenni Beth. Can the guy who thoroughly broke her heart become the man who will help her build her happily ever after?

———

"All about small towns, community, and
sweet and sexy romance." —*Booklist*

"An intriguing premiere...well-developed characters
and sensual romantic tension." —*Publishers Weekly*

For more Lynnette Austin, visit:

www.sourcebooks.com

Every Bride Has Her Day

Magnolia Brides

by Lynnette Austin

———

Cricket O'Malley can't wait to plant roots back home in Georgia, where she's returned to restore an abandoned flower shop to its former glory. The only blemish? Her neighbor's house is even more neglected than her old flower shop, and its occupant seems as surly as he is darkly handsome.

Devastated body and soul after a tough case went south, New York City detective Sam DeLuca thought he'd have no trouble finding solitude in the quiet Georgia town of Misty Bottoms, but his bubbly neighbor seems determined to shine happiness into Sam's life. Sam is equally determined to close himself off, but his heart says otherwise…

———

Praise for *The Best Laid Wedding Plans*:

"Entertaining…the push and pull of emotion feels real." —*RT Book Reviews*, 4 Stars

"An intriguing premiere…well-developed characters and sensual romantic tension." —*Publishers Weekly*

For more Lynnette Austin, visit:

www.sourcebooks.com